The soldier stalked to a waiting mare, Alena over his shoulder

Alena's head spun when the soldier lowered her to her feet and steadied her with a hard hand on her arm. Her robe had torn at one shoulder, and through tears of rage she saw a sudden twinge of remorse darken the soldier's eyes. He reached out to pull the fabric over her naked shoulder, but she recovered enough to strike his hand away.

"Don't touch me again!"

"I'll do more than touch you, woman, if you don't mount that horse right now." His gritted teeth, and quiet, ominous words rasped across Alena's mind like flint striking on stone.

For a timeless moment, the two stared at one another. All thoughts of rank and authority vanished in the sheer clash of wills between outraged female and arrogant male. Alena felt the hot, reckless blood of her Celtic ancestors rise, heritage of a race who loved battle and would charge in wildly, regardless of the odds. With all her soul she wished for a sword or dagger. She would cut out this bastard's heart.

Dear Reader,

Welcome to another great month of the best in historical romance. With summer just around the corner, Harlequin Historicals has picked four titles sure to heat up your spring nights.

The *Royal Harlot* is Lady Leonie Conniston, a British spy whose assignment is to keep the enigmatic Prince Klaus from danger. However, when Klaus discovers her true identity, who will save her from his growing passions? A big book from author Lucy Gordon.

Newcomer Merline Lovelace gives us a sweeping tale set in ancient Britain. Lady Alena has no love for men after a brutal first marriage, but then why does she find passion and comfort in the arms of a *Roman? Alena* is the first installment of the Destiny's Women trilogy by the author.

In *The Fourth of Forever* by Mary McBride, Race Logan is looking for a harmless roll in the hay with "Kate the Gate," but is shocked to discover the woman in question is not at all what she seems.

And rounding out May, Kathryn Belmont's *Fugitive Heart* tells the story of Jeremiah Sloan and Sarah Randall, who pose as man and wife in order to pull off one of the biggest slave rescues of all time. Yet will their feigned marriage make them yearn for the real thing?

We hope you enjoy these titles. Next month, look for a big book by medieval author Claire Delacroix, and the next installment of the Warrior series by Margaret Moore.

Sincerely,

Tracy Farrell
Senior Editor

Please address questions and book requests to:
Reader Service
U.S.: P.O. Box 1325, Buffalo, NY 14269
Canadian: P.O. Box 1050, Niagara Falls, Ont. L2E 7G7

MERLINE LOVELACE
Alena

Harlequin Books

TORONTO • NEW YORK • LONDON
AMSTERDAM • PARIS • SYDNEY • HAMBURG
STOCKHOLM • ATHENS • TOKYO • MILAN
MADRID • WARSAW • BUDAPEST • AUCKLAND

ISBN 0-373-28820-4

ALENA

Copyright © 1994 by Merline Lovelace.

This edition published by arrangement with Harlequin Enterprises B.V.

® and TM are trademarks of the publisher. Trademarks indicated with ® are registered in the United States Patent and Trademark Office, the Canadian Trade Marks Office and in other countries.

Printed in U.S.A.

Chapter One

He wanted her the moment he saw her.

She was standing in the dusty arena, her head, with its wild, tawny mane, thrown back as she laughed in sheer exuberance. A short training tunic clung to her body in damp patches, and her full breasts still heaved from exertion. Straw targets set halfway down the earthen arena gave evidence that she and the small group with her had just finished a javelin contest.

Marcus Valerius reined in his horse in the shadow of a small thatched hut and motioned the patrol behind him to halt. As he ran his eyes slowly over the girl's body in its clinging tunic, he felt a surge in his loins that caused him to shift uncomfortably in his hard wooden saddle.

The soldier grimaced wryly at his discomfort. He was a seasoned veteran, a distinguished legionnaire of Rome. He prided himself on his ability to discipline himself as strictly as he did his troops. That the mere sight of a tousled native girl should make his blood run so thick and hot surprised him. He leaned a tanned arm across the pommel and watched the dusty blonde gather her gear and walk with her companions up the packed dirt ramp leading to the arena gate. Idly he wondered how much of his hard-won gold this laughing creature was going to cost him. Whatever it was, she would be worth it. He ran an appraising eye down her long legs as the group passed through the wooden gate and headed toward the town. She moved with a casual grace that bespoke years of training and exercise.

Marcus lazed easily in the saddle, his gaze focused on the tawny-haired female. As she approached, he noted the gold band encircling her upper arm and the rich bronze markings decorating her leather scabbard. Mentally he recalculated the amount he had decided to pay for her services. He also revised upward his initial impression of her age. As the distance between them shortened, he could see fine lines radiating out from her sparkling green eyes, and a full, sensuous mouth that was all woman. She wasn't beautiful in any classic sense. Her nose was too short, and her limbs were long and lean instead of softly rounded, but she vibrated with life and an unconscious arrogance that the male in Marcus responded to instinctively.

As the group approached the small, travel-worn patrol standing idle in the shade their laughter dimmed. The woman glanced casually at the horsemen, then frowned when she encountered their leader's steady, assessing stare. She broke off her conversation to look directly at him.

Marcus watched her eyes narrow as they ran over his dusty mount, sweat-stained tunic and weathered skin. When she finished her slow, deliberate review, she met his look with a tilt of her chin. The captain smiled inwardly at the antagonism in her stance. After more than two decades of Roman rule, these tribes of northern Britannia were still not totally subdued. Hot-blooded Celtic pride ran in this clan, showed in this woman's arrogant posture. With suggestive deliberation, Marcus slid his eyes down, then back up the long length of her body. As much by instinct as design, his gaze lingered on her breasts before moving up to meet her hostile glare. The woman stiffened at his blatant inspection.

"Thus is Rome's vaunted sophistication." Although her voice was low and musical, the anger in her words carried easily. "These boors are as rude as they are dirty."

The soldiers behind Marcus had no difficulty understanding the woman's Latin, spiced though it was with a crude local dialect. They straightened in their saddles, and several of them reached toward their swords. Their commander stilled them with a negligent wave of his hand.

"It's obvious the lady hasn't had a good look at herself lately, if she thinks us dirty," he commented dryly, the mocking glint in his eyes deepening.

The blonde flushed with anger, as Marcus had known she would. He'd learned long ago how quickly women reacted to any slurs, real or imagined, on their looks. Roman noble or provincial tribeswoman, they were alike in their vanity.

She stopped in her tracks, and the small group closed ranks around her. Her eyes flashed green fire as she stood, hands on hips, chin thrust out.

"Roman pig!" she spat. Her hand closed around the hilt of the sword strapped to her waist. "In our land, men do not call out insults to women passing in the streets. You had best be prepared to back your words with your sword."

A wicked grin spread across the commander's rough-hewn face. He knew he shouldn't lower himself to trading words in the street with an insolent native, but he couldn't resist the urge to prick her arrogance.

"In Rome, women do not parade the streets half-naked, inviting insult. However, my sword is always ready to oblige a female, although I suggest a more private setting for the thrust."

When the crude meaning of his words sank in, the woman gasped. For a startled moment, she stared at him in speechless astonishment.

The youth next to her flushed with a mixture of anger and nervous bravado. Lifting his javelin from his shoulder, he lowered it until the iron tip pointed directly at Marcus. The captain felt a reluctant admiration for the lad's courage, even as his mind assessed how best to handle the threat. The boy knew all too well how dangerous it was to taunt his Roman overlords, but the fierce, proud blood of his tribe would not tolerate any insult to his lady.

He wasn't much more than a child, the soldier noted. None of the males were. Despite their rangy height, the boys sported no trace of red or gold fuzz on their cheeks to indicate budding manhood. The girls appeared slightly older, although none were as mature and well developed as their leader. Marcus straightened in the saddle, intent on defusing the situation with a quiet word before anyone was hurt. The woman's low voice stopped him.

"Nay, Cwenton, do not." She reached out and laid a restraining hand on the boy's arm. Murmuring low, she spoke to him in their native tongue. The boy looked at her uncertainly, then lowered his spear when she held his gaze with a clear, commanding one of her own.

"Wisely done," the captain told her quietly.

The look she gave him would have shriveled a less seasoned man on the spot. Marcus felt amusement flicker once more, although he was careful to keep his face impassive. By the gods, he would enjoy taming this one. He could well imagine the vile curses that trembled on her lips, but she clamped them shut and whirled away without another word. With a curt gesture to the group, she stalked down the dusty lane.

The soldier watched her, an appreciative eye on her swinging hips and trim rear. He made no move to stop her or the rest of the group following in her wake. This was a small town. She would be easy to locate. He would have her brought to him when he was ready to bargain with her husband or kinsman for her services. Right now, after six days in the saddle, a hot bath and several flagons of the locally brewed bitter ale tempted him even more than this blond baggage.

By the time he led his troop up the hill to the Roman camp west of town, the tingling in his loins caused by the native woman was overcome by greater aches. Having arrived in Britannia just three weeks ago, after five years campaigning in the deserts of northern Africa, Marcus was not yet accustomed to this climate. Dampness seemed to seep into each old wound and make him feel every one of his thirty-six summers. A hard, fast week in the saddle visiting the farthest outposts of his new command hadn't helped, either.

He forgot his weariness, however, when the solid walls of the fort filled his vision. A thrill of pride shot through him at this massive symbol of Rome's might. Situated atop a low, sloping hill, the fort formed a perfect rectangle. Two great ditches surrounded it, one terraced just above the other on the hillside. Earth from the ditches had been hard-packed to form a wall ten feet high around the camp, which in turn was crowned by a palisade of sharpened timbers.

Marcus returned the guard's crisp salute as his patrol clattered through the gate and down the wide avenue to the headquarters. He peered ahead, through the colonnaded facade of the headquarters building to the chapel just within, searching for the golden legionary eagle on its pole in the chapel's central place of honor. He could barely see it in the distance, just a bright gleam surrounded by the flags and standards of each squadron and troop, but that glow reassured him as much as it did every soldier entering any Roman camp. As long as the eagle stood, so did their legion.

His small patrol trotted past rows of long wooden barracks on either side of the main street and clattered to a halt in front of the headquarters. The captain dismissed his escort and slid from his mount with a weary grunt. Tossing the reins to a waiting soldier, he returned his second-in-command's salute.

"Come with me while I bathe and change, Lineas. The news of the camp can wait until I've scrubbed some of this dirt from my hide."

"I sent your orderly down to the bathhouse with fresh linen as soon as your patrol was sighted, Prefect," the tribune told him with a wide grin. Tribune Lineas Flavius had served with Marcus before, and knew his habits well. Even in the most frigid weather, the captain insisted on bathing regularly. He claimed he'd never soak all the desert sands from his soul.

"Good." Marcus stretched his weary muscles. "My bones don't take to the saddle as kindly as they used to."

"Aye, you being such an ancient and all," Lineas agreed with a bland look, falling in beside him for the short walk to the baths.

"Careful, pup, you're only a few years younger."

"In age, perhaps, but centuries younger in experience."

"Except when it comes to wenching," Marcus responded dryly, then snorted at the tribune's innocent expression. The whole legion knew of and relished the man's sexual exploits.

As they entered the stone building housing the baths, Marcus grinned to himself, remembering the first time he'd met Lineas Flavius. Like all noble Roman sons, Flavius had to serve his obligatory term in the army before he assumed his future senatorial duties. In his case, however, duty coincided with necessity. His father had hastily purchased his commission and shipped him out to Tunis when two very young, very well connected girls showed up pregnant at the same time, both claiming Lineas as the father. Much to everyone's surprise, including his own, the young lieutenant had taken to the discipline and physical rigor of soldiering as if born to it.

Flavius had served a year under Marcus in Tunis. The seasoned soldier had quickly discerned the new officer's unique leadership potential and superb engineering skills. He had taken extra time with Flavius, sharing his own hard-won expertise and soldiering techniques. Consequently, despite their differences in age and experience, the two men had become fast comrades, sharing many battles, a respectable pile of booty and more than one woman in their year together. Both were delighted to be serving together again in Britannia.

As they crossed the small courtyard fronting the bathing chambers, Marcus ran keen eyes over the stone building that formed the social and cultural center of the camp and provided for their physical well being. The tribune's fine hand showed in its tight construction and the series of earthenware pipes through which water from the nearby river flowed into the bathing chambers. The captain nodded to a couple off-duty troops exercising with weights in the courtyard, then led the way into the bathhouse. The two officers stood in companionable silence while slaves stripped them.

"Remind me to give an extra offering to Mars tonight," Marcus commented as they strolled into the *frigidarium*. "The gods who look after soldiers must have conspired to send you to Britannia before me. Only you would build a bathhouse before finishing the stables or granaries."

Both soldiers hesitated beside the first pool. The icy water would revive and stimulate them before they settled into the serious pleasure of bathing, but it always took some moments to work up the necessary nerve for the first step.

"I must have had a premonition you would be promoted and sent here as commander," the younger man responded, his teeth chattering, as they stood in the frigid water. He wrapped brawny, gold-furred arms around his muscled torso and shot the captain a quick, speculative look. "The betting was you would get command of the Praetorian Guard after your spectacular victories in the desert. After all, the emperor owes much to the hero of Tunis. Your campaigns distracted the people from his excesses, and most likely saved his crown for another year."

"Nero offered me the Guard," Marcus shrugged, settling himself on a narrow marble ledge running the length of the shallow pool. "I am no courtier, though. Not being born to the purple, like you, the intrigues of the court hold no attraction."

"No, it's just like you to pass up Nero's court, with its wild orgies and willing women, to come to the ends of the earth. I tell you, Marcus, the wenches here are about as cold as the damned climate. Colder even than this pool!"

Marcus only laughed. He knew well the tribune had managed to thaw more than his fair share of the local women. Easing out of the cold water, he shook himself like a wet dog. Lineas followed suit, and the two men moved on to the next, lukewarm pool.

Conversation died completely as the tepid water warmed their chilled flesh. Marcus felt the hard days of riding seep from his tired body. After a short time, they heaved themselves out of the second pool and stretched out on stone tables so slaves could scrub and scrape their bodies. That done, they moved to the last, steaming-hot enclosure.

Marcus grunted with pure pleasure as he leaned his head against one of the marble rests lining the pool and let the hot water soak into his bones. Normally the pools would be crowded with off-duty soldiers and officers. The stone chambers usually rang with the slap of the masseurs' hands, the splashes of noisy people jumping in and the sounds of bones rattling and men calling out bets as they wagered their pay in games of chance. Today, a calm, soothing stillness hung over the steaming room. He surmised Lineas had put out the word that the baths were off-limits for an hour so that they would be free to talk. He reached for a horn cup filled with ale set conveniently to hand and took a long, hard swallow.

"Well, Lineas, tell me now the news of the camp. Your dispatches were well written and succinct, but I would have the details."

"It's been as quiet as I reported, Captain. No new raids from the north, and even the local tribes have kept from each other's throats for a change."

Quickly the tribune ran down the week's activities, including the length and direction of patrols, disciplinary actions, supplies expended, the status of engineering projects and, finally, the civil cases he'd presided over. Marcus lazed in the pool, his lean, muscled body relaxed, but his questions to the officer beside him deliberate and probing.

"The only real news is that we had a message from the governor this morn," Lineas told him when he'd completed his report. "He's sending his chief administrator to meet with you. The man arrives tomorrow."

Marcus raised dark brows at the news. "What reason does the dispatch give for this meeting?"

The tribune shrugged. "Only that the administrator is representing the governor on the annual circuit to the kings of the various tribes. While he's in the north, he's to pay a courtesy visit on the young king of this clan, and his regent. The dispatch requests you meet with him tomorrow at noon to discuss a political matter."

"Any idea what this matter could be?" Marcus asked, sipping his bitter ale slowly.

"No," Lineas responded, his thick golden brows furrowed. "Except for the raids from the north, things have been quiet here since the little king's father died in the great rebellion and Rome exacted vengeance. The Lopocare clan is just starting to recover from the penalties we imposed. They have not the strength to foment trouble."

"That's my assessment, also," Marcus said, nodding. "Although I've spent most of my time since I arrived in the saddle, inspecting the outlying defenses, I've seen enough of these people to believe they're now resigned to our rule." Except for one defiant blonde, he thought. And her I will take care of personally. He pushed aside a sudden, vivid image of the haughty woman as the tribune continued his thoughtful, measured words.

"These Lopocares are just a minor clan of the huge Brigante tribe. When their lord rode south to join the rebellion against Rome, the Brigante queen was furious with him. Especially since he was married to her own daughter. So the people here had to endure both Rome's vengeance and the queen's. Combined with the raids from the north, it's a wonder the clan survived at all."

Marcus had been briefed on the local situation upon his arrival. Still, these tangled tribal rivalries were enough to bewilder the most devious politician. Brigantium almost matched the Roman senate for hot-blooded factions and shifting loyalties.

"Why did the old queen put such a weakling in here as regent if the clan was in such desperate straits?" Marcus asked, sipping his beer. "I've only met the man once, but I was not impressed. Mayhap that's the matter that concerns the governor."

"It could be." Lineas placed one arm behind his head, stretching his long limbs out along the marble shelf. He considered the captain's words carefully. "This regent is a weak, simpering pederast who wants only to placate Rome and keep the queen happy. He's supposed to govern until the boy king is of age, but he's really just a figurehead. The boy's mother holds the reins for him and conducts most of the clan's business."

Lazily he turned his head to face Marcus. "Even I deal with her on civic matters occasionally. You will, also, once you settle the defenses to your satisfaction and take over your administrative duties."

His sly innuendo was not lost on his superior. Marcus grinned as he pulled himself up out of the pool. "What's the matter, Flavius? Is the burden of playing administrator in my absence cutting into your wenching?"

"Well, I'll tell you truthfully, Marcus, if I'd known being promoted to senior tribune would mean spending all my time trying to decide who owns what stray calf or how much to fine a farmer for dumping offal in the river above the drinking area, I would have thought twice about extending my army tour," the lieutenant answered, aggrieved.

The tribune continued his running commentary on the burdens of administering conquered territories as the two men stretched themselves out on a long stone table. Marcus listened with half an ear while the slaves oiled and massaged his body. Their fingers worked magic on his sprawling frame, loosening hard knots in the muscles cording his arms and legs, and easing the aches of old wounds. He relaxed under the slaves' ministering hands and grunted with pleasure when they rubbed salve into various puckered scars and tended to his leg. An arrow had pinned him to his saddle many years ago, leaving his left knee a mass of discolored tissue and twisted tendons. The slaves' soothing hands helped relieve some of the constant ache in the joint, made worse by this damnable damp climate.

When he rose from the table, a silent attendant handed him a fresh linen cloth to wrap around his loins, then a clean wool tunic. Marcus fastened on a worn leather belt, instinctively checking to ensure that his dagger and heavy sword slipped freely from their scabbards. After a slave knelt to tie the thongs of his hobnailed sandals, he motioned to Lineas to join him. Together they strolled into the deepening night, heading toward his quarters.

The camp's cobbled streets were crowded now, filled with men who'd returned from their field duties for the evening meal. The soldiers were gathered in groups outside their barracks, enjoying the summer night. Flickering torches provided light for work and play. Some cleaned gear, others gambled on the toss of the bones, others still engaged in the age-old pursuit of soldiers—swapping war stories. All stood and saluted their commander respectfully when he passed.

As the two officers rounded the corner of the long stable building, they spied a cavalry trooper pressed against a pale-haired maid in the shadows. Technically, no women were allowed in the camp except the house slaves who served the needs of the commander and the other officers. There were brothels aplenty in the rough tumble of huts sprawling down the hillside outside the camp, as well as grogshops and traders' stalls to cater to the soldiers' other desires. But Marcus knew regulations tended to be more relaxed on the outer reaches of the empire. Some of the officers had wives or mistresses, or both, with them. Occasionally the ordinary troops would get lucky, as this one had, and bring some native woman back for the night. Lineas grinned and called out ribald advice, to which the soldier replied lewdly.

Marcus was silent as he gazed at the girl's long, pale hair. She brought to mind the woman he had crossed swords with this afternoon. A mental vision of a tangled, tawny mane and thrusting breasts dispelled the lethargy wrought by the baths. He cursed to himself as his body tightened involuntarily.

"Know you a woman with long, honey-colored hair who sports in the arena, training with javelins?" he asked Lineas, although he thought he already knew the answer. Given the tribune's unerring instinct for locating the more succulent pieces, he probably not only knew the woman, but had enjoyed her favors, as well.

The younger man laughed. "Half the women of this tribe are blond, the rest henna-haired. And they've all taken to arms."

The captain shot him a quick, inquiring look.

"I know Rome's policy is to totally disarm a rebellious tribe." Lineas shrugged. "'Twas done here, as well. But with all the men old enough to carry a sword put to death after the rebellion, there was no one left to hunt. Our forces were too thin to feed the entire populace. The women had already taken up bows and spears when I arrived, and I allowed it to continue. If I had not, the peasants would have starved these past winters."

The tribune turned to look at his commander closely. Even in the dim light, Marcus could see the interest flaring in his blue eyes.

"Was there something special about this woman?"

"She caught my gaze, that's all," Marcus answered with a dismissive shrug. He didn't want to set Lineas on her trail unnecessarily. His loins still tight from the memory of her, he decided to ease himself with one of the house slaves until after he sorted out this business with the governor's administrator. Then he would track down the defiant blonde and satisfy the curious lust she'd aroused in him once and for all.

Chapter Two

Lady Alena, daughter of Cartimandua, queen of the Brigante tribe, and widow of Dugald, king of the Lopocare clan, tucked her crimson robe beneath her legs and settled herself happily on the stone floor. She moved a carved wooden horseman forward in short, trotting steps, then laughed delightedly when another figurine swooped across the floor and toppled hers into the rushes. Childish giggles joined her low chuckles.

"Good, Megarric, good. You caught me by surprise that time with your bold attack. A skilled warrior always strikes first."

Alena gazed down at her son's bright golden curls and felt the familiar rush of love the sight of him always brought. And the constant wonder that such a happy child could have come from the seed of her ill-tempered husband. She pushed a finely carved figure in a miniature chariot forward for the boy to attack at will.

"By all the gods, Alena, this time you have gone too far!"

Peganthus, regent for King Megarric in his minority, paced the floor just beyond where the two figures sat and played. He wrung his hands nervously and cast his "niece" an irritated glance, which she ignored. Alena generally paid no attention to her titular uncle. The man was a fool, and she had little patience with him.

"Alena, you must listen to me. You cannot antagonize these Romans. We can barely pay the fines and tributes now. With their camp outside our gates, they'll look for any excuse to raise the levies for grain and foodstuffs. How could you be so foolish as to insult an officer of Rome?"

Two blond heads looked up at the pacing man. The child's face held curiosity and confusion. His mother's held only disgust.

"You should wish to avenge the insult this Roman gave me, Uncle, rather than question my actions." Her words dripped with scorn. "Even the boys with me were prepared to take on the legionnaires, with all their armor and weapons, had I not stopped them."

Peganthus flushed. As usual, Alena's sharp tongue bit into his manhood. Ever since he'd come north to this accursed land three years ago, this stubborn woman had thwarted him at every turn. His bile rose whenever one of the household slaves turned to her for confirmation of his orders or a farmer would request an audience with her, instead of with him, to settle some issue. When Peganthus took her to task for her presumption, she would shrug contemptuously. Or, worse, she'd suggest that when he put the needs of the people ahead of his own greed they would come to him. Once, he'd even threatened force, at which point she'd calmly pulled out her dagger and promised to slit his throat from ear to ear should he dare lay a hand on her. Still, he was regent, appointed by Queen Cartimandua with the blessing of Rome. He tried once more.

"I did not believe my ears this morning when I heard of your conduct yesterday. These are dangerous times. We must be cautious. We have these Romans on our necks, and, even worse, there's trouble within the Brigante clans again. Your father is restless, and challenges your mother's rule."

He paced anxiously back and forth, chewing on his lower lip. "We are like to be caught between them in their bitter feud. I know not how to satisfy them both, and these Romans, too."

Alena laughed and scooted some soldiers across the floor to attack her son's positions. "Oh, Uncle, my parents have been feuding since before I was born. The only reason my mother gave me to Dugald was to ensure he would hold her northern borders while she battled and intrigued against my father."

She sat back while the boy realigned his forces on the stone floor. "It's a good thing the queen is such a prolific breeder. She whelped enough of us to secure her throne all these years through ever more advantageous alliances. I just wish she would leave me in peace for a while, instead of already plotting my next marriage for her benefit.''

Her words made Peganthus even more nervous. He knew his regency would end when Alena remarried and her new lord took over management of her son's clan. As much as he complained about the meanness of the land, sufficient tribute made its way into his private coffers to make him want to retain his regency as long as possible.

In this one matter, he and Alena were reluctant allies. She had no desire to be subject to another such as her dead husband, and Peganthus didn't want to lose his regency. Between them, they'd delayed and hedged and held up the queen's plans for her daughter for nigh on a year. Cartimandua's troubles with her consort helped distract her, as well. Still, the situation was precarious at best.

Peganthus chewed nervously at one dirty fingernail. "You know that an emissary from Londinium arrives today. He supposedly comes with annual greetings from the governor, but it could be on a more serious matter. Mayhap he wishes to increase the tribute, or the levy for slaves. I pray to Adarte he does not get word of your conduct yesterday," he said, returning to his original grievance.

"Oh, Peganthus, cease. What's done is done."

A calm, commanding voice from the corner of the room made him whirl. He eyed the older woman seated on a low stool respectfully. Much as he disliked and feared Alena, he revered Lady Nelwyn, sister to the dead King Dugald. The entire tribe respected this Druid high priestess. The regent approached her, seeking help in managing the stubborn woman who threatened them with her hot-blooded actions. Nelwyn was the only one he knew who could control Alena.

"You of all people should know how dangerous it is to taunt these Romans, Nelwyn. They killed your husband and forbade you to practice your sacred rites. Alena needs to exercise more caution, lest she bring Rome's wrath down on us all once more."

"My husband died fighting, as a warrior should," she replied with unruffled calm. "His soul has passed to another warrior, perhaps Megarric."

Her eyes softened as she gazed down at her nephew's gold curls. After a moment, she turned back to the nervous regent. "As to the rituals, no man, Roman or otherwise, will keep me from appeasing our gods. I do not fear their wrath."

"Bah! You are both hopeless." Peganthus gave up, as he normally did when dealing with these two females, and stalked out of the room.

The older woman slipped the carved stones she'd been fingering into a fold of her robe and clasped her hands loosely in her lap. Placidly she surveyed the two figures sprawled on the floor, their heads close together.

"As much as I hate to concede anything to Peganthus, he's right, you know," she told her sister-by-marriage. "You should take more care with the Latins. They are desecrators of our gods and our ways."

The woman on the floor sighed and pulled herself up. She settled the skirts of her woolen robe around her knees, leaning her elbows on them to prop her chin in her hand. "Aye, I know, Nelwyn. Truly, I did not mean to let the situation escalate so, but I lost my temper."

Nelwyn smiled. Although they were sisters-by-marriage, more than two decades separated her from Alena. When the girl had come as a child bride of less than six summers to her brother, the gray-bearded warrior had summoned Nelwyn and her husband from their homestead. He had tasked his sister with the care of his bride, then promptly forgotten her for the rest of her childhood. Nelwyn had raised the bright, mischievous girl child, and loved her as if she were the daughter she had never borne.

"You tend to lose your temper rather frequently," Nelwyn commented to the impenitent woman before her.

"Aye," Alena replied, her eyes twinkling. "'Tis my worst fault. One of my worst," she amended, at Nelwyn's skeptical look. "However, as you said, 'tis done. With luck I shall never see the Roman pig again, and so shall not be goaded into further unseemly conduct."

At her sister's undignified snort, Alena laughed and gathered her child to her breast, hugging and tickling him until they both screamed with laughter. Deliberately she put the incident, and Peganthus's worries, behind her.

*   *   *

Marcus Valerius left camp just after the sun passed its zenith to meet with the governor's representative. He led a troop of ten cavalrymen, more for show than because of any need for an armed escort on the short ride to the town. His patrol trotted easily, their bronze mail and plumed helmets shining in the dull sunlight that filtered through the scudding clouds.

From long habit, the captain's careful gaze assessed the natives' behavior as he rode through the gates of Corstopitum, the hillfort city that served as the seat of the Lopocare clan. Women crouched in the open doors of round thatched huts while naked children played in the streets alongside chickens and snuffling pigs. The youngsters scrambled out of the way and watched the troop with wide eyes. They were curious, but not frightened, Marcus noted, a sure sign that the vicious repression of this tribe after its lord's rebellion was beginning to fade in the people's memories.

Most of Corstopitum had been burned to the ground in punishment for their lord's actions, but already a thriving town of mud-and-wattle huts had sprung back. A few stone buildings were visible among the huts, as well as a massive long hall built on high pilings for the storage of grain and other goods. Marcus pulled up in front of the king's dwelling. It had been rebuilt in stone, in the Roman style, with wide, shallow steps leading to a portico braced by carved wooden posts.

The regent hurried to meet him as he dismounted. Bowing obsequiously, Peganthus offered to lead him to their visitor. Marcus's lips curled at the man's fawning, but he greeted him with courtesy and followed him into the house to a large chamber to one side of the main hall. A stooped, gray-haired man rose from a leather chair in front of the fire when the two men entered.

"Ave, Prefect Valerius. I bring you greetings from the governor."

"Greetings, Administrator," Marcus replied in a neutral voice, coming forward to clasp the man's forearm. Over the years, he'd dealt with many of the civil servants who governed Rome's far-flung dominions. Most of them were rapacious, greedy bastards, intent only on plundering the provinces of what they could during their three-year tours. Some few bal-

anced maturity with fairness in the discharge of their duties.
The soldier would withhold judgment on this one until he knew
him better.

"I'm sorry to have missed you when you arrived in Londinium, Prefect. Your reputation and honors preceded you. I'm
most pleased to meet the hero of Tunis."

The administrator smiled, his dark eyes glinting shrewdly. He
turned to the hovering regent. "Thank you for your hospital-
ity, Lord Peganthus. I'll call when we're finished."

Thus casually dismissed from his own chambers, Peganthus
bowed low and left.

"In truth, it is most reassuring to have one with your experience commanding the Seventh," the administrator continued when the two men had seated themselves before the fire and
poured wine into elaborately carved and decorated horn cups.

"I'm honored the emperor chose me for this legion," Marcus responded. He kept his words formal and his tone even, but
an unmistakable hint of pride colored his voice.

He had reason to be proud, he well knew. The son of a legionnaire and a freed slave, he'd joined the army at the age of
ten and come up through the ranks the hard way. His daring
and leadership had earned him an early commission and rapid
advancement through officer ranks. Still, this assignment to
command the Seventh was a rare honor for one not of noble
birth.

"You've been more than three weeks in your new command, Prefect," the emissary commented as both men lounged
at ease in their chairs. "The governor would know your im-
pressions of the allegiance of these northern tribes."

Marcus shrugged. "I sent a dispatch to Londinium last week
with my first report. The Brigantes appear to be survivors.
Queen Cartimandua kept most of them out of the great rebellion, and thus preserved her kingdom. Only a few clan leaders, such as Dugald of the Lopocares, defied her wishes and
suffered the consequences."

He swirled the dark wine in his goblet, then continued slowly.
"I see no threat among the Lopocares at this moment. The boy
king is only five, too young yet to inspire anyone's loyalty. Peganthus, his regent, is a weakling. He has no children of his
own to threaten the boy. Nor is he like to, if the rumors are true

about his sexual preferences. The people are just beginning to recover from their punishment for participating in the rebellion. They appear content with the regency and with waiting for the boy to grow into his crown."

The administrator nodded slowly. "We thought so, as well. However, I had long discussions with Queen Cartimandua last week. She worries about this clan. Her own daughter was wedded to their king, yet the man defied her orders and participated in the uprising against Rome. Lately there have been rumors that the widow seeks to ally herself with one of the tribes to the north that are hostile to our interests. Have you had dealings with the woman?"

"No, not as yet. I met the regent and the boy king when I first arrived, but have had little time for local matters since then. My first priority was the perimeter defenses. My senior tribune speaks highly of her care for her people, though," he added fairly.

"I, too, am told she is well loved here. Also that she is the hand behind the king. That, unfortunately, is the problem. The queen worries that the regent is too weak to control these lands or this widow. She wants the woman returned to her court so that she can give her to someone she can trust."

"Cartimandua named him regent in the first place," Marcus responded. "Why did we concur in the appointment, if he is not the right man for the task?"

The older man shook his head. "The only reason he's here is that every male remotely connected to this people was put to the sword after the rebellion. Peganthus was with Cartimandua and did not take part in it. This regency is his reward, though he's done a piss-poor job of it so far."

Absently Marcus fingered the bronze decorations on the horn goblet. He knew there were nuances to the situation that his direct soldier's mind had yet to grasp. "If it's in our best interests to send this woman to Cartimandua, I'll send her."

"It's not quite that simple," the administrator said, hedging. "The queen's hold on her throne is shaky. Her own husband feuds with her regularly. He actually led an armed force against her years ago, and Rome had to send in troops to quell the disturbance."

The administrator shook his head, as if bewildered and disgusted by the eternal feuding of these clans. "In gratitude for saving her throne, Cartimandua kept most of the Brigante clans out of the great rebellion. But we can't trust her. We can't trust any of them after that."

Marcus kept his thoughts to himself. He'd been serving in Germania when stories of the rebellion in Britannia startled the empire. The soldier in him found it hard to believe that a woman called Boadicea could have led an uprising that nearly drove Rome from Britannia's shores. She had left some seventy thousand dead, and three cities burned to the ground, before she was finally defeated. The governor at the time had exacted swift, sure retribution from all the clans who participated in the revolt. Still, he should never have allowed such an uprising to occur in the first place. An uprising led by a woman, still less.

"So the governor would hold this woman, this widow, hostage to Cartimandua's continued loyalty?" he mused.

"Exactly," the older man responded. "He's not ready to give her over to Cartimandua's keeping yet. We don't trust the queen, but we worry at leaving the widow under the eye of such a one as Peganthus. The governor has decided to remove her from the regent's care, and wants you to take her in hand until it is decided where to bestow her."

Marcus barely suppressed a groan. He had his hands full with settling military matters in this wild northern land. The last thing he needed was to be burdened with the petulant demands of a royal widow. A brief assignment to the Praetorian Guard as a young man, and an even briefer marriage to the daughter of a blue-blooded patrician, had given him a decidedly poor opinion of the manners and morals of noble matrons.

"I've told Peganthus that you will remove the woman from his house and that you will oversee the young king's training. You are to use your discretion as to whether the boy should be sent to Rome. We want him loyal to us and our ways, but he needs to know his people, too."

Marcus nodded slowly. Seeing to the boy's training would not be difficult. He'd shaped many young men into fine officers. Caring for the widow was another matter. He had little time or use for females, except in bed. He'd assign the task to his tribune, he decided, grinning to himself as he thought of the tribune's reaction to another administrative duty. Although; if the widow wasn't too seasoned, Lineas would probably make the most of it.

The two men sat comfortably in the big carved chairs and sipped the sour local wine. They talked more of matters in Britannia, and then the administrator pumped Marcus for the latest news from Rome. Being so newly arrived, and having been so recently feted by Nero himself, the soldier had a good firsthand impression of the troubles besetting their increasingly erratic emperor. Gradually Marcus felt himself relaxing under the man's polite, discreet questions. This was a career bureaucrat, one who knew his job and did not try to exceed his authority. Just the kind of assistant a governor such as Maximus needed, the soldier thought. The governor's vague indecisiveness had not impressed Marcus when he'd traveled to Londinium to present his credentials before heading north.

The fire burned low in the stone grate before the two men finished their conversation and word went to the regent to bring the Lady Alena.

Soldier and patrician rose when Peganthus hurried into the room. He turned and called anxiously to a dim figure in the hallway.

"Come, Alena. Your presence is desired within."

Marcus moved back, vacating the leather chair for the lady who followed slowly in the regent's wake. He stood quietly in the shadows while the administrator moved forward, a welcoming smile on his face. The woman who entered didn't see him at first, her eyes on the figure of the other man. But if she did not see him, the soldier recognized her instantly. The dusty blonde might have traded her short, sweat-stained tunic for a rich crimson robe and subdued her tawny mane into a sedate matron's roll, but there was no mistaking the proud look in her clear green eyes.

"Ave, Administrator. You are welcome to the land of the Lopocares, bravest of the Brigante clans." Her words flowed in pure, unaccented Latin as she stood tall and proud, with all the dignity that Peganthus lacked.

Marcus stiffened. The witch, he thought. She used a poor local dialect to taunt me yesterday, when she's obviously been taught the finest Latin by a master. Deliberately he compared this cool beauty to the disheveled wench who'd stirred his lust. He tried to reconcile the shrew who'd flung insults at him in the street with this woman who was widow of one king and mother of another. So much for his plans to purchase her body for his use, the soldier thought sardonically.

"Welcome, Lady Alena." The administrator bowed over her hand. "I bring you greetings from your mother, the queen, and from Governor Maximus. Please, come in. I understand you've not yet met the Prefect Marcus Valerius, commander of the Seventh Legion and newly arrived in your lands."

The woman turned at his words, and Marcus felt a fierce satisfaction at her startled gasp when she recognized him. He bowed slightly and answered the administrator's surprised look.

"The . . . lady and I have indeed met."

She flushed at his deliberate hesitation, but held herself rigid, refusing to give in to the anger he saw glittering in her eyes.

"We exchanged greetings outside the arena yesterday," Marcus drawled.

Surprised, the older man looked from the stiff woman before him to the dark legionnaire. When neither spoke further, he gestured toward the seat by the fire.

"Come, Lady. Take this chair next to me, so we can speak comfortably." He waited until she had seated herself, then continued smoothly. "As you know, each year the governor makes a trip round the province to speak directly with Rome's client kings. Since Governor Maximus could not make the trip this year, he asked me to do so in his stead. He specifically directed me to come to the land of the Lopocares and assess your situation, and that of your son."

Alena nodded regally, but declined to comment.

"I visited with your lady mother as I traveled north. Queen Cartimandua asks that we send you back to her court. She is concerned with your future, and would settle you on someone who could hold this land for your son."

"My mother is ever watchful of her people's welfare," Lady Alena responded noncommittally. "However, I am well placed here, and have no desire to wed as yet."

"You've been a widow for several years now. Your mother indicates she has several good offers for your hand," the older man commented. "But we would mate you with a man who will use your person and your possessions for the good of Rome, as much as for the betterment of the Brigantes."

The woman paled at his blunt words, but forced herself to face him steadily. "I do not wish to wed while my son is yet an infant."

Marcus frowned at the woman's temerity. Noble or peasant, women's wishes in the important matter of marriage were of little concern. The politician responded more gently than the soldier would have in the face of such brazenness.

"I understood he is five years in age. Moreover, he is under your uncle's care during the regency."

Alena made no attempt to hide the scorn in her eyes as she glanced at Peganthus. "My 'uncle' has little time to see to the needs of a small child. Nor is he as familiar as I with the management of the tribe's affairs. I am needed here."

Even a smooth career diplomat could eventually run out of patience. "Nevertheless, Lady Alena, I've come to tell you that the governor is taking the matter of your future in hand. You will be removed from this house and placed under the protection of the prefect until we work out with your mother where to bestow you. And the captain has instructions to see to your son's training."

Marcus could tell the words were an unpleasant shock to the woman. She stiffened and turned her head, giving him a cold stare. Her arrogance did not amuse him this time, as it had the day before, when she faced him, dirty and defiant, in the street. Now he saw it as a direct challenge to his authority. He wanted to wipe that icy disdain off her face.

Without a word, she turned her head back to the administrator. Marcus clenched his lips at the deliberate insult. Not many women, or men, would dare to ignore a prefect of Rome.

The diplomat bowed. "You may retire now, Lady. I leave in the morning to continue my journey, and will negotiate your circumstances with your mother when I return to Londinium. In the meantime, Prefect Valerius will see to your welfare."

The woman stood and faced the administrator. Although both men could see that it went against her grain to plead, she made one more try.

"I have been well and safe in this land for many years. I have little need of this man's attention."

Marcus had had enough. He stepped forward and faced the woman squarely. "You are a rich prize, Lady Alena. Your son will rule these lands in a few years. I will ensure that you are not stolen or given to one whose interests are not also those of Rome."

"And what of my interests, and those of my people?" she asked, her hostility naked now.

"Enough. Gather your things, and be ready to leave within the hour."

At his curt command, she stiffened. For a moment, green flames replaced the icy disdain in her eyes. Her jaw clenched until Marcus could see a line of white bracketing her lips and marring the smoothness of her golden skin. He kept his eyes hard and his stance unyielding in the face of her obvious anger. Without another word, she turned and left the room.

The men stood silent until the servant closed the door behind her, then turned to the cringing Peganthus. Marcus could barely conceal his disgust. One look at the frightened man showed he had no blood kinship to the icily composed, proud young woman.

The administrator issued a stern warning. "The Lady Alena is Rome's ward now. You retain your duties as regent to her son, but with oversight from the commander. Get you gone now, and see to her preparations."

When the regent bowed and hurriedly left the room, the older man turned to the soldier with a rueful smile. "I fear that woman has been too long without the strong arm of a husband to keep her in her place. You'll have your hands full with her."

Marcus relaxed slightly and returned the other man's smile. "I'll manage." He lifted the goblet in a mock salute, then summoned a trooper to send word to the camp to prepare for the Lady Alena's arrival.

Chapter Three

Alena stood trembling in the hallway leading from the main room, trying to still her fiery rage. It had taken every ounce of self-control she possessed to maintain her composure before the Romans. Now, alone in the dim hall, hot anger flooded her veins and caused her to tremble violently. Slowly, painfully, she unclenched her hands from where she'd hidden them in the folds of her robe. She stared down at the deep cuts left in her palms by her fingernails and tried to absorb what had just happened.

A fresh wave of fury hit her as she thought of the administrator's cold words. They would mate her for the betterment of Rome! She ground her teeth in frustration. After holding off her mother all this time, she was to be disposed of so casually by these Romans. Well, they just might have a surprise or two in store for them, she fumed.

"Alena, are you all right?" A quiet voice nibbled at the edges of her fierce concentration. When a hand reached out and shook her sleeve, she whirled, eyes wide and staring.

"Alena, child, what is it? What has happened?"

"Oh, Nelwyn." She sighed, some of the rigidity going out of her stance. "The Romans have decided to take my future in hand. I am to be removed from here and 'protected' until my mother and the governor choose my next husband."

The older woman drew herself up slowly and laid a soothing hand on Alena's arm. "Come, we must talk of this."

"Nay, Nelwyn, I will come to you shortly. I must go to my son first."

The older woman stood silently in the dim hallway and watched Alena hurry toward the young king's rooms. Slowly, silently, her lips moved in an incantation older than time.

Alena stopped just outside the wooden door to her son's chambers and took long, measured breaths. She fought to submerge her anger as best she could, and then she entered the small chamber. The child looked up from his treasured wooden horsemen and smiled. His sunny look clutched at her heart, as it always did. Alena took another deep breath and signaled to the slaves attending the young king to leave.

"What is this, Megarric? Are you refighting old battles?" Smiling, she crossed the room to kneel beside her child. She wanted desperately to grab his small body, to clutch it tight against her breast. Instead, she forced herself to reach out and ruffle his tousled curls.

"Look, Mother," the child said excitedly. "I've got the Lopocares far to the north, about to attack the blue men." He shoved his finely carved wooden figures, then grunted with displeasure when his fingers knocked them over on the rough stone floor.

"Leave them for now," his mother said, drawing him from his mock battle and into her lap. "I would speak with you."

He struggled briefly to be free, then gave up when she put her face into his bright curls and held him tightly. His blue eyes looked up questioningly when she raised her head and gave him a wobbly smile.

"I shall be going away for a while, Megarric. The governor has decided to give me his protection." At his look of childish confusion, she hastened to reassure him. "Only to another house, in the Roman camp. And the governor has also decided you shall receive special training from the Roman's prefect."

The child's frightened look gave way to one of excited surprise. "Truly, Mother? Will I learn to be a soldier, and lead my warriors in battle?"

Alena suppressed a sharp pain. As young as he was, Megarric possessed all the reckless courage and joyous love of battle that characterized her people. Usually she took great pride in his eager, childish daring. Today it hurt that he would accept her going so easily if it meant training with soldiers.

She managed to smile down at him. "Yes, you will learn soldiering. You must pay close attention. Only the gods know how long these Romans will be in our land. If you are to lead our people in these troubled times, you must know their ways, as well as our own."

The boy's face set in mulish lines. "That's why you've made me learn their twisted tongue and haven't sent me out for fostering."

Alena smiled to herself at this old complaint. Most nobles' sons, even royal ones, went to foster with renowned warriors almost as soon as they could walk or stay in the saddle. Long the accepted way for a young man to learn the skills of war, fostering also helped build alliances between the tribes. Megarric should have gone last year, and had fretted petulantly at the delay. Despite her better judgment, Alena could not bear to part with him, and had convinced Peganthus to put his departure off another year.

"Well, now you will learn all their secrets and skills. I will expect you to show me what you learn each day." She sent a fleeting prayer to Epona, the Great Mother, that she would be allowed to see him daily. Bile churned in her stomach when she remembered that the arrogant, insulting Roman soldier would be the one to make that decision.

Swallowing her own thoughts, she stroked her son's head. Crooning gently, she sang stories of the great Celtic warriors he sprang from. Only when a maid came to inquire if she needed anything did she remember the soldiers' orders to ready herself. Gently she kissed the boy, and left him playing on the floor. With one last, lingering look at his bright, sunny face, she left to find Nelwyn.

The older woman sat quietly in her darkened chamber and smiled when Alena entered. Her keen brown eyes surveyed the young woman and saw that the fierce rage that had consumed her in the hall was gone. Alena had a vile temper, but her rages rarely lasted long or carried any grudge with them. They burned cleanly and quickly, leaving a rueful, laughing woman in their wake.

"You will care for Megarric until I sort this out, sister?" Alena moved forward and knelt by the older woman's side.

"Aye, you know I will, child. Tell me what has happened."

Briefly, bitterly, Alena related her conversation with the governor's emissary.

"Why do these Romans seek to take you now, after all these years? Think you they have heard of your dealings with Beorht?"

Alena sighed and shook her head. "I know not, but they must suspect something. They said that they wanted to be assured I did not wed someone hostile to their interests. Beorht certainly is that."

"Aye," the older woman responded dryly. "Of all the great warriors I've known, he is one of the fiercest. Never would he submit himself or his tribe to Roman rule. He wouldn't even submit to Dugald's hand when he came here as a boy for fostering. I was always surprised at the friendship you two children formed."

"He was so brash and bold." Alena smiled, a mischievous twinkle lighting her eyes. "Always fighting and bragging. He couldn't believe it when I bested him at the bow. From that moment, he hounded me. We raced and trained together and played until he grew a few muscles and could finally shoot farther, if not straighter. He was satisfied once he won a few contests."

"Not quite," the older woman drawled. "He matured so much faster than you, Alena. I worried for years he might take your maidenhead before you were of age to consummate your marriage."

Alena laughed up at her. "He tried, sister, he tried. But I would not so forsake my vows."

"Aye, my bright shining one, my *A-leh-nya.*" The soft Celtic syllables rolled lovingly off Nelwyn's tongue. "You are truly named. Even so young, you held true to yourself and your honor. It was obvious to all the boy wanted you. He could scarce hide his stiff rod the last year he was here. 'Twas fortunate the gods sent that omen decreeing Beorht be sent back to his tribe."

"Or that you interpreted the omen to say thus," Alena replied teasingly. "Nay, do not scowl at me. I know you would not manipulate your readings deliberately—unless you believed it most necessary."

Nelwyn's smile faded slowly. "I wonder now if I read those signs aright. Sending the boy away so abruptly ended the first peace we'd had with his tribe in many men's memory. The raids from the north became savage after that. The lad's father swore vengeance for the insult."

"If they had not used that excuse, there would have been some other," Alena offered. "Our clan has always warred with those to the north. Now that Beorht is king, the raids have abated somewhat, though not entirely. He is as war-mad as his father." She sighed and stirred restlessly.

"His last message was most tempting, Nelwyn. He promised to end the raids and rid our land of this festering sore, this Roman camp, would I join with him."

"He would do it, too."

"Have the gods told you this?" Alena asked, wide-eyed. "Did you read it in the entrails of the goat we sacrificed last week?"

"Nay, child," the older woman replied softly. She might, consciously or unconsciously, slant her interpretation of the omens to further a cause she knew to be right, but she would never lie to Alena.

"Oh, Nelwyn, I know not what to do. You are right that only he, if anyone, can rid us of the Romans. It's just . . . I'm loath to subject our people to the ravages his wars would bring, when they are just recovering from the retribution the last rebellion brought us. And I fear the way these Romans come, with ever more troops, scattered across our lands from ocean to ocean. My heart questions whether even Beorht can shake their hold."

The priestess stroked Alena's soft hair thoughtfully. "I, too, worry, child. Since the Romans destroyed our sacred grove at Mora and outlawed our cult, the high priest and priestesses have not been able to hold the annual conclave. I have only whispered messages and travelers' tales to tell me what is happening elsewhere. My heart is filled with bitterness for these invaders. Beorht may be our last chance to throw off their yoke."

"Aye." The younger woman nodded. "Yet he frightens me. He is much as my husband was in his passions. Do you think it wrong of me to hesitate so, because my woman's body recoils?"

"Nay," the older woman responded slowly. She knew well the indignities Alena had suffered at her lord's rough, uncaring hands. "The decision to ally yourself with Beorht must be yours, and yours alone. I will go to the grove, though, and seek some sign to aid you."

She rose slowly and pulled Alena up from the floor. The old habit of looking after the younger woman still governed her. "Come, you must prepare yourself and pack your things. Don't worry about your son. I will tend to him closely, and bring him to you often."

Alena rose, kissed her sister, and left. A frantic Peganthus met her in the hall.

"Woman, what do you mean, tarrying so long? It is past the hour the Romans said to be ready, and you have not begun to gather your things yet. By all the gods, you must hurry."

Contemptuously Alena flung off the hand he laid on her arm and told him, in succinct, colorful phrases, how he and his disreputable ancestors could service the Romans. She left him shaking with helpless rage, and entered her own chambers.

When the given hour had passed, Marcus bade the administrator farewell and went to ready his troops. Mounting his huge, muscled war-horse, he sent word to the woman's uncle that he awaited her.

The late-afternoon sun beat steadily down on his restless patrol. Dogs snuffled in the dirt, nipping at the horses' hooves. Long, slow minutes passed, and still the woman did not appear. Marcus clenched his teeth. As a commander with the might of Rome's legions behind him, he had little patience with anyone who failed to follow orders precisely. And adding to his growing impatience was the fact that he waited here in the dusty, dirty street for a woman who had challenged him twice before. When his horse snorted and shifted once more under his weight, he muttered a vile oath and dismounted. His black brows drew together in a thunderous scowl as he stalked back into the stone house.

"Where is the woman?" he demanded when Peganthus hurried to meet him.

"I've sent for her, Captain. She is in the women's quarters." Nervously Peganthus gestured down the long, dim hallway. "Please, she will come shortly."

Marcus brushed him aside and strode down the passageway. The administrator came into the hall at the sound of doors crashing open and lifted his brows inquiringly at the despairing Peganthus.

" 'Twas not my fault, Excellency. The bitch would not heed my orders and pack. She said Rome could await her pleasure."

They both turned at the sound of screams coming from one of the back chambers. Several maids ran from a far room, crying out in fear. Alena stumbled out the chamber door on their heels. Her hair fell loose from its roll and tumbled wildly about her shoulders as she grasped the doorframe to steady herself. Marcus followed her through the portal.

"Offal!" she screamed as she pushed her tawny mane out of her eyes. "Do not dare to lay hands on me!"

Marcus ignored her tirade and took hold of her arm, yanking her toward the central hall. She lost both her breath and her footing, and fell hard against him. He caught her with an arm around her waist and half carried, half dragged her down the hallway past the two astonished men.

Alena struggled as his arm tightened like an iron band around her and cut off her breath. She beat futilely against his hold, pounding on his rigid muscles and scoring his flesh with her fingernails. As they neared the door, he pulled her upright and set her hard on her feet.

"You have a choice, Lady," he told her grimly. "You can walk out and mount on your own, or I will carry you and throw you across my saddle like some prize of war. Which will it be?"

Tears of pure rage and pain filled Alena's eyes. Her breath came in short, rasping gasps, and she glared up at the hard face of the soldier.

"You bastard!" she spit at him. "I will have your head for treating me so. Dare to touch me again, and your death will be as slow and as painful as I can devise."

She jerked her arm loose and started toward the two other men, who were still watching the scene before them in openmouthed amazement. Before she had taken more than a few steps she felt herself pulled backward by a violent tug on her woolen robe. She whirled again, fists raised, to lash out at her tormentor. The soldier bent under her raised arms and took her writhing form over his shoulder. Her breath left her with a *whoosh* as a hard shoulder cut painfully into her middle. Her head spun dizzily, but she recovered enough to call out to her uncle for help as she was carried from the building.

"Hold, Peganthus." The administrator's cool voice dashed her last hopes. "The governor has given the lady to this man's care. He has the authority to subdue her willfulness as he sees fit."

The soldier stalked to a waiting mare, Alena over his shoulder. Her head spun when he lowered her to her feet and steadied her with a hard hand on her arm. Her robe had torn at one shoulder with the violence, and through tears of rage she saw a sudden twinge of remorse darken the soldier's eyes. He reached out to pull the fabric over her naked shoulder, but she recovered enough to strike his hand away.

"Don't touch me again!" she spit out, and her eyes narrowed to glittering green slits.

"I'll do more than touch you, woman, if you don't mount that horse right now." His gritted teeth and quiet, ominous words rasped across Alena's mind like flint striking on stone.

For a timeless moment, the two stared at each other. All thoughts of rank and authority vanished in the sheer clash of wills between outraged female and arrogant male. She felt the hot, reckless blood of her Celtic ancestors rise, heritage of a race who loved battle and would charge in wildly, regardless of the odds. With all her soul she wished for a sword or dagger. She would cut out this bastard's heart.

Marcus felt his own eyes narrow as he looked down at that tangled hair and those flashing eyes. This was the woman of yesterday, the one who'd challenged him in the street and stirred his lust. A hot flash of desire shot through him. Only his iron discipline, and the belated knowledge that the entire troop was watching the scene with stunned amazement, kept him from grabbing her and throwing her across his saddle.

Alena glanced desperately at the cowering figure of Peganthus. The captain moved deliberately to cut off her view and backed her slowly against the waiting horse with his body. His

massive shoulders blocked everything else from her sight.
Briefly, Alena glanced down at the sword hanging from his
waist in a worn leather scabbard. She bit her lip in frustration
as she realized there was no way to draw and wield it with any
advantage in such close quarters. She looked up to meet his
dark, mocking eyes.

Marcus read the thoughts chasing each other across her face
as clearly as if she'd written her intentions on parchment. By
Mars, these northern tribes bred undisciplined, warlike women.
His blood surged thick and hot at the thought of taming this
wild creature. With great effort, he forced his mind from the
body pressed so close to his and rapped out a short, succinct
order.

"Mount, Lady."

Alena read implacable determination in his dark eyes. And
absolute authority in the harsh, angled planes of his face. She
swallowed the curses that hovered on her lips, knowing they
would do no good. Blindly she turned and reached for the
rough mane with trembling hands. Shaking with rage and
frustration, she struggled to pull herself onto the horse's back.
Hard hands gripped her waist and threw her up into the saddle. Almost before she had time to settle herself between the
four wooden pommel posts, the prefect swung onto his own
mount and wheeled his horse. He reached down for Alena's
reins and jerked her horse after his unceremoniously. The
troops, startled from their fascinated absorption in the drama
under way before their eyes, scrambled to follow.

Alena's face burned with shame as he led her through the
streets, her horse's reins held firmly in his hand. Of all the
characteristics of her people, their love of horses was the one
that most permeated every aspect of their lives. Steeds with
flowing manes and flying hooves decorated their coins. Great
lords displayed their wealth in rich bridle bits and bronzed nave
bands. Warriors fought from horseback or chariot, while
wellborn children, both boys and girls, rode before they could
walk. If this despicable Roman had spent hours searching for
a way to thoroughly humiliate her, he could not have found a
more effective one than taking control of her horse.

By the time they had left the town behind and were climbing
the hill toward the Roman camp, Alena had regained some

semblance of control. Her pride would not let her show any emotion as they passed through the wide gates of the camp and headed toward its center.

The sergeant Marcus had sent ahead to prepare quarters for the lady stood waiting when they drew up in front of a timber-and-stone house across the cobbled square from the head-quarters. The captain dismounted, returned the sergeant's stiff salute, and walked back to assist the lady. Disdaining his help, she slid gracefully from the saddle. The effect was ruined, however, when the edge of her crimson robe caught on one of the pommels.

He watched impassively as she tugged at the tangled fabric. Finally he reached out a strong, tanned hand and ripped it loose. Holding the dark red cloth as if it were a tether, he studied her with narrowed, glittering eyes.

She made a wild sight, with her hair tumbled down her back, her robe half torn off her shoulders and her skirts hiked above her knees. Her anger lit bright green flames in her eyes, and her words came out low and vibrating with heat.

"If you wished to shame me thoroughly, Roman, you have done so. Now release me."

The prefect let the rich crimson wool drop slowly from his fingers. His own voice was just as low, but cold and deliberate.

"You will retire to this house and await my orders. You'll have no visitors without my permission. I'll send your maids to attend you, and servants to see to the house. Praxas here will detail sufficient men to keep you from harm."

With a nod, he signaled to the staring sergeant to take her into the house. She spun on her heel and glared when the man reached out a hand to help her over the threshold. Praxas dropped his hand as if scalded, half mumbling an apology.

"You are a soldier of Rome, man! Do your duty and see the lady inside!"

The prefect's harsh voice whipped both Alena and the sergeant around. Mounted, his armor blazing against the back-drop of the setting sun, he loomed massive and threatening.

Alena muttered a vile oath and entered the house.

Chapter Four

Alena's ready temper usually flared hot but burned quickly. This time, however, it held her in thrall for several hours. She stormed through the house, ranting and cursing, while the servants who had been left to see to her needs cowered in fear. With dire threats and fervent promises, she called on a host of gods to rain down unspeakable horrors on a certain Roman soldier. At last she calmed enough to recognize the unfairness of taking out her anger on the helpless house slaves. She ceased her furious pacing and took several deep, gulping swallows. Slowly, breath by furious breath, she regained her composure.

Gradually Alena controlled herself enough to take stock of the house, which had been hastily emptied for her use. Built in the Roman style, it contained three wings of rooms surrounding a small courtyard. She had never been in one of the invader's homes before, and curiosity, as well as confusion, began to replace the last remnants of her fury. Tentatively she explored the strange rooms and odd furnishings.

She marveled at the luxury of this little stone house. The Celts displayed their wealth in cattle, horses, and rich personal adornment, but scorned creature comforts. Their circular homes, with high, sloping roofs to shed rain and snow, had two or three partitioned rooms, and an open fire pit in the center. Even the king's palace, newly rebuilt in stone with a long corridor and several suites of rooms, was sparsely furnished compared to this house.

Alena roamed from the main room with its cushioned wooden benches and its leather stools, into a large, spacious chamber that was obviously the dining place. It held several

long couches with intricately carved legs and low tables placed
in front of them. Small terra-cotta lamps littered the table-
tops. Behind the dining room was the kitchen, with its great
hearth and its small stone oven. Two kitchen slaves, brought
from the south, eyed Alena nervously when she wandered in.
With her torn robe and tangled hair, she knew she must present a frightening appearance to these soft southern peoples.

Alena ignored them as she continued her explorations.
Across the small courtyard she found sleeping quarters. At least
she assumed they were sleeping quarters. They contained a
raised stone platform with a thick straw mattress and fur coverings. She shook her head in confusion at these foreigners'
strange ways. Why sleep on stone, when the same mattress and
furs could be spread on the floor, she wondered? Shrugging,
she peered into the small rooms that served as slave quarters,
then returned to the central courtyard. Intrigued, she moved
closer to examine an altar set in a niche of the wall at the far end
of the courtyard. It had two carved pillars on either side, with
a triangular stone pediment on top. The back of the altar was
painted, showing three stylized figures. The central figure was
a god of some sort, she supposed, since it sported a head full
of writhing snakes instead of hair. The two figures to either side
of the god held out offerings. Amused, Alena stored up the
details of the small altar to relate to Nelwyn. Imagine trying to
capture gods in paintings and manlike figures, when everyone
knew they were formless, shapeless spirits who inhabited every
river and forest and glen.

Her explorations done, she paced restlessly around the small
courtyard for a while. She retired to the main chamber as the
late-afternoon shadows deepened into dusk, bringing a light
summer chill. One of the servants crept in to build a small fire
in the stone hearth. He timidly offered his new mistress some
watered wine, and she accepted it gratefully. Alena stared into
the flames when the servant left, trying to reconcile all that had
happened in the short space of one afternoon. Tears threatened whenever she thought of Megarric, but she forced them
back. The boy was well attended by loyal servants, and Nelwyn would oversee his education for as long as Alena was gone.
Peganthus would not harm him. He knew full well he would

not survive her wrath for even a day if anything should happen to the boy.

Alena sighed tiredly and slumped on the cushioned bench. Although she despised Peganthus for his weak, sniveling character, she'd found a measure of freedom in his household that she'd never known before. The regent was so frightened of her, he had avoided her whenever possible, leaving her to her own devices most of the time. She had thoroughly enjoyed this unusual state, running both her own life and her son's tiny kingdom until the queen started making plans for her again.

Blast her mother, anyway, Alena thought morosely. Why must she meddle? As many children as she has spawned, could she not have left me in peace in this little kingdom and worked her devious wiles elsewhere? But even as she formed the thoughts, Alena knew such wishes were useless. She accepted the reality of alliances formed through marriage. She herself had been sent north when only five years old to wed the king of the Lopocares for just such a reason.

Her husband, Dugald, had been married before, and had sons aplenty. He accepted the child bride because of her rich dowry in gold and horses, and because he needed a peaceful border with her mother, Queen Cartimandua, so that he could war with his neighbors to the north. Dugald had used Alena's dowry to outfit his warriors, turned her over to Nelwyn, and ridden off to the battles he loved. A long line of sluttish mistresses had seen to his needs during the infrequent periods he was home.

Alena learned at an early age to escape Nelwyn's halfhearted attempts to school her in wifely skills. The older woman cared more for her duties as a priestess than for housekeeping, anyway. Nor did the child wish to subject herself to the petty jealousies of her husband's numerous paramours, some of whom gained thoughts above their station and taunted the little bride-to-be before inevitably being replaced in Dugald's bed by another, fresher mistress.

Almost daily, Alena slipped out of the dark, dank stronghold to wander through the village. Gradually her roaming took her into the surrounding hills and vales. Her husband counted his wealth in horses, and she learned to pick the strongest and fastest to carry her on wild rides through the countryside. She became a familiar sight as she flew across open fields, her hair streaming out behind her.

She knew well that her bright thatch of tangled golden hair and the knowledge that she was bound to the master of this small kingdom protected her. Little by little, she learned to know the people inhabiting the farms and villages, absorbing their names and their ways and their worries. Just as gradually, the people began to share their problems with her when she stopped for a sip of ale or a bite of bread. The child would wrinkle her forehead, take counsel with her husband's steward, and return with an answer whenever possible.

She'd met the boy, Beorht, on one of these rides, and bested him in an impromptu archery contest. Alena's plucky spirit half angered, half amused the red-haired stripling. He would join her whenever he could escape the grizzled old warrior assigned to train the boys fostered with Dugald. He treated Alena with a careless rough-and-tumble affection that brought her many bruises, as well as much laughter.

Almost in self-defense, Alena began to join the few other girls who trained with the boys, to build her muscles and skill. Lopocare women often hunted in the absence of their men, and girls learned young to handle bow and javelin. Soon she was a regular member of a boisterous group of youngsters battling straw enemies hung from trees and shooting at leather targets set halfway down the field. She had a good eye and a natural athlete's skill, and won many of the local contests. In this happy, careless way, the girl slipped slowly through her childhood. She missed Beorht when he was sent away, although his roving hands and increasingly persistent attempts to take her in the grass had become bothersome.

Her childhood came to an abrupt end with her first womanly flow. Nelwyn dutifully displayed the bloody rags to Dugald as proof that his child bride was ready for bedding. Alena fully understood her duty. Although Dugald and his dependents occupied the largest lodge in town, with separate sleeping and living quarters, there was little privacy. Mating occurred regularly at the wild feasts and celebrations, particularly after a successful raid, when the men brought back new women slaves. Alena had often come upon warriors mounted on servant girls in dark corners of the crowded keep. More than once she'd seen her husband, flushed with drink, grunting on top of one of his concubines. She knew what to expect when her husband summoned her to the hall to inform her that the marriage would proceed. He ordered sacrifices, declared himself satisfied when Nelwyn read the signs and said them to be propitious, then formalized the union.

Alena sat quietly through her wedding ceremony, which took place in the main hall of the keep. Just as quietly, she submitted to Dugald's quick breaking of her maidenhead that night. She was not afraid, but found the whole experience unpleasant in the extreme. Her husband smelled of stale beer and old sweat, and it did not occur to him to initiate the child bride gently. His subsequent beddings brought little pleasure and frequent pain. He was a huge, loutish man, who took his ease whenever the need moved him, without bothering to prepare his young wife or ease his passage.

Once, when his drinking made him particularly brutal, she slipped from their bed of animal skins, found his dagger in the dark, and threatened to stuff his man-root down his throat if he touched her again. He was drunk enough to find her childish defiance amusing that time, although she bore many bruises in later years when her attempts to defend herself were less successful.

When Dugald joined the few other Brigante lords who defied Queen Cartimandua and rode south in the great rebellion against the Romans, Alena gave silent thanks for his absence and ruled his lands competently in his name. After the rebellion failed and Dugald took to the hills to evade and harass the pursuing Romans, she saw him only once more. He crept back, late one night, under the Romans' noses, for supplies and arms. He took the time for a hurried, hurtful coupling with his young wife, then was gone. Word came months later that he had been trapped and killed. Alena observed all the proper rituals, but her heart was filled with wild rejoicing. It was only then, as she awaited word of her own fate, that she discovered she carried a babe.

Her mother, Queen Cartimandua, convinced the Romans to spare the noble womenfolk when they arrived to mete out vengeance to the rebellious Lopocare. Cartimandua fully planned to use the women herself by giving them as prizes to allies she could trust. The queen summoned her daughter to her court, but Alena sent word she was with child and could not travel.

Life at Corstopitum under Rome's heavy hand was not easy. As punishment for the tribe's part in the rebellion, the Romans confiscated the lands and goods of the dead warriors and put the town to the torch. The surviving warriors were sent into slavery, and many of the women and children starved or froze that first, harsh winter. Under sanction herself, Alena nevertheless forced the soldiers who took up permanent duty in their area to deal with her.

Reluctantly at first, then recognizing the need if she was to ensure the survival of her son and her people, Alena learned fluent Latin. Ignoring the regent's clumsy attempts to take over leadership of the tribe, she managed its affairs, as she had always done. Distant clansmen sent petitions for her to rule on. She would consult with Nelwyn on all judgments, drawing on the priestess's vast learning and ability to read omens, then persuade the Romans to see to her people's needs.

Eventually the Romans brought slaves from the south to help rebuild the towns and farmhouses. They organized the mating of local women to retired legionnaires and freed men brought up from the south to replace the diminished labor supply. After a year had passed, they even allowed some distant Lopocare lords who had not taken part in the rebellion to assume the management of the outlying lands and swear fealty to the boy king Megarric. The Romans even set up defenses to help hold off the northern raiders, who would steal even the few pitiful animals and women who survived. Slowly, as one year led to the next, order returned. With it came an uneasy mix of Lopocare, Roman, and southern customs.

When Lineas Flavius arrived to take over as senior tribune of the new camp, Alena's life eased somewhat. With his laughing blue eyes, outrageous sense of humor and blatant invitations to his bed, the tribune granted her concessions to ease her people's plight. His teasing and sensual flattery awakened a feminine awareness in Alena that she had never known before, but she had no difficulty deflecting his advances. After her experiences with her husband, she had no desire to subject herself to any man again.

Between managing her tribe's affairs and tending to her babe, Alena filled her days and nights. If occasionally her body ached with strange longings she didn't understand or know how to ease, she worked off the feelings with long rides through the early-morning mists. She also found that physical exercise

helped, and convinced Lineas Flavius to allow her to institute
training sessions for the surviving children in the new earthen
arena the Romans had built outside town. Frequently she
joined in, as she had yesterday, when she met the despised prefect for the first time.

Thoughts of the prefect brought Alena back to the present
with a surge of frustration. Closing her eyes and leaning back
against the rough wall, she wished fervently that the governor
had given her in keeping to anyone but this soldier. Rage surged
through her again as she thought of how he'd handled her.
Even her husband, brutish as he was in bed, had given her the
respect due her rank in public. Since his death, she'd grown
unused to bowing to any man's authority. The regent was weak
and stupid, easily maneuvered. The tribune laughed and teased
and generally gave her what she wished. Their only serious
disagreements concerned his enforcement of the edict against
the Druids, and the amount of tribute the Lopocares should
pay to support the growing camp outside their town. This new
prefect, this Marcus Valerius, would not be as easy to manage,
especially if he roused her ire every time they met.

Alena rose and paced the room restlessly as she considered
ways to get control of her life back into her own hands. She was
still considering her limited options when a noisy clatter announced the arrival of her women. A few moments later, her
timid red-haired maid rushed in.

"Lady Alena, are you all right? I was sore afraid when that
Roman stormed into your chambers and carried you off like
that."

"I didn't exactly enjoy it myself," Alena responded dryly.

Ethelyn blinked. The girl had served her since they were both
children, but Alena knew her strange sense of humor still confused the maid. More than once, she'd marveled that Alena
could recover both her spirits and her laughter after one of
Dugald's visits. And more than once, Alena had tended to the
maid after she herself had received Dugald's indiscriminate
lusts and crawled in pain to her straw pallet.

Alena sighed. "Come, Ethelyn, show me what you have
brought." Together they walked across the courtyard to the
sleeping chamber and dug through the baskets dumped there by
the soldiers. Alena fingered the bright striped and checkered
woolen fabric of her robes as she pulled them out. She had but
three good robes, and even fewer pieces of adornment—only

the thick, twisted torque she wore about her neck on ceremonial occasions, and her armbands. All her other jewelry had been confiscated. She had not wished to burden the peasants by buying trinkets when they were struggling to meet both the queen's and Rome's demands. She'd managed to control the amount Peganthus skimmed off in bribes and extra fines, and knew, almost to a coin, how slim their coffers were. She would not waste their precious reserve on finery, despite the fact that the traders who followed the Roman camps were bringing new and exotic ornaments to their markets, the like of which she had never seen before.

She shook the folds of her robes out and gave them to Ethelyn to hang on the pegs pounded into the bedchamber's stone walls. Finding an old, plain robe in the bottom of the basket, she set it aside. Unfastening the enamel brooch that held the one untorn shoulder of her robe, she slipped out of it.

"Here, Ethelyn, see if you can mend this."

The girl took the robe, then gasped. Alena followed her eyes to the dark bruise marks that marred the flesh of her shoulders and upper arms. Surprised, she rubbed her fingers lightly over the marks. She remembered the captain's hard hold, could feel again her helpless fury when he had handled her so carelessly, but in truth she could recall no pain.

Mother Epona, she prayed, eyes on the bruises, give me strength. Help me with this man. He had irritated her beyond measure from the first moment of their meeting. In their few encounters, she'd allowed him the upper hand when she lost her temper. From now on, she vowed, he would find her cool, calm, and rigidly in control. She would not let this boorish clod of a Roman goad her into losing her temper again. She would discover this man's weaknesses and use them to bend him to her desires. All she needed to turn this potential disaster was a little time and self-control.

Chapter Five

Lineas Flavius rushed through his duties early the next morning. When the buglers signaled the men to their morning meal, he consumed his own breakfast in quick bites. He waited impatiently while the centurions accounted for their companies, then brought in their daily report. Lineas took their reports and confirmed the work details for the day. That done, he strode across the central courtyard of the headquarters building and sent a scribe to request a few moments of the commander's time. He found Marcus at the wide wooden table that served as his desk, reviewing the previous day's dispatches.

He greeted Marcus with a wide grin. "Hail, Prefect. I arrived back from patrol late last night to find a guard posted at the doors to my quarters and myself dispossessed. I understand the Lady Alena had taken up residence there."

Marcus leaned back in his chair and eyed his lieutenant. He waved the younger man to one of the leather chairs facing his worktable. "How well do you know the lady?"

"Well enough," Lineas answered. "I've dealt with her on matters of distribution of food and seed, since her fool of an uncle can't make a decision to save his soul. She's always been most gracious and charming."

Lineas concealed his curiosity behind an impassive countenance, but wondered what in the world was happening. Word of the captain's stormy confrontation with Lady Alena was the talk of the camp. He'd gotten a garbled account of it from his orderly when he arrived at his temporary apartments last night, and it had formed the main topic of conversation at the offi-

cers' mess this morning. There he'd heard wild tales of torn
clothing and the lady being carried out of her house over the
prefect's shoulder.

"Indeed," Marcus drawled, refusing to be drawn out. He
knew well what rumors must be circulating in the camp.

"Come, Valerius," Lineas said impatiently, abandoning all
attempts at restraint. "Tell me what happened. Why did the
governor's emissary come, and what has the lady to do with
it?"

Marcus put down the scroll he'd been holding and detailed,
shortly and succinctly, the rationale behind the visit. Although
he kept any mention of Alena herself to a minimum, Lineas
seemed fascinated by her.

"So the old queen thinks to settle the Lady Alena again.
From what I know of her, the governor is right to be concerned. She's strong-willed, and beautiful enough to turn any
man's mind. He needs to choose carefully who he mates her
to."

"How is it that these native women gain such power?"
Marcus asked in some exasperation. "This one should have
been locked away or married off years ago."

Lineas shrugged. "I don't understand it myself, precisely.
Something to do with their religion, I think. Women serve as
high priestesses and take part in all the ceremonies. Unlike our
Roman women, these have rights under tribal laws. They can
be deeded lands and property, unbelievable as it may be. And
many bear arms."

Marcus smiled inwardly as he remembered again the first
time he'd seen Alena, with her long legs bared and a short
sword belted to her waist.

"There were reports that a good number of women fought
in the rebellion," Lineas continued, unaware of his superior's
distracted thoughts. "I doubt the number was all that large,
although you and I have both seen more surprising things in the
course of wars."

"Whatever number of warlike women may have taken up
arms in the past, it matters not now. The Lady Alena will have
to learn to accept Roman governance of her behavior henceforth," Marcus replied. A now-familiar irritation filled him at
the thought of the lady in his care. He knew it had much to do

with wanting the woman and not being able to take her as he desired. Abruptly he rose and buckled on his short sword. "Call in the troop commanders, and we'll review the disposition of our forces."

Military matters occupied him fully for the next few days, and he delegated care of the lady to Lineas. Conscious of his charge to take the young king's training in hand, however, he did set aside time to visit the boy. He showed up unexpectedly one afternoon at the king's residence and asked to see the child. Marcus bowed slightly, helmet in hand, when Peganthus brought him to the child's room.

Man and boy observed each other carefully. Marcus could see his mother's coloring in the golden curls, but the wide blue eyes that watched him so seriously had no hint of the deep jade green of his dam.

"Ave, King Megarric. I am Marcus Valerius. Part of my duties as prefect of this territory is to see to your training at arms."

The child nodded, his neck craned to look up at the tall, armored man looming over him. When his lip trembled slightly, Marcus knelt slowly before the boy to ease his fear. He had little experience with children, but much with young and frightened recruits.

"I have asked your uncle to have your pony saddled. Will you ride with me?"

Marcus had found the one sure way to banish the child's fears. Megarric had ridden in his mother's arms almost since the day of his birth. She'd strapped him on his first pony herself. His happiest hours were when they rode wildly through the lush valleys and swirling mists.

"Yes, Prefect. I will ride." His formal response came out in a childish treble, but there was no mistaking the eagerness in his blue eyes. Remembering his dignity just in time, Megarric solemnly led the way outside and scrambled unassisted onto his mount. In keeping with his rank, his horse's trappings sported heavy bronze ornaments that tinkled merrily as he rode at the head of the small detachment of soldiers. Megarric forgot even the semblance of kingly deportment, however, when they reached a wide meadow and Marcus suggested they let the horses have their heads.

With a wild whoop, the boy kicked in his heels and took off like an arrow loosed from a bow. A flicker of fear shot through the Roman prefect as he watched the small body being borne off into the distance. He spurred his own stallion after the boy. By the time his great war-horse had closed on the pony, the soldier relaxed. He could see the boy was in firm control of his horse. His short legs barely reached the pony's side, but he had a steady grip on the bridle and leaned forward easily in the saddle. For long moments they galloped side by side, the wind in their ears and the sun beating down on their heads.

When they finally drew up beside a tumbling stream, Marcus watched as the child slid agilely to the ground and allowed his horse to drink sparingly of the cold water. Someone had trained the boy well, he thought.

"You ride like a warrior, King Megarric," he commented as he led his own horse to the rushing water.

The child shrugged, keeping a close eye on his hot pony. Riding was part of his nature, bred into him as surely as his daring spirit.

"Shall we see what other skills you have learned?" Marcus asked when they pulled both horses away before they could drink too much of the cold waters.

The boy looked uncertainly at the man before him. When Marcus fashioned a small sword from broken branches, he grinned in relief. Grasping the makeshift weapon in both chubby hands, he swung back and banged it against the soldier's shins with all his might.

"Ouch!" Marcus jumped back in astonishment. "You little devil, what are you up to?"

The boy giggled in delight. "Mother says attack is always better than defense, especially when you have surprise with you."

Marcus smiled ruefully. He should have known that the hellcat he'd carried kicking and screaming from her house would spawn a fighter. He bent to pick up another branch and barely parried the boy's enthusiastic thrusts. They were both laughing by the time the soldier called a halt. Although Megarric gave no signs of wanting to quit, Marcus could see that his arms had begun to tremble from the weight of the branch and his thrusts were more erratic than planned.

"Enough, halfling, I yield." He smiled down at the child, rank forgotten by both in the shared comradeship of arms. "We will continue another day."

He lifted the boy, now more tired child than cocky warrior, onto his pony, and returned him to his house. A waiting maid-servant took the weary child in her arms. Despite his drooping head, the boy managed a cheeky grin as he disappeared into the house.

Marcus informed Peganthus that he would send soldiers to fetch the child twice weekly, then returned to the camp, well pleased with his afternoon. One of his charges, at least, looked to be manageable.

His other charge, however, proved even more troublesome than he had imagined she would. His first mistake, Marcus acknowledged wryly some days later, was in assigning Lineas to see to her needs. The tribune would not stop mooning on about the lady, either on or off duty. And the guards assigned to her house were no better. The Lady Alena became a favorite topic of conversation at the baths, until Marcus finally snapped irritably that he was tired of hearing about her. For reasons he preferred not to analyze, he disliked hearing other men discussing her lush body and rich coloring. But Lineas seemed particularly fascinated by her.

"Enough, Flavius," Marcus ordered coldly, the sharp edge of anger in his voice halting the tribune's embellished account of the lady's charms in midsentence. Marcus had joined his senior staff in the austere, plain room that served as the officers' mess while they broke their fast, only to find them listening with varying degrees of male appreciation to the tribune's description of his latest visit to the lady's quarters.

The officers looked at Marcus in surprise. The captain's thick dark brows drew together in a frown. He rarely lost his temper or his control with his men.

However, most of the camp had noted his short temper lately where the lady was concerned. His men had begun to walk warily around him. All except Lineas. The tribune grinned at the prefect's irritated scowl whenever the lady was mentioned, and delighted in giving him casual, offhand reports of her graciousness and golden smiles. There was the slight matter of an Arab woman who had ridden off most willingly with Marcus, even as Lineas was bargaining with her husband, that he had long wanted to avenge.

Marcus stood. The men eyed him warily after his harsh order.

"Those of you not on duty this day, get your bows and join me at the stables. I need a hunt to clear my mind and ease my temper."

A long hunt, a fire shared with companions, some dark ale— that was what he needed to shake the irritating woman from his thoughts, the prefect decided.

Lineas grinned at his captain's orders and gathered a dozen lightly armed troops at the north gate of the camp. They broke into a gallop as they followed their commander across the lush green fields. This damp climate might wreak havoc on an old warrior's injuries, Marcus mused, but it certainly sustained a rich crop growth. The hunters soon left the fields and plunged into the woods, spreading out as they crashed through the brush. Gradually, they slowed and worked their way methodically through the thick wood. One of the men caught sight of a boar and yelled as he gave chase. The others wheeled to follow the sound, soon joining in for the kill.

When the band stopped to rest beside a small stream running through a leafy glade, the bloody carcasses of several wild pigs and antlered deer were strung across the withers of their tired horses. The thrill of the chase had erased the last of Marcus's ill temper. He knelt on the bank of the stream beside his men and washed the blood and gore from his hands and arms. Leaving their horses to crop the rich grass filling the small glen, the soldiers settled themselves comfortably on the ground. One of the men passed a leather wineskin he'd had the foresight to bring. Even the sour local wine tasted good after the long hunt. They lazed companionably in the grass, sharing the wine and tales of successful campaigns and hard-won victories.

After a while, one of the men rose to amble to the edge of the clearing. He reached under his tunic to loosen his loincloth and relieved himself. A frown etched his forehead as he straightened his clothes and kicked aside the brush piled against a tall tree.

"Captain, look here."

Marcus rose with a swift, fluid motion and joined him. The other men followed in his wake. Kneeling, the captain ran a hand across a low, squared stone with an oval depression hollowed out in its top.

"What do you suppose it is?" the soldier asked.

Thoughtfully Marcus fingered rough carvings on the sides of the stone, obvious representations of the sun and the stars. "I would guess it's a Druid altar," he replied calmly, surveying the brush piled high on either side of and behind the stone. "If you move that debris aside, you'll probably find bones and animal remains."

"And a human skull or two," Lineas added, looking over the captain's shoulder. "These barbarians have an unholy fascination with heads. The warriors decorate their doorposts with the skulls of their conquered enemies. And they offered the heads of sacrificial victims to their gods before we outlawed Druidism."

Marcus straightened slowly and looked at the thick trees lining the edges of the glade. His gaze fixed on one particularly tall oak a few rods away. Strolling over to it, he kicked at the loose scrub under one massive branch and uncovered a bare, burned patch of ground.

"This was likely one of their sacred groves. When I served in Gaul, I heard tales of Druid practices. There was much human sacrifice, particularly before battle. They would enclose prisoners or sacrificial slaves in wicker cages, hang them from trees and light fires under them. The priests would prophesy the battle's outcome based on their victim's agonized movements."

"No wonder their practices were outlawed," one of the men growled, glancing nervously from the blackened earth to the dark, silent woods around them. "Such human sacrifice is disgusting."

"Aye, though how it differs much from the spectacles of our arenas escapes me," Lineas drawled as he poked at the scorched ground with the tip of his bow. "Nero's latest sport is feeding helpless, unarmed men, women and children to wild beasts to satisfy the blood lust of the crowd."

One of the senior centurions nodded. "The emperor has found new fodder in a fanatic sect, called Christians, after their prophet. I saw over two hundred of them savaged at the festival in Jupiter's honor when last I was in Rome."

Marcus sent his tribune a quelling glance. Criticism, even implied, of the emperor or his habits bordered on treason. The prefect could allow no hint of disrespect in front of the men, although he had his own doubts about Nero's orgies of blood. In Tunis, he'd had to detail a special detachment just to crate and handle the thousands of lions and wild panthers shipped to Rome for the spectacles. He'd seen those same animals in action, as Nero's guest, before leaving for Britannia. These so-called games sickened him. Death in battle he accepted. The atrocities committed in war's aftermath he could understand, if not always condone. The mindless, frenzied blood lust of a screaming crowd made his own blood run cold. Deliberately he put the emperor and his excesses from his mind and focused on the problem at hand.

"From the way the grass is growing back, it would appear that there have been no sacrifices here in many months. Still, I want patrols sent out regularly to check. Catullus, take one of the stags and leave it at the stone altar. Although we do not agree with the way these people honor their gods, it's not wise to offend them."

The men nodded, relieved. Like most of Rome's auxiliaries, they came from the far corners of the empire, bringing their customs and their beliefs with them. They worshipped a wide host of gods, their own, as well as Rome's. No need to risk an arrow or a spear from an unfriendly tribesman just because one of the local deities was slighted.

The hunters returned to camp with the rest of their trophies just as the bugle sounded for the evening meal. They clattered through the gates and headed down the broad *via principalis* toward the headquarters, weaving their way through clusters of soldiers on their way to their barracks and a hot evening meal. Smoke from a hundred kitchen fires curled out of the barrack's chimneys and filled the darkened evening with the tantalizing scent of roasting meat.

After giving the carcasses to the quartermaster to be dressed and distributed, the officers separated to wash, then gathered in the mess to dine and celebrate their hunt. Marcus joined the centurions and tribunes in the officers' mess for the long evening meal. Course followed course, and amphora after amphora of wine vanished as the convivial group toasted the hunters' skill and marksmanship. By the time he made his careful way to his own quarters, Marcus had lost all traces of the irritability that had plagued him in recent days. He fell into bed still half dressed, bellowing for the kitchen slave who saw to his needs. She slipped into his bedchamber, trying to gauge his mood. Normally she enjoyed his skilled lovemaking, but lately he had been abstracted and less attentive in his love play.

"Come, little one. I will not bite. At least not so as to cause pain."

She giggled at his lopsided grin and slipped her tattered robe from her shoulders. He tugged her hair as she leaned over him with one knee on the raised sleeping platform. Laughing, she tumbled into his arms, then gasped as he rolled over and fastened his mouth on hers.

Marcus tried to summon his usual enthusiasm for the willing maid, but even in the depths of his wine-induced passion a fleeting vision of long, lean flanks and shining gold hair filled his mind. Disgusted, he forced the image from his mind and attended to the business at hand. But at the final moment of climax, when the little maid screamed her pleasure, the Lady Alena filled his thoughts and robbed him of any measure of satisfaction.

Chapter Six

The next morning Marcus awakened with a pounding in his skull and a throat that felt like raw leather. Easing his arm from under the maid's head, he forced his protesting body from the bed. He grabbed his linen tunic from the floor and left the bedchamber, heading for the baths. Perhaps the icy waters of the *frigidarium* would stop the fierce throbbing in his head.

By the time he returned, his body tingled from immersion in the cold waters, and the ache in his temples had eased. He ate a light breakfast, then sent a servant to rouse the suffering Lineas from his bed with orders to join him within an hour so they could call on the Lady Alena. He had put off his business with the woman long enough.

Alena heard his arrival from the kitchens, where she was instructing the servants in the preparation of some of her preferred dishes. As long as she was to be immured in this admittedly luxurious prison, she intended to run it to her satisfaction. Since she had little knowledge of kitchen skills, both she and the hapless cook she was trying to instruct were frustrated and short-tempered.

When a maid came running with the news of the captain's arrival, Alena wiped her hands on the cloth tied around her waist. She cursed the man for sending no advance word so she could ready herself. As it was, she wore one of her oldest, most serviceable tunics. The gray robe hung to the floor in shapeless folds. It was fine for when she was romping with Megarric, rolling in green fields and wading in streams, but she had wanted the armor of her finest robes when she met this arrogant Roman again. She considered ignoring the summons brought by the frightened maid and taking time to change, but the memory of what had happened the last time she kept this man waiting was too fresh for her to take the chance.

She wiped her hands and tunic as best she could and walked slowly to the main chamber at the front of the house. She reminded herself of the promises she'd made to stay calm, to stay in control, to learn this man and his weaknesses. Alena entered the *solarium* quietly and waited for him to acknowledge her.

Marcus had to look twice at the woman before he recognized her as the lady he'd come to dictate terms to. She'd covered her hair with a dull gray cloth and wore a tunic his house slaves would disdain. He shot an incredulous look at Lineas, who shrugged and shook his head. The suspicion that the woman deliberately offered insult by appearing before him dressed in rags crossed his mind, only to be dismissed. Still, he had difficulty reconciling the slatternly figure before him with either the laughing wench of the street or the icy matron of the administrator's visit.

Alena withstood his silent scrutiny until her patience wore thin. She decided not to cater to his boorishness and took the initiative, since he seemed disinclined to offer her even a simple greeting.

"Hail, Roman. I'm sorry I had no notice of your visit to prepare a fire in this chamber. However, I've sent for wine and cheeses, and I bid you be seated until they come."

She had turned to smile a greeting to Lineas when a hard voice stopped her.

"My name is Marcus Valerius. You may call me 'Captain' or 'Valerius,' but not 'Roman,' and not in that tone of voice."

Alena blinked. No man had ever dared speak to her thus, not Peganthus, not even her husband in his worst moments. She bit back an angry retort that sprang to her lips and took a deep breath.

"Very well, Captain. Please sit and tell me what brings you here."

Marcus stood, arms crossed, eyes narrowed. What was the woman up to? What did she think to accomplish with this meek, drab mien? He moved to a wooden bench, motioned to her to sit on the one facing it, and waited until she had seated herself before continuing.

"I am here to settle your circumstances until the governor and the queen decide where to bestow you. I would have you know what I expect of you in the weeks to come."

Alena felt a flush creep up her face at his clipped, authoritarian tone, but forced herself to stay calm. She kept her head down and refused to look at either the captain or his lieutenant. She knew that if she looked up now her anger at being spoken to so would betray her.

"What do you expect, Captain? I want to know so we may avoid any repetition of the treatment I experienced at your hands when last we met."

Despite herself, Alena could not keep the acid hint of her dislike out of her tone. She raised her head slowly, fixing her eyes on a point just over his left shoulder.

The prefect sat back on the wooden bench and surveyed the stiff woman from under half-closed lids. He hadn't missed the temper in her voice, however she might have tried to control it. He held his response while two slaves brought wine and trays of fruit and cheeses and set them on a low table in front of their mistress.

"I expect word from the governor by the new moon. Until that time, you will keep to this house and behave quietly and modestly. I will send food and fresh game. You will not contact your uncle, nor will you admit anyone that I or Tribune Flavius do not authorize. The governor has fears for your safety, and I am charged with holding you fast until he sends for you. Do you understand, Lady?"

Alena felt the last threads of her self-control slip at his low, deliberate words. How dare this ignorant, pig-headed Roman imply she had ever behaved immodestly? Did he think she would submit so meekly to such strictures? Her anger boiled over, and her eyes flashed green sparks. She rose abruptly from her chair and advanced on the man seated opposite her.

"Do you question my conduct? Do you dare tell me how to act? You are nothing but a common soldier, offal that Rome tosses from its shores to float endlessly on foreign tides. Do not presume to dictate behavior to your betters."

Marcus rose, as well, amusement glinting in his dark eyes. It hadn't taken long for her to shed her docile manner. The little cat couldn't change her spots, after all. She had less self-control than his rawest recruit, but twice the foolhardy bravado, he decided. She knew all too well how easily he could control her with brute strength, but still she came at him with eyes blazing and anger radiating in every line of her long, lush body.

His amusement fired Alena's rage. The lout dared to laugh at her. She looked wildly about the room for something to use as a weapon. Lineas took a hasty step backward as her gaze locked on his sword. Seeing nothing else to hand, Alena whirled and came within arm's length of the captain.

"Do not laugh at me, pig," she warned. "I have skewered men for less than you presume to."

Marcus stood, unmoving, arms crossed over the linked mail of his cuirass. Much as the man in him might enjoy the sight of her heaving bosom and the flush painting her cheeks to bright pink, the soldier in him could not allow such defiance to pass.

"Cease your ranting, woman, or else I shall take you across my knee and beat you until you have not breath left for such empty threats."

He took her arm and thrust her down on her bench. She tried to rise, but his hand tightened warningly on her soft flesh and held her until she stopped resisting.

Lineas took an involuntary step forward. In his dealings with Alena, she had charmed him completely. Although he barely recognized this spitting cat as the same woman, he disliked seeing her treated so.

Marcus fired a hard look at his lieutenant that stopped him in his tracks, then dismissed him with a quick jerk of his head. The younger man gave Alena a quick assessing glance before he straightened slowly. His respect for the man overcame his concern for the woman. He knew Marcus would not harm her unduly, although he suspected she would not like his disciplinary methods, however temperate the captain might consider them. He spun on his heel and left.

A long, heavy silence filled the *solarium* after the door closed behind the tribune. Alena looked down pointedly at the restraining hand, so dark against the pale skin of her arm. The strong grip did not loosen until she craned her neck upward to

meet the prefect's gaze directly. He was so close, Alena could
see hazel flecks in his intent brown eyes and the faint white line
of an old scar that ran from the corner of one eyebrow across
his temple to bury itself in his crisp black curls.

Slowly Marcus lifted his hand and moved away. "Look you,
Lady, I like this stewardship as little as you, but I will keep you
safe and fast, whether you wish it or not. This period can be as
pleasant or as rough for you as you make it. If you will curb
your temper, we can discuss sensibly how we are to proceed."

He held her eyes with a hard, steady stare until she finally
broke the deadlock to look away. She swallowed and made an
obvious effort to gather the shreds of her dignity. Marcus used
the few silent moments to take a leisurely inventory of her
averted profile. Nose too short, he decided, chin too squared,
surprisingly dark brows too thick. Obviously the Roman matron's predilection for plucking the brows into a thin line had
not spread to this land yet. But, by Venus, what skin! Soft and
golden and completely free of paint or artifice. And what incredibly long, dark lashes, shading eyes the color of a deep
forest pool. Although her hair was hidden under a gray cloth,
he remembered well the way it hung, tangled and wild, below
her waist. His fingers itched to reach out and pull the cloth off.
For a few moments, he allowed himself the luxury of imagin-
ing the feel of her silky mane. Desire licked at his veins as he
waited quietly until she turned to face him once more.

"You are right, Captain," she said through clenched teeth,
swallowing her anger. "We must deal better with each other
and with this . . . this situation."

"Good." He nodded approvingly, knowing how much the
words had cost her. "We seem to have struck sparks off each
other from our first meeting. We must both learn to temper our
words and our actions."

Alena's brows raised in surprise.

"Think you I do not know that I have antagonized you?" he
asked, a smile tugging at one corner of his lean cheek.

"Aye, you have. Deliberately!" Indignation and irritation
laced her retort.

"Perhaps, at first," he admitted, his smile open now.

"At first! And your orders this day to behave—modestly,
was it not? That was not intended as insult?"

"In truth, it was not. I admit to a poor choice of words. I am more used to dealing with soldiers and warriors than a woman's sensitivities. Come, let us cry *pax*. I will do what I can to make this time as comfortable as possible for you. Do you cooperate, the days will pass quickly and your future resolve itself."

"I understand." Alena clenched her jaw. She would have liked to walk out on this arrogant pig, but did not quite dare. Besides, she had yet to address her main concern. "I would ask—beg—only one concession."

"Tell me what you wish, and I will tell you if it is possible."

Alena bit her lip at his quiet authority. She hated having to ask him for anything.

"I would like to have some time with my son. I am used to spending hours with him each day and . . . and miss him," she finished lamely. *Miss* was hardly the right word for the aching void that spread through her each time she thought of Megarric.

Marcus kept his face impassive while he considered her request. It surprised him. Most Roman matrons assigned their children to nurses and teachers, having little contact with them almost from birth. His own wife had certainly never shown any desire to have their infant daughter near. She had died birthing his son, cursing the child that brought her such pain, and taking it with her into death. Their daughter had died of cholera not a year later, while he was in Tunis.

He searched Alena's clear eyes for some sign that this was a plot to undermine his authority. He noted the way she forced herself to hold his look, and knew how much this request must have cost her pride. He decided to be magnanimous, but keep a close eye on the child.

"I will have him brought to you here twice weekly, after his training sessions. That will have to do until I'm comfortable with the arrangement."

Alena's face paled. "Training sessions? You have begun training sessions?" Visions of sweating, exhausted young men driven by whips and chains danced before her eyes.

"He spends two hours one day with my master-at-arms and the same another day with the master-at-horse. Although I doubt we can teach him much there," Marcus added under his breath.

Alena buried her hands in the folds of her shapeless gown to hide her clenched fists.

"He is only a babe yet, Captain." She despised herself for the trembling in her voice, but couldn't help herself. "You will instruct your men to have a care to his person?"

Marcus thought of the way the little devil had whacked his shins and bit back the reply that his men had better watch out for themselves.

"Aye, Lady, they will be careful. And you yourself may see how he does when he comes to you." He rose and moved slowly across the room toward her chair.

Alena rose, as well, and forced a slight smile she hoped would pass for gratitude. It galled her to owe this Roman any favor.

"It will have to do, then, Captain."

"What do I get in return for this concession, Lady?"

She looked up, surprised. She had not understood they were bargaining, and she cast about in confusion for something to offer him in exchange. She had few coins or jewels with her, and she couldn't offer the furnishings from a house that did not belong to her. She thought of her horse, but one glance at the solid bulk of the man before her dispelled that idea. Her mountain pony would break under this man's weight. She shrugged and looked up at the man standing next to her.

"I have naught here to offer you in exchange for these visits, but if you tell me what you deem they are worth, I will try to arrange it."

Marcus laughed gently at the confusion in her eyes. Until this moment, he had thought to barter visits with the boy for her continued good behavior. That thought vanished as he looked down at the soft jade of her eyes, framed by those ridiculously thick lashes. He knew there was only one thing he wanted from this woman. Unfortunately, he couldn't claim it. Instead, he would settle for a tantalizing taste.

"Don't worry, Lady. I won't deny you your request. I will take this to seal the bargain, though."

Before Alena realized his intent, he slipped a callused palm around her slim neck and abruptly pulled her against his body. His mouth lowered to cover hers. Too surprised to resist, Alena felt his firm lips against her own. For the first time, she experienced a kiss that was not painful. Warmth and sensual pleasure enveloped her, and her eyes widened as an unfamiliar tingling fluttered low in her belly. Before she had time to fully savor this strange sensation, the Roman slipped his other arm around her waist and drew her hard against him. Her full breasts flattened against the massive planes of his chest.

He slanted his lips over hers to deepen the kiss and thrust his tongue against her closed lips. Alena stiffened as memories of her husband's painful hands and biting teeth banished the tentative, pleasing sensations. She reacted instinctively and fought her way free.

Marcus gave a grunt of pain as her sandaled foot connected solidly with his shin. Damn, this she-cat and her cub would permanently cripple him, he thought. When she followed her kick with hard fists beating against his head and shoulders, he put her away from him firmly.

"By Jupiter, woman, it was only a kiss. If you didn't want it, you should have said so, instead of melting in a man's arms like that."

Alena burned with shame at the memory of that brief interval of surprised pleasure. It galled beyond words that she could have yielded, even for a moment, to this Roman, when she had held herself stiff and unresponsive under her husband's pawing for so many years.

Marcus met the woman's angry, accusing glare with a frowning one of his own. The first stirrings of guilt nagged at the edges of his mind. She was in his care, and he should have exercised more control. Still, she needn't have reacted as if she were some frightened virgin. She'd been wed, and she knew well the feel of a man's body against her soft flesh. He turned abruptly and strode for the door, leaving her standing in the middle of the chamber in her long, shapeless dress. At least that accursed head covering had fallen off.

Chapter Seven

Lineas Flavius watched with undisguised interest as events unfolded over the next few days. Neither Marcus nor Alena would speak of their confrontation to him, but the tribune took sardonic glee in his captain's continued temper where the lady was concerned, as well as in her haughty disdain whenever the prefect's name came up in their conversations.

Lineas found himself a regular visitor in his own home, both for help with his unwelcome administrative duties and to press his so-far-unsuccessful campaign for the lady's favors. He was there late one afternoon, working both issues. He'd been hounded by the quartermaster for several days over Peganthus's claim that he could not meet the grain levy this month. From habit, the tribune knew better than to waste his time with the dithering regent, and he brought the problem to Alena.

"No, Tribune, we cannot sustain a higher grain levy this year. In fact, we must reduce it."

"I cannot make such a decision without consulting with the captain."

"You agreed with me readily enough on adjustment of the tribute before."

A merry smile twinkled in the tribune's dark eyes at her tart rejoinder. "Aye, but that was before the prefect's arrival. He brought with him an additional squadron of Tungarian cavalry. Now we have forty more men and mounts to provide for. I cannot authorize a decrease in the tribute when in fact we need more fodder."

"Tribune Flavius, you know the rains destroyed the spring crop this year. If you tax the peasants further, they will have no fodder for their own cattle and oxen. Which means a reduced late-summer planting, which will in turn mean a desperate winter—for your precious Tungarian cavalry, as well as for my people. Even the Prefect Valerius cannot expect starving people to produce what they do not have.''

Flavius grinned at the ice that frosted her voice at her mention of the captain. "Nay, he is not so unreasonable. Truly,'' he added at her undignified snort. "But he would expect me to find a solution to this damnable business.''

"Can we not provide additional tribute in some other form?'' Alena asked, her brow furrowed in thought. "There is a craftsman in a village not far distant whose saddles and bridles are known as the finest in our lands. My husband's warriors prized his work most highly. He is old and withered now, but I could send leather and iron and several promising boys to help stoke the fires and shape the iron for him. You will need gear, as well as grain, for your additional troops. Let us supply the gear, and you can buy grain from the south.''

Lineas sat up, alert and very interested in her proposal. Celtic horsemen were acknowledged as the finest in the known world, and the Roman cavalry had learned from them the use of saddles and iron shoes to protect their horses' hooves. Additionally, the troops squabbled incessantly and cast bones for the highly decorated bronze eyeguards and bits taken from vanquished British warriors. They would give much for such superb accoutrements.

"Aye, Lady, that would be a fair exchange. If you think this man is capable of producing the gear, I will have the quartermaster and master-of-horse draw up a list of what we need and what it is worth to us.''

"We will negotiate that last point when I see the list, Tribune,'' Alena told him, a mischievous glint in her eyes.

Lineas groaned. "By Hercules, I will probably end up paying you tribute by the time you are done with me.''

Alena's bright, lilting laugh rang out. "Well, at least you are forewarned. I will take whatever I can get from you!''

Without a flicker of an eyelash, Lineas took this opportunity to resume their long-standing, more personal banter. "I would give you much, much more. You know that, Lady Alena.''

It was Alena's turn to groan as Lineas reached out and took her hand in his. He stroked it gently, his grip tightening when she tried to tug her fingers loose.

"Lineas Flavius, is there not a word for *no* that you Romans understand?"

He eyed her shrewdly even as he ran his thumb lightly across the back of her hand, over and over. "Who else have you had to say no to, I wonder?"

"You may keep wondering, Tribune, and release the lady's hand."

Both Alena and Lineas jumped at the prefect's deep drawl. Heat rose in Alena's cheeks as she snatched her hand free and sprang up.

"I apologize for the laxity of my servants in failing to announce you. They will not be so remiss again." The chill in her words made a marked contrast to the flush in her cheeks.

Marcus noted both as he unfolded his arms and levered his shoulders from the portal. Absurdly, the laughing rejection he had just witnessed pleased him. Not many women resisted the tribune's smooth tongue and less-than-subtle courting for long. Deep in his gut, he wanted no other man claiming this woman's smiles, at least not while he had to watch.

"I told the maid not to bother announcing me," he told her blandly before turning to the tribune. "You are dismissed, Flavius."

The younger man pulled a wry face at his peremptory marching orders, but took them in good humor. He made a smiling farewell to Alena, saluted Marcus casually, and left.

As the captain waited for the ring of hobnailed sandals on stone floor to fade, he wondered if the wash of soft pink that colored the lady's cheeks sprang from embarrassment at Lineas's heavy-handed courting, or if she was remembering their last meeting. Marcus certainly was. The feel of her warm lips and her sweet, honeyed taste filled his mind until he gave himself a mental shake and broached the reason for his unplanned visit.

"I am on my way to the *gymnasium* where King Megarric trains. I thought you might like to see how he does on the field." Even knowing how much this woman valued her small son, he was unprepared for the flame that lit green fires in her eyes.

"Yes," she breathed, and all animosity was instantly submerged. "Yes, I would. He has told me of the training sessions, but I would see for myself how he progresses." And see for myself that he is not abused, Alena added silently, although in truth the child gave no evidence of fear when relating his experiences with the Romans. She left the *solarium* hastily to collect her bright green-and-blue patterned cloak.

Alena was silent as she rode through the camp beside him. Marcus wondered if she thought of the last time they had ridden together, when he'd held her reins and brought her to the camp under protest. This time she controlled her own mount. He couldn't help but notice how the woman moved with an easy, liquid grace to her horse's rhythm. Or how her robe hiked up to show long, bare legs dangling on either side of the wooden saddle. A familiar clenching gripped his loins. Involuntarily his thighs tightened, and his muscled gray stallion leapt forward. Marcus reined in the horse, a tinge of red coloring his high cheekbones. Juno help me, he thought disgustedly, what was it about this particular female that roused him so?

The *gymnasium* consisted of a rough cleared area at the base of the hill west of camp, surrounded on three sides by a low stone wall. Here the cavalry trained and, on feast days, paraded and performed colorful exhibitions of their skill. Today the field was empty of all but two riders, although a number of off-duty troops lounged beside their horses on the grassy verge. Marcus reined in beside them. The soldiers scrambled to their feet, and the decurion in charge greeted Alena courteously. He followed her anxious gaze to the small boy trotting docilely beside a burly trooper mounted on a huge, barrel-chested mare.

"He's a likely lad," the decurion said with a chuckle, eyes on the field. Megarric gave his pony a sharp kick and leaned forward as his small horse broke into a furious gallop. He left his astonished riding instructor in the dust.

"Aye," Alena returned, maternal pride glowing from every pore. The boy turned his pony just short of the stone fence and galloped recklessly back toward his mother and the towering captain.

"Hello, Mother. Hail, Marcus Valerius." Dust swirled as the child reined his horse in within inches of the watching captain. "I don't like riding in this little arena."

Marcus hid a grin at his decidedly royal tone. "Nevertheless, Your Highness, you will practice here, at least at first. You must learn to control your horse in close quarters, with sounds of battle ringing all around you. If you learn your lessons well, I will take you afield another time."

Expecting a tantrum, Marcus was pleased when the child appeared to weigh his words carefully, then nodded in agreement. The captain signaled to the waiting men.

"Perform your maneuvers, with the king in your midst. I would see how he works his horse in formation."

Mother and mentor watched the child closely. Even surrounded by hulking troops, his bright gold curls were clearly visible. Alena's lips curved in a proud smile as Megarric turned his pony right, then left, in perfect measure with the experienced troop. At the decurion's crisp order, the horsemen quickened their pace. The troop cantered the length of the field, turned, and galloped toward the arena's open end. Halfway down the field, the left rank raised their javelins and threw them in a sure, practiced arc at a padded wooden stake. At the end of the field, they turned their mounts and charged again, so that the right rank could loose their weapons. Even from a distance, Alena could hear her son's clear, childish voice demanding he be given a javelin for the next run. She slanted a laughing glance up at the soldier next to her. The taunt that hovered on her lips was lost, however, as she and Marcus turned toward the sound of a furious galloping behind them.

"Captain, word has just come of an attack on our outpost at Cilurnium. The messenger reports that the Selgovae, backed by Caledonian savages, have stormed the walls. Tribune Flavius is forming a troop and awaits your instructions in the headquarters."

"Escort the lady to her quarters," Marcus ordered tersely, then turned to the still, wide-eyed woman beside him. "The decurion will bring King Megarric to you shortly."

The sun hung low in the sky when Marcus led two companies of cavalry and light infantry out of Corstopitum for the

fort at Cilurnium, some fourteen miles west. The cavalry was
fully armored, with helmets, mailed body armor, and bronze
greaves to protect their shins. Each man carried two iron-tipped
spears and a rounded shield slung close at hand on the horse's
withers. The infantry was also armored, although they wore
lighter mail, since they would run alongside, holding the horse's
manes to keep up. A horse-drawn light catapult and supply
wagons brought up the rear. The fourteen-mile march would
take a regular infantry unit almost a full day. Marcus knew
from long experience that his mixed cavalry and light infantry
could cover this distance at a forced march in less than four
hours.

Local boys pressed into service as guides took them along
beaten-earth roads through the gathering dusk. Twilight deepened into full darkness before Marcus allowed a brief halt beside a roaring stream to rest both horses and men. Towering
oak trees bordered the stream on either side, forming a thick
canopy over their heads and shutting off all sight of moon or
stars. The prefect stood lazily, patting his gray's dusty neck as
it drank in the cool water. For all his relaxed stance, though, his
eyes roamed constantly over the thick undergrowth just yards
away.

"I don't like these woods, Captain. They're too dark and
crowding."

Marcus turned as a short, stocky centurion came to stand
beside him. Like most of the army's professional officers, the
centurion had worked his way up through the ranks and showed
both his experience and his brutal toughness in his scarred face
and bulging muscles. Nervously the man slapped his vine-staff
swagger stick against his left leg.

"'Tis said the natives have secret glens here where they hold
strange ceremonies and sacrifice virgins to their gods."

Marcus grinned in the dark. "I doubt there are many virgins left in this area since the legions have come. Such tales are
more likely spread by the Britons to keep us away from the
cattle they have hidden. Still, this darkness—and quiet—are not
to my liking, either," he admitted.

To a man who had spent so many years under the desert skies
of Numidia, the thick trees were claustrophobic. Marcus felt
himself growing more tense. He listened for some familiar

sounds over the noisy lapping of the horses and the quiet murmurs of his men, but heard nothing else. The hairs on the back of his neck began to rise. Straightening, he gave the centurion beside him a soft order to pull the men back from the stream to the center of the road. With a quick, silent movement, he slipped his heavy cutting sword from the leather scabbard attached to his mount's side.

The centurion had just issued the order to remount when a guard's strangled shout rang out. The stillness shattered as the woods around them filled with wild cries. Marcus heard the deadly whir of arrows slashing through the trees to fall in vicious arcs around scrambling soldiers. The first rush of arrows ended in cries of pain, mingled with shrill screams from wounded horses. His troops turned to face dark shapes now crashing out of the brush on both sides of the clearing. The dim apparitions shrieked and banged iron swords against shields to create an unholy din of noise and confusion.

Marcus felt his blood rush through his veins as he lifted his sword and thrust himself at a dark figure lunging through the ranks of his men. He gave a grunt of satisfaction as his blade slipped past the man's hidebound shield and buried itself in his chest. Warm blood spurted over the Roman's arm and chest. He planted a foot firmly on the fallen man's chest to free his sword. One corner of his mind registered that his foe was naked, his body covered with some kind of blue paste streaked with white designs. He turned just in time to parry a spear thrust at him from behind. The ragged iron tip ripped along his right arm with a burning sensation. Marcus offered a fleeting prayer to Mars, god of war and protector of soldiers, that the tip was not poisoned and swung his sword in a vicious arc.

He fought with fierce concentration, as did his men. Slowly the rigid training of the soldiers overcame the wild, undisciplined charges of their attackers. The two companies of Romans gradually pulled back into rough squares, their shields overlapping to form an almost impenetrable barrier. Native warriors, their blue now streaked with blood and sweat, charged futilely against the solid phalanxes. Battle cries ended in screams of rage and pain as they ran into the spears thrust through the screen of shields. The Roman cavalry circled as best they could in the narrow clearing to attack from the sides, slashing viciously with their long cutting swords at the naked, unarmored Britons. The clearing was littered with writhing bodies before the remaining attackers finally broke off to run, crashing, into the brush. Marcus led his men into the thick scree, mercilessly slashing and stabbing.

He halted his troops before they could be lured into a trap. He didn't know the territory well enough to follow the fleeing enemy in the dark. The soldiers returned to the road, chests heaving from their wild run, blood still pumping. They lit torches to survey the damage and quickly dispatched the wounded enemy, hanging the bodies from trees as warning to anyone who might think to challenge Rome's might. They had no time to interrogate the wounded or secure prisoners, but they did strip the naked corpses of the few ornaments they wore and gather what weapons could be found in the darkness.

The centurion came to report the loss of two men and three horses. His worried glance took in his superior's blood-spattered tunic. "Are you cut, Captain?"

Marcus eyed the dark stains covering most of his body. He started to shake his head, only to feel the beginning of a fiery pain in his arm. "I've taken a spear tip, that's all. See to the seriously wounded first."

It took only a short time to bind the wounded soldiers and place them in the supply wagon. In the interval, the Romans wrapped their fallen companions tightly in their cloaks and buried them in shallow graves. Marcus offered a hurried prayer to Pluto, god of the underworld, to speed their journey across the river Styx, then ordered the march resumed. An hour later the column left the thick woods behind them and halted at the edge of a wide clearing that gave a view of the camp they had come to relieve.

Moonlight bathed the clearing in an iridescent glow, softening the shapes and debris of a ferocious battle. In the dim light, the soldiers could barely make out silhouettes of carcasses and overturned chariots littering the sloping hill leading up to the fort. Faint sounds drifted over on the wind from inside the camp's timber walls.

"Think you our men held against the attack?" the centurion whispered.

"Aye," Marcus answered slowly, "else the camp would be burning still. But bring the catapult forward and we'll soon find out."

While he waited for the artillerymen to position the catapult, he called his officers together and issued terse instructions for the disposition of the troops. The two decurions commanding the cavalry moved their units off quietly in the darkness to cover the back and sides of the fort. The infantry formed ranks at the edge of the forest on either side of the road leading to the camp's main gate. For security, additional scouts and infantry were sent farther back in the woods to augment the rear guard, in case their earlier attackers should return.

Marcus wrote a brief message on three separate pieces of parchment and gave them to the artillerymen. Swiftly the men wrapped the parchment around orange-size shot to fire into the camp. If they aimed well, at least one of the missiles should sail over the wall and into the camp.

Marcus watched intently as the shot flew into the darkness, then settled down to wait. Long, tense moments later, the front gate opened and a small troop clattered out. Their flaming torches clearly illuminated the red crests on the soldiers' helmets and the gold unit insignia of the detachment. Relieved that the camp had held, Marcus led his men inside.

After the relief column had been bedded down and the wounded moved to the hospital, Marcus and his officers crowded into a small room in the square building that served as the outpost's headquarters to hear firsthand a report of the day's events.

"The Britons attacked at noon, Captain," the centurion in charge of the camp explained. "We had no warning at all. Half the men were on patrol, which is what saved us."

He rubbed a weary, begrimed hand across his eyes. "The first attack was disorganized, more a wild charge of chariots and horsemen making a mad dash for the gates. We lost five men who were on quarry detail, but the rest managed to withdraw to the fort in good order. I led a countercharge, and we pushed them back into the woods to the north. But our scouts reported a large force massed in the next valley, so I withdrew and sent messengers to you and riders to find our men out on patrol. They had to fight their way through, but all returned in time to help repel the second attack at dusk." He paused to take a long, hard swallow of ale.

" 'Twas strange, though, Captain," the deputy commander continued, hulking forward on his wooden bench. "The second attack was almost a feint. They did not use the larger force that had been reported. It was almost as if we were a diversionary tactic."

Marcus fingered a sword taken from one of the natives in the ambush of the relief column. The iron blade was half a foot longer than those used by the Romans, and the hilt was decorated with intricately carved, swirling bronze designs.

"I begin to think the main force was waiting to ambush us on the road. They were well positioned, surrounding the only watering place between here and Corstopitum. They knew we would come to relieve you. It is the who and the why of the attack that puzzle me."

"From the bodies we examined, most of the warriors appear to be Selgovae," the post commander offered. "They're well-known for their vicious lightning raids, and their custom of never taking male prisoners. 'Tis said they're a most barbaric, fierce people, Captain. They live naked, even in the coldest of weather, in hide tents, and possess their women in common. Rumor has it they can survive half-submerged in swamps for many days, living off roots and bark."

The man paused, considering his words. "Of late they've changed their tactics somewhat. They used to charge recklessly at us. They were so wild and undisciplined it was easy to overcome them with our weapons and armor. Now they plan their strikes and try to draw us out."

The deputy nodded in agreement. "Their old leader died, and they have a new one, a red-haired giant called Beorht. He's a cunning bastard. No matter where our patrols strike, he seems to have word of it, and hits in another valley just over the ridge. It's almost as if he were deliberately taunting us, thumbing his nose at Rome's authority."

The prefect smiled and offered a suggestion of what the barbarian chief could do with his thumb and his nose that had the men roaring. They went to bed in considerably better humor, congratulating themselves for having had the luck to get a commander who would deal with these savages properly.

Although he'd made light of the natives, Marcus Valerius took the attack seriously. Knowing he had to allay the superstitious fears of his soldiers, he ordered a formal sacrifice. At dawn the bugler called the entire garrison to the open courtyard in the center of the fort. The centurions stood at the head of their infantry rank and file, the decurions in front of their massed cavalry troops. The legion's standards fluttered bright red and gold in the early-morning breeze.

Marcus took the officers' reports and personally officiated at the sacrifice of a small bull to Aeon, the highest god in the Mithraic cult. Mithras, the bull-slayer of ancient Persian legend, had spawned an all-male cult that was especially popular with army men, since it stressed such qualities as truthfulness and fortitude. Many of the senior officers had endured long, elaborate initiation ceremonies, lying on coffinlike slabs in total darkness, washed in bull's blood. Only those who had progressed to the fifth of seven grades, as Marcus had, could officiate at ceremonies.

At his nod, the centurion swung a heavy stone hammer and felled the bull with one clean hit. Blood from the animal's slashed jugular splashed into a small stone basin, its vivid color mirroring the bright red banners of the legion.

"Aeon is pleased, soldiers of Rome," Marcus pronounced. "The kill is clean, and the blood flows red and thick. We will avenge our fallen comrades this day with the blessing of the great god of boundless time."

With the skill of long practice and the art of a consummate commander, Marcus praised his men's skill in turning back the attack of the barbarian hordes and exhorted them to even more courageous action in pursuing and destroying this enemy of Rome.

He spent the next several weeks ranging the borderlands of the Selgovae. A full scale attack on their stronghold to the north would have to wait until the major campaign planned for next spring, but he was determined that the tribe should pay for its presumption. He concentrated instead on their outlying camps, nestled in the crags of surrounding mountains. With surefooted locals as guides, they found and destroyed several such camps.

"Disgusting, isn't it?"

The burly Sergeant Praxas leaned against his spear after one particularly fierce skirmish and watched their native guides gleefully detach heads from lifeless, and several not-yet-lifeless, bodies. They hung the gory trophies from belts and saddles, to be taken home and displayed as honored trophies.

"They believe the head is a man's soul, the seat of his being. By taking a warrior's head, they take his power, as well." Marcus watched the grisly scene calmly. There wasn't much he hadn't seen in his years of campaigning.

Late one night, his company slipped up on an enemy camp, almost invisible in the craggy hills. They struck at dawn, fought a bloody, vicious battle, and wiped out a good number of the band. By the time Marcus returned to Corstopitum several weeks later, he felt a satisfied weariness in his bones. Although he hadn't captured the elusive Beorht, he'd dispatched a good number of his men. The northern reaches should be quiet for a time.

Lineas met him at the steps to his villa and shook his head at his captain's begrimed, stained appearance.

"You're getting too old to be leading these raids, Prefect." His sober words didn't offend Marcus. The tribune simply stated fact. Rarely did senior commanders lead their men personally in battle. Their persons were too valuable to risk in combat. Most often they directed operations from a high, safe vantage point.

"Aye, I know I should delegate these tasks to young pups like you, Flavius," Marcus returned as he slid from his horse and led the way into his quarters. "But I like to know the scope and character of my foes. I wish to be ready for the campaign next spring. What news, Lineas?"

Although Marcus demanded a steady stream of dispatches to keep in touch with his headquarters, he knew the runners were always days behind when they reached him.

"Not much here. A traveling merchant brought rumors that old Queen Cartimandua is having marital difficulties again." The tribune grinned at Marcus as he handed him a goblet of wine. "Last time, she needed Roman troops to keep her consort in line."

Marcus grunted. Talk of the old queen brought her daughter to mind—not that she had ever been completely out of it.

Alena had warmed his thoughts and his blood on more than one dark night as he lay wrapped in his cloak on his leather cot.

"The queen is demanding the Lady Alena's return again," Lineas said, as if reading his thoughts. "She wants to be assured of her own ally in this land if her husband should try to raise the tribes against her."

"She can demand all she wants. The lady stays here until I order otherwise. How is she?" he asked casually, his eyes on the dark wine in his goblet.

Lineas gave a rueful laugh. "She's well, but has too much energy for such confinement. Since you left, she's become . . . somewhat involved in the camp's activities."

"What activities?"

"She's taken over direction of the public works."

"What?"

"And organized weekly games between our soldiers and the local champions."

"Lineas . . ." Marcus began, his brows drawing together in a scowl.

"And has a solid phalanx of troops sworn to protect her with their lives."

"I thought I gave orders she was to see no one without permission! Can't you control one admittedly headstrong female?"

Lineas gave his superior a sheepish look. "I swear I don't know how it happened, Marcus. I vetted everyone who had business with her. I didn't think there was any harm when the chief engineer asked permission to consult her. Her people refused to cooperate on a building project until she concurred. Then the quartermaster asked her advice on levies of meat from the outlying farmsteads. After that, she just . . . assumed control."

"By the gods, you're serious," Marcus breathed in disgust. "I'm too tired to deal with this tonight. I need a hot bath, some decent wine, and a long sleep. I'll see to the lady tomorrow."

Chapter Eight

Due to the demands of his vast civil and military duties, it was late the following afternoon before Marcus found time to ride to the house holding the lady.

A timid red-haired maid answered his knock and blanched at the forbidding sight of the tall, stern soldier. She stammered so incoherently at the prefect's request for her mistress that he brushed past her and entered the house. Laying his helmet on a marble table, he followed the sounds of laughter and high, childish shrieks to the central courtyard.

Standing in the pillared shadows, he watched the woman and her child in fascination. She wore that damned gray sack again, but it proved its value this time as she lay on her back on the tiles. The child bounced on her stomach, shrieking as she tickled him, and the lady squealed as loudly as the boy himself.

Marcus folded his arms and leaned against a stone column. His eyes gleamed in pure male appreciation as Alena waved her legs in the air when the child bounced harder. The gown slid back to reveal her long, slender calves and thighs. A familiar ache tightened his groin, and he kept still until both woman and boy had exhausted themselves with their play and lay side by side, giggling.

"Good afternoon, King Megarric."

His deep voice, coming out of the shadows, caused them both to jump. The boy scrambled to his feet first, while the mother struggled feverishly to pull the disreputable robe down over her knees and stand.

"You're back!" The boy ran to him delightedly, shrieking anew as Marcus swung him up in the air.

Alena stilled her agitated struggles to watch, tight-lipped, while her child laughed down into the face of her worst enemy. When the boy subsided, the tall Roman turned to face her.

"Lady."

Alena scrambled to her feet, flushing with mortification at what he must have seen. She swore silently that she would personally whip every servant in the house if this man ever entered unannounced again.

"Captain," she replied, her voice low. Telling herself sternly that it didn't matter a whit if the prefect only ever saw her in her oldest robes, she invited him to the *solarium* for wine.

He motioned gallantly for her to precede him. Cheeks burning and head held high, she did. He followed, the child still in his arms. A flustered servant met them in the hall and eyed the captain nervously.

"The escort is here for King Megarric, Lady. I told them you were with the captain and they should wait."

Wordlessly Alena turned and held out her arms for the boy. She buried her face in his tumbled curls for a long moment, then set him down.

"Go with Ethelyn, Megarric. I will see you in two days, when next you come."

She managed a smile for the boy. His blue eyes clouded and his sunny smile faltered, but he bade the soldier a polite farewell, then went with the girl.

Neither Alena nor Marcus made any move to break the silence after the child's departure. Alena battled the ache she felt each time the boy left, then led the way to the *solarium*. She waited until the hovering slave had poured out watered wine and left before she spoke.

"Lineas Flavius said you were in the north, Captain. Are you just returned?"

Her polite mention of the tribune triggered a frown of displeasure on the soldier's face. "Yes," he answered shortly.

Alena stiffened. She folded her arms across her chest and surveyed him with cool disdain.

"And I returned to find you have taken over running most of the camp, Lady. My quartermaster comes daily to consult, the master-at-arms took your suggestion of weekly games for the local youth, and I understand you sent a squad of men to bring in horses from the valley to the south."

"They were running wild," Alena told him with a shrug. "We are short of mounts in town. Your men might as well have some useful occupation, besides their everlasting quarrying for stone, and road-building. As to your other concerns, I'm used to directing the affairs of this kingdom. The ass you Romans installed as regent cares only for his warm hearth and chilled wine. Someone must do it."

By the end of her short speech, Alena had regained her spirit. She lifted her head and tossed her tangled mane over her shoulders to glare at the Roman. When his eyes narrowed dangerously, she bit her lip and forced herself to moderate her tone.

"The reports said that you destroyed several of the Selgovae camps."

"Great Jupiter, does even the administrator report to you now, with the latest dispatches?"

Glancing up, Alena caught traces of exasperation warring with amusement in his dark eyes.

"You're supposed to be under close watch, yet you know more of the camp news than most of my own men."

"Your administrator knows I have an interest in the matter. The Selgovae have long harassed our borders and raided within our lands. Until the Romans arrived, we warred mostly with them."

"And now?"

"Now there are few Lopocare warriors left to war with anyone, as you well know. We must rely on your troops for protection, or ally ourselves with the northerners against you. The choice is not a welcome one."

"You are forgetting the third, and only, choice."

At her questioning look, he continued. "Your mother would install a strong warrior here as your husband, who would hold the lands for Megarric and Rome."

"I would you not utter my son's name and that of Rome in the same breath! They are not the same."

To her surprise, the big man opposite her took a deep breath and nodded slowly in agreement. "Nay, they are not. You're right. We don't wish to destroy you or your people, you know. If you cooperate, your son could well be recognized as one of

Rome's client kings, and rule his lands, just as your mother does, with little interference.''

"My mother is hardly the example I wish my son to follow," she flashed. "Cartimandua sucks Rome's teat greedily and holds her throne only with your backing. Her own people, led by my esteemed father, no less, have sought to dislodge her several times.''

"And have failed, Lady." Marcus leaned forward intently. "If your father could not overcome her, with well-armed warriors behind him, how do you think to defy your mother's wishes with none to support you?''

Alena bit her lip. She'd like nothing better than to throw Beorht's offer in this Roman's face. Although she had had no direct word from him, she knew the recent attack was a signal, a demonstration. He was showing his ability against that of the Romans. From the information she'd charmed out of the unsuspecting officers, she knew the captain's excursions north had inflicted serious, but not disabling, casualties on Beorht's forces. The Selgovae would retreat to their hidden strongholds and regroup. Whether they could gather the strength to defeat these Romans was the question that burned in her mind each night. Swallowing the urge to speak more of the captain's excursion north, she made a noncommittal reply.

"I do not defy my mother. I only seek to delay until I decide what is best." Alena stood and moved across the small room, anxious to change the subject. "I did not have time before you left to thank you for your care of my son. As you may have gathered, he is most precious to me.''

Marcus nodded, going along with the change of tack. "He is a good child. You've done well with him.''

Alena stared at the unexpected praise. As far as she could recall, these were the first kind words the man had ever spoken to her. She was still staring when he stood and gathered the folds of his cloak in preparation for leaving.

"I promised him release from the riding arena, as I recall. I plan to take him with me as I familiarize myself with these lands. You may join us tomorrow, if you will.''

"Yes," she breathed, her eyes lighting up. "I've been shut up in this house for years, it seems. I crave the sun and the wind and a horse under me.''

"Until tomorrow, then, Lady."

Marcus was halfway back to his quarters before he realized he had not resolved the matter of Alena's meddling in the affairs of the camp and the kingdom. He would settle it on the morrow, he decided.

He did not, however. Instead, he found himself so absorbed by the woman as she rode with unalloyed pleasure beside her small son that he pushed the whole matter of her conduct to the back of his mind. For most of a gloriously sunny afternoon, they rode the length of a verdant green valley, returning just as the horns sounded to call the men to the evening meal.

That ride set the pattern for the days and weeks to follow. With the child between them and a troop following discreetly behind, they rode out to villages and farmsteads in surrounding valleys. The late-summer weather cooperated, giving them weeks of sunshine, only occasionally sprinkled with soft, drizzling mists. Marcus learned much of the people and their conditions, and shrewdly assessed Rome's hold over the land. He also saw firsthand how Alena ruled the people with a firm hand in Megarric's name. In each town or village or keep, the vassals and farmers knew her and brought their problems to her with every expectation of solution. He began to understand just how much she belonged to this tribe, and what she might risk for it.

Late one drizzly afternoon, they stopped at a small freeholder's farm nestled in the low hills some leagues to the west of the camp. Marcus was silent while the farmer discussed with Alena a reduced tribute due to the death of his only milk cow in calving. The lady made sure Megarric was included in the conversation, and prompted him gently in his responses to the man. The matter would have to be referred to Peganthus, as regent, but from the determined look in Alena's eye and the pleased look in the farmer's, Marcus knew the issue was settled.

"You seem to know every woman and child in the kingdom, Lady," he commented as they accepted foaming horns of ale from the freeholder's wife.

Alena shrugged and took a swallow of ale. "I came to this kingdom as a small child. Lady Nelwyn tried to teach me house

husbandry, but I escaped her most days and roamed the hills
and valleys. The people here know me well."

Marcus tried to reconcile her freedom with the circum-
scribed life of Roman girls. He doubted his wife had ever ven-
tured out of her father's house unescorted before she was
brought to his own villa as a bride.

"And when you grew to womanhood, did not your husband expect you to take over the chatelaine's duties in the
keep?" he asked idly, a watchful eye on the young king, who
was showing his small, burnished sword to a gaggle of ragged
children.

"Dugald spent most of his time away in one war or another."

Marcus turned, curious at the coldness that crept into her
voice when she mentioned her husband. Unaware of his careful scrutiny, Alena relaxed in her saddle and kept her gaze on
the children. After a few moments, she continued.

"He loved the fight, almost regardless of the cause. The men
went with him, of course, all but the very old and the crippled,
so I administered tribal matters and saw to our vassals' property and families. I'm much better at that than spinning and
cooking," she finished, flashing him an impish grin.

He smiled back. For long moments they sat in companionable accord, sipping the bitter ale, until excited, childish shouts
broke the stillness. The prefect turned to the difficult task of
convincing the young king that he shouldn't take the grunting
piglet in his arms back to the palace to raise.

Alena sat easily on her shuffling horse, wondering how she
could feel even the smallest niggle of contentment in this man's
company. He had not touched her since that one kiss, weeks
ago. Gradually she had allowed herself to relax in his company. She had even, despite herself, begun to notice the man as
much as the Roman. She told herself that his lean, whipcord
strength and dark curling hair held no attraction for a woman
more used to big-boned men with fair or reddish hair. But every
time her eyes drifted to the corded muscles of his thighs as he
galloped next to her or to the strong, blunt hands that held his
reins so lightly, she had to force herself to look away. She was
woman enough to recognize the strange stirrings his raw mas-

culinity raised, and strong enough in her pride to suppress them.

Except late at night, in the privacy of her chamber. Then she tossed and turned restlessly and let her rebellious thoughts dwell on those first moments of surprised pleasure when he had pressed his lips to hers. She marveled that one man's kiss could be so different from another's. That her husband had tasted only of ale or fetid breath, while this soldier could taste of dark, honeyed wine and intoxicating maleness.

Watching him hand the squealing, mud-covered pig back to the farm children with as much ceremony as if he were handling the emperor's crown, Alena shifted uncomfortably in her saddle. She knew little of his past or his private thoughts. He rarely spoke, and then never of himself. But in the weeks they'd ridden together, she'd watched his quiet authority with the men and the careful way he noted every detail of the land and the people. She was grateful for the manner in which he underscored Megarric's role and even allowed her the semblance of authority with her people.

A grudging respect for the huge, dark soldier grew in her, although she took pains to conceal it. Sitting quietly on her horse, watching him give the farmer and his wife a thoughtful farewell, Alena allowed herself a brief moment of hope. Perhaps this strange truce between them could be extended. Perhaps she would not have to give herself to Beorht, or to whomever her mother intended for her. She thrust the thought from her mind, promising to savor it later, and turned her horse's head to follow Marcus and her son through the farm's gates.

They returned from their ride late that afternoon, stopping first at the hilltop fort to leave Megarric and to take wine with Peganthus. The regent had lost all but the most superficial trappings of authority, and knew it. He fretted and stewed and drove the tribal elders almost to distraction in council meetings. Less and less did anyone turn to him; the days of his regency were numbered. Still, he treated Alena with reluctant courtesy under the prefect's watchful eyes.

A glowing, golden full moon hovered over the horizon when Marcus and Alena finally headed back toward camp. Their small troop cantered across the wooden bridge over the river that separated the Lopocare stronghold from the fort. Sprawling down the hillside beneath the fort was the *vicus*. Alena marveled that such a jumbled city could have grown so quickly outside the camp, with its motley citizenry of merchants, craftsmen, common-law wives and prostitutes. In the last traces of twilight, she could see the brothels opening their wide doors and the women strolling out into the street to ply their trade. They wore that curious, bulky garment the Romans called a toga, once the dress of wellborn Roman women, but now shunned by all but streetwalkers. The anklets above their bare feet tinkled as they walked along in twos and threes, seeking customers. A tall, swarthy woman, her face coated with thick paint, called out to the passing troop and bared one pendulous breast. Alena glanced sideways at the prefect and caught the amused, appreciative look in his dark eyes. A shaft of pure feminine pique shot through her. She might not want this man's attentions, but, irrationally, neither did she want him ogling other women in her presence.

When they drew up in front of her quarters, the guard posted at the door came forward to lift the lady from her saddle. The captain slid from his horse and waved the guard away. He strode back to wrap his hands around Alena's middle. Lifting her easily, he let his hands linger on her firm waist. When she raised her face to look up at him, she saw moonlight gleaming on the silver that threaded his dark hair at the temples. She moistened her lips, suddenly nervous.

With a terse command, he dismissed the rest of the troop, keeping her in his hold until the ring of the horses' iron-shod hooves against the cobblestones faded in the distance.

"Do you plan to assault me?" Alena asked. "Here, in the street? Did that whore fire your blood so that you forget yourself with me?"

A slow, wicked gleam came into his eyes. "Nay, you need not fear that any whore could make me forget 'tis you beneath my hands. And I don't plan to assault you in the street."

He let go of her waist, trailing his hands lightly down the swell of her hips. Alena pushed herself out of his hold, and the interested guard jumped to open the door.

"Here in the house, however, is another matter."

The door had barely closed behind them before Alena felt herself grasped lightly from behind and pulled backward so that her buttocks nestled against his thighs and her stiff, unbending back was cradled against his chest. His huge arms wrapped around her, just beneath her breasts.

"Don't be ridiculous." She pushed ineffectively at his forearms, trying to loosen their hold. "I have only to scream and the servants will come running."

"Aye," Marcus agreed genially, nudging aside the wisps of hair at her ear. His warm, moist breath sent a frisson of sensation darting down her spine.

"You abuse your authority. And your responsibility. And... Stop it!" she gasped. His tongue had begun to trace the delicate swirls of her ear. She jumped when it entered the inner cavity.

"Aye," Marcus agreed once more. He stilled his busy tongue at her command and withdrew, only to bend and run it lightly along the cords of her neck. Now he used his teeth, as well, taking sharp little bites, then soothing them with warm, velvety kisses.

Alena hunched her shoulder and wondered frantically why she didn't scream. His tongue and his sharp, nipping kisses distracted her, confused her. They hinted at pain and domination, but sent only tremors of pleasure throughout her body. If it were anyone but this Roman causing them, she would give herself up to the dark sensations coursing through her. As it was, they so distracted her that she didn't even realize his hand had closed over her breast until he lifted its heavy weight and squeezed gently. She jerked back, inadvertently fitting herself even more intimately against the cradle of his thighs.

Marcus drew in a sharp breath when her nether cheeks pressed against his manhood. He loosed his arms and turned her so that she faced him. "If you intend to scream, do so now, Lady. For I plan to kiss you thoroughly."

Alena stared up at him, her palms flattened against his chest. She couldn't remember ever having been so confused. Or so aroused. Her mouth opened, only to release a shallow, panting breath. Fierce male satisfaction flamed suddenly in the dark eyes holding her own. Deep within her, she knew that the moment when she would have called a halt was gone. With a deep sigh, Alena consigned her confusion and doubts to the gods, and gave herself up to the feel of his lips covering her own.

This time she felt no fear at all, only hot, delicious desire. She held herself passive in his arms, but if her body was still, her mind and her senses rioted. She tasted salty maleness. She felt stiff bristles brush against her chin as he slanted his mouth over hers. She heard his rasping breath and grunt of satisfaction when he pulled her close, eliminating all space, and any doubt about the state of his desire. Before her lids drifted closed, she saw his dark, waving curls, lightly sprinkled with silver. And she smelled him. All of him. Old leather and wet wool and the unmistakable tang of the barnyard. Unable to stop herself, she gave a low, smothered giggle.

Marcus lifted his head and frowned. "It would appear that my attentions afford you some degree of pleasure, if not that which I anticipated." A tinge of affronted male pride colored his voice.

Alena bit her lip to hold back more laughter. "Mayhap you should plan your advances more carefully, Captain. For a time when you have not been wallowing with piglets. The, uh, aroma does distract somewhat from your kisses."

Her eyes danced as Marcus glanced down at his mud-stained tunic. When he looked up again, a slow, easy smile tugged at the corners of his mouth.

"I will bear that in mind, Lady."

He left Alena leaning against the wall, still laughing softly.

Marcus carried the low, musical sound of her laughter inside him through the darkened streets, past barracks and granaries and administrative buildings. It teased at his senses even more than the feel of her breast or the touch of her lips. He frowned in the darkness, wondering what it was about this female that threw him so off balance, and what in the name of all the gods he could do about it. His disquiet only deepened when he found Lineas Flavius waiting for him in the outer room of his private apartments.

For once, the tribune's brown eyes were solemn. "A dispatch from the governor just arrived, Captain. You— What is that smell? Have you been mucking out stables?"

Marcus sighed at the young man's puzzled frown. "No, but I did save the royal household from acquiring a particularly filthy little pig as its latest resident. King Megarric accepted the gift from one of his tribesmen. I had to exercise all my diplomacy in returning it."

Brows raised in amazement, Lineas gaped at his captain. "Since when do the duties of the commander of the Seventh Legion of Horse include handling barnyard animals?"

"Since the boy and his mother seem to expect it. Enough about the blasted animal! I wish now I had skewered the damned thing and ordered it up for dinner tonight. What do you here, Lineas?"

The tribune shook his head in confusion. Marcus watched him struggle to contain his curiosity. He sighed, knowing that highly colored accounts of the commander's latest outing would be circulating in the camp before the moon fully rose.

"Your business, Tribune?"

The young man's face settled into serious lines. "The governor has sent word that the Lady Alena is to be delivered to the queen. Cartimandua has evidently persuaded him to agree to a match."

"Let me see the dispatch." Marcus felt his jaw clench as he scanned the few lines on the parchment scroll embossed with the governor's heavy wax seal.

The message was brief, indicating only that the governor had agreed to the lady's disposition and that Alena was to be brought to Isurium, Queen Cartimandua's capital, with all dispatch. The governor himself would meet Valerius there to learn firsthand of the success of his efforts in the north and discuss plans for a military campaign in the spring. Marcus rolled the parchment up and slapped it against his leg. After long, charged moments, he turned to the waiting tribune.

"Send a message to the lady that she's been summoned. Tell her to be ready to travel tomorrow. Take the boy to her in the morning so that they may say farewell. I want you to assume personal responsibility for his care while I'm gone." With those terse commands, Marcus turned and left.

Lineas watched his commander stride away. He, along with most of the camp, had speculated freely about the prefect's growing involvement with the Lady Alena. Despite the collective opinion that the captain should bed her while he had her so conveniently to hand, the general consensus was that he hadn't. Which was highly unusual for a man with his record of success with women, Lineas mused. Knowing from personal experience that the captain's lust almost, but not quite, matched his own, he was as surprised as the rest of the men at his restraint. It was obvious he desired the native woman. Well, they had a long journey ahead of them, the tribune thought. If the captain was to have her, he'd best use this opportunity. Lineas could speak with full authority on the many ways a man could enjoy a woman while managing a full day's march.

Chapter Nine

Marcus cursed under his breath as he led an escort of fifty foot soldiers and twenty mounted troops to the lady's quarters the next day. He was late getting started, having been detained all morning by the mass of administrative and military detail that needed attending before an absence of several weeks. Just when he believed the routine business done, a supply train had arrived from the south with a cache of gold coins. The amount had had to be verified and stored in the vault beneath the altar in the small camp chapel. It would be disbursed, minus deductions for food and clothing, to the troops on their monthly payday the following week. His calm, competent administrator had counted the coins thrice before requesting the commander's seal on the transmittal vouchers. Marcus concealed his impatience with the man, but felt his irritation growing with each passing minute. By the time he finally set out to collect the lady and begin the long trek south, he wore an ominous scowl.

Alena's own temper mounted with each passing hour. Fury was the only weapon she had to hold back the frustration that threatened to overwhelm her. To think she'd imagined a half truce with these accursed Romans! To think she'd allowed the lingering laughter she'd shared with the commander to tease her during the long night! After such silly musings, the terse message to prepare to journey to Isurium had come like a bolt of lightning. Lineas Flavius, when he brought Megarric early this morning, had confirmed the summons, but given her no further details.

With a sense of stone walls closing in on her, she sent a trusted servant with a cryptic message to Nelwyn. She knew word of her summons would find its way to Beorht in his northern stronghold within a matter of days. Whether he would come for her, or whether she would take him if he did, was uncertain, but at least he would know of her mother's plans.

She managed to keep her voice light during her brief visit with Megarric. From their earliest days together, she'd been frank with the boy about tribal matters. The child would rule a vast territory someday, and must understand the realities of politics. He had long known that his mother would remarry, that it was only a question of when. He furrowed his brow as his mother explained her departure in as calm and steady a voice as she could manage. Since Alena had few details to share apart from the bald fact that she'd been summoned, he absorbed what he could, then settled happily to play with her for the hour they had together.

Marcus arrived well past the sun's zenith. Alena had been waiting, packed and ready, since early morning. She was furious when a slave showed the prefect into her *solarium*.

As he entered, Marcus noted with grim satisfaction the bundles wrapped in hide waiting beside the door. He half feared he'd have to carry her kicking and screaming to her horse again.

"Hail, Lady Alena. I'm pleased you're ready." He took a moment to run an appreciative eye over her. He'd begun to think loose, baggy sacks were all she possessed. At least she was decently dressed this time, looking much different from the tousled companion of his rides. Today she wore a long rose-and-red patterned tunic that clasped at her shoulders with enameled pins. Belted by a thin strap that wrapped around her waist and crossed between her full breasts, the tunic showed off her figure to perfection. Her maids had woven her hair into an intricate series of braids, pulled back from her face with a golden clasp. Despite his general irritability, or perhaps because of it, Marcus took time to absorb the pink-and-gold aura she presented.

Tapping her foot impatiently, Alena suffered his appraising stare. Their brief, unspoken peace of the past few weeks was gone, shattered by the governor's summons. Once again this soldier represented unwanted authority over her and the small kingdom she held for her son.

"When you are through gaping, Captain, I would suggest we begin this journey. Since you neglected to inform me of how I was to travel, I've had my horses brought round and saddled. I would prefer not to keep them standing longer than they already have been." She picked up her cloak and started toward the door.

Marcus crossed his arms over his chest and did not move. Alena was forced to stop as she neared the solid frame blocking the exit. When she looked up into his hard, dark eyes, she saw in them only the Roman commander. There was no trace of the man who had tossed her son in the air and ridden companionably with her across the hills. Nor of the man who had kissed her and laughed with her just the night before. She swallowed and tried again.

"Come, Captain, we have a long journey ahead. I would that we might make it in at least some semblance of dignity."

"If you desire to keep your dignity intact, Lady, you will curb that waspish tongue of yours. I warned you before, I will not take that tone from you. We will leave when I decide we are ready."

Even as he spoke the words, Marcus recognized the reason for their harshness. He wanted to distance himself from this woman, to remind her, and himself, of their respective roles. His duty was to deliver her to the governor. Hers was to present herself for marriage. He would do his duty, but suddenly the task seemed onerous. After a brief, tense silence, he turned and walked out of the room. Alena heard him give orders for her bundles to be loaded on pack horses.

Marcus scowled as Alena came out of the house with a timid maid in her wake. In truth, he had given little thought to the lady's personal needs. He was used to traveling hard and fast with his troops. The prospect of being saddled with an additional woman only deepened his irritation with the whole venture.

The maid, Ethelyn, watched as her mistress mounted with the help of one of the soldiers, then fearfully approached the horse held for her. She was bred from a long line of house slaves, and had never ridden a horse before. But she had grown up almost alongside the child bride, and she worshiped the young mistress who treated her with casual kindness. She would protect the Lady Alena with her life, if necessary. She would even mount the evil-looking horse shuffling impatiently on the cobbled street. Swallowing her fear, she reached for the horse's mane, then gave a frightened squeak when a burly, black-haired sergeant seized her to toss her up into the saddle.

Praxas grinned and rubbed his hand along her bare calf as she scrambled for balance. "Don't worry, little dove, I'll make sure you don't fall off."

The frightened girl gaped down at him. She barely understood his fractured attempt at her dialect, but there was no mistaking his suggestive leer. She kicked her leg free of his hand, squealing again when the horse shifted under her. Praxas laughed and held her mount's leads in one hand as he swung onto his own.

Marcus watched the interplay with a grim look. His lips thinned as the sergeant moved into place, the little maid bouncing up and down and clutching frantically at the saddle's crest with each movement. Alena ignored his dark scowl and turned her head forward.

Their route lay directly south, from Corstopitum to Queen Cartimandua's chief city of Isurium. The soldiers had just finished a paved road connecting Corstopitum with the major cities and forts to the south. While not as smooth or as broad as the famed Via Fosse, which slashed diagonally across southern Britannia, from the great fortress at Lincoln to the southwestern tip of Wales, the new road was still a great improvement. It ran straight and narrow, mile after mile, a monument to the soldiers' dogged determination and backbreaking labor.

Marcus had planned their first stop an easy day's ride south. The Romans had constructed roadhouses at planned intervals to ensure the safety and convenience of travelers. With their late start, however, the sun began to slip down behind the thick trees lining the road while they were still many leagues from the roadhouse. The fact that they would have to spend the night in the open only added to the captain's growing irascibility.

He gave orders for the troop to make camp in a large open field. With the ease of long practice, the soldiers began to erect a temporary fortification. Using the tools they carried in a hide bundle slung from a pole over their shoulders, one crew of legionnaires dug a deep circular ditch. A second crew piled the earth from the ditch into a rampart and rammed sharpened stakes into this protective wall. The senior centurion in charge inspected their work critically and laid his vine staff across the shoulders of more than one man who did not dig fast enough or pack the earth firmly enough.

Alena watched the work in progress with great interest, the sergeant Praxas and her wilting maid beside her. She marveled at the discipline of such men, who would dig before they would eat or rest from their long march. From the corner of one eye, she saw the prefect striding toward her. Quickly she slid off her horse and turned to face him. She would give him no further excuse to put his hands on her.

"Lady, you will stay within the perimeter of the camp at all times. Praxas will see to a tent for you and your maid."

She shook out the folds of her bright, multicolored cloak and sent him a look of disdain. "These are still the lands of my tribe. Surely you don't fear attack here?"

"I don't fear anything. However, I prepare for the worst. Your person is valuable to both the queen and the governor. I don't want you taken."

"No, it wouldn't do for me to be taken before I served my purpose, would it?" Her eyes were cold as she turned away with a swirl of her cloak.

An hour later, after inspecting the fortifications and the disposition of the guards, Marcus returned to the leather tent erected for him in the center of the camp. His orderly helped him unarm and took charge of his weapons. Relieved of his constricting armor, Marcus strolled outside, then settled comfortably on a small folding stool within a circle of officers. He reached for a wineskin held out by one of the junior centurions. A low whistle stopped him with the skin halfway to his lips.

"Look at that," the centurion said. He nodded to where Alena sat on her cloak outside her small tent, the maid beside her. The setting sun turned her hair to molten gold, and a dazzling smile lightened her eyes as she bantered gently with the young soldier assigned to cook for the camp. Marcus stared, mesmerized, at the smile. It softened her face and gave her a breathtaking beauty in the soft light. He glanced around the small camp and saw that every other man was staring, as well.

"Crap," he muttered. He had too many years of soldiering under his belt to underestimate the effect of females, in general, and this female, in particular, on the troops. Stifling an exasperated sigh, he lumbered to his feet and crossed the short space to where Alena sat.

"Eat your meal and get to bed. We have a long day and hard miles ahead of us tomorrow."

Alena blinked at his authoritarian tone, and the last traces of her smile faded. The young soldier scuttled away with his pot to serve the rest of the company. Marcus felt a flicker of regret as the light went out of her eyes, but he kept his face impassive.

Alena slammed her plate down and rose. The startled maid clambered to her feet and cowered behind her mistress.

"I find I'm not hungry, Captain. Something has put me off my food." She turned to enter her tent, only to find her arm held in a hard grip. She almost lost her balance when he whirled her back around.

"You will eat, Lady," he told her quietly. "I intend to travel hard tomorrow, and will not have you fainting from hunger or weakness."

"I have never fainted in my life." She spit the words at him. "I assure you, I will not hold up your march. I'm as eager as you to be released from your stewardship."

Alena refused to acknowledge, even to herself, the hurt his words engendered. The man made no effort to disguise his eagerness to finish his journey and be rid of her.

"Sit down and eat." He bit out each word. His hand tightened warningly on her arm, and he started to force her down.

"All right!" she snarled. She pulled free with a vicious jerk and sat, her back to him. Marcus stood over her, legs parted, hands on hips, until she took a bite of roasted hare and began to chew.

The officers eyed their superior warily as he stalked back to his stool. The captain's black scowl discouraged any further comment. Marcus ate his own meal slowly, his dark eyes on the woman by the fire. He tried to understand what it was about this stubborn, irritating female that made him want to force her into submission. He had endured the whining petulance of his wife for the months they had lived together, without once feeling the urge to manhandle her. This blond witch could infuriate him as easily and as effortlessly as she roused him. Strong, conflicting urges raced through him. He wanted to take her across his knee and beat the haughty disdain out of her, as fiercely as he wanted to lay her down and thrust into her long, ripe body.

Taking a long swallow from the wineskin, he forced himself to acknowledge that what he felt most toward the Lady Alena was frustration. He had wanted her from the first time he'd seen her, and been denied. He'd been given glimpses of a laughing, vital woman, had tasted her warmth more than once. Now she treated him with cold contempt. And soon he would hand her over to another man to use. Marcus cursed, long and fluently, as he settled himself on his leather cot. He wished this damnable journey over.

By noon the next day, his frustration had built to explosive limits. He'd led the column out early, with the women traveling in the center for protection. The trouble began when they stopped at midmorning beside a small stream to allow the women to refresh and relieve themselves. He watched impatiently while Praxas lifted the wilting maid off her pony, then caught her in his arms when her legs collapsed under her. The burly sergeant laid the maid on the grass, then called out to her mistress.

Alena brushed him aside and knelt beside the sobbing girl.

"I'm sorry, Lady Alena. I can't get back on that beast again."

"Hush, Ethelyn. Let me see to your hurts." She turned to glare at the interested troopers, who dispersed themselves in a loose circle with backs turned.

Alena lifted the girl's shift and gasped. The maid's thighs were rubbed raw and streaked with blood.

"Great Mother!" she whispered. "Why didn't you tell me of your pain? I could've bound your thighs with linen."

She dropped the shift quickly as a shadow fell over the woman's prone body.

"I'll need salve and linen strips, Captain," she told him crisply. She would've preferred not to speak to him at all, but the girl's pitiful condition demanded attention.

"Praxas!" The sergeant hurried back to the small group at his commander's sharp call. "Bring saddle soap and linen. 'Tis all we have, Lady," he said sharply at her indignant look. "If it works for Roman saddle sores, it will work for this silly female's, as well."

When Ethelyn was cleansed and bound, she sobbed pitifully at the order to remount. A red-faced but grinning Praxas took her sideways across the crest of his saddle, where she clung to his arms like a monkey.

Marcus strode toward Alena to toss her up on her own horse, but she forestalled him by swinging into her saddle. His eyes narrowed, but he made no comment.

By midafternoon they had reached the small village of Lavatra. Marcus decided to halt there and let the wretched maid rest rather than push on to his planned stop, some leagues distant. The local chieftain welcomed the Romans profusely and offered use of his own house. This consisted of a large thatched hut with a single long room. A hide partition stretched across one end to divide the sleeping quarters from the common area. Smoke curled up from a blazing fire in the center, to escape through an opening in the thatch. Marcus inspected the quarters and thanked the chieftain graciously for his generosity. Directing that the women be installed on one side of the hide partition, he left to see to the disposition of perimeter guards.

His orderly, a fresh-faced young soldier just out from Rome, helped build a fresh straw pallet for the maid and piled furs on a leather cot for the lady. Alena gave him a warm smile of thanks and bit her lip to keep from laughing when the gangly boy tripped over his own feet as he backed out to the other side of the partition. She could hear him moving about, arranging his commander's things and settling down to polish the already shining armor.

Alena cared for Ethelyn as best she could. She rubbed soothing ointment on the girl's thighs and bound them in fresh linen. She sent the orderly for the chief's wife, who provided herbs and wine, which soon had the girl deep in a drugged sleep.

As the late-afternoon sun beat down on the thatched hut, Alena decided to wander outside for some air. She saw quickly that the village didn't offer much in the way of diversions. It consisted of small round huts with high, sloping thatched roofs. Pigs wallowed in the muddy street alongside equally dirty children. The youngsters stared as the lady, skirts held high, picked her way carefully down the lane. The sound of shouts and hearty male laughter lured her to a meadow at the far end of the village. Drawing near, she saw that the soldiers had laid out a crude archery range. Several of them were lined up shoulder to shoulder to shoot at painted leather targets tied to sheaves of hay.

Alena watched the contest with interest, comparing these foreigners' skills with those of her own tribe. Their bows were shorter, and therefore not as powerful as the ones Alena was used to. The Romans no doubt employed them at close quarters, probably from behind the protection of their massed troops, she surmised. Brigante warriors used longer bows and would loose their arrows from wildly galloping ponies at far greater distances. Alena stood quietly through a few rounds and gathered from the frequent exchange of coins that the stocky Praxas was the troop champion. On impulse, she strolled over to him.

"Well done, Sergeant. Although you don't appear to have much competition here." Alena lightened her mocking words with a wide smile.

Praxas cast a shrewd eye over her. He'd been with the captain the first time they saw this woman, sweaty and stained from a javelin contest in the arena. He guessed she had some skill at the bow, as well.

"Would you care to try your hand against me, Lady?" he inquired politely.

"Aye, that I would, Sergeant." Alena took the bow offered by one of the grinning soldiers and tested its pull. "By the gods, it feels good to have a bow in my hands again, even if it is one of these stunted ones you Romans use. When you grow a few muscles in your arms and chest, I might let you try mine."

The men laughed at her good-natured heckling. They could see the woman knew what she was about. She laid a notched arrow across the bow and lifted it, sighting along her out-

stretched arm. After a few practice shots, she declared herself
ready. A trooper hurried to tie a fresh skin, with its crudely
painted red circle, around the haystack. The contestants agreed
to three rounds of five arrows each.

"You first, Lady." Praxas grinned at her. "I would get the
measure of my opponent."

Alena threw off the light mantle she wore over her shoulders and wished heartily for one of her short, sleeveless training tunics. She borrowed a leather thong from one of the
troopers to tie under her arms, just above her breasts. It would
keep the dangling cloth of her robe out of the way of her drawn
bowstring. Another thong tied her long hair back out of her
eyes.

"I'm ready, Sergeant. Be prepared to take my measure and
hand over all your winnings!"

With that, she stepped up to the mark, whipped an arrow out
of the quiver, laid it across the bow, pulled it taut, then released it, all with such blinding speed that the watching men
gaped. The feathered shaft buried itself inside the painted circle, but high and to the left. With a slight frown, she repeated
the process with the same lightning speed, this time centering
the shaft almost perfectly. She put three more arrows well
within the mark before turning to her opponent.

"Your turn. Let me see that famous Roman skill."

Praxas gave a huge grin, showing gaping holes where he'd
lost teeth in various battles over the years, and stepped up to the
mark.

The contest was in its last round when Marcus and the senior centurion returned from a long meeting with the chieftain. Marcus had used the time to glean what he could of both
the people and the terrain. Attracted by the shouts and whis-
tles, the two men walked over to watch the contest.

The prefect's brows drew together in a thunderous scowl as
he watched his charge take up her bow with a ribald comment
on her opponent's ancestry—or, more precisely, his lack of it—
which apparently somehow contributed to his lack of skill. The
men roared, and Alena laughed, as well, throwing back her
head in a pose that reminded Marcus so much of the first time
he'd seen her that his blood began to pound.

"In the name of Jupiter, doesn't that female know any better than to flaunt herself before the men like that?"

The centurion turned in surprise at his captain's low, angry words. He'd thought the contest the very thing to break the monotony of the unexpected delay and was thoroughly enjoying the sight of the lady, laughing and natural in the sunlight. Only after his commander's muttered words did he notice how her full breasts thrust against the robe tied tightly by the leather thong. Or how the late-afternoon sun outlined her long legs in perfect detail through the thin fabric of her gown as she took a wide stance and sighted an arrow. The muscled centurion swallowed and tore his eyes with great reluctance from the vision in front of him.

"Exactly." Marcus drawled to the man's red face. He could barely pull his own eyes from her lush figure. A familiar heat spread through his loins. Only by the sheerest exercise in self-discipline was he able to keep from walking over to the group and flinging her over his shoulder. He wanted to take her into the dark woods, lay her on her back on a thick carpet of grass, and . . .

A loud shot cut off his vivid mental picture. Praxas had loosed his last arrow, which missed the center mark by a hair.

Alena grinned in sweaty triumph. "Good, but not good enough, Sergeant. However, I'll give you another chance to redeem your honor, not to mention your coins."

"No, you will not."

The entire group fell silent as the prefect strode into their midst. He stalked toward the woman and took the bow from her hand.

"That's enough. Get back to your quarters and stay there."

Surprised, Alena flushed at his abrupt orders. "I am no babe or peasant to be ordered about thus." She crossed her arms and stood her ground with a mulish expression.

Marcus ground his teeth in exasperation. The stubborn wench would test him yet again. He would not have it. He reached out and took her arm in a hard grasp.

All the fear, frustration and fury Alena had experienced since meeting this man exploded in her. How dare he humiliate her so in front of his men! She'd be damned if she would allow him to manhandle her again.

"Get your hands off me, Roman. I'm tired of being mauled and pulled about."

When she tried to wrench away, Marcus tightened his grip and pulled her off balance against his side. Beside herself now with rage, and the hot, reckless passion of her race, Alena pushed at his hard body to right herself. She grabbed his wide leather belt for balance. Before she even realized her intent, her hand closed around the handle of his dagger, and she whipped it from its scabbard. With a violent pull, she freed her arm and faced him, the gleaming knife held low and pointed at his groin.

"Touch me again and I swear I will geld you," she spit out.

Chapter Ten

A stunned silence fell over the group of soldiers, broken only by the faint, distant calls of birds, and Alena's panting breath as she crouched, knife in hand. For long, tense moments, no one moved.

"Give me the dagger." The words were low, slow and coldly furious.

"Nay, never." Alena felt real fear at the look on the prefect's dark face, but she would not back down now.

His eyes fixed on the crouching woman, Marcus slipped his heavy woolen cloak from his shoulders. Without speaking, he wound it slowly around his right forearm. His jaw clenched in fury as he began to circle her. He knew he could disarm her with little struggle, but a fear that she would be hurt in the process tightened his gut and added to his blazing anger.

Praxas recovered abruptly from his stunned amazement. One look at his captain's dark face told him he had to do something, fast. Marcus Valerius would have disemboweled any trooper who dared defy his authority so, and the sergeant greatly feared for the woman's safety. Taking advantage of the lady's total concentration on the captain, he moved up behind her. For all his size, he made no sound as he edged forward on the balls of his feet. He seized her wrist and flipped the dagger out of her hand with a vicious, bone-wrenching twist. When she whirled and would have lashed out at him, he caught her other arm and held her fast.

"Enough, Lady," he growled. "You've gone too far."

Alena stared at him furiously. Just moments ago they had been companions, sharing the thrill of testing each other's skill. Now he turned cold eyes on her and held her in a painful grip.

"Take her back to her quarters and see that she stays there," Marcus ordered.

Praxas hurried Alena away. The men parted silently to let them through and cast nervous glances at the captain. Although he was known throughout the legion as a fair man, they were unsure how much of the blame for this extraordinary breach of discipline would fall on their shoulders.

"Get back to your posts."

With palpable relief, the men scrambled to gather their gear and obey the captain's clipped order. Marcus held himself rigid as they scattered. He didn't trust himself to move until the red mists of fury swirling within him subsided. Long years of discipline stood him in good stead as, gradually, forcefully, he brought himself under control. Just as he would never strike a soldier or order punishment in anger, he would not deal with the woman as she deserved until he could view the incident with less heat. But deal with her he would.

"Captain, 'twas not the lady's fault."

Marcus turned to see the beefy sergeant standing at attention behind him.

"I thought I told you to see to her detainment," he snapped.

" 'Tis done. She's within, and I've posted two guards at the door. But I couldn't leave it thus. I encouraged the lady in the sport, Captain. I deserve the punishment for letting her cross the bounds."

Marcus studied the man's red, perspiring face and rigid stance. He knew Praxas had well over twenty years of service under his belt and was close to winning his retirement, with full honors and land grant. Of all the senior legionnaires detailed to his personal guard this weathered sergeant was the most reliable. He made sure his troops always appeared in polished, shining armor, and he drilled them constantly. Few men in his troop sported scars on their back from the centurion's cane.

"I have not yet determined what punishment to impose," Marcus said, his tone even. "However, I don't hold you responsible for the lady's ungovernable temper. I suspect she acquired that long before you arrived in this land," he added dryly.

Somewhat reassured by the prefect's measured words, but still worried, Praxas held his stance.

"I would take whatever punishment you fix, sir."

"If I decide that you should do so, you will. Now get you gone." Marcus admired the man's willingness to take the blame and the penalty, but he was not about to have his decision pre-empted. He returned the sergeant's stiff salute and dismissed him.

Deliberately, Marcus avoided the chieftain's hut for the rest of the afternoon and evening. He told himself it would do the Lady Alena good to stew over the price she would pay for her defiance, but in truth he could not decide what that punishment should be. He knew he should take a whip to her for defying his authority in front of the men, but the thought of bruising and breaking her golden skin left a bad taste in his mouth. He wrestled with the problem through a dinner of wild pig roasted over an open pit and two flagons of wine.

When a group of officers called to him from a dirt hut they had commandeered, he pushed the dilemma to the back of his mind and went to answer their calls. The soldiers had discovered that the owner had hidden several urns of the bitter local beer, as well as his numerous progeny, in a ramshackle shed behind the hut. The farmer danced about in frantic worry as the soldiers pulled the urns and two brawny girls from the shed, but his cries disappeared magically with the coins tossed his way. The girls were tearful, but not terrified. It was soon obvious that they had entertained warriors before. They swilled the ale the soldiers poured down their throats, cast off their rags and performed with zest, if not with any particular skill, on the raucous soldiers.

Marcus watched in amusement as the now-drunken girls scrabbled in the dirt for the copper coins his men tossed during their performance. When one of them approached him, rubbing her dangling breasts with dirty hands, he grinned, but passed her into the willing arms of the centurion. Their uninhibited lust heated his blood, but he couldn't bring himself to share their sweaty favors. The hour was well past midnight by the time the ale and the girls were finished and Marcus made his way back to the chieftain's hut.

Alena lay wide awake in the darkness. She heard the Roman blunder into the small room. In the dim light of the banked fire she saw his form silhouetted against the scraped-hide partition. Through half-shut eyes she watched as he removed his mantle and baldric, then bent to unlace his sandals. In mingled astonishment and distaste, she listened to the lewd army ditty he hummed off-key. So the man had drowned his evil temper in drink while she had been walled up in this steaming hut for hours with only her maid and her fears! She had forced herself to tend Ethelyn, still deep in her drugged sleep on the straw pallet, while she tried not to think what would happen to one who dared take a knife to a Roman, and a senior military commander, at that. The realization that she had been penned up, fearful and nervous, while he had been out swilling wine all these hours made her furious.

"Roman pig!" she muttered into the straw pillow.

She regretted the words the instant they were out of her mouth. A deadly silence replaced the humming, followed by a loud crash as the hide partition was torn violently from its moorings. Alena scrambled upright on the bed and clutched the fur coverings to her chest. The Roman moved to stand at the foot of her bed.

"You had done better to feign sleep, Lady. I had thought to postpone this meeting until morning, but find I can stomach neither your temper nor your tongue one minute more."

Marcus surveyed the disheveled creature staring up at him in the dim light, taking in her tumbled hair, lit to a soft gold by the dying embers, and the white skin of her shoulders, glimmering beneath the thin shift. He felt his blood rise, hot and heavy, in his veins. A deep, instinctive certainty filled him. 'Twas time.

One last shred of sanity told him he was about to cross an invisible yet indelible line. He knew the ale and the uninhibited orgy he'd witnessed had shredded his self-control. He knew he shouldn't even have come in here, tempting himself with the sight and the smell of her. But he also knew it would take half his legion to pull him out at this point.

Alena watched him draw the leather strap from around his waist, and felt her stomach clench in fear. Clad only in his short woolen tunic, he loomed, huge and menacing, over her. The fire backlit his dark hair, shadowed his eyes, made the bulging muscles of his arms and thighs gleam. With a quick indrawn breath, she scurried to the far side of the bed, seeking to escape him. But she didn't move fast enough. His hand snaked out and grasped her ankle. Frantically she kicked and struggled against the band of iron clamped around her bare leg. She heard his low laugh as she twisted and turned, panting furiously. The bed furs fell to the floor, and her shift rode high on her thighs as she was pulled slowly, steadily, across the low bed.

Marcus grabbed her other, flailing leg. He held her ankles wide apart as she writhed and bucked to free herself. Her frantic movements caused the thin shift to ride higher, baring most of her thighs and the shadowy triangle between them to his hungry eyes. He tightened his grip as the need to possess her became a low, painful burning in his gut. Abruptly he released her ankles and pinned her to the furs with his body.

Sheer surprise took Alena's breath away. She expected a beating. She would fight it with all her strength, but she was ready for it. She was not prepared for the way his heavy, muscled body slammed into hers. He was solid as a rock, and just as immovable. Panting with mingled fear and fury, she pounded at his shoulders and back. He grunted when one fist connected solidly with his ear. With a swift twist of his arms, he caught her wrists in one huge hand and stretched them out over her head.

Alena struggled furiously to free her wrists, but could not loosen his iron hold. She tried to work one leg between his, thinking to knee him in the groin. He blocked her maneuver with a rolling motion of his hips that ground the rocklike hardness of his straining member into her belly. When she lay for a moment, panting, trying to gather her strength and breath, he ran his free hand over the body stretched tautly beneath him.

"By the gods, woman, you are made to pleasure a man. I've had many a sleepless night these past weeks, thinking of this moment."

Alena gasped as he levered himself off her enough to reach the neck of her shift. With one sure motion, he ripped it open and laid a heavy hand against her breast. Expecting pain, she tensed. When he kneaded the white flesh gently, rolling and tugging its nipple between thumb and forefinger, she sucked in her breath in sheer surprise.

"Stop, Prefect," she panted.

"I can't, woman, and I won't." Flames flickered in the dark eyes above her. "I've wanted you since the first time I saw you, dirty and proud, in the square. Tonight I will have you."

With a great effort, Alena heaved herself upward, trying to dislodge him and shake his hand from her throbbing flesh. He laughed softly as he rode her bucking body. When she stopped, gulping air into her flattened lungs, he bent and took the captured breast in his mouth. He pushed the soft flesh up and suckled steadily on the now-taut peak. Alena felt a flash of fire radiate from her nipple that startled her with its intensity. When he took the tender tip between his teeth, the fire spread from her breast to her belly.

Panting, she stared helplessly at the dark head bent over her breast. He loosened his grip on her wrists enough to ease the pressure, but not enough for her to free herself. He settled himself solidly between her spread thighs. She closed her eyes and waited for the pain she associated with coupling, but this heavy man sprawling over her controlled his strength as much as he controlled her. He held back, content to suckle and torment and rouse sensations totally outside her experience.

"Don't do this, Roman," she whispered when he raised his head and slid upward along her body.

"Don't do what?" he asked softly. "This?" His free hand kneaded her breast.

"Or this?" He bent his head and bit gently at her lobe.

When his wet tongue pushed into her ear, exploring its delicate whorls, her eyes widened in sheer surprise. "Wait. Wait," she panted desperately.

This time he loosened his grip enough for her to free her hands and push against his chest. Even in the dim light he could see the startled confusion in her eyes. With a sigh, he struggled to control his raging fires. He had neither the patience nor the desire to woo this woman as if she were some frightened maid, but he knew the pleasure would be greater for them both if he took some time to ready her. His hand slid from her breast, over the shift twisted around her waist, to the smooth curve of her stomach. Soft flesh quivered under his fingertips. He nuzzled her ear and stroked her belly, over and over, up and down. Deliberately he moved his hand lower still until it buried itself in the tight curls guarding her womanhood. He used one knee to pry hers farther apart, so that his questing fingers could stroke and probe the damp crevasse between her thighs.

Alena lay trembling in the darkness, her fear replaced by confusion as ripples of hot fire shot through her loins. Eyes wide, she stared up at the dark face hovering over her. This man was awakening sensations she had never experienced before. She was unused to pleasure of any sort in coupling. Long-submerged desires slowly flooded her veins. She lay still and tense under his probing hand, wondering desperately how this detestable Roman could work such strange magic upon her body. She didn't understand it, and her mind gave up trying to sort it out.

All she knew was that this probing, thrusting hand was rousing a growing swell of . . . something. She wasn't sure what it was, but for the first time in her life it was pleasurable, and suddenly, fiercely, she wanted it to continue. She relaxed her leg muscles and gave him full access. Her hips lifted as he rubbed his palm against her mound and thrust his fingers deeper into her velvety softness.

Marcus felt her stiffness give way even as he heard the soft moan far back in her throat. The last shreds of his control almost gave way. Sweat broke out on his brow, but still he held back. Now that the moment was here, perversely, he didn't want to hurry it. The ale and his own lust pounded in his skull, and his blood sang in his ears. Over the roaring, he heard the soft, panting sighs of the woman beneath him. The sound filled him with a fierce, flaming satisfaction. He worked his hand slowly, in and out, back and forth, until her legs writhed under the heavy weight of his and her breath came in throaty sobs.

"Alena, open your eyes. Look at me." His voice rasped unsteadily. "Look at me!"

He stilled his hand and leaned heavily on her body to quiet her. Slowly, as if weighted with stones, her lids flickered open.

In the dim light he could barely see the green rim, so dilated were the pupils. He read confusion in their dark depths, and dawning desire, but no fear. He gave a grunt of primitive male satisfaction, and a slow, feral grin spread across his lean face.

Alena stared up at his dark face. She felt him against every part of her body. Long, hair-roughened legs held her own legs wide apart. His man-root pressed into her thigh, hot and turgid. His hand, huge and calloused and incredibly gentle, rested against the core of her womanhood. She longed with all her being to close her eyes and shut out the sight of him, to pretend it was anyone other than this man who burned against her. She wanted to give herself up to the waves of pleasure still throbbing in her loins.

"No," he commanded roughly when her eyes fluttered shut. With one hand tangled in her hair, he shook her. "I want you to know with whom you lie."

At that moment, Alena hated as she had never hated before. And desired as she had never, in all her years, desired anything or anyone. She would do this, she decided, this once she would do it for herself alone.

"Finish it, Roman," she whispered.

Marcus held himself rigid over her for a long moment, fighting the swamping rush of heat her words brought. When the corded muscles in his arms stopped quivering, he reached down and worked his loincloth loose. Settling his weight firmly on her soft body, he thrust his tongue into the dark sweetness of her mouth. His knees widened her, and suddenly, fiercely, he pushed into her tight, wet sheath. Hard hands held her head still for the wild plundering of his mouth, while his lower body forced her into an even wilder rhythm. He rode her long and hard, until the ale and the sweet, dark taste of this woman swept through him. He arched, emptying himself into her with a rasping groan.

Alena grunted as the man collapsed on top of her, breathing heavily. Her hips moved involuntarily against his, until she felt his man-root slip from her and trail wetness across her thigh. She wanted to cry out, frustrated beyond belief, although she wasn't experienced enough to recognize the feeling for what it was. All she knew was that this man had taken her beyond fear to some near-sensation, and then left her aching and twitching against him like some kitchen slut. Like one of her husband's own drabs, she thought with a surge of self-loathing.

"Get off me, you pig," she snarled. She heaved at the sweaty shoulders pinning her to the hide.

Marcus rolled to one side, still caught in the aftermath of his release as much as in the effects of the ale. He kept his hand anchored in Alena's tangled hair and a heavy leg across her stomach to hold her until his senses stopped reeling. He wasn't capable of coherent thought, but he knew he couldn't let her go yet. When she continued to push and fight him, he turned her easily on her side and pulled her stiff body against his, her buttocks and back hard against him.

"Wait, little one, wait."

His whispered words made no sense to her, and she fought to unwrap the arms locked about her waist.

Marcus sighed and tightened his hold. He'd better finish what he'd started before this she-devil unmanned him in his weakened state.

"This time is for you. Lie still."

He breathed the words into her ear, and his hand reached around her hips to bury itself between her legs. The feel of his seed on slick flesh sent a shaft of satisfaction through him so hot and so deep that it began to rouse him once more. He whispered dark, delicious promises in her ear.

Alena blushed a fiery red in the darkness. Roaring heat spread from her bosom to her shoulders to her face. Never had she heard such erotic words. Never had she imagined that a man would play with a woman's body so, or hold himself back while he did. Gradually the frustration still raging in her loins took on a new, sharper edge. She closed her eyes, willing herself to forget the man behind her, focusing only on the soft, rasping words and the feel of his hands. One played between her thighs, the other moved upward to shape and knead and tease at her aching breasts. When his hot tongue slipped into her ear, she yelped and jerked her entire body.

Marcus groaned when her backside butted against his now-aching shaft. His hands moved harder, thrust deeper, rubbed faster. He felt her dew wash him, mixed with the thick stickiness of his seed. Once more he tongued her ear, and whispered wild, sweet, explicit threats.

In a rushing, swamping tide of heat, Alena exploded. Blood swept up from her loins to wash over her in white-hot waves. Her body arched and she cried out, a deep, wrenching moan from far back in her throat. Marcus held her tightly while shudder after shudder wracked her body. Every male instinct cried for him to enter her, to ride this tide with her, but he gritted his teeth and held back. A deep, totally alien urge wanted her to have this moment for herself. Somehow he sensed she had not known pleasure before.

Long moments later, the world righted itself. Alena opened her eyes. In the sputtering light of the small fire, she saw the torn leather partition, the furs scattered across the dirt floor, the prefect's sword belt tossed among the furs. She moaned and rolled onto her stomach to bury her face in her hands.

Marcus eyed the round buttocks and long, white thighs displayed so delectably. His hand reached out, shaped itself to fit her quivering curves.

Her flesh jumped under his hand. "Get out!"

Marcus bit back a rueful grin and dropped his hand to his side. He didn't understand this woman in all her fiery moods, but he knew her well enough by now to know that her temper was fast replacing the remnants of slackened passion. He was in no condition to deal with it, or with her. The bed tottered as he rolled into a sitting position and bent to pick up his belt. He glanced back at Alena, still lying on her stomach with her face buried and her rear bared. He reached out and pulled her tangled shift down to cover her buttocks.

"Get out of here!" she screeched. She rolled away from his touch, against the far wall, knees drawn up and eyes spitting green sparks. She was embarrassed beyond tears, furious with herself for her wild, thrashing moans, totally confused by what had just happened. She needed time and privacy and quiet to sort all this out. Her eyes followed the prefect as he stood, looked down at her once more, then turned and left.

Long after the wooden door to the hut had banged behind him, Alena stayed crouched against the rough stone wall. Finally, when she knew with certainty that he would not be back, she straightened her cramped limbs and pulled the furs back onto the bed. She lay still in the flickering darkness, willing her

mind to stop its chaotic churning. The effort proved too much.
However desperately she wished to, she could not seem to form
any coherent thought. Groaning, she rolled over and covered
her head with a fur.

Chapter Eleven

Alena woke the next morning to the sound of the orderly rummaging through the packs scattered on the far side of the room. The youth turned when he heard her struggle to free herself of the twisted coverings and sit up on the bed. If the boy wondered at the torn hide partition, he didn't mention it. Nor did he imply that there was anything unusual about his captain choosing to sleep wrapped in a cloak on the floor of the hut next door when all had been prepared for his comfort in this room.

"Hail, Lady Alena. The captain bids you rise and refresh yourself so that we may continue the journey as soon as the horses are loaded."

Alena pushed the tangled hair from her eyes and tried not to grimace at the youth's cheerfulness. She was stiff from lying taut and sleepless most of the night. Her shame and her confused, bitter anger surfaced when she saw the boy glance from her to the torn partition and back again.

"Leave me. I will dress and see to my maid. You can tell your captain we will continue the journey when I'm damned well ready."

She bit her lip at the boy's rounded eyes. With a tired sigh, she softened her words.

"Please, bring me bread and ale to break our fast, and I will see to my woman. We will be ready shortly."

"Shortly" turned out to be well over an hour. Alena cleansed herself in the bowl of tepid water left by the orderly, then bathed Ethelyn's face and hands until she woke from her drugged sleep. The maid's thighs were still red and sore, but a fresh application of balm and thick linen strips soothed the pain. Alena fussed with their bundles, stretching out the last of her packing. To the depths of her soul, she dreaded leaving the comforting dimness of the hut and facing the prefect.

Marcus waited with restrained impatience outside the chief's hut. A raging guilt clashed with the throbbing in his skull from the ale's residue and left him uncharacteristically indecisive. Twice he started into the round building, then stomped away. He paced restlessly, setting and resetting several deadlines for departure in his mind. He had resolved to storm the hut, fully intending to drag the blasted woman out whether she was dressed or not, when she finally appeared.

"Are you all right?" he asked curtly.

"It's a bit late to be worried about my well-being, Roman," Alena snapped, her confused insecurities submerged in a healthy anger at his peremptory tone.

Marcus clenched his jaw and signaled to the waiting Praxas to take care of the timid maid, then led Alena to her horse. He turned her to face him, tilting her chin up so that she was forced to look into his eyes.

"I would apologize for last night, Alena, except I find I am not sorry at all." He held her face firmly when she tried to turn her head away. "I know I have violated my duty to care for your person, and will take what judgment the governor decides as a result. It will not happen again."

"Pah! Your assurances don't carry much weight with me at this point!"

"I give you my word," he growled. "I want yours that there will be no more displays of temper such as you treated us to yesterday."

"Or what, Captain?" Her voice dripped with venomous sweetness.

"I'm serious, Lady. We have a long way yet to travel, and I can't have you undermining my position with my men. I'll have to take more stringent measures, do I not have your word."

"You would trust the word of a woman?"

"I will trust your word," he said quietly.

She looked up at him in silence for a long moment. "Nay, I cannot give it," she said finally. "What you would deem a display of temper, I see as fighting to maintain my being, my dignity. I will fight you however and whenever I can. You must take whatever measures you will."

A muscle twitched in the soldier's dark jaw as he stared down at her set face. In the harsh early-morning light, he could see the bluish shadows under her eyes from her sleepless night.

"Get you horsed," he ordered tersely.

When the troop was mounted, he placed the two women within a protective shield of horsemen, with Praxas detailed to guard them. The foot soldiers strung out in a double row behind, their shields hung across their backs and their gear strapped to hide packs carried on long poles over their shoulders. Marcus swung into position at the head of the column.

Ironically, now that she was assured she need not worry about the prefect abusing her person further, Alena's mind could not seem to free itself from the incident in the hut. Swirling, secret thoughts filled her mind, products of a healthy appetite long stunted. In all the years of her marriage, she had never experienced the sensations the Roman had aroused. Despite her shame, she couldn't stop her thoughts from returning to this unique experience of coupling without pain. Not just without pain, she amended, but with hot, sweet, overwhelming pleasure. Heat flooded her face whenever she remembered the way his hands and mouth had made free with her. No matter how many times she forced herself to cease thinking about the previous night, it took only a flash of the prefect's crested helmet or his swirling red cloak to cause her cheeks to flush and her mind to fill with dark images.

Marcus kept the women in the center of the column and himself well away from them throughout the day. Despite his best efforts, his gut clenched every time he allowed himself to think about what had happened. Instead of lessening, his desire for the tawny-haired wench grew with each passing hour. Now that he knew the feel of her ripe breasts and her warm, slick softness, he wanted more. He wanted her willing this time, and eager. The ache of desire grew in his loins with every passing step. Grimly, he increased the pace. He'd better deliver the woman and get back to soldiering, or he'd be a damned cripple for life, bent over in the saddle and weak from wanting. He made sure Alena and her maid were housed well away from him and under heavy guard when they stopped at a wayside road-house that night.

On the afternoon of the following day, he pulled to the side of the column and rode back toward her.

"We reach Catterick this afternoon, Lady. I know the commander of the garrison well. You will be able to rest comfortably and refresh yourself."

She nodded coolly. Marcus stared down at her, piqued by her coldness, even as he knew it protected them both. Still, he had an urge to see the ice melt somewhat in her eyes.

"Catterick is a rich trading center, with goods from the four corners of the empire flowing in. Perhaps you will wish to find some toy or trinket to send back to King Megarric." His ploy worked. Alena's breathtaking smile broke through.

"Yes," she breathed, "I would like that. I ... worry about him."

Marcus heard the tremor in her voice and shook his head. The woman astounded him. How one female could combine so many dimensions, from spitting, clawing she-cat to soft, loving mother, was beyond his male comprehension.

"I'll arrange an escort for you when we arrive. Until this evening, Lady." He rode off, inexplicably pleased with himself for that brief, sunny smile.

Hours later, her smile annoyed him tremendously.

They made good time and reached Catterick by mid-afternoon. As promised, Marcus arranged an escort for her with the camp commander, who waited to greet them. The grizzled veteran handed Alena down with every deference due her rank and enlisted his wife to see to her comfort. The portly, gray-haired woman, swathed in a long white robe that only added to her comfortable bulk, cheerfully took Alena's arm and guided her into the villa.

At first, Alena felt reticent with the older woman. She'd had no dealings with wellborn Roman women before. Her fierce pride would tolerate no slight from the wife of one of her country's conquerors.

Julia Petronia soon put her at ease, however. The woman had traveled to many distant lands with her husband, living in tents and dirt huts and palaces. She'd long ago learned to take people as she found them. She helped settle Ethelyn in a cool, spacious room, then took Alena under her wing.

The two women spent several hours wandering the vast forum that covered nearly a square block in the heart of the city. Alena tried not to stare as Julia led her through crowded stalls filled with every imaginable good. She fingered delicate amphorae full of wine from Rhodes, olive oil from Hispania, and rich spices from unknown eastern lands. One merchant held up glassware from Syria for her fascinated inspection, while another tried to tempt her with delicately hammered silver bracelets. Julia watched the younger woman's eyes widen as she fingered a thin green fabric shot through with golden threads, then laugh and shake her head at the shopkeeper's importuning.

"You should take that cloth, dear," Julia advised. "The color would be exquisite with your eyes."

Alena smiled and shook her head. She was too proud to admit she had only a few copper coins. Peganthus had refused to send her any money while she was under the Romans' care.

"You know, Marcus Valerius gave me a purse to see to your needs," the older woman mentioned. When Alena stiffened, she added shrewdly, "You should use it. You owe it to your rank and your tribe to appear at your best. Besides, most of it was probably taken from your lands, anyway."

Alena turned to assess the stolid matron. "It undoubtedly was," she responded coolly.

"Now don't get on your high horse with me, dear." Julia patted her arm. "I've seen too many lands and too many people. In this world, the strong men take what they will. It's usually left to women like us to pick up the pieces and straighten out the mess they leave."

Alena laughed in agreement. The two women finished their shopping in perfect accord and left, the shimmering green material neatly wrapped and tucked under their escort's arm. Alena herself carried a small sword, its hilt of hammered silver, chased with figures of strange, slant-eyed warriors, for Megarric.

"Now," Julia said with a sigh as they came out of the forum, "come with me. The baths are the best part of the day."

Alena hung back. "Ah...I think I should rest, Lady Julia."

"You will, dear, you will," Julia replied with a twinkle in her eye as she took Alena's hand and led her firmly toward the baths.

With some hesitation, Alena followed her hostess into the awesome building that housed the baths. A wide, columned portico surrounded the rectangular edifice, built where a bend in the river wound its way through the town. Alena mounted the marble steps slowly, feet dragging. Her tribe was not overly concerned with cleanliness, bathing in streams and rivers when the opportunity presented itself. Since the Romans had occupied the encampment outside her town, she'd heard many tales of the soldiers' preoccupation with bathing. She thought it a strange custom for warriors. It didn't take long, however, for her trepidation to change to pure, unadulterated pleasure.

The pace was leisurely, luxurious, and totally relaxing. Julia chattered about inconsequential matters as they were shepherded from pool to pool. A whole regiment of attendants brought wine and cheeses, patted them dry with warmed, scented towels, and rinsed their hair. They finally reached the third, sensually hot, scented pool. Julia introduced her to a number of other women who lounged there, catching up on or inventing the latest gossip. The other women slanted curious looks at the tall, sun-streaked blonde, who had to be shown the bathing ritual. More than one matronly glance lingered enviously on her flat belly and full breasts. An hour later, Alena groaned in sheer feline satisfaction as she stretched naked on one of the marble tables while slaves massaged scented oil into her skin.

By the time she and Julia returned to dress for the evening meal, Alena was more relaxed than she'd been in months. Julia sent a maid to help drape the shimmering green fabric into long, clinging lines. The maid crossed a thin golden rope between Alena's breasts and wound it around her waist several times. Ethelyn pushed the girl aside to dress her mistress's hair herself. She pulled the curling mass back into a flowing mane and anchored it with golden combs in the manner of their people, then helped Alena fasten a heavy golden torque around her slim neck.

"You look breathtaking, dear," Julia said with genuine warmth when she came to escort her guest to the dining chamber. Most Roman women were not invited to join male guests at formal dinners, but then, Julia was not like most women.

"Where did you get that magnificent necklace?" she asked as they walked through the villa.

Alena fingered the heavy gold collar. "It was part of the dowry I took to my husband. Within our tribe, it's as much a badge of rank as a decoration. I don't wear it often, because it's so heavy, but this seemed a special occasion."

The men seemed to think so, too, when the women joined them. Marcus watched her being introduced to the other officers with outward calm, but his jaw tightened when he saw them run admiring eyes over her long, lithe figure, which was outlined to perfection by the clinging material. When Alena settled herself on one of the long couches, leaning negligently on her left elbow, the draped fabric opened to show the shadowy cleft between her breasts. Marcus felt an almost overpowering urge to cross the room and cover her with his cloak.

The meal turned out to be one of the longest Marcus had ever endured. He watched grown men make perfect fools of themselves, rushing to fill Alena's goblet or pass her choice bits of meat. She accepted their attentions shyly, tantalized as much by this, her first meal with Romans, as by their flattering courtesies. She tasted every dish presented, from the delicate pheasant eggs and roasted oysters in the first course to the seven different meats in the second. She recognized veal and boar and venison, even covered in thick, unfamiliar sauces, but viewed the slithery black mass her host scooped up on a thick slab of bread with a distinct lack of enthusiasm.

"Try them, Lady. 'Tis only lampreys in honey sauce. You slide them down your throat and follow with a quick sip of wine.

Alena glanced quickly around the room. The officers all reclined at their ease, using fingers and spoons to scoop healthy portions of the slimy mass from serving bowls placed on low tables before them. Even Julia threw her head back and swallowed a large portion with every appearance of enjoyment. Only the prefect, sitting across the room and scowling at her for some unfathomable reason, appeared not to enjoy the dish.

Alena promptly took the slab of bread her host offered, tossed her head back, and slid the black mass into her throat. She managed a half swallow before her hand came up to cover her mouth and she turned her back to the watching room.

The officers laughed when she faced them once more, red with embarrassment. Julia nodded to the slaves to clear the dishes away and bring the second tables, loaded with puddings, pastries, fresh fruits and cheeses. Gratefully Alena took advantage of the distraction to cleanse her throat with long, soothing drafts of light wine.

Marcus watched the other officers lap up her unaffected manner and shy smiles. If the fools only knew what a hellcat lay under that honey coating, he thought sardonically.

"She's a lovely young woman."

The softly spoken words broke into his thoughts. Marcus turned to his hostess. "Sometimes," he agreed dryly.

"Who does the governor plan to give her to?" Julia asked casually.

"I don't know, Lady Julia. He and her mother, Queen Cartimandua, have arranged a match." Marcus frowned into his wine. "My instructions are only to deliver her to Isurium with all speed."

"Harrumph! That old baggage would sell even her unborn, were she young enough to carry any, to further her ambitions."

Marcus turned to survey his hostess. "Do you know Cartimandua?"

"Aye. My husband was in charge of the auxiliary cohort sent to quell her husband's revolt some years ago. In gratitude, the queen petitioned the governor at the time for his promotion and command of this fort. The queen has called us to her court several times since for feasts. They surpass even tales of Nero's wildest orgies. The lady has a lusty appetite."

Her words conjured up images of the queen's daughter that made Marcus shift restlessly. He turned to survey the object of his suddenly heated thoughts.

"By the shades of—"

Startled by his low exclamation, Julia glanced up. She followed the direction of his eyes to see her husband, somewhat the worse for his wine, leaning over his guest with a decidedly

foolish smile on his face. He was laughing at some remark
Alena had made, his hand laid companionably on her arm,
when he glanced up to find himself skewered by two pairs of
cold eyes. He swallowed at the prefect's hard look, but posi-
tively blanched at his wife's poisonous glare. Quintus Nuntius
dropped his hand as if scalded.

"Will you excuse me, Lady Julia?" Marcus said, rising
smoothly from the low couch. "I thank you for your hospital-
ity, but we must leave early in the morning."

Julia watched the tall soldier stride with unconscious authority across the room. Alena looked up in surprise at the figure looming over her and shook her head, not yet ready to
retire. It was a flushed and furious young woman who crossed
the room a few moments later, her arm firmly held by her escort, to give her thanks to her hostess and make her farewells.

"Let me go, Prefect," Alena ordered through stiff lips as he
led her from the dining chamber. She tried to pull her arm
loose, but he only tightened his grip and lengthened his stride
until she had to half run to keep up with him.

"What in the name of all the gods is the matter with you?"
she cried when they reached her apartments.

"I mislike seeing you flaunt yourself," he replied. It was
unfair, he knew. She hadn't put herself forward. She didn't
need to. The men had all but fought for her merest smile. He
wasn't about to admit, even to himself, the sheer male rage that
had coursed through him when he saw the older man lay his
hand on her. Instead, he focused his anger on her.

"That robe is an invitation for any man to touch you, to see
what lies beneath. And that scent you've drenched yourself in
is enough to put a corpse in heat."

"Do not judge every man by yourself, Roman," Alena spit
out. She was so incensed she could cry. This stupid, pigheaded
man had ruined all her pleasure from the baths and her new
robe with his sneering looks and accusations.

"Don't fool yourself. There wasn't a man in that room tonight who wasn't itching to see if the taste is as good as the
smell."

Without thinking, Alena swung her hand in a vicious arc.
Before it could connect, Marcus caught her arm in an iron grip

and twisted it behind her. He slammed her up against his chest, her arm held fast and the combs tumbling from her hair.

"I could have told them that it is," he got out grimly, before slanting his mouth over hers in a bruising kiss.

Alena closed her eyes and forced herself not to respond. Her mind repeated over and over like a chant, Do not feel him, do not breathe him, do not think about what the touch of his lips does to your senses.

"Open your mouth, woman," Marcus growled, incensed by the way she held herself so rigid and unresponsive. Wrapping a thick rope of her hair around his fist, he pulled her head back for his kiss. His tongue forced its way between her trembling lips and danced with hers.

"Ah, you're like honeyed mead," he murmured, nibbling and biting at her lips. His hips ground against hers, thrusting his swollen manhood into her lower belly. Desperately Alena fought the urge to give in, to loose her awakening sensuality, to give full rein to her hungry appetites.

Marcus released her arm and bent to sweep her up against his chest. He carried her across the chamber to the sleeping platform. The scent of him filled Alena—a warm, musky mansmell that tickled her nostrils and tingled along her nerves. She kept her eyes closed as he laid her on the bed, and waited, breath suspended, wanting and fearing his touch at the same time.

"Open your eyes, Alena. Look at me."

Startled, she opened her eyes to see him studying her with fierce concentration.

Marcus wanted to see her eyes, to read in their green depths what she was feeling. He saw confusion there, and the beginnings of heavy-lidded desire, but no fear. He gave a grunt of savage satisfaction.

"I swore I would not take you again, woman, and I will not. Much as it pains me," he muttered.

Alena stared up at his face, its harsh planes etched in stark relief, seeing the raw flame flicker in his dark eyes. She knew he wanted to forget his oath, wanted to fit his body to hers and pour his seed into her. Her muscles tensed at the thought— whether from desire or from disgust, she knew not. She breathed a silent sigh when he muttered a vile curse and sat up.

"You know this is not finished between us," he growled, his back to her.

Alena scrambled to the far side of the platform and slipped from the bed. She tried to straighten her robe, but her shaking hands slid uselessly over the rumpled green fabric.

"There is nothing between us. Only the heavy hand of Rome that takes me from all I love and leaves you a conqueror in a hostile land."

Marcus stood and faced her, his expression harsh. "You go to your fate, woman. I but do my duty."

"Pah!" Alena cried, angry now that this man could hold her one moment and dismiss her as a piece of goods to be bartered the next. "I go to the fate you Romans have decreed. It's not my wish, and I do not intend to accept it meekly. You may bow to your marble gods in their stone temples, but mine are alive. They're in the air and the trees and the hills around us, and they call out to me."

"You have no choice. You must accept your lot. What can you do to alter the course the governor has chosen?"

When she shrugged and turned away, Marcus felt his sexual tension drain as doubt snaked through his belly. Half-buried suspicions, submerged in the weeks since they had begun their rides together, came alive. The idea that she might be plotting some dangerous act to avoid the plans for her ate into his consciousness. He cared now not so much what she might have planned, only that it might cause her hurt. No one defied Rome's decree without suffering the consequences, and particularly not the widow of a rebel king.

Marcus strode around the bed and caught her by the arms. "Listen to me, Alena, you have no choice in this." He was suddenly afraid for her. She was so wild in her anger, so proud, she could very well be putting herself in danger.

"There is always choice. You would be wise to remember that, soldier."

Marcus stared down into her angry, defiant eyes for a long moment. He would get no more from her, he realized. With a curt order for her to be ready to ride with the first light, he left. His last act before throwing himself down on his own bed was to place a guard at the Lady Alena's door.

Chapter Twelve

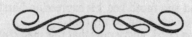

A changed, charged atmosphere surrounded the captain the next day. He made a quick farewell to his host and got the entourage moving early, keeping them to a rapid pace. As they moved along deserted stretches of the narrow road south of Catterick, Marcus felt his hackles begin to rise. The doubt Alena had planted in him grew with each passing mile. He would not rest easy until he had her safely within the thick walls of the Roman camp outside Isurium.

His soldier's instinct for trouble proved true. The enemy struck just after midday. The troop had halted beside a flowing stream and the women had been allowed to go a brief distance downstream to tend to their private needs. Alena was just about to dismount when wild shouts scattered the stillness and blue-painted bodies crashed out of the brush all around her. Above Ethelyn's shrill screams, she heard a deep, guttural voice call her.

"Here, Alena. Get you behind me."

She turned to see a huge, naked warrior, his head a nimbus of flaming red hair.

"Beorht," she gasped. He grinned even as he swung his sword in a vicious arc. The guard assigned to her fell under his slashing blow, blood spouting from neck and chest. Beorht reached out for her horse's bridle and pulled the mount away from the scene.

"Hold her," the warrior king ordered two of his men, then rushed past to lead a wild charge on the Romans. Raucous, whooping shouts mingled with the sound of swords beating against iron-bossed shields and the shrill neighing of horses.

The attacking warriors bore down on the main body of soldiers bent low as the air around them filled with arrows arcing over them in both directions.

Marcus leapt into his saddle at the first shout. Viciously he cursed himself for not listening to his instincts and keeping a tighter formation. And for letting Alena out of his sight. He pulled his shield from the leather ties holding it under his saddle blanket and raised it just in time to deflect a shower of arrows. With a quick, short jab of his iron spurs, he raced his gray stallion across the clearing toward the wave of blue-painted horsemen.

A huge, heavily muscled giant with flowing red hair leaned forward and kicked his horse toward Marcus. His tough mountain pony crashed into the solid wall of the stallion's chest. The two horses skittered sideways, their riders slashing and jabbing while they fought for balance. With the sounds of battle closing all around them, the two managed to turn their mounts and attack again.

"We meet, Roman."

A wide grin split the blue face of the warrior, and he swung his long iron sword. Metal sliced only air as Marcus wrenched his horse's reins back and leaned low on its withers. The Roman jerked upright and swung his own sword. It caught the man under his upraised arm, slicing through muscle to the bone beneath.

The giant grimaced, then quickly switched his sword to his left hand. He swung wildly and hit Marcus on the side of his helmet before the momentum of the horses separated them once more.

Beorht wrenched his horse around, intent on rejoining battle with the Roman captain. He had recognized his enemy immediately, not only by the shining eagle embossed on his cuirass, but also by the cool, icy-eyed authority he emanated. White teeth flashed in a blue-streaked face as the chief of the Selgovae measured his man. This Roman was a worthy opponent, one whose head would bring much power and honor when it hung from his saddle. He would take him, even with his injured arm hanging bloodied and numb at his side. Beorht took the leather reins in his teeth, swung his sword in a wild circle over his head and charged recklessly back across the clearing.

From the corner of one eye, Marcus saw the chieftain wheel his pony and begin back toward him. He jabbed at a naked warrior, thrusting clean through his unprotected neck, then pulled his sword free and spurred his stallion through the melee toward the bellowing chieftain. He swore viciously and deflected his horse at the last minute as two Roman cavalrymen crossed in front of him, heading for the same target. Before he could bring his mount around once more, grasping hands pulled at its bridle. He spent the next furious seconds slashing and slicing to free himself and his horse. Corpses littered the ground under his mount's trampling hooves by the time he fought clear.

Panting, the cool air searing his heated lungs, Marcus surveyed the battle scene. He heard the centurion scream hoarsely above the incredible din to bring the legionnaires into formation. Protected by a solid wall of shields, the soldiers began to advance. Marcus parried a long spear thrust at him by a running native and looked across the clearing to where the giant who had attacked him still fought. Although his every instinct urged him to go after the man and finish him, Marcus knew Alena was the target of this ambush. He wheeled his horse and spurred it downstream.

"Praxas, the women!" he shouted to the burly sergeant as he charged past. The man grunted and swung his sword in a wide arc that nearly lopped off a bearded blond head, then whirled to follow his captain.

Marcus cursed as he saw horses disappearing around a bend in the stream. Alena was bent low over her saddle, riding hard. A naked, blue-painted warrior rode on either side of her, one of whom held the little maid. The prefect spurred his own horse mercilessly. His stallion's long legs ate into the hard ground. The sergeant's horse pounded behind him.

Alena looked over her shoulder and saw the Roman in wild pursuit. Her breath caught on a ragged sob and she kicked her horse savagely. The men beside her fell back to take on the attackers, but Alena dared not stop. She knew she would have only this one chance.

"I've got them, Captain," Praxas shouted as he fitted an arrow to a bow pulled from behind his saddle. He took down one of the blue warriors on the first shot, then turned to intercept the one who held the maid. Marcus thundered past, his whole being intent on the flaring, brightly colored cloak of the woman before him.

Alena hugged her horse's neck and kicked it savagely with her sandaled heels, forcing the panting creature into the swift flowing stream. She knew her mountain-bred pony could never outrun the Roman's huge war-horse. Her only hope was to cross the stream and try to lose him in the thick woods on the opposite bank. Her mount splashed through the water and leapt onto the bank. Heart pounding, Alena felt its hooves scrambling for purchase, then cursed when the soft mud gave way.

Marcus watched with equal parts fear and grim satisfaction as her horse slid down the bank and fell back on its haunches. Alena threw herself out of the saddle and rolled clear just as the animal slipped, thrashing, into the water.

Desperately Alena clawed at the roots of the bushes lining the bank, trying to pull herself up and make for the shelter of the trees. Her drenched skirts tangled around her knees, denying her purchase on the steep slope. She heard the steady drum of a horse's hooves in the water behind her. Almost crying from mingled fear and exertion, she scrambled over the top of the bank.

"Take one more step and I swear I won't answer for my actions," Marcus panted as he pulled his horse up the bank and swerved it in front of her.

Alena pushed her tangled hair out of her eyes and looked up. The expression in the captain's eyes made her heart flutter with fear. She stepped back, only to fall to her knees to keep from tumbling backward over the bank.

"You'll spend a lot more time on your knees before this is over, woman." His voice harsh, Marcus bent and twisted his fist in her robe, pulling her to her feet.

"Get up behind me." His grip shifted to her arm. With a vicious tug, he pulled her up and almost over his horse's rump. When she clutched at him awkwardly to keep from tumbling off, he reached back for her other arm and dragged it forward.

Ripping a leather lacing from his saddle, he wrapped it tight around her wrists. Alena bit her lip as the leather cut into her flesh.

Marcus swung his horse back through the shallow stream. He felt his lips curl in a grim smile when the woman behind him was forced to grab his belt to keep her balance. Her position was awkward, but it kept her secure and his arms free for battle.

The fight was over, however, by the time he arrived back at the scene.

"What losses, Centurion?" he snapped as he cut the laces binding Alena's hands and slid from the saddle.

"Only one, sir," the older man replied. "The savages melted back into the brush when you took off after the lady. We accounted for half a score of them, though," he said with satisfaction.

Marcus surveyed the bloody clearing. There was no sign of the red-haired leader among the bodies littering the field. "Hang the corpses from the trees, and let's get going. I want to be within walls by nightfall."

Alena sat mute as he gave his orders. She rubbed her bruised wrists and wondered what would come next. Her mind numb, she comforted Ethelyn when the girl came running over and clutched her leg, sobbing. One of the pages offered her a skin of wine that she accepted gratefully. Marcus flashed her a dark look when she whispered her thanks, but kept silent. Gradually she realized that the men didn't know she had attempted to escape. They seemed to think the prefect had rescued her from the savages and would keep her safe. For some reason, he did not say otherwise. She was too drained emotionally—and too frightened, if the truth be known—to understand the captain's motives. He would tell her in his own time, in his own way, why he did not expose her to his men.

When Marcus swung back into the saddle, he told her brusquely to put her arms forward again. Biting back a weary sigh, Alena wrapped her arms around his waist and felt him bind her wrists, although not as tightly as before. Once again she was forced to clutch at his belt when he spurred his horse into a fast trot. The foot soldiers jogged in a silent column behind them.

They made Beldae before dark. The small town sat atop a rolling hill, surrounded by wide ditches and a palisade of sharpened stakes. Marcus commandeered a large stone house in the center of town and, after a brief inspection, escorted Alena to a room at the back of the house.

"But, Lord, this is only a storeroom. It has no windows or comforts for the lady," their host protested. A wealthy merchant, he had filled his house with fine tiles and rich furnishings. He could provide better for his unexpected guests.

"It'll do. Send wine and meats," Marcus said grimly before he shut the door in his host's confused face. He turned, leaning his back against the wooden door, to face the woman standing in the middle of the small, airless room.

"When was this afternoon's ambush planned?" he demanded, his voice low and hard.

"It was not planned, at least not by me," she replied wearily.

"Don't toy with me, Alena, not if you value your hide," he warned her, his jaw set in a tight line. "These raiders were from the northern lands, beyond Corstopitum. Their leader is the one called Beorht?"

"Aye."

"The chieftain of the clan called Selgovae?"

"Aye."

"He has not been known to raid so far south before. Was he after you?" Marcus didn't really need to ask, but he wanted to see how the woman would answer.

"He knew I was on my way to Isurium. I sent him a message before we left." Alena met his eyes with an unwavering look. "But I did not think he would dare come this far into territory controlled by Rome."

She surprised him with her frank response, and angered him with her duplicity. "How long have you been communicating with him?"

"Since shortly after my husband was killed." She raised a shaking hand to brush the golden tangles from her face. Disgusted by this sign of weakness, she lowered her arm and hid it in the folds of her tattered robe. "He wants me. Or my son's lands. I'm not sure which. Both, I suppose, since we seem to go together."

"You would wed with this savage?" Marcus asked angrily.

"One savage is as good as another," she snapped back. "At least the man promised to take me to wife before he took me to bed."

"Be careful, woman," Marcus ground out through clenched jaws. "You're playing with your life here. Should the governor find out you conspired with this outlaw who flouts Rome's authority, you would not live long enough to wed or bed anyone."

"Aye." Alena sighed. Her spurt of defiance drained away, leaving her tired and strangely weak. "I've known Beorht long, since I was a child. He is wild and fierce and determined to keep his lands free of Rome's heavy hand. He would even align himself with the Caledonians to the north, long his enemy, to stop your armies."

"If you have known him so long, why did you wait to go to him?"

Alena shrugged, doubting that this soldier would understand her reluctance to bind herself to a man who was, she suspected, even rougher and more forthright in his passions than her husband had been.

"I thought to keep my choice open as long as possible, I suppose. Too long, it appears now."

"I told you last night, you have no choice in this matter."

"And I told you there are always choices. I made the wrong one, that's all."

Marcus stood still, a muscle jumping in his jaw. He was afraid to let himself touch the woman, for fear he would beat her. His heart still pounded whenever he thought of her desperate, wild ride. The realization that he'd almost lost her left him confused and angry. It wasn't that he had come close to failing in his duty to keep her fast. It was something more, the unfamiliar rush of panic that had swept over him when he saw her horse disappearing around the bend. He didn't understand the fear that had gripped him when he thought her gone. Or the bitter anger he had felt when he realized she wasn't being carried off, she was fleeing.

"Do what you will, Captain. I am too tired to care anymore." Alena sank down on a wooden crate.

Whatever Marcus would have replied was lost when a timid knock sounded on the door. Ethelyn entered at his terse bark, a wooden tray in her hands.

"Put it down and get out," Marcus ordered.

"But my mistress needs me," the girl whimpered.

"Get out."

"Go, Ethelyn," Alena said when the maid looked about to defy the captain. She would not have the girl suffer unnecessarily.

Marcus grabbed the door as it swung behind the frightened girl. "I'll be back for you at first light." He shut and bolted the wooden panel behind him.

Marcus sat silent through the long supper the merchant spread before him. Half of him listened and made polite responses to the man's light conversation about his travels, while half still seethed with anger and worry over Alena. Finally, after the last libation to Hercules, patron of merchants, had been imbibed, Marcus excused himself and retired.

Dismissing his orderly with a curt nod, he undressed himself. Stretched out in a chair before the fire, he rubbed his aching knee absently and tried to unweave the tangled web of Alena's plotting. He knew now that Beorht's attack on his northern outpost and his ambush of the Roman relief column had been deliberate. The chieftain would show his strength to the woman to convince her to come to him.

Why would she do it? The question nagged at him as the fire died slowly. Why would she align herself with a barbarian when the governor had promised to give her to one who would hold her lands? Her defiant words about wanting to make her own choice flashed through his mind. Marcus shook his head. The lady realized now she had chosen wrongly. What she didn't realize was that her decision had sealed her fate. After today, the soldier knew with deep, unerring certainty that she would not go to Beorht. Or to anyone else. He relived the moment when he had seen her riding off between the two warriors and made a silent vow to Mars, god of all soldiers, that she would not ride away from him again.

In the dark, airless room, Alena spread her cloak on the floor and tried to find a comfortable position on the hard-packed dirt. She was drained, both emotionally and physically, in a way that she could not remember ever having been before. For the first time in all her adult years, she wanted to cry. She despised tears as the ploy of weak women, but tonight she felt weak and helpless and hurt. Huddled on the hard floor, surrounded by bleak darkness, she knew that she had come to the end of her hopes. Tomorrow would bring her to her mother's court and a new husband. She tried desperately to block out the remembered pain of the marriage bed.

Slowly, insidiously, her mind fastened on the prefect. Not on the cruel way his hands had lashed hers this afternoon, but on the way they had played with her and brought her to her only taste of pleasure. Mayhap her unknown husband-to-be would couple as this Roman did. The thought brought her small comfort. Instead, a queer little pain, entirely unrelated to her aching wrists or her bruised arms, lodged next to her heart. She drifted off to sleep, unaware of the tears that trickled down her muddied cheeks.

It seemed as if her head had barely touched the hard-packed dirt before a sharp rap on the wooden door awakened her.

"The captain says to rise, Lady," Ethelyn whispered as she entered the small room. She balanced a pitcher of water in one hand and a tray of bread and cheese in the other. "He wants to reach your mother's court today."

Alena sat up slowly, every muscle in her body stiff. She grimaced when she looked down at her tattered, muddy skirts. Ruefully she wondered what the rest of her must look like.

"Pour the water out for me to wash," she told the girl. She would have given much for a bit of soap or her wooden comb, but she settled down on the floor to rub a rag over her face and muddy legs. She used her fingers to comb out her wild tangles as best she could. Ethelyn watched her, lips pursed, then left the room with a quiet word to the guard. She returned moments later, clean robes over her arm.

"Here, Lady," she offered in a breathless rush.

"The Roman deigns to give me use of my own clothing?" Alena asked tartly as she slipped out of her tattered woolen robe and pulled on the clean one. She fingered the familiar green-and-blue plaid gratefully.

"No. I didn't ask him." A mischievous smile brought a gamine beauty to the red-haired maid's small face. "Praxas got it for me from our bundles."

Alena glanced down, taken aback by the rosy blush that covered her maid's cheeks. "Be careful," she told the girl dryly. "These Romans would as soon mount you as their horses. Sooner," she amended.

"I wouldn't mind, mistress. It's been too long since I had a man."

"You would lie with him willingly?"

"I've felt his shaft poking at my behind often enough these last days, riding in his lap as I did. He is well armored. I have an itch to feel it poke elsewhere." The maid grinned, totally unabashed in her earthy honesty.

Alena felt her own cheeks redden as the memory of how the prefect's iron rod had filled her washed into her mind. And into her body. She brought her legs together to still their sudden trembling.

"Enough," she snapped at the maid. "We'd best get us outside and see what this day will bring."

It brought hard riding, and her first sight of her mother in almost two decades.

Chapter Thirteen

"So, daughter, you have finally acceded to your queen's wishes and come."

Alena knelt on the paved floor, her head bowed as her mother's sardonic voice washed over her. In truth, she could do little else. She was so weary from the ruthless pace Marcus had set for the final leg of their journey that she wanted to crumple to the hard stones and weep.

"Get up, get up," Cartimandua ordered impatiently. "Come, sit here beside me."

Alena struggled to rise. Clumsy with fatigue, she stumbled over her skirts. The prefect leaned down and took a firm grasp of her arm, helping her to her feet. She pulled free with a determined jerk and gave him an angry glare before moving toward a small stool beside the queen's chair. Cartimandua watched her daughter approach, then turned to the much more interesting prospect of the Roman prefect.

Marcus stood at ease, helmet under his arm, while the queen of the Brigantes openly inspected him. He could see only a faint resemblance between mother and daughter. Cartimandua had the same tawny shade of hair, worn in high rolls on her head and held by an ornate gold comb, and her eyes sparkled with green lights. But the woman seated in the richly carved wooden throne was big and coarse, for all her finery. Where Alena's body had been honed through years of exercise and riding into long, clean limbs, the queen had rolls of flesh hanging from her arms and settled about her middle. Even the differences in their age wouldn't account for the excess, Marcus thought dispassionately. He'd learned that Cartimandua meant "sleek pony" in the Celtic tongue. If so, the queen had long outgrown her name. Moreover, there was little similarity in their demeanor or their expressions. Where the daughter had a clear, sun-darkened complexion that showed her every emotion, the queen's heavily painted face held a shuttered, calculating look.

Still, despite her coarseness, Cartimandua exuded an earthy ripeness all her own. When the queen shot Marcus a look of frank sensual approval, he saw the truth of Lady Julia's description of the queen as a lusty old baggage. Meeting her heavy-lidded eyes, he well understood the marital problems her absent husband must have experienced over the years.

"Seat yourself, Marcus Valerius, and take wine." Graciously the queen waved the soldier to one of the hide chairs scattered around her own seat. "Governor Maximus told me much of you when last we met. He believes that if anyone can pacify the northern reaches and bring them under Rome's banner, you can."

"It can be done," Marcus responded, keeping his gaze from Alena's averted face, "but not without some effort."

"The northern tribes have long harassed Brigantium's borders. I had thought my daughter's husband would hold them. I gave him gold and arms enough in dower." Her voice held a hint of acid as she slanted a sharp look at the woman seated beside her.

"Dugald kept the northern borders for many years, Mother Queen," Alena said quietly. She had no love for her husband, but, for all his faults, he had been a bold, courageous warrior.

"Until he turned traitor to me and his tribe and joined the rebellion against Rome," Cartimandua snapped.

"He thought to save the Lopocares and their ways." Alena was discovering she could be as bullheaded as her mother. "He saw how Rome built marble temples to house strange gods and forbade our priests and priestesses their rites. How other nobles' lands were confiscated and given to retired soldiers for settlement. When the Iceni were forbidden to carry arms and could not protect themselves from raids, even though they had been Rome's allies for many years, he felt he must act."

Marcus cursed Alena silently and willed her to quiet. She damned herself with every word out of her mouth. Although they had talked little of her past, Marcus had gleaned from the bits and pieces she had let drop that her marriage had not been a happy one. Damn the misguided sense of honor that led her to defend Dugald now.

"Your husband was a fool," the queen snapped.

"You chose him for me, Lady Mother," Alena shot back.

After a startled moment, the queen's massive bosom heaved in a raucous chuckle. "Aye, I did."

Her daughter's sudden spirit pleased her. Cartimandua had birthed many babes, and from many fathers, if the truth be known. Of necessity, she'd had little time for any of them, except perhaps her eldest sons. That this one possessed some of her own feisty temper gratified her. She'd not want to have whelped a weakling.

"This time, I will do better," Cartimandua responded, still chuckling. She didn't miss the flash of green fire in her daughter's eyes at the promise.

"I've chambers prepared for you in the women's quarters. You may go to your rest. Your king and father returns tomorrow, and we will talk more then."

Alena bit her lip at the abrupt dismissal. Her hackles rose, as they always did when someone ordered her about. She'd been too long her own mistress to bow meekly to anyone, even this huge, fierce woman who owned her.

Marcus read the expressions chasing across Alena's face and gritted his teeth. He knew her so well by now that he could see clearly the signs bespeaking imminent explosion, from the defiant light in her eyes to the color staining in her cheeks. Swiftly he rose to intervene before the stubborn woman put her neck on the block irretrievably.

"We thank you, Majesty," he said smoothly. "The Lady Alena was put in my care by Governor Maximus himself. He charged me to bring her to Isurium, which I have done. But I will hold her until the governor arrives and you conclude agreements for her disposition. I've sent runners to the Roman camp for quarters to be prepared for us."

With a slight bow to the queen, Marcus slipped his hand under Alena's arm, marking his possession.

A hush fell over the long hall as the motley crowd sensed the sudden tension radiating from their queen. Several huge, fair-skinned warriors rose silently to their feet. For long moments only the sounds of the crackling fires and the dogs snuffling in the reeds covering the stone floor disturbed the silence.

Cartimandua studied the man before her. There was calm determination in his stance, and all the weight of Rome's authority behind him, but no arrogance. His dark eyes met hers steadily. She knew well the Roman sense of duty, and this soldier believed he was doing his. For a brief moment she weighed her long loyalty to Rome against the outcome of contesting this man's claim to the woman he held so firmly.

"Take her, Prefect," the queen told him finally. "I'll expect you when the sun is directly overhead tomorrow, and we'll discuss this further."

Cartimandua had not kept her throne through all these years by wasting energy and blood on small battles. She would work out her daughter's fate with the governor when he arrived. In the meantime, she'd learn more of this soldier who commanded the troops spread across her nothern borderlands.

Marcus let out an imperceptible breath and bowed once more. He'd gambled and won—this time, at least. Taking Alena from her mother's roof far exceeded his authority, but only he knew that at this point. He'd have a lot of explaining to do when the governor arrived.

"Why did you do that?" Alena asked as he led her into the dark courtyard and signaled to his waiting troops to bring their mounts.

Marcus subdued the urge to shake her and tried to make her see the dangerous ground she was dancing on. "You're a worrisome burden, and I should be glad to be rid of you, but for some reason I was loath to see you bare your neck for the strangler's knot. If you had spouted one more word in support of your husband's treason, you would've been even more suspect than you are now. I thought it best to remove you from your mother's hold until both of you cool your tempers."

"You but delay the inevitable, Prefect. I cannot and will not change what I am. I suspect my temper comes from my dam. There will likely be many clashes between us."

Marcus spun her about to face him. "Listen, you little fool," he growled. "You have not your mother's wiles or long experience. Do not think to match wits with her. You will be crushed in the process."

"Why do you always seek to school me to obedience, Roman? I haven't survived this long through obedience. I didn't give in meekly to my husband, nor to Peganthus in his doddering regency, nor to Rome. I cannot go quietly to the fate the governor and my 'mother' decide for me without at least trying to shape it to my will."

"Great Mars, give me patience," Marcus muttered.

By the time he had her and her maid settled, with two guards at the door to her quarters, he was content to stretch wearily in front of a roaring fire with a foaming mug of ale and exchange news with the commander of this small camp. The grizzled centurion chafed at being separated from his legion for this largely administrative post in the Brigantian capital. He'd heard much of Marcus Valerius, and the two men spent a companionable hour trading war tales. When the soldiers rose to seek their beds, the centurion offered his guest the use of his prettiest house slaves for the night. Marcus refused the offer with a laughing reference to age and hard rides, then spent the time while he was readying for sleep wondering why he had done so.

It wasn't as if his body did not need ease. He'd been in a constant state of arousal for weeks. Ever since meeting the irritating woman in his care, he admitted wryly. He propped both hands under his head and stared up at the painted fresco on the ceiling, wondering at the effect the Lady Alena had on his mind and body.

He'd never met any woman quite like her. It was not just that she aroused his lust with her wildness and long legs and soft, golden skin. She stirred something deeper in him, something he'd never felt with another woman. He wanted to possess her, all of her, not just her body. He wanted her warmth and her passion and her laughter. He wanted to shield her, almost as much as he wanted to beat her at times. Tiredly he stretched under the thick furs. Soon, he told himself, soon.

Although Marcus Valerius spent a restless night, the Lady Alena appeared to have slept exceedingly well. He ran a jaundiced eye over her clean, waving hair and scrubbed countenance when they met just before noon the next morning. Even the drizzle turning the world around them to dreary gray could not dull her shine.

"You appear to have recovered from the ravages of your journey well, Lady," he commented as he led her to her horse.

"Much as I hate to admit admiring anything Roman, I've taken to this strange custom you have of soaking your bodies," she replied calmly. "The centurion was kind enough to escort me to the bathing chambers while you were with the men."

Marcus scowled and held her reins. "Did he also accompany you into the chambers?" The question was out before he could stop it.

Wide, surprised eyes looked down at him. "Is such a thing permitted?" Alena had little false modesty about her own or others' bodies. Many of her tribe's warriors, her husband included, had often wrestled and fought naked. Still, the thought of men and women together in the languorous environment of the pools was . . . interesting.

"Men and women bathe together in many places," Marcus admitted as he mounted and they wheeled their horses toward the gates. "But not in my camps. It's not good for the discipline of the men."

"No, I would imagine not." Alena's voice held an amused note.

Marcus slanted her a quick, assessing look. That she could jest after the emotional turmoil and exhaustion of their journey, even as she was on her way to be introduced to her prospective mate, was a measure of this unusual female. The soldier doubted there were many women who could find humor in such circumstances.

In truth, Alena's spirits and natural optimism had revived with the long rest and the visit to the baths. Moreover, she'd sent Ethelyn early this morning with one of her precious gold armbands to find a priest to offer sacrifices and read the omens for her. The maid arrived back only an hour ago, breathless and wide-eyed with excitement. She reported that the ancient one would prepare sacrifices at dusk, but had seen a flock of ravens alight on a stone wall even as she passed him the armband. That there were seven ravens in the flock and that they immediately flew north, the priest had interpreted as excellent omens. He would send further word by sundown. Fortified by rest, a long, soothing session at the baths and the heartening words of the priest, Alena faced the coming session with her mother and her unknown suitors with confidence. The gods would work for her yet.

During the short ride from camp, Alena's eyes widened at the city she'd been too weary and disheartened to note the previous night. She found Isurium much changed from what she could remember of the city of her birth. In its collage of ancient Celtic structures and gleaming new Roman-style public buildings, it reflected the enduring twenty-year alliance between Brigantium and Rome. The old timber-and-stone ceremonial hall that had occupied a prime position on the highest hill of the city was gone, replaced by a huge, colonnaded forum teeming with shops, and a lively open-air market. On the far side of the forum stood a monstrous basilica, where the tribal council met and the elected magistrates dispensed legal decisions under the watchful eye of the queen. Alena gaped at the size of the structure, almost two hundred feet in length and a good sixty feet across. Surely every one of Isurium's four thousand inhabitants could fit in it, if necessary.

Surrounding these imposing buildings was a curious mixture of old and new. Traditional round mud huts sat side by side with long rectangular buildings of wood and stone. Alena leaned low over her horse's withers to peer into the open fronts of these long structures. They were houses or shops, or both, she decided. It appeared the residents lived and worked in the back and spread their wares in front to offer them to passing customers. The streets still reflected the old city, twisting and winding in haphazard fashion instead of following the straight grids the Romans loved so passionately. But many of them were cobbled now, with wide gutters on either side filled with flowing water to carry off sewage. Only a short distance from her mother's palace they passed the site of new public baths under construction. The sharp ring of chisels on stone, the shouts of engineers and the groans of slaves hauling huge slabs of stone on wooden rollers created a din unlike any Alena had ever heard.

By the time they reached the palace, Alena's wonder at Isurium's changing character had turned to cynical appreciation of her mother's gift for political survival. While the Lopocares and the other tribes who had tried to throw off Rome's yoke starved and scrabbled to meet the fines and taxes, Cartimandua and the others who had remained loyal grew fat and prospered. Inside the rambling wooden palace, she took a scornful inventory. Instead of rough wooden walls, these were covered in thick plaster, with a painted frieze of graceful swirls in the Celtic manner. Evidence of the queen's wealth was everywhere, from the chased silver mugs set in a rack above one fireplace to the red glazed Samian bowls filled with sweetmeats and fruits set out on low wooden tables throughout the long room.

Alena pushed aside her private thoughts on the opulence of the hall to greet the queen with quiet courtesy and the king, her father, with frank curiosity. She'd rarely seen Venutius as a child and had only vague memories of her sire. She was not impressed with the man seated before her, nor was he much interested in this long-distant daughter. He brushed her greeting aside impatiently, barely waiting until she'd seated herself once more on the small stool her mother indicated before addressing the prefect.

"You will be gratified to hear Governor Maximus arrives tomorrow."

Marcus kept his face impassive as he surveyed the titular king of the Brigantes. In truth, he little liked what he saw. Although big and brawny, his flowing red hair only lightly streaked with gray, the king did not match his wife in presence. He had a habit of shifting his eyes away when in conversation. Additionally, Marcus Valerius could summon little respect for a man who'd been restored to his throne and his wife's bed only through the might of Roman swords.

The centurion had given some of the details of the turbulent relationship between Cartimandua and Venutius last night. The marriage was a dynastic one, Venutius being from the northeastern reaches and Cartimandua from the southern part of Brigantium. Together, they ruled the largest kingdom in Roman Britannia, one that stretched from sea to sea across the entire northern part of the province. Their reign had been a stormy one. Eight years ago Venutius had fanned the anti-Roman, antifeminine elements of his tribe and led a band of lords in bloody revolt against their queen. Cartimandua, in turn, took several members of his family prisoner. She used her long loyalty to Rome to gain the governor's support in this intertribal war. With the help of two cohorts of auxiliaries, she won a fierce battle just south of Catterick and put down the rebellion. Although many lords lost their heads, Venutius miraculously survived and retained his title as co-ruler. He must be exceptionally well endowed, Marcus thought cynically as his eyes raked the king.

"Aye, Lord," he responded finally. "I am aware of the governor's arrival. He sent a messenger to the camp, as well."

"Did his message indicate his agreement with our plans for our daughter?"

"It said only that the governor had agreed to consider her marriage." Although he didn't look at her directly, Marcus caught the way Alena stiffened on her uncomfortable stool.

Cartimandua spoke for the first time. "There are two offers for her. Both lords are here to present their case." She heaved herself forward in her massive chair, tugging at the bright red-and-gold patterned draperies that covered her bulk. Beckoning imperiously to a tall warrior with flaming red hair, she called him forward. In a land of big, raw-boned men, this one stood out for his astounding height and breadth. He appeared young, younger even than the woman he would wive. A second or third son, looking for his own holdings, Marcus guessed as the behemoth stumbled awkwardly forward. The young lord seemed incapable of speech and stood mute, his face as red as his hair.

The second suitor strolled forward when the awkward silence stretched. "If I am permitted to speak for Lord Berk, as well as myself, I will say we're most anxious to get this matter settled, Lady Queen."

Marcus disliked the man's smooth voice. Much smaller than the huge red-haired lord, this suitor was whipcord-lean and battle-ravaged. His hair showed more gray than dark, and his smile exposed jagged gaps. He wore a once-fine woolen tunic, its rents inexpertly mended. This one is dangerous, Marcus thought. Lean and hungry and dangerous.

"I, too, wish the matter settled, Lord Eadgar," Cartimandua replied. "Now that my daughter is here, we will review your offers and consult the priests. If the omens are propitious, the marriage will take place tomorrow, after the governor's arrival. I have organized a hunt for this afternoon. It'll keep you busy and provide meat for the feast tomorrow.''

"I would join the hunt, also."

Cartimandua swiveled her head in surprise at her daughter's cool tones. She started to deny the request abruptly. After all, it had taken her years to get the stubborn woman here. She wanted to take no chances of losing her now. She swallowed the harsh denial even as it formed on her lips, however. The girl would be well guarded, with both her eager suitors hovering over her. Mayhap she would entice them with her lush body and comely looks. If the fools became besotted with her, Cartimandua could lower the dower she'd pledged.

"If your guardian permits, you may go," the old queen said slyly. If aught happened to the woman, Rome could share the blame. "He is much protective of your person."

"I have no objection." Marcus shrugged. He needed some action, as well. Suddenly the long hall seemed overcrowded with perspiring bodies and greedy suitors. He welcomed the thought of an afternoon in the wet, cool air.

When the pack of horsemen clattered out through the town gates a short time later, the drizzle had turned to a fine, driving rain. Alena and a few other adventurous women rode in the center of the group. Their horses threw up thick clods of mud as they left the main road and headed across sloping fields toward the thick forests barely visible in the distance. Beaters sent out earlier by the queen began thrashing the bush and yelling wildly as soon as they saw the horsemen crest the far hill.

Marcus felt the thrill of the chase surge through him as he and several other men took off in pursuit of a large horned buck that broke cover and bounded across the fields. He gave a yell as wild as any of his companions' and leaned low in his saddle. Letting his horse have its head, he reached for his bow. The buck swerved and crashed back into the woods, three riders closing fast on its tail.

When the small group rejoined others some hours later, they were bloody, tired, and as close companions as conqueror and conquered could be after sharing good sport. His fellow hunters had impressed Marcus with their deadly skills at bow and javelin, and they'd cheered when he chased down a huge boar and slashed its throat in one daring charge.

The hunters tossed their bloody prizes to the bearers, who would gut and skin the carcasses. Marcus leaned against a tree, sharing a wineskin with his companions. His gaze roamed around the group gathered at the fire. For the first time, he noted Alena's absence. He noted that several of the men were missing, as well. Including the Lord Eadgar.

"Have you seen the Lady Alena?" he asked one of the other men who'd just ridden into the clearing.

"Aye, she was after a boar in the south fields some time ago," the man replied. He wiped wine from his lips before adding with a grin, "Eadgar was hot on her tail. He'll have his hands full with that one, I'll be bound. She looks to have her mother's temper, but her body would make a shrewish tongue easier to bear. I'd keep her so busy humping she'd have no breath for nagging."

Marcus felt his jaw tighten when the men around him laughed and offered ribald comments on how to tame one such as Alena. As the comments became more explicit, his eyes narrowed dangerously. He spit a short stream of wine and swung up onto his horse.

"I would remind you the woman is daughter to your queen," he snapped. Giving the reins a sharp tug, he kicked his mount into a gallop and headed toward the south fields.

Chapter Fourteen

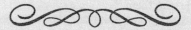

Alena enjoyed the hunt as much for the exercise as for the opportunity it gave her to pursue her own ends. The cool, mist-filled air and the strenuous gallop cleared her head and renewed her confidence. She and her small group brought down several deer and wild dogs, then rested briefly beside a small stream to wash away the blood and gore. As she had known he would, Lord Eadgar had sidled up beside her mare early in the hunt and stayed with her most of the afternoon. She gave no sign that she noticed him throughout the long chase or even during the short rest. Only after their group remounted and split up did she deign to spare the lean man at her side a glance.

She would have spoken then, but a great boar crashed out of the brush directly across an open field from them. Both man and woman took off, spears in hand, wild yells ripping from their throats. The animal tore through the woods, then doubled back and charged its pursuers. His sharp, curving tusks caught Eadgar's horse alongside its belly, ripping open a gaping wound. The horse screamed in pain and went down on its knees. Eadgar leapt clear and turned, spear in hand, to meet the enraged boar. Alena yelled wildly to distract the animal and charged. Her spear thrust cleanly through the boar's throat even as the animal spitted itself on the javelin Eadgar had wedged into the ground before him.

"By the gods, that was closer than I like the hunt to be," Eadgar said with a laugh. He straightened from his crouching position and walked over to where Alena had slid off her horse and leaned against it, panting.

"You have a strong arm for such a clean thrust, Lady."

"I get much practice in Corstopitum, Lord Eadgar," she told him. "Those of our men who did not die in battle were put to the sword, so the women hunt for most of the meat. The boys are only now reaching the age and strength to bring down animals such as this."

"I know well what you have endured," Eadgar said. "My own father and brothers were killed by the Romans. I chose to stay with Cartimandua, but I find it difficult even now to sit at the same table with them."

Alena shrugged. "The years ease the pain, even as the land turns green once more. I don't hate them for their drive to conquer as much as I fear the loss of our ways. I worry my son will not know whether he is of Brigantium or Rome. Whether he will rule as a Lopocare king or a provincial administrator."

"You know I would not let that happen, Lady." Eadgar moved to stand directly in front of her. "I have a substantial troop who serve under my standard. I would bring them north with me and provide you and your son the protection of a warrior clan."

"I know what my mother wants of this match," Alena said, her eyes searching his. "She seeks a strong, loyal vassal to hold the northern territories and send tribute regularly. What does she offer you in return? My son will inherit the lands and riches. What do you gain?"

"I gain a holding of my own, at least until your son reaches manhood," he answered, just as steadily. "I will receive gold and arms to refit my men. I will ride with the Romans, much as it galls me, when they strike north, and perhaps gain more land, this time my own. And I will gain your body for my use. After meeting you, Lady, it is no small incentive."

Alena brushed away the hand he lifted to the shoulder clasp of her robe. "Don't try to convince me you're suddenly swept by passion. I'm not a green girl who needs wooing." She took a deep breath and played her hand.

"I cannot give you land, but I can give you gold. I have some that was buried and thus missed by the Romans. It would outfit your men and perhaps allow you to purchase land elsewhere."

Eadgar's pale eyes narrowed suddenly. "You seek to buy me off? Why should I settle for your offer, when I could have all?"

"You would not enjoy the holding, Lord. I am used to ordering the tribe, and the people turn to me. Moreover, the Romans have built a permanent camp in our town. You would have little authority," she told him baldly.

Unwittingly she had pricked the festering sore of this landless noble. It galled him that he could call no keep his own, could establish his authority over no domain.

"You overstep yourself, woman," Eadgar warned. "Were we to wed, I would be master of my keep."

"My son's keep," Alena reminded him relentlessly. "And I call no man master."

"You would call me so."

"Not unless you beat it out of me. And I know well from past experience that the beating lessens the pleasure of submission."

"Not necessarily, Lady."

Eadgar's low, silky reply sent shivers up Alena's arms. Suddenly nervous, she backed away, but not quickly enough. Eadgar reached out and grasped her brutally by her upper arms. He pulled her up against his chest and smiled, a thin, sneering twist of his lips.

"Some men prefer pain to spice their pleasure," he told her as he deliberately tightened his hands on the soft flesh of her upper arms.

"Let me go, Lord Eadgar." Alena's voice was as low and steady.

"Soon, my dear. First I would taste these— Ummph!"

Alena leapt back as the man doubled over, his hands cupping his groin. "You said you liked pain. You have it," she told him viciously, swinging around to clamber into her saddle.

"Not so fast, you bitch." Eadgar recovered enough to grab her robe. Panting and still bent over, he pulled at the cloth.

When Alena whirled around to face him, she had a dagger held in one hand. "Touch me again and you will not live to regret it."

"I would take the lady at her word, were I you."

Alena and the wounded lord both spun around to stare as Marcus Valerius straightened from where he had been leaning against a tree.

"You beast! How long have you been there?" Alena cried.

"Long enough."

"You would stand there and let him maul me?"

"Nay, I would not. But I would stand there while you mauled him," Marcus told her dryly. "Get on your horse. You have maimed the man enough."

"This is not your business, Roman." Eadgar straightened painfully and moved between Alena and the approaching soldier.

"You err." Marcus sent him a look of hard promise. "She is my business, and I dislike you laying hands on her. Do not do so again while she is in my care. Get mounted, Alena. Now."

Marveling that the man she alternately hated and cordially disliked could suddenly appear so welcome, Alena pulled her horse a safe distance from the glowering Eadgar and mounted. She trotted to the Roman's side, and he swung easily up behind her.

"Be still," he admonished when she protested his taking the reins in his own hands. "I left my mount some way back, and will take us both to him."

They were silent as they rode through the dim forest. Light rain pattered on the leaves overhead and showered them as they passed, causing Alena to shiver. At least, she told herself, it was the cool drizzle and not the prefect's hard thighs pushing against hers that sent tremors through her lower body. For the first time since the ambush, she was more aware of Marcus as a man than as a Roman commander. She tried to keep her eyes from the strong arms that circled her waist, to hold herself stiff and away from his hard chest.

Marcus breathed in the damp, musky scent of her hair just beneath his chin. He smiled to himself at her rigid, awkward posture. Deliberately he tightened his arms so that they held her around her ribs and brushed against the sides of her breasts with each jogging step of the small horse.

"That was not wise, you know. Such a lean, hungry man will not be bought off with a few pieces of gold when he could have all."

" 'Twas worth a try, anyway," Alena said with a shrug. She reached up impatiently to brush back the stray hairs that tickled her ears, stirred by his hot breath.

"He will make a most unpleasant husband after this little tryst in the woods."

"Aye." She sighed. "I had not planned that part." She closed her eyes a moment and leaned back, only to jerk upright again. "I suppose I shall have to work on the other one, the mountain."

Marcus was confused. He had his own plans for the woman, but wished to understand her schemes. For the life of him, he could not follow the workings of her mind. "If you buy off the boy, you leave the field clear for Eadgar."

"No, I had not thought to buy him off. I knew that would only work with Eadgar. He is the one who frightened ... who worried me most, the one I knew I had to be rid of. Once he was out of the way, I would have used some other tactic on the mountain."

"Like what?"

"I'm not sure," Alena mused, thinking hard as they rode. "I've not had much time to take his measure. Perhaps I would play with him, seduce him, then challenge his manhood and shame him away. That might have done it. He has the look of one easily led by his rod."

Marcus disliked both her words and the image they provoked. At the thought of Alena seducing that huge, youthful warrior, his arms tightened to rigid bands.

"You make free use of your body, woman. First you offer it to the brigand from the north, now you would lay it out for this beardless boy."

"Stop it, Prefect." Alena pushed at the arms crushing her breasts. "It is my body. If my mother and the governor and everyone else is willing to barter it, why should I not, also?"

Marcus muttered a low curse and lifted his leg over the mount's back, swinging them both out of the saddle. As soon as they hit the ground, he wrapped his fist in her hair and held her face up to his.

"If you wish to sell yourself," he told her with deadly calm, "tell me your terms."

"Are you mad?" Alena cried, pushing at his chest.

"What are your terms, Lady?" His hard fist held her steady. "Think for a moment. I could rid you of either suitor, of all suitors, including that oaf from the north, by claiming you myself."

"As what?" She spit. "Your whore? Your concubine for as long as you're in this land? Who would have me when you left? I doubt even Megarric would support a mother who whored for the Romans."

"You'd be well cared for. I would see to that. Few would dare revile one under Rome's protection."

"Nay. Nay. I thank you for your generous offer." Scorn dripped from every word. "But I would rather have Eadgar's cruel hands on me than shame myself and my people by lying with one who would trample us and our ways under his heels."

"You have lain with me once already. I could take you again, now, should I wish it," Marcus told her coldly.

"Aye, you could, and forswear your oath. Is your word given so lightly, your honor so valueless?"

"That oath is the only thing that keeps me from throwing you down right here and filling you with my seed."

The blunt words hung on the air between them. Alena stared up at him, shocked. She wanted to scream her fury at his insult. She wanted to cry with hurt. And, even more confusing, she wanted to shut out the sudden, searing memory of this man coming inside her, filling her, pleasuring her in that dim, dark, stone hut. She did none of these things, could do nothing except look up at him with wide, confused eyes.

Slowly, reluctantly, Marcus eased his hold.

"I'm sorry," he told her with a sigh. "I know you only seek to use what few weapons you have in this idiotic quest you have to control your destiny. But there is no dishonor in what I offer you. The arrangement is an accepted one in Rome. The agreement would be sealed by the scribes and recorded. You would be respected and revered by my men for as long as we are together, and well settled after. I meant you no insult."

Some of Alena's fury abated at his quiet words, although the hurt lingered. "It may be your custom, but it is not ours. I would be your slut, your leman. Such women are lower than serfs here, and have no rights. I would be shunned by my own people and not part of yours. No, Marcus Valerius, I will not have it."

Her eyes filled with a soft mist, and she turned her head away. "If I must, I will accept the Lord Berk. At least he is manageable. And I will have some honor in the arrangement."

Marcus studied her averted face intently. No, Lady, he thought, you will not have the young lord.

They didn't speak during the ride back to the capital. Nor did they exchange any words later that evening, during the long dinner laid out in the queen's hall. Marcus brought Alena to the palace just as slaves finished laying boards across trestles and began bringing in heaping platters of food. After they paid their respects to the queen and her consort, Marcus found himself seated beside Cartimandua. Alena, he noted, was assigned a seat farther down the boards, beside the mountain. His jaw ground audibly when he saw her smile up at the hapless Lord Berk. So she had decided to launch her campaign already.

Cartimandua followed the line of his eyes, and her own hardened.

"I am unused to being ignored, particularly in favor of my own daughters," she told him bluntly.

"Your pardon, Lady Queen," the soldier replied, tearing his eyes from the sight of Alena smiling seductively at the blushing youth. "I fear I take my duties too seriously at times."

"As you did this afternoon, when you removed my daughter from the overheated advances of one of her suitors?"

"Is that what he told you?" Marcus laughed. "The Lady Alena is much like you yourself, I would guess. She removed herself, with little help from me."

"Not so much like me, after all, Valerius," the queen murmured, her fascinated gaze on his white teeth and the strong column of his throat as he laughed. "I doubt I would have defended my honor quite so vigorously."

She had his full attention now. Even with her thick paint and sagging breasts, this woman's blatant sensuality could capture a man's interest. Marcus leaned closer, his eyes full of sheer male appreciation of her unabashed womanliness.

Alena glanced up from her position halfway down the table, and her mouth dropped in astonishment. She completely forgot the husky youth beside her as Marcus lowered his curly head closer to her mother's golden one, a lecherous grin on his face. Her mother, by the gods! Alena's eyes flashed to her father, sitting to the queen's other side. Venutius was either too inured to his wife's ways or too drunk to care. He lolled in his chair, a cup held loosely in his hand.

"Lady, you must tell me more of Corstopitum." Berk took her arm gently in one huge fist and tried to turn her back to him. A shy, awkward youth, made fun of because of his size, he had emerged slowly from his stammering shell under Alena's skillful banter.

"Aye," she murmured, her face turning back to the warrior, but her mind's eye on the head of the table. She barely noticed when Lord Berk speared the choicest morsels of mutton for her from a huge silver serving platter, or solicitously spread mustard and salt on flat unleavened bread before carving strips of beef. But she certainly noticed when Marcus Valerius did the same for the queen.

The rest of the long meal passed in a confused haze for Alena. For the first time, she saw Valerius as another woman must. Her eyes widened when he laughed at something her mother said and threw back his well-shaped head. His dark curls glinted in the firelight, and a light dew of sweat from the crowded hall glistened on the muscles roping his arms. His short white tunic seemed designed to display heavily muscled shoulders and long, sinewy legs. He leaned back in his seat and propped one sandaled foot on the side of her mother's chair. Totally bewildered by a sharp stab that could only be jealousy, Alena turned away. She could not bear the sight of his thigh resting so close to the queen's own leg.

So, she thought, he would try the daughter first, and if she won't whore for him, he'll take the mother. Abruptly she stood.

"I have eaten my fill, Lady Mother. I find the hall too close, and would take some air."

The queen waved a negligent hand, dismissing her to turn back to the man at her side. Alena gritted her teeth and forced a tight smile.

Young Lord Berk clambered awkwardly to his feet, almost knocking the man next to him off the bench in his haste. He ignored his irate neighbor's angry curse and trailed after Alena.

Marcus watched the two of them leave and tried to tell himself to ignore them. The lady could work her plans and schemes as she would. Tomorrow she would be settled. Despite all his stern admonishments, however, he could not take his eyes from her until the wooden doors closed behind the mammoth figure of her suitor.

"Again?"

He turned back to the queen with a rueful grin.

"Once more, I apologize. I've learned the hard way that it's best not to leave your lady daughter to her own devices too long. I usually end up with either a knife at my gut or under full-scale attack. If you will excuse me, I'll see to this last night of my guardianship."

"Go, go..." Cartimandua waved him away petulantly. "I dislike sharing a man's attention with any other woman, even— particularly—my own daughter. I begin to be as anxious as you to end this guardianship of yours, Captain."

Marcus laughed, bowing over the queen's hand. He nodded briefly to the besotted king and made his way out of the crowded hall. As he had suspected he would, he found Alena in the courtyard surrounding the hall, almost smothered in the arms of the youthful Lord Berk. He watched from the shadows, thinking that he was rapidly having a surfeit of the lady's suitors.

Alena, eyes wide open and mind working furiously, suffered Lord Berk's clumsy kisses. Arms the size of young trees closed around her and pressed dangerously against her ribs. 'Tis not so bad, she thought as he mashed his eager lips down on hers. Compared to her husband's and Lord Eadgar's punishing kisses, the boy at least showed a respectful, if overwhelming, passion. 'Tis not so good, either, her rebellious mind responded. Not compared to the prefect's warm, hungry lips molding her own and coaxing responses she cared not to remember.

Marcus straightened abruptly when the boy's beefy hand moved down Alena's back and cupped her buttocks, lifting her half a foot off the ground. She squealed indignantly and pushed herself away from him.

"'Tis late, Lady. I would take you back to the camp now so that you might rest for the ceremonies tomorrow."

Both woman and boy whirled as Marcus strode out of the shadows. Alena prayed fervently that the overcast night would hide the red staining her cheeks. She was embarrassed to have been seen kissing this stripling, this child in a man's body. And doubly embarrassed by the way his massive rod stood straight out, tenting the fabric of his robe. She saw the captain's eyes gleam wickedly as they moved from her burning face to the boy's evident desire.

"If you laugh, I swear I will kill you," she said furiously as Marcus bade the bewildered lord good-night and walked her away.

"You've done enough violence for one day, Lady. Two men are disabled with aching loins. You don't need to spill my blood, also." His voice was even, but Alena could hear the amusement in it. Embarrassment and chagrin fired her ready temper.

"Damn you, Valerius, you're not one who should speak of aching loins. From the way you all but hung over my *mother*, it would appear you have invitation to ease yours there."

"Be quiet, you little fool," Marcus warned her, all amusement gone. "The woman is your lady queen, and this is her ground. She will not tolerate much more from you. Come, I'll take you back to camp."

Alena rode silently beside the equally quiet soldier, their escort cantering behind them. Her head ached miserably, and she wanted nothing more than for this awful day to be over.

When they pulled up in front of her quarters, Marcus slid off his horse and came around to her. For a moment he studied the drooping woman. He couldn't see her face in the dark, drizzly night, but he could feel her almost tangible despair.

"Come," he ordered softly. He caught her as she slid from her horse. This is the last time, he thought, his arms filling with her warm, tantalizing length. By tomorrow this damnable guardianship will be ended. He wrapped his arms around her.

Alena looked up at him, weariness and a dull, unfamiliar resignation in her eyes. "Do not, please. I cannot stand much more this day. 'Tis over. You have done your duty. Now leave me be."

Marcus frowned down at her. He hesitated, wanting to give comfort, but unsure what he could or should say at this point. This dispirited, tired creature in his arms was so unlike the Alena he knew that it worried him.

"Go to bed now." The soldier pushed her gently toward the door. "You're exhausted. I would be, also, had I unmanned as many warriors as you have this day. What happens tomorrow will happen."

As he hoped, his words put an angry sparkle back into her eyes. "You may be content to wait upon the will of the gods, Roman. I believe they expect us to take more of a hand in our fate."

"We've had this argument before. Your fate is sealed, Alena. Go to bed."

Marcus stood silently as she turned away and strode into the house. Thoughtfully he eyed the guard standing beside the portal. He turned away with a brusque order to put an extra guard at the back of the house this night. Thanking the gods that his damnable duty as keeper would be over the next day, he rode to his own quarters.

Alena dismissed the sleepy Ethelyn and disrobed herself. In her linen shift, with only a light loincloth and breastband under it, she lay down on the sleeping platform to consider her options. She'd thought earlier of escape, had contemplated riding off during the hunt, but she knew the prefect would track her down before she could travel far. Besides, escape would lead her only to Beorht. She would have gone with him the day he came for her, in the heat of battle, although the secret recesses of her mind knew she had been fleeing from the Roman that day, rather than running to Beorht. Now it was too late for either. Tomorrow she would have to take one of the lords her mother had chosen.

She sighed and turned over to bury her face in the soft silver-fox fur. Alena knew which lord would be her husband. She would be bound to that lump of a boy. She'd made sure, in those few moments in the dark courtyard, that he would best whatever offer Eadgar made—if he made any, after that scene in the woods. That much of her fate, at least, she had shaped to her desire. Berk was not so bad, she told herself. He was strong and clean and whole. Definitely whole. He would be manageable, at least. She should be grateful, she thought dispiritedly. At least she would be wedded, not living as a whore, as a certain soldier suggested. The insidious, rebellious thought crept into her mind that becoming leman to a man who brought her such blazing pleasure might not be such a bad fate after all. Alena groaned and pulled the furs over her head.

Chapter Fifteen

Marcus Valerius, Prefect of the Seventh Legion, donned full dress regalia for his meeting with Governor Trebellius Maximus. He pulled on a short white tunic, banded in gold at the hem and sleeves, then stood still while his orderly fastened on his bronze breastplate, with its shining insignia of rank. The boy knelt to clasp silver greaves to each leg, then slipped his captain's ceremonial silver dagger and sword holder onto his wide leather belt. Marcus tightened the belt around his lean waist. With a careful hand he draped a long red woolen mantle across his shoulders. His outfitting done, he tucked his heavily embossed helmet, with its red crest, under his arm. With a smile to his young orderly, he stepped out of the tribune's house to survey his escort.

He could see Sergeant Praxas's fine hand in the gleaming, polished troop standing at rigid attention. The sergeant himself headed the column of foot soldiers. In front of them was a cavalry troop, with the decurion in charge mounted and waiting. The red woolen banner with the legion's symbol, a raging bull embroidered in gold and bronze threads, whipped in the breeze. The legate's own standard, a golden eagle with a silver wreath around its wings to show the special honors the Seventh had won, remained in Corstopitum with the main body of the legion. Still, even without the golden eagle, Marcus took pride in his small detachment. They well represented Rome's might.

He and his troops lined up in front of Cartimandua's palace for the governor's arrival. Marcus stood to one side as the queen welcomed the lean, ascetic man who ruled Britannia in

Rome's name. Trebellius Maximus returned her gracious greeting and that of Venutius, then turned to his senior commander in the north.

"Hail, Valerius. Well met. I see you survived your guardianship. My administrator tells me the lady was less than enthusiastic about being put in your care."

Marcus could well imagine the account the governor must have had of Alena carried kicking and screaming from her uncle's house. Aware of the queen's avid interest, he gave a noncommittal nod. "She was not happy about it, Excellency, but 'tis done."

"Almost. Come, let us settle this matter of the lady's disposition, so that the sacrifices can be made and the marriage concluded. Then I would have time with you, Valerius, to discuss your excursions in the north."

Cartimandua led the way into her vast hall. She waved away all of her people but the lords involved, waiting until the men settled themselves comfortably and slaves brought wine and cheeses before beginning.

"I have two offers I'm considering for my daughter, Excellency. Both men are renowned warriors and can hold the northern lands for me—for Brigantium." Cartimandua corrected herself when her consort stirred angrily in his chair. "Lord Eadgar has served us faithfully for many years. He raised no sword against Rome in the rebellion. He has a troop of fifty men and ten horses he would take north with him. I've told him I will dower my daughter with two chests, one of gold and one of arms. Since the woman brings her former husband's lands, it is sufficient."

Marcus felt a slow disgust infuse his veins. Granted, dowries were serious matters, but the callousness with which the queen bartered away her flesh and blood repelled him. Not once did Cartimandua show any concern for or interest in how these men would honor her daughter. His jaw tightened as she continued.

"The other who would have her is Lord Berk, youngest son of Aellyn, king of the Atribates. He brings only twenty men, but promises rich trading with the tribes to the south. I've long sought to expand the markets for our goods. With the roads

Rome has brought to our land, trade with the south is now possible.''

"I—I will bring more warriors, Lady Queen."

Cartimandua looked up sharply as Lord Berk spoke up.

"I promised the Lady Alena last night I would raise the number to two score men, each with their own horse. My father will honor this," he stammered.

The queen sat back in her chair. Her eyes narrowed as she considered this offer.

Lord Eadgar shot the youth an angry glance, then turned to the queen. "I can raise no more men, but you may keep the chest of arms you offer as dower. My warriors are adequately provided."

Cartimandua's green eyes gleamed. "I see you are both taken with this marriage. It must be the woman who has sparked these new offers. So she has stirred your lust. It seems she is more my daughter than I'd realized. Her blood runs hot, I'll warrant. Such a prize is worth more than I first considered."

Marcus reached into the folds of his mantle and pulled out a small leather bag. With a curt gesture, he tossed it on the table.

"Cease your haggling. I will take the lady to wife. I want no dower, and give you these gold marks to seal the bargain."

Five faces turned to him in blank astonishment. For long moments, no one spoke. Then all recovered at the same time and broke out in an excited, angry babble of voices. After a moment, the governor silenced them by the simple expedient of crashing his open palm against the wooden table. He rose and signaled to the soldier. "Come with me, Valerius. I would discuss this with you privately."

The two men moved to the far end of the hall.

"What is this, Prefect? You are a hero of Rome. Nero himself chose you for this post, for the honor commanding the new Seventh Legion. You can do much better than a native woman, however valued she may be in this land. You should wive a Roman woman who can help further your career and fortunes."

"I've had a well-bred Roman wife, Excellency. She left my bed cold and me bored. This woman heats my loins, and I would have her."

"Then take her, by all the shades! But you need not do so in marriage."

"I've already done so, but the taking has only whetted my appetite. I am not proud of abusing my charge of her. I will accept whatever penalty you deem appropriate for so using one you left in my care."

The governor waved aside this interesting piece of news with an impatient hand. "That matter can be resolved once this question of marriage is settled. If you desire the woman so much, why not just set her up as concubine? We can delay any marriage as long as she is under your protection."

"You underestimate the lady in question," Marcus returned blandly. "She informed me she would not be my mistress."

Maximus gasped. "You asked her?"

"Aye." He grinned, then took pity on the man's obvious amazement. "You've not seen her, Excellency. She is wild and spirited and has ridden my lust mercilessly since the first time I saw her. She's wedged under my skin like a burr. The thought of her going to any other disturbs me greatly. Give her to me, and I will ensure her son holds the northern reaches for Rome," he finished in a low, determined tone.

Trebellius Maximus eyed the man before him. Having no military experience himself, he stood in awe of this man's reputation and achievements. His one previous visit with Marcus, newly arrived in Londinium to present his credentials, had greatly reassured him about the troublesome northern territories. Maximus had difficulty enough controlling the haughty, independent commanders of the other legions. This one, with his calm manner and steady, even demeanor, he trusted instinctively.

The governor stroked his chin, deep in thought. Much as it went against the grain to allow someone he liked and trusted to waste himself on a native woman, he began to see advantages to the match. Marcus Valerius would be in his debt for this, literally and figuratively.

In a quick mental exercise, the governor calculated just how much the soldier had won in honors and how much bride tax he could pay. Even more important, however, with this woman as wife, Valerius would have a personal stake in increasing Rome's territories to the north. More than anything, Maximus wished to win some glory from this dismal tour. He needed dramatic gains and a triumphal return at the end of his tour to win election as first consul of the Senate. With this man leading his campaign north, such honors would surely come. Still, it was risky. What if this woman turned the prefect's loyalty? Characteristically, Maximus vacillated.

Marcus watched the governor's thoughts chase themselves across his face with sardonic understanding. Maximus represented the worst of Rome's seniority system. Wellborn, but with little talent, and afraid to make the smallest decision. The soldier would not allow such a weakling to decide his fate.

"I will have her, Governor." He kept his voice even, but made sure Maximus heard the steel underlying his words.

"All right, Prefect. I only hope you may not come to regret this."

"I'll probably regret it thrice daily." Marcus laughed, at ease now that his plans were coming to fruition. "Most likely I'll have to lay in a cord of thick birch rods before I bring the lady to heel, but doubt not, she'll soon learn who her master is."

The governor smiled at his wry statement. "I suspect you might well wear out your arm and a whole forest of switches before the Lady Alena bows to any lord, from all I've heard." He took the captain's arm and led him back to the waiting group.

Cartimandua watched their return with narrowed eyes. It was obvious that the governor had agreed to the match. Her mind worked furiously. Many Romans took local wives, of course, but none of any rank. She considered what this could mean for her tribe and for her personally. As she ran every angle through her fertile mind, she could find only positive benefits from such a close alignment with Rome's might. She sat back as the two men returned to her table, her mind made up.

"I agree to marriage between the Prefect Valerius and the Lady Alena," Maximus announced.

"But I do not!" King Venutius's chair clattered to the floor as he stood angrily. "This is my daughter and my kingdom. It is not for Rome to dispose of either without our concurrence."

"But we do concur, Venutius." Cartimandua also stood and faced her husband squarely. "'Tis much to our advantage to have Rome hold our northern borders."

"To your advantage, Lady Wife." Venutius sneered. "You would sell your daughter, just as you have sold your soul, to please our conquerors."

"These 'conquerors' spared your life and your throne, you ass," Cartimandua hissed at him. "You tried once to flex your muscles. You raised your sword against them, and me, only to be brought back like a whipped dog. It took all my persuasion and more gold than you're worth to buy you out of that one. Although why I bothered is something only the gods understand."

Totally oblivious of the others, husband and wife stood toe to toe. Their rage glared hot and passionate, and arguments that had long divided their house spewed from their angry lips.

Marcus eyed the parents of his bride with growing disfavor. Had they no more sense than to air their grievances before the governor? He shook his head over the passionate Celtic nature that cared little for subterfuge or discretion and sent Maximus a stern look. If the governor did not soon end this appalling display, he would do so himself.

"Enough!" Maximus stepped between the angry couple. "This match is to both Brigatium's and Rome's advantage. 'Tis done. Valerius will take the lady to wife."

"And her lands, Prefect? Will you also take her lands?" Cartimandua turned to the one she knew wielded the real power in this drama. She wanted the agreement between them spelled out clearly.

"No, they belong to her son. I will hold them for Megarric until he is of age."

"She must be more of a woman than even I credited her with," Cartimandua muttered, spite tinging her voice.

Marcus tightened his jaw. "Have the sacrifices made. I will give the priests a double offering to make sure the signs are propitious. I want the ceremony and the feast done this night."

With that, he and the governor left. Cartimandua dismissed the two would-be suitors and turned to the unpleasant task of dealing with her surly spouse. She would convince the dolt to show some semblance of acceptance of this match or skewer him with his own sword.

The two Romans repaired to another, smaller room. Maximus offered a tentative toast and called on the gods to bless this union. Marcus accepted his hesitant congratulations with a wry smile, then suggested they discuss more pressing military matters. The governor listened attentively to the captain's assessment of the Selgovae and Caledonians, and agreed with his estimate of the men and material necessary to push north the following spring. The sun rode low in the afternoon sky by the time the prefect rode to collect his bride. He dismissed his troop when they arrived back at the camp, took a deep breath, and entered the small stone house where Alena was held.

Alena had spent the day in growing impatience, waiting for her summons. She had ridden into town early in the morning, under escort, to consult with the priest. Out of earshot of the soldiers, the drooping, rheumy-eyed elder had confirmed that the organs of a rare white calf, purchased with her gold armband, held only hopeful signs. They foretold that she would live long in the north and wield a strong woman's power.

"What kind of woman's power?" Alena asked, nettled. Her precious ornament should have purchased more than this sparse prophecy. "The power of a queen mother? Of a warrior queen? Or of a wife over her husband?" It shouldn't be too difficult to exercise the latter, with Lord Berk as her mate.

"Nay, I cannot tell you more, only that the gods bless your union."

For a moment, Alena wondered suspiciously if her mother had bribed the old man to ensure her docility in this match. Priests were known to find all kinds of favorable signs if the offerings were right. She sighed, eyeing the doddering old man. She'd get no more out of him. With the escort dogging her heels, she wandered through the narrow, twisting streets of Isurium for a while, trying to work off her nervousness. When she dared delay no longer, she rode back to the orderly Roman camp perched on its hill outside the town.

Ethelyn met her upon her return to her rooms, her eyes glowing with excitement and her arms full of a loosely wrapped bundle.

"Look, Lady. I have never seen fabric such as this. It glows green, then blue, as the light strikes it. It came just a few moments ago."

"My lady mother would have me do her honor at this marriage, it seems." Alena fingered the soft, iridescent linen. She remembered well the first time her mother had given her in marriage. The queen had sent her off with a ragged doll and a stern admonition to obey her lord. It would appear the governor's presence called for more costly display.

"Come, Lady, they will call for you soon. Let me fix your hair."

In her eagerness to show her lady at her finest, Ethelyn made up in enthusiasm what Alena lacked. She washed and brushed Alena's hair until it crackled and shone like burnished gold, then wound it into a thick coronet of braids. Among the braids she wove dark green vines and leaves as a symbol of the ancient life force of the mother earth. Stripping her mistress naked, she rubbed scented oils on arms, legs and breasts before binding her lightly with linen at her loins and chest. Finally she draped the shimmering green-and-blue cloth in rich folds over one shoulder and across her breasts.

Alena peered into a beaten metal mirror to fasten the robe at her shoulder with an enameled brooch. She fingered the delicate pin lovingly. It had been a bride gift from Nelwyn many years before, the only one the child had ever received. The pin swirled and curled in intricate spirals and ended in a trumpet shape. Alena loved it less for its beauty than for the fact that it came from Nelwyn, her sister-by-marriage, her foster mother, her teacher and only friend. The pin firmly in place, she picked up the heavy gold torque, symbol of her rank, and fastened it around her throat. The thick necklace always choked her with its weight. Today, its tight, smothering fit matched her mood.

Alena surveyed herself in the mirror once more, then gave her head a determined shake. She was as ready as she would ever be. She slipped on a pair of low sandals, gave Ethelyn grateful thanks for her care and went to take a noon meal of fruit, cheese and wine in the small antechamber that served as dining and guest room. The light delicious Tuscan wine, served in a chilled clay amphora, soothed her nerves. She filled her drinking bowl once more.

By the time she heard the clatter of horses' hooves drawing to a halt on the street outside her small house, she'd downed most of the contents of the amphora and felt decidedly relaxed. With a langurous movement, she turned her head to survey the man who strode into the *solar*.

"Is this the same woman I have seen in shapeless gray sacks and covered in mud from toe to ear?"

Somewhat unsteadily, Alena stood as Marcus strolled into the room. A flush of pleasure filled her at his sweeping, admiring look, but was lost to a wave of dizziness. She clutched the table beside her for support. "What are you doing here? I thought you were to meet with the governor."

"I was. I have."

"Well, you can get yourself gone again, Roman. Your guardianship is ended. I need be bothered with you no more."

His dark eyes narrowed as he surveyed her swaying form. Alena lifted her chin and waved her arm, intending to dismiss him regally. The effect was spoiled, however, when her unsteady arm knocked the heavy clay container from the table beside her. It shattered on the stone floor. Alena hopped back, squeaking in dismay as the last of the wine spattered her robe. She bent down to rub the spots, only to bang her forehead against the edge of the table. With a curse, Lady Alena sat down hard, her rump landing on the stone floor with a distinct thud.

Marcus watched her rub futilely at the stained robe, and a smile tugged at the corner of his mouth. The little wretch was as drunk as a trooper. The shattered jug held only a few dregs of wine. If she'd downed the whole thing, he doubted he would bed a conscious bride this night.

"Come, Lady. I see you have celebrated your wedding somewhat prematurely. But you must still make an appearance and exchange vows with your groom." He knelt to lift her from the floor.

"Oh, yes, my groom. Do you wonder why I fortify myself with wine? Would you not, if you had to bed an oversize child this night?"

Marcus felt his bride clutch his arm and sway, as if the floor tilted strangely under her.

"Alena, there is something . . ."

"Aye, something disgusting about this, is there not? Although I suppose most women would not whine so." She pushed herself away and peered uncertainly up at Marcus.

"The boy has proven himself in battle, I'm told, and he's certainly well enough armed to perform nobly in the marriage bed."

"Alena!"

"What? You saw him, standing at attention, about to poke a hole in my mother's outer wall. Do you not think he will perform his marital duties well this night?"

Marcus reached out and took the swaying woman in hard hands. "Listen to me. The boy can perform all he wants, this night or any other night, but he will not do so on your body."

Every vestige of color washed out of Alena's face, and she clutched at the prefect's red mantle. "By the gods, Marcus, she did not give me to Eadgar! Not that vile, pain-loving worm!"

"Nay, nay, calm yourself, woman. You will not wed Eadgar the worm."

Alena blinked up at him. It was obvious she heard, but did not understand, his words. She opened and shut her mouth several times, but no sound emerged.

"Alena, listen to me." Marcus shook her gently, trying to get her to focus. "I have taken you to wife. The governor agreed. All the sacrifices have been made and the gods, yours and mine, appeased. We have only to exchange vows in front of six witnesses, as Roman law requires, and 'tis done. The feast this night will celebrate our union, yours and mine."

He looked down at her expectantly. Wide, confused green eyes stared back at him.

"Did you understand me? I said we are to wed."

Alena's thick, dark brows drew together uncertainly. After a long, still moment, she groaned. "I need a chamber vessel."

"What?"

"I need a chamber vessel. I'm going to be sick."

Blank astonishment filled his soldier's mind. Then he threw back his head and gave a shout of laughter. Of all the reactions he'd imagined she would have to his news, this was certainly not one of them. He'd expected raging anger, or denial, or mayhap even tears, although he'd not known Alena to indulge in such a weakness. But he hadn't expected his bride to retch in his arms.

Affronted by his laughter, Alena pulled herself free and stumbled from the room. She barely made it across the small courtyard to the bedchamber before she bent, sides heaving, over a clay bowl. Marcus followed her, laughter still rumbling in his chest.

"Get you gone. I will tend to your mistress."

He pushed the protesting Ethelyn out of the room and closed the door in her face. Biting his lip to hold back his laughter, he held Alena until her retching stopped, then laid her gently on the bed. He found a pitcher of fresh water on a wooden chest and brought her a brimming cupful to rinse her mouth. When she finished, he filled the cup again, dipped a corner of her ruined robe in it and began to wipe her face. Alena groaned and tried to push his hands away.

"Let me clean you." He held her head firmly and continued the soft, gentle stroking.

"Go away! Please!"

Alena kept her eyes squeezed shut. She'd never been so mortified in her life. That this Roman should see her sick and puling was abominable. This man, of all men, who laughed at her and taunted her and— She opened her eyes and clutched frantically at his hands.

"What did you say before, about the governor agreeing and sacrifices made?"

Marcus sat back on his haunches beside the bed and surveyed his bride. Vine leaves hung from her disordered hair, her face was a pasty white, and her robe was not fit to use as a saddle blanket. And he wanted her with a fierceness that almost overwhelmed him.

"I would have you, Alena. On your terms, since you would not accept mine. We will wed this afternoon."

"Wed?" she whispered. "Do you jest?"

When he shook his head, she lifted a trembling hand to her mouth. The room still whirled around her, and her thoughts spun just as wildly. Her words, when she could frame coherent thought, came out through numbed lips. "We cannot wed. You are of Rome, of my people's conquerors. You worship different gods, you live in strange houses, you . . . you write in books." Her voice rose to a panic-filled screech.

"Our ways are different, but not so different you cannot learn them."

"And what if I do not wish to learn them? What if I do not want any part of you!" Alena shouted. Her own voice struck against her skull like a sword beating on a helmet. Involuntarily she moaned and pressed her fingers to her aching temple.

"Then I must make you want me."

Marcus reached for his trembling bride. Calmly he unclasped the pin holding her robe at her shoulder. She gasped in surprise and tried to catch the loose fabric as it fell to her waist. He leaned down and took firm hold of the material. Ignoring Alena's vociferous protests and flailing arms, he unwound the soiled linen. Unable to stop him, Alena rolled helplessly across the bed as the robe was pulled out from under her.

Marcus looked down at the sprawling, panting woman and felt every drop of his blood begin to heat. Naked except for her white breastband and loincloth and that monstrous, barbaric torque around her neck, she fulfilled his every erotic dream. He swallowed thickly. Moving with jerky strides across the room, he pulled her soft, rose-colored robe from a wooden peg. Shaking out its voluminous folds, he leaned over and swaddled the surprised woman completely.

"What are you doing?" she gasped, struggling to free her arms from the tight bonds of wool.

"Ridding your head of wine fumes. I refuse to take a drunken bride."

He lifted her easily and strode toward the door. Holding the swaddled bundle against his chest, he reached down to open the heavy wooden panel. Ethelyn fell against him in a flutter of nervous hands and swirling robes.

"What have you done to my mistress? Lady Alena, are you all right? Where are you going?"

Both Marcus and Alena ignored the little maid, who followed them across the courtyard and out the front portal. Marcus because his hands were full with his struggling, cursing bride, Alena because her head whirled dizzily and her stomach heaved from the sudden movement. She barely heard Ethelyn's twittering, frantic cries. The maid screwed up every ounce of courage she possessed and tugged ferociously but ineffectually on the captain's swirling red cloak to stop him.

"Calm yourself!" Marcus bellowed at her. Both women jumped, Alena as much as her binding would permit, Ethelyn clear back against the stone wall. The prefect shook his head at her terrified face and moderated his tone.

"I take your lady to her marriage ceremony. Get you inside and clean her chambers. We will return late."

Marcus took his reins from the gaping guard, swung into the saddle with Alena balanced under one arm and galloped out of the small camp.

Chapter Sixteen

Held sideways against the Roman's unyielding breastplate, Alena struggled to rid herself of the effects of the wine. Fresh air rushed against her face and helped clear some of her dizziness, although the jarring gallop did little for her rebellious stomach. She took long, gulping breaths and let her body settle into the horse's steady gait. The roiling in her stomach gradually subsided, but the tumult in her mind did not. She kept turning the prefect's words over and over in her jumbled thoughts. Marriage, to the Roman, agreed to by the governor! The camp was far behind them before she even realized they rode away from, not toward, Isurium. She bit her lip in confusion when Marcus pulled his horse off the main road and slowed to take a leafy path into the forest.

Marcus gave a small, satisfied grunt when he reined in at the edge of the clearing where the hunters had gathered the previous day. Yesterday, the glen had been filled with noisy beaters, busy skinners, stamping horses and laughing, bragging huntsmen. Today, no sound except the rush of a wide, bubbling stream disturbed the late-afternoon stillness. With Alena held firmly in his arms, he dismounted and strode over to a thick, grassy verge beside the silvery water. Bending one knee, he laid his bedraggled bundle on the soft grass and sat back on his heel to examine his bride. As he'd known it would, the ride and fresh air had cleared her head. Her eyes were free of their dizziness, and soft color brushed her cheek. He reached down and began to unwrap the rose wool.

"What are you doing!" After struggling to free herself from the tight swaddling throughout the ride, Alena now locked her fingers around the fabric and clung to it.

"I'm undressing you."

"You pig! You would take me here, in the grass, like some common slut?"

"Do not overrate your charms, Lady Wife-to-Be." His low voice teased her. "Could you see yourself now, you would understand why we are here."

With a swift, sure tug, he pulled the gown from her tight grasp and from her body. Clad only in her thin linen breast-band and loincloth, Alena scrambled to her knees in the thick grass. When his hands reached out to pull the thin covering from her breast, she tried to knock them away. Marcus made short work of the flimsy linen strips, despite Alena's determined struggles. Taking both of her wrists in one iron fist to stop the blows she rained on his head and shoulders, he stood, pulling her naked form up with him. Before Alena had any idea what he intended, she found herself flying through the air to land squarely in the middle of the deep, rushing stream.

Icy, crystal-clear water closed over her head, and she sank like a stone. Her rump bounced off the pebbly streambed. She managed to get her legs under her and pushed up, floundering and almost screaming in her rage.

"Whoreson! Bastard! Son of a diseased mule!"

Icy, crystal-clear water streamed over her as she fought to find her footing against the rushing current. Her foot slipped on a rock and she went down again, arms flailing.

Marcus stood on the bank, feet spread wide and arms crossed over his massive chest. He watched his bride surface once more. She pushed her straggling hair out of her eyes and let loose with a stream of curses that made his brows rise. The soldier in him admired her spectacular range of invective, while the man in him ran hot, appreciative eyes over the water glistening on her golden skin and her puckered nipples thrusting boldly out at him. He watched as she made her stumbling way back to the grassy bank. She stood at the edge of the steep bank, shivering in the frigid water, but too proud to scramble out on her hands and knees before him or to beg his help.

Marcus reached down. "Take my hand."

"Get you back. I will get myself out."

"Take my hand, woman. You're turning blue. It looks better than the pasty green you were before, but I have no more desire to wed a lump of ice than a drunkard."

Alena shot him a poisonous glare. Grudgingly she put her hand in his. With one easy motion, he pulled her, dripping and shivering, from the water.

"Here, take my mantle to dry yourself."

She wanted to fling the red wool back in his face, but its rough warmth in her icy hands convinced her otherwise. Shaking, she wrapped the voluminous folds of red around her. Gradually her teeth stopped chattering and the warmth enveloped her. She burrowed her face in the wool and inhaled the dusky male scent of its owner. Flinging up her wet head, she glared at him.

Marcus tried hard to swallow a grin at the figure she presented. Bits of vine still straggled from her dripping hair. The mantle covered her in great drooping folds from shoulder to knee. Her long, bare calves showed white below the red cloak. And she wore an angry, proud, defiant look that made the blood in his loins surge hot and thick. With a rueful sigh, he reached out, grabbed the folds of the mantle and pulled her against him.

Alena stiffened and pushed at him in outrage. "Do not dare to touch me!"

"I fear I must," he told her. "If nothing else, it will warm you."

"You rutting pig," she gasped, her words muffled against his chest. "Do not disguise your mauling with such feeble excuses!"

Marcus smiled down into the wet, tangled skeins just under his chin. His arms held her stiff, resisting body easily. He began to run his hands up and down her back, her buttocks, her sides. The rough wool under his hands shaped itself to her body and fired his own.

"Nay, Alena, do not fight me. Not this day. This day I claim you as mine."

"I must always fight you, Roman." Alena ground out the words through gritted teeth. "You may claim my body, but not my spirit."

The dark eyes lightened as a smile tugged at the corners of his mouth. "Then I must settle for what I can get."

His hands parted the red wool. Instinctively, in a gesture as old as womanhood, Alena wound her arms across her chest to cover her breasts from his avid gaze. Anger and embarrassment washed over her face, and her eyes slid to the dagger in its silver-embossed scabbard on his leather belt.

Marcus laughed. "Nay, woman. The only dagger between us this time is the one I will wield." With a quick motion, he laid her down on the thick grass, on top of the rough wool cloak. His hands on her shoulders held her still.

"We will bind our lives together this night, Alena. I would that we should bind our bodies, here, in the clean, clear privacy of this glen, instead of in front of drunken, leering witnesses."

Vivid memories of her first wedding flashed through Alena's mind. Rough hands had pinched and prodded her tender virgin flesh when they stripped her for bedding, and her husband's coarse jests had echoed those of the avid guests. Suddenly the quiet glen seemed infinitely preferable as a bridal bower. She bit her lip and stared up at the determined eyes above her. Her mind still rebelled, but her heart knew this soldier would not be denied.

"All right," she muttered angrily. "If you must be ruled by your rod, be done with it."

Marcus's dark eyes glinted with amusement at her less-than-loverlike invitation to join his body to hers. He would have to see what he could do to turn the anger in her to some other, equally heated emotion. Kneeling, he unbuckled his thick leather belt and tossed it to the grass, just beyond her reach. He struggled with the leather straps that held the two pieces of his ceremonial breastplate together at each side and shoulder. When it finally clattered to the ground, he shed the short white tunic underneath, then knelt to remove his greaves and sandals.

Lying stiffly on the red wool, Alena watched as the man stripped himself. No stranger to nudity, she ran her eyes over the thick columns of the muscled legs spread before her, past his linen-covered loins, to his trim waist and solid rib cage, crisscrossed with old scars. This was a man among men, she acknowledged reluctantly. His massive shoulders, furred with dark, curling hair, blocked the filtered sunlight completely. When he stood and loosened his loincloth, any thought of lying passively under him while he grunted his way to completion fled. Wildly she calculated her chances of escape. If she could make it to his horse before him . . .

"Do not even think it."

Marcus dropped to his knees beside her, cutting off her view of the grazing stallion. His rod jutted up stiffly between them. Alena gasped and tried to scramble back. Stifling an oath, Marcus stilled her. Marshaling every ounce of iron discipline at his disposal, he schooled himself to patience. His blood pounded in his ears and filled his aching shaft. This woman would be his wife, and he would have her. But this time he would have her open and willing beneath him. One brown hand reached out to tug at the tumbled remains of her braided coronet. He unwound her hair and loosened the fat braid, raking his fingers through her thick hair until it spread in an unruly mass across her shoulders and down her back. Plucking the last of the vines out of her tumbled curls, he rubbed the green leaf between his fingers, over and over.

Alena stared as if mesmerized at the dark green leaf slowly shredding in his hand. Although one part of her mind still weighed and discarded increasingly improbable escape plans, she knew their coupling was inevitable. A tiny shiver of anticipation danced up her spine. When the last bit of green fell from his fingers, she looked up. His hot, hungry expression made her swallow. Her shivers spread, becoming a tingling that tightened her nipples and caused strange swirlings deep in her belly. Alena wanted desperately to scoot backward, away from this looming male, but she forced herself to remain still and stiff. Her pride would not let her cringe away from him, not even when he reached out and brushed one knuckle against the crests of her swelling breast.

Unhurried, Marcus stretched himself out beside her. He propped his head up on one hand and let his eyes roam over the woman lying stiffly beside him. Amusement warred with the heat in his dark gaze at her rigid posture, at the eyes staring straight up at the branches of the tree above them. She would not remain so detached for long, he vowed. Lightly, teasingly, he brushed his palm across the tight bud of her breasts. Her muscles twitched involuntarily, but still she would not look at him. He took one nipple between his thumb and forefinger. Pulling gently, he rolled and twisted it into a red, turgid peak. With a lazy movement, he rolled half on top of her and took the swollen nipple between his teeth.

Alena gasped and squeezed her eyes shut. Streaks of fire spread across her aching breast. His tongue flicked back and forth against the incredibly sensitive bud, and it took all her willpower to remain stiff and still under him. Dimly she heard him chuckle, and then his marauding mouth moved to her other breast. He kneaded the soft, swelling flesh as his wet tongue laved her. Leaving a hot, moist trail across her chest and up her neck, he nuzzled the tender flesh just beneath her ear. Alena began a desperate incantation in her mind to the earth mother, praying for strength, for the power to resist, for—

The prayer ended abruptly when he bit playfully on her lobe. The tiny shaft of pain turned to fiery waves of a sweeter sensation as his tongue pushed into her ear. She gave up all attempts to remain still. Turning in his arms, she pushed against the broad planes of his chest. Her head butted painfully against his chin.

"That's better. I mislike making love to a corpse."

Alena could feel the laughter rumbling deep in his chest under her fingertips. Sweet mother, how could the pig laugh at her at such a time? She curled her hands into his thick chest hair, unsure whether to claw him or tear out his hairs, one by one. Before she could do either, she was flat on her back once more with his full weight on her and his mouth swooping down to stop her sputtering protests.

The last vestiges of playfulness left Marcus. His tongue pushed past her teeth to plunder the dark, honeyed recesses of her mouth. One hand buried itself in her hair to hold her head steady for his devouring kiss, while the other pushed and pulled and shaped her breast. He forced his knee between her legs, prying her resisting thighs apart. Impatiently he slid his hand down to tangle in the thicket of curls between her legs. A hard, flat palm on her mons pinned Alena to the ground while his fingers parted the folds of her womanhood and found the sensitive nub at their center.

Unable to move under his monstrous weight, hardly able to breathe, Alena felt him on every part of her body. His tongue teased hers unmercifully, thrusting in and out of her mouth in a heavy, panting imitation of the mating ritual. His chest crushed her breasts and irritated her nipples beyond bearing as rough hair rubbed against her. The hot, pulsing length of his rod thrust into her belly, wetting her skin with its oozing secretion. And his hands, Great Mother Epona, his hands! The one tormenting her womanhood lubricated itself with her wetness, then thrust two thick, demanding fingers into her core. Alena had only a brief moment to wonder at the lack of pain before hot waves of pleasure began to heat her skin and burn across her mind. She took great gulping gasps of air when his mouth left hers, only to let it all out in a small scream when his lips closed over her breast once more.

He was less than gentle now. His teeth worried her nipple with fierce little nips that made her writhe helplessly beneath him. Impaled on his thrusting fingers, legs spread wide, her aching breast radiating fire down to her belly, Alena felt dark, pulsing heat gather in her loins, heat such as she had felt only once before. She was so lost in the swamping sensations, she didn't realize Marcus had raised himself off her until cool air touched the sweat on her fevered body. She opened her eyes to see him staring down, fierce male dominance darkening his skin.

"Keep your eyes open. I want you to see who it is that takes you now. Your lord, your husband."

His hand closed over her mound to still the flicker of defiance that arced through her. With a quick twist of his body, he brought his rod down and rubbed it against her cleft. His fingers held her open, vulnerable, while the dripping tip teased and rubbed and brought her own wetness gushing forth. Satisfied that she was ready, he slid into her sheath. A quick thrust seated him to the hilt. Sweat beaded his brow as he raised himself on trembling forearms.

Alena swallowed convulsively when he began to move inside her depths. Her hands came up of their own accord to wrap around the straining muscles of his arms and steady her against his slow, sure thrusts. His hips ground into hers, pressing her deep into the thick grass. To ease the pressure, she lifted her legs and wrapped them around his thighs. Her eyes widened when he groaned and used her raised hips to delve even more deeply into her.

Fiercely, his eyes locked to hers, Marcus rode her. In and out, harder and harder, until he felt his own pleasure begin to rise uncontrollably. Propping his weight on one arm, he slid his hand down between their slick bodies to rub her center once more. His knowing fingers made her gasp and scream and arch her back as her pleasure exploded in hot, pulsing waves.

Grunting with the primitive satisfaction of knowing he had satisfied his mate, Marcus gave himself up to his own pleasure. The last shuddering contractions of her tight little sheath gripped him as he surged fully into her once more. Two, three lunges, then his seed spewed forth, hot and gushing and incredibly thick.

Finally, when his breath returned and his sight cleared, he rolled off her. Gathering her limp form into his arms, he settled her on top of his still-heated body. With a flicker of amusement, he saw that her eyes were wide open. The little cat had kept them open as he'd ordered, all through their wild coupling. For once he couldn't read the expression in those deep green pools. He reached up and twirled a strand of her tawny hair between his fingers thoughtfully.

"We may not worship the same gods or share the same customs, but we at least have one thing in common. We find pleasure in each other's bodies. 'Tis not a bad basis to begin a marriage."

Alena folded her arms stiffly on his chest, forcing some distance from their sweat-slicked bodies. "I am ashamed of what you made me feel," she said. "The pleasure comes and goes quickly, the shame stays with me. And that is not a good foundation for a marriage."

Her words nettled him. Why couldn't the stubborn wench just accept her fate and build on this shaky beginning? His brows drew together, but he took a deep breath before responding. "There's no shame in what passes between a man and his wife."

A dark shadow passed over her eyes, and she rolled off him to stare up into the leafy canopy above them.

"Much you know of it. There can be shame, and pain, and many other hurtful emotions."

"And honor, and pleasure, and comfort in each other's company," Marcus replied, leaning over to examine this unfamiliar Alena. He'd seen her icily proud, and flaming with rage. Laughing in the sunlight, and panting in the throes of passion. But this was the first he'd seen her shadowed with painful thoughts. A fierce anger surged in him at the thought of what her first husband must have done to cause such dark memories.

Alena turned to face him, her golden hair spread against the velvet-green carpet of grass. "And did you have such a marriage, Prefect? One filled with comfort and love?"

"Nay. My wife coveted my honors and war prizes, but had little use for me. She stayed in Rome while I spent most of my years abroad. She died birthing our child, screaming curses at me all the while. But my parents had such a match."

From the way her green eyes narrowed, he could see that Alena was intrigued. She relaxed and nodded, urging him to continue.

Marcus settled in beside her. A private person, he rarely spoke of himself or his past. But he realized he would have to share something of himself if he and his wild bride were to bridge the huge gulf that separated their worlds.

"My mother was an Egyptian slave, brought to Rome as a child by a wealthy merchant. She was part of his stable of concubines and bore her first child when she was barely twelve summers. It was sold at the babe market."

Stretched out in the grass, Marcus stared up at the shady branches, letting his words roll softly as they would. "The merchant died soon after she birthed me, her second child. His wife sold off all his pretty toys. The little Egyptian was bought by a legionnaire, just retired and returned to Rome. He was looking to set up house for himself and needed a housekeeper and bed partner. Luckily, he grew to love her."

He rolled onto his side, propping his head on one hand while the other traced lazy circles on her belly. Alena pushed his hand away, with a tart command to finish what he had begun.

"I'm trying to," he told her with a laugh, spreading his hand across her warm flesh.

"Nay, not that. Tell me more of your parents. How came they to love from such an inauspicious beginning?"

"Who knows what causes one to love another?" Marcus shrugged. "All I know is, he freed my mother, wed her, and gave me his name. He gave me much love, as well, and his profession."

He had no words to convey the wonder of the bond between his delicate mother and the rough, grizzled man who had cared for them both. Or the intense love that had grown between him and his adopted father over the years. The old soldier had fashioned the boy's first wooden toy sword, had taken him into the hills above Rome to run and build his muscles, had nurtured him on stories of campaigns in far-off lands. And when Marcus was just ten, the old legionnaire had used his life savings to purchase the boy a place in the military *gymnasium*. There he had trained and won a place in the most elite of Rome's legions. In his mind, Marcus could still see the pride and love that had gleamed in his father's eyes when he returned, many years later, carrying the vine staff that symbolized his rank as centurion. A very junior centurion, it was true, but an officer nonetheless. Only the hardiest and most skilled legionnaires made it to officer rank.

"I envy you your parents, soldier," Alena told him slowly. "Mine have had little use for me, other than as a pawn."

"Have you known no love in your life?" he asked her gently.

"Oh, aye. Nelwyn gave me all any child could want. She's a very learned priestess, and took me into the forests and glens often. She let me ride and roam at will—or rather gave up trying to stop me," Alena amended, a mischievous laugh in her eyes. "And I have Megarric."

Her simple words hung softly in the air. She could not begin to express what she felt for her child. Nor did she need to. Marcus had seen them together often enough.

Alena turned on her side and propped her head on one hand, totally unconscious of her nakedness. "How do I explain this marriage to my child, Prefect? How do I raise him to be king of the proud Lopocares, if I myself have succumbed to their conquerors? He, and all my people, will despise me." The words were torn from her heart.

Marcus heard the panic in them. Deliberately he kept his voice level and calm as he reached out one hand to stroke a knuckle down her cheek.

"They will not despise you, or treat you with anything less than honor. You must trust me to see that Megarric is trained well for his rule. I would not rob the boy of his heritage."

Alena saw the quiet strength in his eyes and knew he spoke the truth. She had seen how her son responded to this soldier. For the first time she began to wonder if perhaps they could make this strange union work.

Marcus watched her expressive face, absorbed in the way her eyes mirrored her every thought and the way the shadows played across her high cheekbones. The rustling shadows brought him to a gradual realization that the sun was setting behind the trees. Much as he would have liked to continue this rare moment of peace between them, they were already late. Very late. He stood and reached a hand down to her.

"Come, 'tis past time for us to show ourselves at our wedding. They've probably already begun the feast without us."

Alena ignored the hand he held out to her and scrambled to her feet. She grimaced when thick wetness oozed down between her legs, then blushed a fiery red when she saw the knowing grin on the Roman's face. She picked up her crumpled breastband to wipe herself clean.

"You could at least turn your back," she told him tartly.

"Nay, I regret I don't yet trust you enough to turn my back when weapons are handy."

His dancing eyes mocked her, and he delighted in the red that stained her shoulders and cheeks. Unconcerned with his own nakedness, he leaned lazily against a tree, arms crossed, and waited for her to proceed.

Alena threw down the soiled breastband and turned her back to don her rumpled clothing. With unabashed pleasure, Marcus ran his eyes over the clean, curving lines of her back, her rounded buttocks, her long, long legs. Incredibly, his manhood began to stir again. Shaking his head, he moved toward his own scattered garments. He'd better get her wedded before he killed himself, and her, with the bedding.

Chapter Seventeen

Alena's face burned when they drew up in the courtyard of her mother's palace. She'd done the best she could to tidy herself, but she knew she must make a most disreputable bride. The rose wool robe hung unevenly about her, tied at the waist by a leather thong taken from the prefect's saddle. She'd draped the material precariously over one shoulder, but with no pin to clasp it, she feared she would spend the evening holding herself together. Another leather thong caught thick bands of hair back from either side of her face, leaving most of the unruly mass to hang in wild disarray down her back. Her lips still throbbed from the Roman's rough kisses, and her every instinct told her to burrow into some deep hole and hide.

"You look beautiful."

She looked up quickly to see if Marcus taunted her with his soft words.

"Truthfully, Lady. There's not a man here who will not envy me for the wild creature I have captured. Or at least cornered," he amended quickly when she frowned. He bit back a grin, but saw that his words had their desired effect. Alena straightened her shoulders and lifted her chin in a way that reminded him forcefully of their first meeting outside the dusty arena. At that moment, he vowed silently to handle her so that she would not completely lose her air of haughty defiance. It irritated him as much as it challenged him, but he knew this woman would not fascinate him half so much were she meek and compliant. He would gentle her to his touch and curb some of her wild ways, but he would not break her spirit. Confident, sated, well satisfied with his prospective wife, he escorted her into her mother's hall.

Alena needed every ounce of her willpower to keep her head high and walk the long length of the hall. It was unbelievably crowded. All the great Brigante lords had been invited to the feast, and many had brought wives and kin. They stood shoulder to shoulder with Roman officers in bright crimson mantles. And every one of them, Alena was convinced, stared with avid, curious eyes at the rumpled bride and her unlikely groom.

As Marcus had predicted, the festivities had begun without them. An army of slaves scurried back and forth refilling tall pitchers of honeyed wine and frothing ale, while a bard entertained the appreciative guests. Alena caught a few words over the din of the crowd. He sang of the raven-goddess Morrigan, whose sexual appetites lured brave warriors into battle with each other and death. The bard's very explicit description of how one hapless warrior lost his life, and his organs, to the vengeful goddess made Alena slant a tight smile up at the tall soldier beside her. Marcus grinned back and leaned over to whisper something in her ear. Her smile widened and, to her own surprise, she laughed.

Queen Cartimandua broke off her conversation with Governor Maximus and looked up to see the errant couple grinning as they negotiated the crowded hall. Her eyes widened, then narrowed in furious anger when she took in her daughter's appearance. By Adarte, those were grass stains on the woman's robe! Envy of her own daughter rose, hot and bilious. She would have given much to romp in the grass with one such as this Roman. Her thoughts showed clearly on her heavy face and her sensual, drooping lids as she surveyed the couple in front of her.

The simple greeting Alena was about to offer died at the lascivious look on her mother's face. Instinctively she moved closer to Marcus. He stepped smoothly into the breach.

"We took longer than anticipated to...prepare ourselves for the ceremony, Lady Queen. Our apologies if we kept you waiting. If you will assemble the witnesses, we are ready now."

"From the look of your bride, you've prepared her most well, soldier." Spite dripped from every word. "Normally, the bedding follows the vows."

Marcus stiffened. Queen or not, he would not allow this old bawd to insult his woman. But before he could speak, Alena stepped forward.

"We make our own traditions, Mother." Her voice was low and dangerous, and her eyes were filled with green fire. "Remember that when you mate Celt to Roman. What results is something expected by neither."

The governor rose hurriedly from his couch to step between the two women. "Yes, well, let us conclude the ceremony. Come, sign the contracts and make your vows."

Alena looked blankly at the sheets of parchment brought forward by one of the scribes. Her heritage and her rich, beautiful language were too elusive to be captured by the scribblings of men. She knew not how to write, and scorned the written word. Once more, Marcus took control.

"With the blessing of our godhead, the emperor Nero, and the great god Jupiter and his mate, Juno, who rule the heavens, I set my seal to this contract of marriage. I, Marcus Valerius, prefect of Rome, take the Lady Alena to wife. In front of these witnesses, I vow to protect her person, honor her body, and fill her womb with children of my seed."

He bent and signed the parchment with a quick flourish. Half holding his breath, he turned to Alena.

Her eyes met his in a long, steady look. The noisy hall faded from her consciousness, and there was only this man before her. He stood tall and proud in his uniform of Rome. Involuntarily her gaze fastened on the bronze eagle emblazoned on his breastplate, the symbol of his rank. Of his authority. Of his dominance over her lands. The eagle burned into her mind, held her eyes.

Marcus didn't move. Calmly he watched the expressions chase each other across her face. He knew she had no choice and would—eventually—give her oath. But the gods alone knew what fireworks she might treat them all to first.

"Great Taranis, woman, we've waited long enough this night." Alena blinked at her father's harsh, slurred words. "Your lady mother is not about to lose the gold this man paid for you, so give your damned oath and end this farce."

Alena shot Venutius a deadly look that reminded him so forcefully of her mother, his wife, that he blanched. She turned back to Marcus and looked up at him steadily.

"I swear by Anu, mother of the gods, that I, Alena of the Lopocares, will take only this man, Marcus Valerius, to husband. For as long as he lives."

She picked up a small knife from the low table before her mother, drew its sharp blade across her finger without a single flinch or flicker of an eyelid, and made her mark in blood on the parchment.

A rustling tide of whispers broke out in the crowd at her curt, stark oath, but Marcus was unperturbed. Her words bound her to him. That was sufficient.

By the time a full dozen of the highest-ranking guests had signed or made their mark in blood, the hall rang with shouts and toasts. Huge, hairy hands reached for Alena, and she was passed from man to man, with hearty kisses and ribald advice on how to handle a lusty male. Marcus downed bowl after bowl of honey-flavored wine in response to the toasts. When he decided enough men had pawed his bride, he strode down the hall to collect her and take her to the couch reserved for them between the queen and the governor.

Alena must have conversed with the governor, seated just to her right, but ever afterward she could not remember a word they shared. She took long, steadying drafts from the double-handled loving cup set before her until Marcus reached over and took it out of her hands.

"I refuse to tend to a retching wife more than once this day," he told her, his voice low and teasing.

"Then you are in luck, Roman. I do not want you to tend me, ill or otherwise." Her honey-coated voice almost, but not quite, disguised the sting of her words.

Marcus laughed, refusing to let her ruffle his satisfaction. He reached down and pulled a succulent morsel of roast boar, dripping with sauce, from a delicate bowl and lifted it to her lips.

Alena put a hand up quickly to catch the dribbling sauce, then licked her fingers greedily. The stringy meat, flavored with garlic and wild onions, was delicious. She suddenly realized how hungry she was. Her stomach growled ferociously, protesting its emptiness. She filled her pewter bowl with huge chunks of boar and venison and mutton swimming in a glutinous, greasy sauce sweetened with thyme and rosemary. Scooping the meat up with pieces of flat unleavened bread, she set to with her normal healthy appetite. When she would have washed her meal down with fine Mamertine wine, a gift from Governor Maximus, Marcus took the silver drinking bowl and swallowed half its contents himself. He signaled to a waiting slave, who refilled the half-full bowl with water, and handed it back to his indignant wife.

He ignored her decided scowl. Instead, he gave his full attention to the dish of mounded goose liver surrounded by mushrooms and asparagus being presented to him. With elegant courtesy, he scooped a generous portion out and offered it to Queen Cartimandua.

The older woman took the pâté and leaned back to survey her new son-by-marriage. The thought of this man as her "son" made her mouth turn down in something very close to a pout.

"I hope this marriage brings what you want out of it, Marcus Valerius. If this daughter is anything like her dam, she will not be an easy wife to manage."

"If she lives up to half her mother's reputation, I will be well satisfied." The glint in his dark eyes told the queen exactly which reputation he referred to.

Cartimandua gave a bellow of laughter. "By the gods, soldier, 'tis well Alena decided to give her oath. Else I might have declared the offer invalid and made my own proposition to you."

"We both gave oaths, Lady Queen. I intend to honor mine, and see that the Lady Alena does, as well."

There was no mistaking the iron in his words. Cartimandua sighed and put the image of this man, naked and gleaming with sweat, from her mind. She'd done many things in her lifetime, but never yet had she taken her own sons or sons-by-marriage to her bed. There were plenty of others to choose from, she decided, not without a last, lingering tinge of regret.

"Do you also intend to hold to your oath to keep the borderlands for King Megarric? My sources tell me Beorht of the north will be most displeased when he hears of Alena's marriage. You may find him as difficult to handle as your new wife."

"I will manage both."

"You had best start now." Cartimandua nodded to the woman at his far side.

Marcus turned to see angry green eyes glaring at him and the queen. Swallowing a grin, he gave his full attention to the woman stretched out on the eating couch next to him. With quiet courtesy he fed her the choicest sticky sweetmeats, bits of fruit, and pungent crumbled goat cheese. They washed the food down with sweet, cool wine, carefully watered by the attending slave.

As the long feast rose to a crescendo of noise and riotous toasts, Marcus found it harder and harder to respond politely or listen to the songs of the storytellers. He barely noticed when guests staggered outside to be sick or when the governor disappeared for a long period with the brawny slave girl who'd been feeding him sweetmeats from her own lips. Marcus found his eyes, and his lusts, centered entirely on his wife. His eyes kept straying to Alena's red, moist lips sucking on juicy bits of fruit or to her long, shapely legs stretched out beside him. When she leaned forward and her rose wool drape slipped from its precarious hold to show a lush white breast, Marcus stood abruptly and pulled her up beside him.

He bowed to Cartimandua and to the governor, and gave the lolling King Venutius a brief nod. "My lady wife and I thank you for this gracious feast. We will make our farewells now."

"The night is not yet half-over, Prefect," the queen protested. "There are yet games, and dancing slaves from the East, and more wine."

"I'm sure the guests will enjoy them, Highness. The groom has other matters to attend to yet this eve."

Ignoring Alena's indignant gasp, he deftly extricated them both from the milling throng of well-wishers. His troop, not quite as polished and precise after hours celebrating their captain's wedding, formed up behind them for the short ride back to camp. They broke out in raucous song halfway there. Alena caught only snatches of their words, which seemed to be addressed to a rather active god who had descended to take a human bride. She turned to Marcus in silent query.

" 'Tis the traditional Roman marriage hymn, *'Hymen, a Hymenaee, Hymen.'* Although they seem to be adding their own variations to the basic theme," he told her with a grin.

She spent the rest of the short trip listening with astonishment to the improbable, imaginative, incredibly acrobatic activities of the newly married god.

When they arrived back at her quarters, Marcus dismounted and strode back to lift her from the saddle. Instead of setting her on her feet, he held her high in his strong arms and carried her across the threshold to the soldiers' shouts of *"Talassio!"*

"An ancient cry of fertility," he told her, kicking the door shut on the bellowing troops. His arms tightened around her when she struggled lightly to be set down.

"Roman tradition calls for me to carry you across the threshold, lest you stumble over it. That would be a bad omen for our marriage, and we don't need any more difficulties than we already face." His breath lifted the wispy curls around her ears as he carried her through the *solar* to the bedchamber at the back of the house.

"If this were Rome, you would anoint the door with oil to smooth our new life together and leave your sandals outside on the stoop to signify the life you leave behind."

Ethelyn awaited them in the small bedchamber. She jumped up when the looming form of the captain filled the door, her mistress in his arms.

"What have you done to her?" she cried, running forward, fists clenched, forgetting her fear of the Roman in her concern for her lady.

"Quickly, wife, tell your woman you are not hurt, before she unmans me."

Alena looked up, her green eyes glinting. "I'm not sure I can offer such assurances," she replied blandly. "You have used me most hardily this day."

Marcus stared at her. Did she play with him? Or had he unknowingly hurt her in his fevered groping? Doubts swirled through him.

Ethelyn's anxious voice interrupted them. "Lady, are you all right?"

"Aye, more or less," Alena admitted wryly, taking pity on the worried girl. She pushed at the massive chest under her palm, demanding to be set down.

Absurdly relieved, Marcus only gripped her tighter. "Your lady is in my care, this night and henceforth," he told the trembling maid. "You may retire."

Ethelyn turned in confusion to her mistress. Sighing, Alena nodded. She would have to break this new husband of the habit of ordering her slaves about arbitrarily.

Marcus waited until the stout wooden door closed behind the maid before he set Alena on her feet. When she would have moved away from him, he stayed her with a gentle hold on her arm.

"In the, ah…press of more urgent concerns when I came for you this afternoon, I neglected to give you your bride gift."

Alena eyed the small parcel he held out suspiciously. Having received few gifts in her life, she'd not learned to accept them graciously. Impatiently Marcus thrust it into her hand. "Open it."

Her fingers awkward, she unwrapped the packet. The thin leather wrapping fell away to reveal a glittering mass of gold and green. Alena held the necklace up to the light of the fire and gasped at the web of gossamer gold links, studded with bright, flashing emeralds. She had never seen anything so fine in her entire life.

"I would that our courtship and wedding had been more— conventional, Lady Wife. Perhaps this bride gift will help you forget some of the less pleasant memories and let us start fresh."

Alena eyed him speculatively. "Is this a bribe? Think you this bauble will make me into a docile, submissive Roman wife?"

"I doubt any bribe could accomplish such a miracle," Marcus told her bluntly, irritated at her lukewarm response to his gift. "That will more likely take my strong arm and several hardy switches. Nay, do not fire up. Just take the gift in the spirit in which it was offered."

Her ready temper flared. "I do not want your offering. These links have too much the look of a slave collar, for all their sparkling stones. I will not wear it."

Teeth clenched against his own temper, Marcus eyed his wife grimly. There was a time and a place for defiance, and this was not it, he decided. "You will wear it, and nothing else, I think," he promised.

He made good on his promise. Hours later, he pulled a sleeping, wildly tousled wife into his arms. His last conscious thought, as he gently fingered the stones crushed between her full breasts, was that the emeralds' glow could not begin to compare with the green fire that flamed in her eyes when she moaned with passion.

The celebrations in honor of their marriage lasted for three days. Cartimandua had planned the festivities well to impress her often rebellious lords with her great wealth and her solidarity with the powerful Roman governor. The bridal couple were honored in a great processional that wound through the streets of Isurium. Senior Brigante magistrates led the parade, their brightly striped and patterned robes proclaiming their individual clans. Behind them, white-clad priests and priestesses marched, followed by acolytes leading a menagerie of beasts to be sacrificed. Marcus and Alena came next, in the place of honor, in a gleaming white chariot gilded with gold and bronze decoration. They were followed by the governor, and then by the Brigantian king and queen in their own richly decorated wicker chariots. The rest of the guests streamed behind, and the city's inhabitants joined in the long, merry march as it passed. By the time the procession made its way to the huge basilica crowning Isurium's highest hill, it had swelled to thousands.

In front of a milling, cheering throng, Marcus once again pledged to hold the land of Lopocares in the name of King Megarric and in keeping with the agreements between the Brigantes and Rome. Alena passed among the crowd with a basket of flat unleavened bread, a symbolic sharing of the wealth and riches of her new marriage and a prelude to the feast to come. The governor and Queen Cartimandua gave gracious speeches, Venutius a curt, almost surly one. Finally, acolytes led forward a huge white stallion, and Marcus himself stepped forward to dedicate the first sacrifice.

A low rumble of uneasiness drifted across the crowd. Marcus knew well the Celts did not object to sacrifice. On the contrary, offering such a magnificent beast to the gods would meet with their approval. But he knew many still held to the old ways, which mandated ceremonies in quiet glens and dark forests. His voice rang out across the crowd, commanding and sure.

"I, Marcus Valerius, prefect of Rome, dedicate this sacrifice to Mars, the god of soldiers. In this land, he is known as Rigisamus, the god 'most royal.' I offer this beast in the hope that he will bless the union of soldier of Rome and princess of Britannia." Turning, he reached for Alena and pulled her forward.

"Cleverly done," Alena told him, her low voice barely audible over the wild cheers of the crowd. "You would lull their fears by using their own gods to gain your ends."

Marcus shrugged and led her to their waiting chariot. "I've served in many lands and known many gods. I respect them all."

"Yet you would deny us our most ancient ways of worship."

Marcus waited until the chariot began its slow, rumbling way before he responded. He leaned easily against its side, one hand holding the iron grip to steady himself as wooden wheels bounced over uneven cobblestones, the other hand around Alena's waist.

"If you speak of Druidism, yes. 'Tis not that Rome denies your gods, only the power of the Druid priests and priestesses. With their enclaves and meetings, they link the tribes and incite them against Rome. The Druid caste has been eradicated in Gaul these many years, yet the people still worship their gods in peace. Only here, in the remote hills of Britannia, do people still cling to old ways and old priests."

Alena clutched the side of the chariot for support as it bounced over a rut. She would have continued the argument, but Marcus forestalled her.

"Let us save this discussion for another day. Today I wish only to enjoy the games and the feast and the sight of my wife in all her finery."

His eyes drifted down over her, lingering on the swell of her breasts filling the blue robe she wore, then back up to dwell on the heavy gold torque around her neck. He forbore from commenting on the fact that she had not worn his bridal gift. If she wore it only for him, as she had last night, in wild, abandoned nakedness—and she would, he vowed!—he would be well content.

Alena flushed under his gaze. It combined elements of a hot desire she was beginning to recognize all too well and a new, decidedly proprietary gleam. She saw his eyes linger on the heavy twist of gold that circled her neck, and her chin went up. She still carried marks where the emeralds had pressed into her flesh. Erotic images of how those marks had gotten there burned across her mind, and she turned away to fling coins to the cheering crowd, her face red.

She had little to say to her new husband as they presided at the games in their honor. Local warriors demonstrated their skills with sword and spear and wildly exuberant chariot races around the huge earthen amphitheater outside Isurium's town walls. Although professional gladiators were beginning to appear at the games in Rome's capital to the south, Londinium, the northern tribes still held to their own ways. Alena found herself caught up in the excitement of the games, cheering lustily for her favorites and commenting shrewdly on the skill, or lack of skill, of the warriors. She presented prizes of gold coins, minted especially for this occasion, to the winners with laughing grace.

Marcus, too, enjoyed the games, although he gained more entertainment from watching his wife than from watching the contestants. She threw herself wholeheartedly into the events. He had a shrewd suspicion that she probably itched to grab a javelin and join the sweaty competitors in the games. And could probably best most of them, if she was as skilled with the spear as she had shown herself with the bow. For the first time in many days, he relaxed. He put the weight of his responsibility for the unsettled northern border out his mind. He kept his eyes away from the queen and her surly consort, and all the political problems they represented. He responded politely when the governor addressed him, but for the most part ignored Maximus. The man's nervous airs did not sit well with him.

Instead, Marcus gave himself up to the pageantry that swirled around him, and to the deep, visceral pleasure that just the sight of his golden-haired bride brought. A smile tugged at his mouth when she screamed invective at a seemingly hesitant contestant in the bear-baiting. He compared the vibrant, glowing creature beside him to his pallid, cool, always proper first wife. Marcus grinned, thinking how shocked Lavinia would have been if he had tried with her some of the things he had done with, and to, Alena in the early hours of the morning. He might still have to coax and tease and torment his native wife until she forgot it was a Roman who held her, but now that her passion had been unleashed, it grew more glorious and more tempestuous with every coupling. 'Twas as if it had been held in check and only now allowed to be unleashed. Once again Marcus wondered how her dead husband could have mishandled her so, to have left her natural sensuality untapped. He felt his loins tighten as he remembered how he'd had to take her hand and force her to explore him, to touch him in the ways that brought a man pleasure. Suddenly the sun seemed too hot and the crowd too loud. Marcus cursed under his breath, shifted uncomfortably in his chair, and heartily wished the games and the feast to follow were over.

Chapter Eighteen

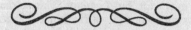

Lady Nelwyn sat in a high-backed leather chair, fingering the small stones in her hand with slow, measured strokes. Her nephew played happily with his toy warriors on a rug laid by the stone hearth.

"I don't know how you can be so calm, Nelwyn. This marriage is as much a shock to you as to me, yet you sit there fingering your stones as if 'twere of no account."

Nelwyn turned to survey the regent as he paced back and forth at the far end of the hall.

"'Tis done, Peganthus. I do not waste my energies ranting against what the gods have wrought."

"But Alena will be under this Roman's thumb. She'll have to submit to his ways and forsake ours. Think you she'll continue to support your practice of the sacred rites?" he asked spitefully.

"I doubt I will live to see the day Alena is under any man's thumb," Nelwyn responded, refusing to be drawn. "If Dugald could not contain her, brutal as he was, do you think this Roman can?"

"Do not underestimate him! This soldier's only been in our land little more than a month, yet already he spreads Rome's tentacles well beyond the borders with his string of forts and detachments. Even Beorht was driven back from his last attempt to shake them loose."

"This Roman is but a man, Peganthus. He's not invincible, nor invulnerable. There are ways to bring even the boldest warrior to his knees."

"What do you mean?" The regent's watery blue eyes sharpened with interest. "Do you speak of spells or incantations? Or poisons?"

Nelwyn frowned and slanted a quick look at the child. Megarric paid no attention to the adult conversation and played contentedly with his toys.

"I speak of nothing, yet. I'll wait and see how events unfold, and read what omens the gods send."

"Well, you may wait, but I cannot. This soldier sent word that my regency ends when they arrive home." Peganthus threw himself down in a leather chair beside Nelwyn and stared disconsolately into the fire.

"You knew it would end in any case with Alena's marriage. Now you can return to the south, to the stable of boys you had to leave when you came here."

Peganthus flushed at Nelwyn's quiet words. Alena's adamant refusal to allow him to bring his playmates into her son's home still rankled. He bit at one dirty fingernail and recognized he'd get no support from the woman beside him. Not for the first time since the curt message had arrived advising him of the marriage and the expected date the couple would return, he gave a vile curse. Reluctantly he rose to oversee the packing of his personal possessions and the secret cache of gold he had hoarded during his years of regency.

Three days later, Alena leapt from her horse and ran into the palace of the king of the Lopocares. She had no concern for dignity in her eagerness to see her son. Megarric, along with Nelwyn and Peganthus and the surviving Lopocare lords, awaited her in the great hall.

Marcus followed in her wake. He waited quietly while Alena greeted her son with joyous laughter and ferocious hugs that had the boy squealing with excitement. Finally she released him and moved to one side. Marcus crossed the room to stand before the boy. Soldier and child stared at each other solemnly, and then Marcus went down on one knee.

"Ave, King Megarric. I have taken your mother to wife and given my sacred pledge to care for her person with all honor and respect." He ignored the small snort Alena gave over the child's head. "I pledge, as well, to protect your rights as king in this land, in accordance with the treaty between Brigantium and Rome.''

When the soldier finished his short speech, Megarric flashed an uncertain look up at Alena. After a moment, she nodded. Although she'd never admit it to the arrogant soldier who was her husband, his public pledge of support for Megarric did much to loosen the knot of tension that had built within her with each passing mile of the long trip home. When Megarric's clear, childish treble accepted the soldier's pledge and the lords present each came forward to reaffirm their own oaths, the knot loosened an inch more. She stepped back to allow the child his dignities and joined Nelwyn in a corner of the room.

Nelwyn slipped an arm around her sister-by-marriage. ''Welcome home, child.''

''Oh, Nelwyn, 'tis good to see you. I longed so for your wise counsel these weeks.'' Alena buried her head in the older woman's shoulder, as she had so many times before.

''We must talk later, child. I would have you tell me with your own lips how this strange marriage came about.''

''Aye,'' Alena replied, straightening. ''Although, for the life of me, I'm still not sure myself. I yet panic in the night, when this Roman reaches for me, thinking it all a dream.''

Nelwyn frowned into her sister's clear green eyes. ''Does this man use you painfully?''

A wash of pink stole up Alena's neck and colored her cheeks. Nelwyn's frown deepened.

''Nay,'' Alena answered finally. The color in her cheeks deepened to a bright red. ''But he makes me do things I would never have imagined possible between two people!'' Her low voice vibrated with indignation.

Nelwyn stared at her, astonishment widening her brown eyes, then tried unsuccessfully to smother a long, low laugh.

''Oh, Alena, do you finally become a woman? Nay, do not fire up at me.'' Still smiling, the older woman put a placating hand on Alena's arm.

''I see no cause for humor, sister.'' Alena stiffened in offended dignity. But that pose lasted only a moment. The urge to confide in the calm, quiet woman was too ingrained and too natural for her to take umbrage at her gentle laughter. ''Oh, Nelwyn, I'm so confused. I don't understand how this Roman can make my anger rise with his arrogant ways each day, and my body flame with strange passions each night." And each morning, she thought, and frequently each afternoon. Such as the afternoon, when Marcus had called an early halt during the long journey home. The flush on Alena's face spread to her shoulders as she remembered some of their more innovative couplings.

"'Tis the way of men," Nelwyn told her dryly. "They infuriate us with their often stupid or childish ways, then come at us with hot hands and dripping rods. They think mating will banish all the irritants of the day. And it usually does. Nay, do not look so surprised. My marriage was most satisfying. I loved my warrior, even though I sometimes wondered how the man ever found his way to the stews to relieve himself, let alone to the battlefield."

For a moment, Nelwyn's eyes held a smiling, faraway look, as if she cherished a vision of happy occasions. Alena remembered well her sister's husband. He had been a bluff, hearty warrior who loved nothing more than a fierce battle. He had often brought as many or more heads home to decorate the door of his dwelling as Alena's own husband, Dugald. He had followed Dugald in the rebellion against Rome, and been killed early in the fighting. Nelwyn had taken the news of his death with her characteristic calm, stating only that she knew his soul had passed immediately to another warrior, one who would gain much from the spirit of such a man. But she'd shut herself away in her quarters for several days.

Now her soft voice commanded Alena's attention. "Listen to me, child. I oft regretted that Dugald made no effort to temper his lusts with you. Many times I tried to convince him that gentleness with a woman brought more pleasure than did pain, but he had no care for anyone's need save his own. It hurt me to watch your womanhood crushed before it even flowered. If this Roman brings you pleasure, take it. Learn from him about your woman's body. Take what he offers while you can."

Alena's brows rose incredulously. "You would counsel me to submit to one whose troops took our lands?" she said, her voice low. "One whose governor takes our wealth to feed Rome's coffers?"

"Nay, not submit. 'Tis not in you to submit. But as long as you're locked in marriage with this man who awakens your passions, use him. Learn your body's secrets, and taste some of the pleasure the gods have given us. But keep your heart and your spirit to yourself."

Alena wanted much to take this subject further, but was called back to the ceremonies at hand by an excited Megarric. She kissed her sister-by-marriage with real affection, then joined her son.

Nelwyn stayed back, away from the focus of activity, and turned speculative eyes on the tall soldier who dominated the room. Even surrounded by the hearty, muscled Lopocare lords, the Roman's towering frame dominated the long hall.

As if sensing her eyes on him, Marcus turned to meet Nelwyn's gaze. Dark, almost black eyes looked steadily into still brown ones. The soldier felt a tingle run along the edges of his spine. He knew of the Lady Nelwyn—Alena had mentioned her often enough—but for the first time he felt the power of the strong, silent personality his wife had hinted at. His face grave, he crossed the room to greet her.

"Hail, Lady Nelwyn. Alena has spoken of you often, and with great affection."

"She has told me of you, as well, Captain."

A rueful smile tugged at one corner of his mouth. He could well imagine how Alena had described him to this woman. "I would that we might become friends, lady. You have much influence with Alena, and could school me in how to care for her."

Nelwyn's brows rose. "I suspect you're not one to be easily led where your heart does not want you to go, Marcus Valerius. I will wait, and watch, before I give you any advice or hold over one who is most dear to me."

Marcus nodded at her calm words, his respect for the woman increasing by the moment. In this land of hot-tempered, impetuous people, it was refreshing to find one so measured and thoughtful. He bowed and went to collect Alena and Megarric. They would ride with him to the parade planned in their honor.

* * *

Lineas Flavius stood at the head of troops massed in rank
after glittering rank in the long, open *gymnasium*. The entire
legion waited to welcome their captain and his bride. Squad-
rons of foot soldiers and cavalrymen stood proudly behind their
colorful regimental banners, in their finest parade dress. Red
plumes danced in the breeze atop elaborate ceremonial helmets, and burnished armor sparkled in the sun. Shields embossed with jutting heads of dragons and tigers hung from the
soldiers' arms and the saddles of the cavalrymen. Even the
horses were richly caparisoned with silver and gold, sporting
intricately carved facepieces with elaborate medallions and
eyeguards. Glittering, ornate bridles and nave bands tinkled
merrily as the horses and men shifted in eager anticipation of
the celebrations to follow.

When the captain's huge ceremonial chariot, pulled by
enormous matched grays harnessed four abreast, swept up the
hill and onto the training field, the massed troops gave a loud,
bellowing cheer. Lineas Flavius greeted his commander with a
crisp salute, then swept Alena off her feet for a bride kiss that
had her blushing, the troops grinning, and Marcus smiling
wryly.

"Enough, Flavius," he told his second-in-command when
Alena shot him a helpless, flustered look over the tribune's
muscled shoulder. "Remember the lady is my wife."

"Much as I envy you for walking off with such a prize,
Captain, I take consolation in the fact that you now leave the
rest of the field open for me. Somehow I suspect your bride will
leave you little energy or interest for any other women."

The tribune smiled to himself when he saw the quick, possessive look his captain gave his new wife. Obviously Marcus
had used the long journey south to good effect! With formal
courtesy, he turned to greet Peganthus and the other Lopocare
guests and showed them to their seats under the bright canopy
set up especially for this occasion.

Alena delighted in the breathtaking equestrian display put on
in her honor. At a signal from Marcus, trumpets poured high,
clear notes out across the afternoon air and a line of cavalrymen galloped to the center of the training arena. They lowered
their bronze face masks carved with every imaginable likeness,

from snarling lions to images of goddesses of war. Standing in a long, straight line, they lifted embossed shields as another squad of horsemen thundered down the field toward them. While the crowd roared, these cavalrymen rode past at full gallop and threw light dummy javelins decorated with long, streaming tails at the other men's shields. Alena held her breath and Megarric screamed with delight as the javelins flew with deadly accuracy at the line of men sitting solidly in the middle of the arena. A decurion called out points for each hit scored.

The javelin contest was followed by a demonstration of skill with bows that made Alena's fingers itch. Watching the rain of arrows that sped unerringly toward straw targets, she longed to feel a taut bow and hear the singing whir of an arrow as it rushed past her ear.

As a special treat, a detachment of North African light horsemen amazed the crowds with a dazzling display of horsemanship. They rode without saddles or bridles, guiding their horses in intricate whirlwind maneuvers by only the slightest pressure of their knees and low, muttered commands. As impressive as their skills were, however, even they paled when a troop of mounted Lopocare warriors rode into the arena to present a special tribute to their lady. The Lopocares' reputation as the finest horsemen of the Brigante tribe, who were without question the best in all Britain, was well deserved. Shouting fiercely and banging swords against shields, the warriors pounded across the field in bold, reckless, heart-stopping charges, passing within inches of their onrushing opponents, only to wheel with blinding speed and charge again. Marcus watched the show closely, impressed. The maneuvers reminded him all too well of Beorht's fierce charge, when he had almost succeeded in stealing the Lady Alena. The prefect began to revise his estimation of what it might take to defeat the tribes to the north.

The *hippica gymnasium* was drawing to a close, the last mounted promenade about to begin, when trouble broke out. Later Marcus would discover it had begun when one legionnaire rode too close to a panting native pony, causing the animal to shy. It bumped against a nearby Lopocare lord and tumbled him into the dust. Smothered laughter broke out, and the lord sprang up, incensed. He dragged the careless legionnaire from his horse and went at him with all the reckless Celtic love of a fight, fists swinging and feet kicking. Within moments, the fight became a melee.

"Flavius, get the other officers, on the double!"

With a deliberate, angry stride, Marcus crossed the field and waded into the brawling men. He laid the flat of his sword against helmeted troops and reached down to fling men aside as if they were straw dolls. Centurions came running and slashed their vine canes across the backs and legs of thrashing men, aiming for white-clad soldiers, but hitting as many brawling Lopocare as Romans. All around him Marcus could hear the lusty shouts of spectators, held back from the fray by their officers and their fear of the tall commander mercilessly knocking heads together. Marcus struggled through the tangled, heaving mass of combatants, who grunted and cursed and gave wild roars of victory when opponents went down before swinging fists or butting heads.

Gradually, a new sound began to rise over the din of the fight. A thundering began far down the field and rolled toward the sprawling, roiling pile of humanity. Marcus turned, chest heaving, when the men around him fell back. His eyes narrowed in disbelief when he saw his massive ceremonial chariot, pulled by four panting, galloping grays, pounding down the long field directly at them. All around him, men scrambled aside frantically as the chariot raced relentlessly toward them.

Alena held the sawing leather reins in a hard grip, using every ounce of her strength to control the madly racing horses. She had not handled four abreast before, and the heavy wooden chariot was much different from the light wicker ones of the Lopocare. It took all her skill to keep the plunging beasts headed straight forward in a steady, pounding gallop. She frowned in fierce concentration and braced herself well back on one leg to compensate for the violent pull of the reins. Her eyes narrowed in grim satisfaction when she saw the men ahead of her scramble madly out of the path of the oncoming chariot. Only one man stood, tall and immobile, directly in front of her. Muscles bunching, arms aching, Alena pulled back on the reins. The snorting, plunging grays danced to a stop just a few feet from the prefect.

Alena jumped down lightly and tossed the reins to a gaping soldier. A sharp pain shot through her shoulders from the pull of the reins, but she was too heady from her wild ride to care. She flashed a smug, triumphant smile up at her husband.

"I thank you, and your men, for arranging such entertainment in honor of our wedding. There is nothing Lopocares enjoy more than a display of skill and a good fight."

When Marcus stood silent in front her, her saucy smile deepened. She turned to survey the combatants scattered around her. One by one, sheepish grins broke out on bloodied, bruised faces. She made a full circuit, noting that the Lopocares had certainly held their own against the Romans, if the swelling eyes and bloody noses were any indication. Her survey complete, she once more faced her impassive husband. Why did the man not respond? Did he not realize how she had defused a potentially dangerous situation? Her green eyes flashed an unmistakable command.

"I'm glad the ... festivities pleased you, Lady Wife," Marcus said at last. "Although I doubt the brawl was part of the planned activities, in your honor we will consider it so and forbear to punish those involved."

His words were even and courteous, and only Alena was close enough to note that a cold, furious light burned in his dark eyes.

The men released a collective sigh of relief at the captain's words. Brawling was second nature to these rough and tumble legionnaires, but generally things did not get out of hand to such an extent. Alena couldn't help preening when one of the Romans called out a compliment on her skill and the rest of the men took it up in a ragged cheer. She grinned and nodded graciously.

Her grin slipped when Marcus stepped forward and clasped her arm to lead her to the chariot. His light touch caused the ache in her shoulder to flash with white-hot pain. But she recovered immediately and pinned her smile back on her face. Not for the world would she spoil the dashing image she'd created with that mad, wild ride.

"Keep your smile in place," he hissed as he took the reins from the trooper and headed them back down the long arena.

"I am! It is! What ails you, anyway? Why do you frown at me?" Alena bit her lip as the wheels rumbled over the uneven ground and tongues of fire shot up her arm to her shoulder. Some of her triumphant smugness faded.

"We will speak later."

"Do not take that curt tone with me. I am not one of your troops to be ordered about. What ails you?" The pain in her arm, and her pigheaded husband, were making her angry.

"Think you I want or need your assistance to control my men?"

Alena blinked as he speared her with a furious look. Her mouth dropped open in sheer surprise. "My people were involved, as well! At least *I* managed to stop the fight," she told him nastily. She almost, but not quite, regretted her hasty words when the prefect's mouth thinned to a grim line and a muscle jumped furiously in his cheek.

"You could have killed half of them, and yourself, as well, did you not manage to stop those horses."

"Well, I stopped them, did I not? Surely you had no doubt of my ability, standing foursquare in my way as you did." She pressed back involuntarily against the side of the chariot when Marcus turned on her.

"You idiot, I thought to grab the horses when they flew past. My burliest cavalrymen can barely control these beasts. I was sure they had bolted with you."

Thoroughly indignant now, Alena opened her mouth to tell him exactly what she thought of him and his opinions of her skill with horses, but he yanked abruptly on the reins to pull the chariot to a halt beside the canopied area. She had to grab at the sides of the chariot to keep her balance, then bite her lip viciously as her shoulder screamed in protest.

"Mother! You were so brave! You drove four horses!"

For the first time in her life, Alena was less than pleased to hear her son's piping voice.

" 'Twas not so difficult, Megarric."

"Yes, but four horses all at once! How did you do it?"

Alena ignored her husband's sardonic look. "I just did it. But I must say, I liked it not. 'Tis too unwieldy. Our lighter chariots and short, fast ponies harnessed two together are easier to maneuver."

When Megarric grabbed her wrist and would have pelted her with his usual spate of eager questions, she eased her arm out of his grip unobtrusively and deflected his attention to the parade about to begin.

Alena passed the next few hours in a haze of pain. She smiled and nodded when the final review passed by and the troops honored her with stiff raised-arm salutes. She even managed to swallow her groan of dismay when she saw the trestle tables set out in the field next to the arena. Great Mother, it would take them the rest of this day and most of the night to consume a whole roast oxen, huge, sizzling haunches of venison, mounds of wild game and a dazzling array of side dishes.

Desperately she took a silver chalice brimming with wine from a passing slave and downed the contents in long, gulping swallows. Ignoring her husband's frown, she signaled for the slave to fill it again. An involuntary spasm crossed her face when Flavius came up and lifted her hand for a kiss, but she responded to his laughing, bantering praise for her daring ride with a credible semblance of light-hearted nonchalance. Hours later, long after the sleeping Megarric had been taken back to his quarters and the men had offered toast after toast to the captain and his bride, Marcus told her quietly it was time to retire. Alena almost sobbed in relief as they left. It took every ounce of her concentration to hold herself upright during the short chariot ride to the commander's house at the center of the fort.

"You need not do this again," she protested when Marcus swept her up in his arms. "We fulfilled this tradition in Isurium."

"Be quiet, woman," Marcus snapped as he strode through the echoing halls. "Only the fact that your face is white with pain and you look about to faint keeps me from stripping you bare and beating that luscious rump of yours black and blue. The matter of your conduct this afternoon will have to wait, but be assured we will return to it."

Wisely Alena focused on the first part of his low tirade and ignored the rest. "I never faint!"

"You may well wish to, ere this night is done. I suspect you've dislocated your shoulder with your mad stunt." With a care that belied his curt tone, Marcus placed her on his wide sleeping platform, which was piled high with furs.

Alena marveled at the gentleness in his fingers as he unpinned her robe and peeled it down. "How did you know I was in pain?"

"I suspected when you did not hold your son. I knew it when even half a flagon of wine would bring no color to your face." He probed lightly at the discolored flesh of her shoulder.

Alena gasped, then bit her lip at his quick look. He shook his head in disgust.

"I knew I should have removed you from the banquet long ere this," he muttered, more to himself than to Alena.

"Why did you not? Not that you could have done so, had I not wished it." Even with searing, blazing agony making the edges of her world turn dim, Alena could not let this man think he would rule her.

"Like a fool, I thought to let you savor your moment of triumph. The men will honor you—as much for the punishment you spared them as for your reckless horsemanship." Marcus sat aback on his haunches beside the bed and studied her shoulder.

Despite the pain, Alena managed a smug smile.

"Smile while you may, wife. I fear you will not like the next few moments. I must reset that shoulder."

Alena watched, wide-eyed, while Marcus stood and removed his mantle, then unbuckled his wide leather belt. Her eyes locked on his strong hands as they slid the dagger and sword holders from the belt, then brought the thick leather to her lips.

"Here, bite on this. 'Tis the best I can do. I would give you a sleeping draft, but I fear to take any more time. If your shoulder swells much more, I'll not be able to feel the bones slide back into place."

Alena stared at the leather, swallowing.

"Take it. Or give yourself up to the pain that beads your brow with sweat. Stop fighting it. Let it take your consciousness."

"I told you, I do not faint," Alena snapped. She took the heavy leather between dry lips and bit down, hard.

The last thing she saw, before the world exploded in blinding, white-hot pain and then faded altogether, was the stark planes of her husband's face as he leaned over her.

Chapter Nineteen

"Raise your arm."

"I cannot."

"Raise your arm, woman."

Alena shot her lord a poisonous look. Gritting her teeth, she lifted her injured arm inch by agonizing inch out of the warm water. When it finally reached shoulder height, she lowered it again. Sloshing water over her short linen shift, she turned to the man standing next to her in the shallow pool. "May we cease now?"

"Nay. And do not cast such angry looks at me. 'Twas your recklessness that caused the injury, and your stupid pride that would not let it be tended to quickly. Lift it again."

Alena clamped her teeth shut over the retort she wanted to make and concentrated instead on exercising her arm. She'd learned the hard way in the weeks since she'd injured herself that her husband was relentless in the regime he had imposed for her recovery. He'd enlisted Lady Nelwyn's support immediately. Under their combined dominance, Alena found herself drugged each night to deaden her pain and confined to bed each day until she thought she'd go mad from unaccustomed inactivity. It was many days before Marcus allowed her to rise, and many more after that before he removed the bindings and permitted the first tentative movement of her arm. She'd torn several muscles in her shoulder, and it was taking far longer than someone of her volatile temper expected for it to heal properly.

"Again."

"Great Mother, I will not! 'Tis enough for this day." Alena turned and swirled through the water to the edge of the pool. When she would have swung up onto the shallow marble ledge, strong hands gripped her from behind and turned her in the water. She found herself sitting on the hard ledge, with warm water lapping softly over her hips and her husband lodged firmly between her thighs.

"I suggest you curb that temper of yours, Lady Wife. You know 'tis only your injury that has kept that white rump of yours from sporting bruises even more colorful than those that have decorated your shoulder these many weeks."

Alena spread her hands on the wide ledge and leaned back. Undaunted, she grinned up at her towering husband. She'd heard that threat too many times now to take it seriously. "You might have had some difficulty explaining to your men how I sustained new injuries."

"You don't need to remind me how near my soldiers are to idolizing you," Marcus drawled, his hands still on her wet, slick waist. "The dolts still mistake your foolishness in hiding your injury for bravery."

Alena couldn't help feeling a smug pride at his words. In truth, her popularity with the men continually surprised her. Tales of her hurt had spread rapidly throughout the camp. When one shy trooper had brought her a beaten gold pin as a token of his squadron's regard for her daring, she'd smiled and chatted and put the awkward youth at his ease. Word of her kindness had leaked out, and to her own amazement and her husband's amusement, soldiers had begun to visit regularly. Even Nelwyn, who came daily, often found herself in conversation with curious, friendly soldiers far from home and anxious to talk with women other than the prostitutes who serviced them.

Alena had not hesitated to use her sudden popularity to see to her own people's needs. She plotted and schemed and dictated orders even from her bed. When Marcus had finally allowed her to rise and move about the camp, she had begun meeting regularly with the senior administrator charged with civic matters. Major decisions were, of course, referred to Marcus and given Megarric's ceremonial blessing. But within weeks she'd insinuated herself firmly into the workings of the camp. Only she, and her stubborn lord, knew how much her shoulder pained her or how serious the injury was. He still forced her to take drugged wine each night so that she could gain surcease from the ache, and held her firmly in his arms. And he tormented her each day, pushing her almost beyond her own considerable endurance with these damned exercises.

Marcus held his dripping wife in his hands and watched her thoughts chase themselves across her incredibly expressive face. In the months of their marriage, he'd learned to read her well. He smiled to himself at her smug complacency.

"Know you there is a ceremony tomorrow to dedicate the little temple to Epona, the horse-goddess? The one built by the Tungarian Cohort in your honor?"

"Aye, I am to officiate. Why do you ask?"

"I'm told the goddess bears a striking resemblance to a certain haughty blonde." Slowly, almost casually, Marcus slid his hands up her waist to cup her lush breasts, outlined to perfection under the wet linen shift. "I've never made love to a goddess before."

Deliberately he leaned into the ledge and let the rock-hardness of his member press against her core, spread open and vulnerable. He grinned when Alena's eyes widened.

"Marcus! You cannot, not here! 'Tis near the dinner hour. The men will come to use the baths soon."

"I've left a guard on the door. The men will understand if their lady's exercises take a bit longer than normal." His hands left off playing with stiff, peaked nipples to drift downward. Firmly, he pushed her legs wider apart and tugged her wet loin covering aside.

Alena gasped and tried to scoot back on the ledge. "Cease!"

"Nay, wife. I think your shoulder has healed enough for you to resume your duties. If I do not ease myself on you now, I'll not be able to walk upright back to our quarters. These past weeks have been as much a strain on me as you, although our pains were different."

An arrested expression appeared in the clear green of his wife's eyes. "Do you expect me to believe you have not taken your release on another woman—a house slave or whore—all this time?"

"You may believe what you wish," Marcus told her, more interested in ridding himself of his own loincloth than in her curious words. His need had driven him far beyond the capability of speech at this point. After weeks of holding an unconscious wife in his arms each night, and gritting his teeth each time her backside rubbed against his crotch or her breasts brushed against his chest, he knew that if he did not take her now he would burst. He gave up trying to undo the wet folds of his loincloth and ripped it aside with a grunt. One hand parted the flesh of her womanhood, and the other wrapped around her hips to pull her forward. Aided by the warm water and the residue of the oil he'd used to massage her arm, he slid into her with satisfying ease. Feeling her firmly lodged, he lifted her legs to wrap them around his waist and raised her off the ledge completely.

"Ah!" For long moments he held himself rigid, enjoying the exquisite sensation of her tight heat around his shaft. "By the gods, Alena, do you injure yourself to such an extent again and deny me this, I swear I will not be responsible for my actions."

"Well, of all the— You did not need to deny yourself my body, Roman. The way you and Nelwyn drugged me, you could've rutted the night long and I would not have known it."

Marcus tightened his arms around her waist to still her indignant wiggles. "Hold, or this coupling will be over before it's even begun!" When she stilled, he smiled down into her eyes. "Nay, I would not take you drugged. I want you wide awake and fully responsive when I do this to you. And this."

When they left the baths an hour later, Marcus grinned to himself at the embarrassed greeting his lady gave the men waiting to enter the bathing chambers. Even in the early darkness of the October night he could see the heat staining her cheeks. But she spoke graciously to each man who called to her and held her head high.

He felt a familiar tug of pride at the way she handled his rough soldiers. Her daring won their hearts, but her laughing humor provided the grease that smoothed over the inevitable clashes that rose between hot-blooded Lopocares and often supercilious Romans. On more than one occasion these past weeks Marcus had stayed his hand, letting Alena establish her own authority with his men. Behind the scenes he'd reined in some of her more outrageous demands for her people. And behind the closed doors of their bedchamber they'd had some raging, shouting arguments. But generally he had granted the concessions she'd requested or wheedled or stormed about. If this uneasy marriage was to succeed, 'twas important that she, and her people, recognize Rome's willingness to work with them.

And succeed it would, he vowed to the starry, silent night. Now that the damnable ache in his loins had been relieved, he felt more hopeful of their future than he had since their often stormy marriage began. As he escorted Alena through the busy streets of the camp to their quarters and listened to the respectful greetings his men gave her, his confidence grew. He and his fiery, stubborn, incredibly passionate and fascinating wife would maneuver their way through this delicate business of blending two cultures.

"No."

"But 'tis the winter solstice. Our most holy time of the year."

"No, Lady Wife."

Alena bit her lips in frustration at the quiet but adamant words. She surveyed the group of officers standing to one side and wondered briefly if they would help. She knew most of them well by now—had taken meals with them often and listened to their tales of home and wives left behind and jealous mistresses plaguing them here. But she knew also their fierce devotion to their captain. Nay, they would not help her in this matter. She turned back to her husband and tried her haughtiest tone.

"You do not understand the importance of this day to my people, Prefect. The sun takes its shortest ride across the skies, and if the proper sacrifices are not made to the gods, darkness will swallow the earth. You will remove the sanctions from the glen for this one night."

"Nay, I will not."

Alena watched Marcus come around his massive desk and lean against it to face her squarely. Without taking his eyes from her, he dismissed the group of interested officers. "You may wait without. We'll resume this meeting once my lady and I have finished."

She stood, silent and angry, until the men left and her husband continued.

"I've told you, your people may offer prayers and sacrifices at the temple or some other agreed-upon holy place. But the rituals must not be done in the Druid way or by Druid priests."

Alena opened her mouth to argue, but he forestalled her with a cold, hard look.

"Enough. I've given in to most of your wishes, Lady Wife. I've even allowed your warriors to take up their arms again and patrol the borders, despite my concern they might be tempted to align themselves with this Beorht to the north. But I cannot and will not allow you to resume the Druid practices that were outlawed years ago. You will obey me on this." He held up a hand when she sputtered angrily. "I will not discuss it further."

Alena swallowed her rage at the curt finality in his tone. Although she and Marcus disagreed frequently, she was used to more give-and-take in their arguments. From the hard look in his dark eyes, she could see that the irritating man was not about to yield on this issue. Without another word, she whirled and strode from his office. She gave an angry nod to the milling officers and flung an abrupt command to an attending guard to have her chariot brought to her quarters immediately.

Storming across the broad *via principalis* to their house, she called to Ethelyn to bring her warmest cloak and boots. By the time she'd pulled on the knee-high leather boots lined with soft rabbit fur and fastened the heavy cloak of rare white fox fur over her shoulders, the chariot awaited outside. She took the leather reins from the stablehand and wheeled the wicker vehicle down the paved street toward the camp's main gate. With unthinking skill, she maneuvered the two frisky horses through the usual pedestrian and mounted traffic within the gates and through the crowded streets of the sprawling town outside the gates. With the settlement behind her, she gave the horses their head.

Cold, stinging wind whipped against her cheeks as the iron-clad wheels raced over the frozen ground. Alena held her face up to the thin sunlight and willed the icy cold to clear some of the anger and frustration from her churning mind. She couldn't understand how Marcus could be so stubborn on this one issue, when he'd given in on so many others. And on this, the one thing she wanted to give Nelwyn in return for her care and support.

When she finally drove up the steep hill leading to the Lopocare stronghold some hours later, she was numb with cold but had worked most of her anger out of her system. She found her sister in her rooms.

"He's so pigheaded, Nelwyn. I don't understand why we can't find common ground on this matter. We've managed to do so with all the other problems that have plagued us these last months. Usually, after this much discussion, we find some compromise between Lopocare ways and Roman rule."

Alena paced her sister's spacious rooms, a steaming goblet of hot honeyed wine in her hand.

"'Tis a wonder the walls of the fort are still standing after some of your more spectacular 'discussions,'" Nelwyn teased her gently, laying aside her sewing.

Alena turned with a rueful grin. "Aye, I think the Roman has oft regretted his hasty decision to wed one of such...um... uncertain temperament. Boiling me in oil was the kindest of the punishments he promised last week, when he returned from one of his everlasting tours of the outposts and found I went out after those raiders."

"I believe your lord's objection was not to your leading the patrol to the scene so quickly, nor to your assisting in tracking the bandits. 'Twas your participation in dispatching them he took exception to."

"Well, for the love of Mars, why does he think I train in the arena each day with bow and javelin? Only to exercise this accursed shoulder? I cannot sit idly by and watch others, less skilled, chase clumsily after rogues who kill and maim our people."

"Calm yourself, Alena." Nelwyn smiled. "His concern was for your safety. In that he has my support."

Alena threw herself into the wide leather chair beside her sister's. "Oh, Nelwyn, never mind that stupid incident. I calmed the Roman eventually. I can usually bring him to some understanding of our ways. But on this matter of the solstice ceremony, I cannot move him. He'll not permit it."

"'Tis not for him to allow or not allow, child."

"But he's had the stone altar removed from the glen and will likely post guards, now that I've made such an issue of it."

"Guards may be overcome."

Alena straightened slowly in her chair. The first tinge of uneasiness crept along her spine. "Using force against his men would mean harsh penalties." She felt a strange reluctance to upset the delicate balance these past months had brought.

"Nay, not force," Nelwyn continued in her calm manner. "Do not forget, the Romans also celebrate this night. They offer sacrifices and hold a great feast to their god of the sun, Apollo, so he will bring back the light after these months of early darkness. We will use their own gods to serve ours."

"What do you mean? Do you think the guards will all get drunk and leave their posts? They will not, Nelwyn. They would not risk my lord's wrath."

Alena had seen the swift, sure retribution given soldiers who shirked their duties. Usually infractions were punished by caning or fines or extra duty, sometimes by reduction in rank. But she knew that the penalty for sentries who deserted their posts was death by stoning. Their own companions would throw the stones, in brutal retaliation for their having put lives at risk by leaving them open to unknown enemies.

"No, I do not think the guards will get drunk, either. But they might accept a mug of steaming ale to warm them on such a cold night. The ale will have herbs in it to ensure the soldiers neither see nor hear what happens in the glen this eve. They will awake in a few hours, none the worse for their short sleep."

Alena gnawed uneasily on her lower lip. Subterfuge sat ill with her. She would rather bluster or shout or force her way, winning some arguments and losing others openly. Still, Marcus had proved so recalcitrant on this matter. "It might work," she said slowly. "But 'twill be difficult for me to slip out this night. I've pleaded the cause so strongly, Marcus will be suspicious."

"I don't think you should come, child. I will take Megarric. As king of the tribe, he can accept the readings of the omens. At least he has separate quarters from the Romans, so 'twill not be difficult to slip him out. Our people will understand that you do not come. They know you cannot leave your lord's bed without bringing Roman wrath down upon us all."

Alena felt her face turning red with embarrassed heat. The matter of their living quarters had been the first of the spectacular "discussions" between her and her new husband. On the very night of their marriage feast at Isurium, when they lay sweating and sated, Alena had thought to take advantage of her husband's lazy satisfaction. Leaning across his wide, furry chest, she'd informed him she would continue to reside in the Lopocare fort with Megarric. But she would come to the Roman camp whenever Marcus summoned her to see to his needs, as well as for ceremonies and to conduct tribal business.

Her face still flamed whenever she remembered how the animal had responded to what she thought was a gracious offer. He'd rolled her over, pinned her to the furs and proceeded to show her just why she would be in his house, and in his bed, every day and every night. It had been many days after that before she could bring herself to talk to him, and weeks before she would admit he was right in insisting that the young king should maintain separate quarters, with daily visits from his mother. It still hurt to think that her son did well without her constant presence. Sighing, she turned back to the matter at hand.

"I will be at the glen, Nelwyn."

She brushed off Nelwyn's cautions and left to take her son to the festivities at the camp.

Alena thought the ceremonies that night in honor of Apollo would never end. She tried to give them her attention, but responded mechanically to the toasts and stilled her growing nervousness with wine. She kissed her son and sent him off with a heavy escort at a reasonable hour, then steeled herself to endure the rest of the entertainment that followed. As hour after hour passed, Alena felt the knot of tension in her belly tighten until she wanted to throw up. Instead, she schooled her face to impassiveness and held herself still when Marcus finally shut the door to their chamber and pulled her to him. His thumb eased the furrow between her brows.

"Do you still sulk about the bans on Nelwyn's practices this night?"

"I do not sulk."

"Aye, just as you do not faint."

Alena refused to respond to the gentle teasing in his voice. She pushed herself out of his loose hold and crossed the room to begin disrobing. Her hands shook so, she wished greatly for Ethelyn's services, but Marcus had banned the maid—and everyone else—from their chamber when he shut the door. At length she worked loose the knot of her girdle. She hung it and her robe on the peg pounded into the plastered wall.

"Do you wish for some ale?" She made the offer coolly, turning to face her husband.

Marcus looked up from where he sat on the sleeping platform, unlacing his boots, and nodded. "If it will warm your blood a bit and improve your temper, let us share some."

Alena walked to the low wooden table beside the hearth and lifted the heavy clay pitcher she'd left on a tray earlier. She swallowed, her dry throat aching for a taste of the thick, foaming ale. Walking back to Marcus, she offered him a brimming goblet.

He stood to take it from her hand and emptied half its contents in long, sure swallows.

"That does much to wipe the heavy taste of those sweetmeats from my tongue. How Flavius found such sticky fruits in this season amazed everyone."

Alena nodded without speaking. She was in no mood to discuss the tribune's notable reputation for foraging at this moment. Her eyes fastened on the strong column of her husband's throat as he swallowed once again. Willing her hands not to tremble, she lifted her own goblet and took a sip.

"Come here, wife."

An hour later, Alena raised herself on one elbow and gazed down at her sleeping husband. His lashes lay thick and black against the stark planes of his cheekbones, and his body gleamed in the dancing firelight. With infinite tenderness, she ran her hand through the dark pelt on his chest, down the hard muscles of his belly, and across his flanks. Her fingers touched his flaccid manhood lying across one thigh. She stroked its spongy length lightly and gulped back a nervous laugh. Tonight was the first time his spear had not found its target. He had succumbed to the drugged wine before bringing either of them to their peak.

Easing her long hair from under the dead weight of his arm, she slipped from their bed and dressed hurriedly in the dim light. With her cloak thrown over her arms, she bent to tug the furs over her husband's still form. Casting him a final look, she left the bedchamber. Her soft boots made no sound on the tiled floor as she sped through the darkened house. She waited until the sentry marching slowly to and fro outside the prefect's quarters turned away, then eased past him in the darkness and headed for the stables. Over and over she rehearsed in her mind the excuse she had ready for the stablemaster. King Megarric was sick. He needed her. She must go to him immediately. So absorbed was she in her frantic thoughts that she screeched in surprise when hands reached out of the darkness and fastened in her hair.

"Ho, wench, where do you speed to with such haste?"

Before she could even scream, Alena found herself turned about and pressed firmly against a broad chest. Heavy wool filled her mouth and muffled her indignant cry.

"Hmm, Apollo has sent me a special gift on this night."

A merry, slurred voice sounded above her head, even as rough hands grasped her buttocks and crushed her against a hard frame. Her fur cloak was no protection from their groping. When one of the hands reached up to wrap itself in her hair and tug her head back, she opened her mouth to protest. Before any sound could escape her lips, they were covered in a hot, hard kiss. Alena couldn't breathe under the voracious onslaught, let alone pull herself free. Finally she wiggled one arm free and slammed a balled fist into the man's side with every ounce of her strength.

"Dammit, wench." The man bent over in pain, almost pulling her to the ground with him by the hand wrapped in her hair.

Alena struggled to regain her balance and stared at the dim figure beside her. "Lineas. Great Mother, Lineas, is that you?"

The groaning man straightened, and she could finally make out his features.

"You pig! You idiot! How dare you frighten me so?"

Bile churned through her stomach, and Alena heard her voice rise to a screech. She took a deep breath and tugged again at her hair. "Loose me. At once. Megarric is ill and I must go to him."

The man beside her shook his head and stared at her in the darkness. By the light of the waning moon, she could see confusion warring with the dregs of his drunkenness across his features.

"Lady Alena? What are you doing here by the barracks so late?"

"I told you, you drunken swine. I received word Megarric is ill, and I go to him. Loose me."

"What does Marcus mean, letting you go by yourself this night! Half the camp is drunk, and the other half ruts with anything and everything female. Even the mules aren't safe."

Desperation surged through Alena as the man before her shook his head once more and struggled to understand the situation. She tugged at the knot of hair still clenched in his fist.

"Lineas, let me go. My son needs me."

"How got you this message that he's ill? It could be a trick. The gates are shut tight, and the centurion in charge would have reported any opening to me."

While Alena tried frantically to think of some plausible explanation, he leaned down to peer into her face.

"What in Hades is going on here, Alena? Where's Marcus?" Suspicion sharpened his voice.

"Let me go, Lineas. Please."

"Nay. I'll take you back to your quarters and check with Marcus. If he desires that you travel through this black night to your son, I'll accompany you."

"He sleeps, Lineas. He drank too much wine at the festival. Please, don't delay me further."

Alena wanted to scream with frustration when the tribune sucked in a sharp breath. She bit her lip, realizing her mistake at once. Marcus was never in his cups, at least not that she had ever seen. He was too disciplined ever to let his men see him thus, and Lineas knew it. The tribune let go of her hair, only to take her arm in a hard hold. Unceremoniously he pulled her after him through the darkened streets.

He gave the guard outside the prefect's quarters a curt order to stand by, then strode into the house. Alena refused to meet the guard's surprised stare, or those of the servants who stumbled from their beds at the noise. She gave a silent prayer of thanks when Lineas slammed shut the heavy wooden door to their chamber behind them and dropped the bolt.

"What did you do to him?"

The words came at her, low and cold and simmering with wrath. She looked to where Lineas pointed, at the huge form of her lord sprawled naked across the bed. He must have thrown off the furs she'd covered him with. Even from across the wide chamber, she could see how deathly pale he looked.

For one endless moment, Alena felt her heart stop in her breast. Great Mother, had she given him too much of the sleeping herb? He should be resting peacefully. Instead, he lay as if ready for a bier. She should have asked Nelwyn how much to dose him with, she thought in sudden, desperate fear.

Lineas grabbed both of her arms and shook her, hard. "You bitch, what did you give him?"

"Only the herbs Nelwyn left here weeks ago, when my shoulder pained me too much to sleep. I swear it, Lineas." As shaken now as Lineas was angry, Alena almost sobbed the words up at him. "I only wanted him to sleep a few hours."

Lineas flung her away from him and went to lean over his captain. Alena followed, too frightened to pay any attention to the angry look he shot her. He took hold of one of the captain's arms and heaved, trying to pull the unconscious man to his feet. Alena choked back a cry when Marcus slid heavily back to the bed. Lineas grunted and tried again. This time, Alena grabbed his other arm and pulled with all her might. Both of them nearly tumbled to the floor under the captain's dead weight.

"Put his arm across your shoulder— No, your good one, you stupid female. Now walk with me. We've got to wake him. Unless you want me to send for the physician and have it spread through the camp that you tried to poison the commander, you'd best pray we wake him soon."

Chapter Twenty

For the first time in her life, Alena wished for pain. She stared with unseeing eyes at the stunted landscape in front of her, oblivious of trees twisted and bare in the cold wind and rock-hard clumps of earth thrown up as horses galloped by. Only when Megarric rode past and waved wildly did she rouse herself and wave back. Blinking back unaccustomed tears, she watched her son wheel smartly and lean forward to charge the targets set well down the field. She huddled in her fur cloak, miserable beyond belief.

She wished the Roman would beat her. Or starve her. Or lock her in their quarters. She wished he would do anything except continue to treat her with such coldness. Although she would never have believed it during those long years with her brutal first husband, she was coming to realize that there was another kind of pain, and that it hurt almost as much as being struck with a heavy fist.

Stubborn pride kept her from admitting to Marcus how much his coldness hurt, even after all these weeks. Even when Nelwyn counseled her to go to him and beg his forgiveness. Even when her own heart ached each time he took her quickly, without the love play she'd grown to enjoy, as if he needed relief but didn't particularly care who or what provided it. At his command, she still slept in his bed, but she found none of the warmth and companionship she'd experienced there before.

In public, he still treated her with respect, standing by her side at ceremonial functions like the one yesterday, when they had celebrated the beginning of March, the month most sacred to military men. Yet even when they stood side by side, he was apart from her. More and more he devoted himself to his duties, driving his men and burying himself in plans for the coming campaign to the north.

Although she'd lost Marcus, Alena had regained a measure of the tribune's trust. That long, horrible night they labored together, dragging Marcus up and down the sleeping room, bathing his face and hands with cool water, murmuring fervent prayers to their respective gods, they'd gone beyond lady and lord, Roman and Lopocare. They'd found a common bond in their utter determination to keep his friend, her husband, alive. She knew Lineas had tried, in the weeks since that awful night, to tell Marcus of her own efforts to fight the effects of the drug. She'd overheard them arguing late one evening when they'd come back together from some function or other. Although the words had been indistinct, enough of them had come through for her to know her rash act had destroyed the fragile trust between her and her husband forever.

Alena sighed and buried her nose in the soft white fur of her cloak. Mayhap a visit to Nelwyn would help.

"I will not discuss my wife or my treatment of her with you, Lineas. I tell you as a friend and as your superior, hold your tongue."

Marcus stared coldly at the angry man in front of him.

"You may be my superior, but you're a pigheaded ass of a friend. Don't you realize the entire camp wonders at the way you treat your lady? Especially since you couldn't keep your hands off her not two months ago."

"Let them wonder. And shut your mouth."

"Marcus, I tell you this—"

"Cease, Lineas Flavius." The hard words stopped the younger man in midsentence. "We have more important matters to worry about than one female. Assemble the officers in the headquarters within an hour. That's all."

Marcus stood stiff and unyielding until the tribune saluted and left. When the door slammed behind him, it took all the iron discipline Marcus possessed not to pick up the gold replica of his legionary eagle and heave it at the wall. The urge to smash something ate at his innards like carrion feasting on rotten flesh.

He knew full well that his frustration was due solely to his wife. How could he feel such anger toward her, yet want her so badly that his hands shook whenever he was near her? How could he have let himself trust her, have let down his guard so that she could overcome him so effortlessly? His rage at her duplicity did not lessen with time, nor with the knowledge that no one else knew of his stupidity. None but he and Lineas were aware of what she had done. And the Lady Nelwyn, whom Alena had insisted on sending for that morning when he was still too weak to protest.

Marcus knew his anger simmered unabated for so long because he'd come close to losing himself completely. He'd thought he knew her so well, thought he could read her every expression. Like a fool, he'd believed his wooing and gentle hand had tempered her wildness. And then to be taken in by a ploy the veriest idiot would have seen through! It would be a long time before he trusted anyone, especially any woman, again.

Pushing the turmoil that had plagued him for the past two months from his mind, he forced himself to concentrate on the plans laid out on his desk. By the time his officers were assembled, he had himself back under control.

"We leave in three weeks. The latest reports say the snows have melted enough to allow our wagons and siege engines to pass. Our main column will cross the Tay here and strike straight for the Selgovae stronghold at Eilon Hill. The second column, from the Ninth *Hispania* Legion, will circle to the east. Unless this Beorht rides out to meet us elsewhere, we will take him by main assault on his stronghold."

"When will the Ninth begin their move?" Lineas kept his voice even.

Marcus frowned. "They should've sent word last week that they're ready to leave camp at Lindum. I've sent riders south with queries for the commander. We should hear something within the next few days."

"Captain, this barbarian stronghold looks to be impregnable."

"Aye, it's well defended, not so much by man-made defenses as by its location."

"If we are to believe the two prisoners taken last week, the fortress has never been taken."

"Men whose feet are being held over flames will say anything," Marcus reminded the officer. "But I don't underestimate the task ahead. It will be difficult." He leaned over to study the leather map closely.

"See here, how Eilon Hill is set on a promontory? These two wide rivers rush south on either side of the cliff. The only reasonable approach is from the north, where the land slopes up to form the cliff. That's why the Ninth will circle east, pass the fort, and double back to assault from the north. Our forces will encircle the base of the cliff. The two special squads we've trained will scale the sheer face of the cliff and be the first over their ramparts. The rest will follow on rope ladders.

"You will see that your men carry extra lengths of rope in addition to their regular load of armor and weapons. I hope to take this bastard in his den, but don't discount the possibility he may pick his own ground. We must be prepared for battle anytime and any place once the march north begins."

Marcus threw himself into final preparations for the campaign, as much to avoid Alena as to see to the thousands of details necessary to put his legion on the march. He spent most of his days and the long hours of the night closeted with his officers. Dispatches from the governor urged him to press north, even as they ranted about the lack of initiative and outright disloyalty of the other commanders. Of the four legions stationed in Britannia, Maximus could trust only the Seventh, he wrote. And still no word came that the Ninth was preparing for the march.

"I like it not, Lineas."

The tribune watched with troubled eyes as Marcus paced his office the night before they were scheduled to leave.

"The commander of the Ninth sends bland assurances that he will 'follow his orders, consistent with the needs of the empire.'"

"'Tis this trouble over Nero, Marcus, I know it. By Hades, half the empire is against Nero since he hied himself off to Hellas and walled himself up with pretty boys and spouting orators. Rumor has it that the governor of Gaul urges Maximus to join in the rebellion. But the other legions here will not follow Maximus to the privy, much less in rebellion against our emperor."

"I know, I know, Lineas. Nor will I join in any such madness. As yet, Maximus does not openly advocate rebellion. He has not the guts to do so."

Marcus slapped a rolled leather map against his leg impatiently while he paced. "But if we don't press forward now, when we're ready and most likely to catch this bastard Beorht weakened after the long, hard winter, we'll lose the edge. Maximus himself urges me to go, despite the uncertainty with the other legions."

"We can't go without the Ninth, Marcus. Even the most conservative estimate shows this barbarian's forces outnumber ours four to one."

"We can go, and we will. Not having the Ninth's strength will make the task much more difficult, but I will not allow the Seventh to be recorded by the scribes as a legion that shirked its duty."

"Marcus, 'tis suicide."

"Nay. Reckless, mayhap, and daring, but I'll put my men up against this savage any day. No more arguments, Lineas. You know in your heart you'd do the same. Come, let us join the others in the mess and see if there's any ale left. We might as well enjoy ourselves while we can."

The next morning, Marcus stood beside his wife in the cold, damp air. His impassive face gave no hint of the ferocity with which he'd taken her as dawn streaked the sky above the camp. Even with half a barrel of ale in him, he hadn't been able to bring himself to speak the words of peace that his imminent departure urged. Instead, he'd shaken her awake and covered her body with his. He'd stayed hard and hot and hungry, arching over her and slamming against her softness again and again. Half of him had wondered why she didn't fight him, but the other half had exulted in her wild responses and sobbing, panting cries when he took her to her peak, relentlessly, repeatedly. There had been no words between them when they finished, but he'd held her hard against him and hadn't loosed her until dawn streaked the sky.

He stood beside her now in the watery light, watching the sacrifices made to propitiate the gods, but breathing in only her clean, tangy scent. One of his hands was clenched around a small package. Throughout the long ceremony, he worried the leather-wrapped package, turning it over and over in his fingers. Gripping it tight, he strode forward to exhort his massed troops to victory. His breath hovered on the frost-filled air as he told them of the glorious battles to come and the honor they would bring Rome and their legion. He finished his rousing speech to a roar of cheers and hoarse battle cries. While the centurions lined their men up to depart, the commander bade his wife farewell.

"Here, Lady Wife. I would have you wear this."

"What is it?" Alena looked down in surprise at the small package in his hand.

"Not shackles, if that's what you fear. Though 'tis what you deserve."

Alena's eyes lit with the green fire he knew so well. Her words spilled forth, as if bursting from a dam.

"Oh, for the love of all the gods! You are the most stubborn, pigheaded fool that ever walked the earth! I'm tired of slinking about and feeling guilty over that accursed night. And after this morning, I thought you had put it behind you, as well."

Marcus felt a dull heat creep up his cheeks. Half the damn squadron of light cavalry leaned forward in their saddles, listening with great interest to Alena's steadily rising voice.

"Be quiet, wife. This morning was to remind you of your place and to keep you stiff and sore and out of trouble for the weeks I'll be gone. Though I doubt that last is possible," he muttered.

"You bastard! I hope you take an arrow in that fat prick of yours. I hope your horse stumbles so much you get boils and saddle sores the size of oranges on your arse. I hope— Umph!"

Marcus heard his men's shouted laughter as he silenced the woman in the only way he knew worked with her. When he lifted his mouth from hers, she was panting and gasping for breath.

"Here, take the damned gift." His fingers tore away the leather wrapping. "I had it made as an offering for the New Year, but felt disinclined to give it then."

At the New Year, he'd still been sick as a dog from her drugging, and more inclined to horsewhip his wife than give her gifts. Without waiting for the protest hovering on her lips, he grabbed her hand and shoved a ring over the middle finger. He folded her hand into a fist, wrapped his own around it and held them both up between their bodies.

"I should be back within a month. And when I do come back, if I hear you have not behaved with the circumspection of a vestal maiden, I swear I will beat you black on one side and blue on the other."

"You pompous ass."

The words were low and quiet, but held an unmistakable hint of relieved laughter. Inexplicably Marcus felt the day lighten around him. He looked down into Alena's gleaming eyes and kissed her again, hard.

Five weary days later, Marcus halted his troops on the crest of a high hill. Ahead of him, for as far as the eye could see, stretched swirling mists and dark, rolling hills. He twisted in his wooden saddle and looked back. Behind him, the long length of the Roman column snaked down the hill into the distance, until it, too, was swallowed by the gray mist. Marcus sat calmly in the saddle while a scout rode toward him at a furious pace and reined his horse to a dancing stop just paces away.

"Ave, Prefect. Centurion Catullus sends word that the way is clear for two leagues yet. He has dispersed the first cohort of infantry in a defensive perimeter and set the vanguard to preparing camp in a flat valley just over the next hill. There is a river to cross, swollen with the winter's snows, but fordable."

"Well done, soldier. Take word back to Catullus the main body of troops arrives within an hour."

Marcus shifted in his saddle as the troop rode off. Bracing himself on one of the four wooden pommels, he lifted his backside up for a brief respite. He smiled when he remembered Alena's fervent prayer that his posterior be afflicted with boils.

Away from her distracting presence, he'd had the long hours of the march to think about her, and about them. Mayhap he'd been too severe. He suspected his pride was hurt as much as his faith in his wife. The ring he'd given her was his first attempt to heal the breach. He'd finish the task when he returned.

Calling to the trumpeters to signal forward march, he led his men to the flowing river. Sending half the cavalry upstream to break the force of the current and the other half downstream to catch any equipment carried away in the crossing, he sat on the near bank and watched the mass of infantry struggle through the frigid, chest-high water. The men piled their gear in their shields and balanced the lot on their heads, but more than one lost his footing and his baggage. It would take hours to sort out the many bundles caught floating down the river.

Finally the long column wound its way onto the high plain where they would camp. Marcus noted with approval that the pioneers had already completed the first earthen rampart around the plain and laid stones to mark lines for tents. The men would soon have the leather tents erected and their first hot meal since the previous eve in their bellies. With weary satisfaction, he rode to the officers' encampment.

"Any word of the Ninth?"

"Nay, Lineas. I received another dispatch from His Excellency, Governor Maximus, however."

Marcus stretched his long legs out in front of him with a tired grunt. Dampness and hard days in the saddle wreaked havoc on the old injury to his knee. He massaged it absently while the tribune settled himself on a camp stool.

"Well, what is it this time?" Lineas asked. "Two days ago a frantic, exhausted rider brings us an urgent message to turn back and go to the governor's aid. Less than an hour later another, even more exhausted horseman comes with word to press on, that the Twentieth Legion rebels but the Ninth holds and will come to us."

Marcus tossed him a small scroll. "Supposedly Maximus has settled his differences with Caesus Pontius, commander of the Twentieth. The governor swears he will not join with the governor of Gaul against Nero. And he's ordered the Ninth to head north with all speed."

"Think you they will arrive in time?"

"Nay. I've tangled with this Beorht twice now. All my instincts tell me he will not let us take the battle to him. He will choose his own time and ground. And it will be soon."

Marcus took no satisfaction in the fact that his grim prediction proved true when the first waves of screaming, blue-painted warriors came streaming over a low hill two days later. Just moments before, galloping scouts had brought word that the vanguard was fighting off a vicious assault from the north. Marcus signaled the trumpeters to sound the attack just as the main body of the enemy broke cover and charged. The ground rumbled with the thunder of chariots and pounding horses. A hoarse roar of war cries filled the air, accompanied by an ear-splitting din as swords beat against shields and chariot sides.

"Great Jupiter!"

Over the rising tumult, Marcus heard the tribune's low words. He gave his friend a quicksilver grin. "Looks like Beorht invited all the tribes of the north to this little party."

"Aye. May Mars guide your hand and Hercules give you strength, Marcus."

"And you, Lineas." The prefect lowered the face guard of his helmet. With a vicious kick, he goaded his horse into full gallop.

Chapter Twenty-One

"Great Mother, will you please cease your pacing!"

Alena turned to look at Nelwyn in surprise. Rarely did her sister's calm voice ever contain a hint of exasperation. "I'm sorry. I didn't realize my restlessness disturbed you."

"Nay, it does not disturb me," Nelwyn replied with a droll look. "I just do not wish to have the stones in my floor replaced. You are wearing such deep ruts in them, I am like to trip."

A reluctant laugh bubbled in Alena's throat, and she crossed the room to throw herself into the hidebound chair beside the older woman.

"'Tis good to hear you laugh again, child."

"Oh, Nelwyn, I've not had much to make me feel merry of late. That accursed husband of mine has sent not one private word to me since he left on his campaign. The only message I've received was through the quartermaster, telling me to send an extra levy of grain from our winter stores. They've found less forage than anticipated on the march."

"I don't recall you ever being distraught because you had no word from Dugald during his absences."

Alena flushed. It was true she'd felt only relief when her first husband left on his eternal tribal wars or raids north. But she wasn't quite ready to admit, even to herself, how different this second marriage of hers was. How much she cared what happened to the pigheaded Roman she'd been wedded to. She cast about in her mind for some response that Nelwyn would not see through immediately.

"Nay, don't try to find excuses for how you feel, child. When you're ready, you will hear what your heart tells you."

Sighing, Alena twisted the gold ring encircling her middle finger. A bloodred carnelian the size of a pigeon's egg gleamed dully in the early morning light. The heavy ring weighted down her hand and reminded her constantly of the man who'd given it to her.

"It seems my heart is as confused as my head," she said reluctantly. "My pride would not let me cry forgiveness for that accursed solstice eve, but pride has been poor comfort when my husband turns away from me in the night with barely a word. I think mayhap I have more of my mother in me than I would wish. It seems this Roman has awakened my passions, and now I—I crave his hands on me."

"Only his hands, Alena? Do you miss only his body?"

Alena sprang out of the chair and resumed her pacing. "I don't know!" she wailed. "I don't know what I miss. The stubborn mule did not smile or say one kind word to me for two months. And just when I had resigned myself to a cold bed for the rest of my days, he kisses me in front of his men and gives me this token."

She whirled and went to kneel at Nelwyn's feet. "I don't know what to make of the words carved on this ring. Marcus said he purchased it for me before…before I nearly killed him. But surely he would not have given it to me now did he not feel some softening in his heart."

"*Anima Mea.*" Nelwyn murmured low as she rubbed her finger lightly over the letters carved in the bevel that held the gleaming red stone. "My heart."

"My soul. My being. My person. My chattel! I don't know what it means, Nelwyn, and every man I ask at the camp gives me different answers."

"You must ask the one who gave it to you. Only he can tell you its significance."

"Aye, if I ever get the chance to ask him anything." Alena let her head sink down on Nelwyn's knee. Fears and doubts swamped her again. "I fear he may never return to me from this benighted campaign. The men at camp talk of nothing but the revolt of the other legions in Britannia against the governor.

They fear that the Ninth will not come. Indeed, it is almost too late now."

"Have you no faith in your lord's abilities?"

"Aye, of course. But he's only a man, and outnumbered four to one by Beorht's forces."

"At one time you would have been pleased to see Beorht defeat the Romans and drive them from our lands." Nelwyn's calm words struck into Alena's soul.

"Aye." She raised her head and spoke slowly, as if bringing dark thoughts into the light of day for the first time. "But of late I've come to see the wisdom of my mother's path. She's ruled with the blessing of Rome for nigh on three decades. The Brigantes have not lost their independence, or their ways—except for the practice of Druid rites. 'Tis only when rebels like Dugald, or Beorht, think to challenge Rome's might that disaster follows. These past months since the Roman and I wed have brought unheard-of peace to our land. Even the Lopocare lords are ready to swear fealty to Rome, through Megarric."

"So you've given your loyalty, if not your heart, to Rome."

Alena looked up into Nelwyn's brown eyes. She saw no condemnation, no scorn, only calm acceptance. "Do you think me weak to have given in to this man? To Rome? Do you still hate them for forbidding our rites?"

A soft sigh escaped Nelwyn's lips, and she turned to look out the open window. Early-spring sunlight danced on green shoots just showing in the garden outside her chambers. She gazed at the scene for long, silent moments. Finally she turned back and stroked the tawny head at her knee.

"Look, child. See the green pushing up from the dark earth? A new life cycle begins. The gods give us this wondrous gift each year, to begin afresh. There was turmoil and scorched earth and stunted crops for many years until your lord arrived. Now the grass springs up anew, and our people are at peace. Many of our old priests and priestesses are gone, but mayhap it is as well. 'Tis time for a new way."

"The Roman way?"

Nelwyn leaned her head against her high-backed chair and smiled. "Nay, not the Roman way, nor yet the way of our fathers. A new way, where we take from both to build anew. With

you and this lord of yours to guide Megarric, mayhap the new
will be stronger than the old."

Alena felt much of her own doubt and insecurity fade with
her sister's soft words. The two of them sat, quiet and filled
with their own thoughts, until a slave came to tell Alena her
escort awaited.

"I must go, Nelwyn. I promised to take Megarric to ride this
afternoon. He, too, frets at the absence of my lord. He's come
to see the Roman as his own special captain of the guard."

Alena found Sergeant Praxas waiting at the head of the small
troop. Giving him a speculative look, she allowed the beefy,
red-faced man to lift her into the saddle. He'd grumbled and
complained for days when ordered to stay behind and take
personal charge of the Lady Alena's protection, but her teasing—and Ethelyn's saucy taunts—had soon removed the scowl
from his face, if not the restlessness from his soldier's heart.

"Hail, Praxas. I'm glad to see you this morn. Come, ride
ahead with me. I would speak with you."

The sergeant swallowed convulsively and threw Alena a
nervous look. She suspected he knew well what was coming.

"Ethelyn could not attend me this morning. She was bent
over a bowl in her quarters, retching. When I went to see her,
she confessed she's been ill for some weeks now. It seems her
belly swells with your child."

"Ah, Lady...'tis possible."

"'Tis more than possible, Sergeant," Alena told him dryly.
"'Tis indeed fact. What do you intend to do about it?"

"I don't know, Lady. I've tried to tell Ethelyn that common
soldiers are forbidden to marry while on active duty. 'Tis a
harsh law, but one made to prevent distractions or divided
loyalties."

"Pah! If your leaders think laws can prevent men and
women from coupling, they must all be too old or too twisted
in their tastes to know what happens outside their musty
chambers."

She paused, and Nelwyn's words came full-force into her
mind. "'Tis time to change such old and contrary ways. You
will take Ethelyn to wife, even if we must change the old laws
and customs. I shall see to it."

Praxas grinned, showing wide-gapped teeth. "If my lady so commands. In truth, I told her many times I wanted to take her into my keeping, but she would not leave you, Lady. I've even rented a house in the settlement outside camp, and have all in readiness."

Alena smiled at him. "Well done, Sergeant. We will celebrate your nuptials with all ceremony and feasting when the men return from the campaign."

The grin faded from the beefy face opposite her. "Aye . . . if they return."

"Is it so desperate? Tell me truthfully, Praxas. I get only carefully worded reports from the centurion left in charge of the camp. He does not want to worry me."

"Aye, Lady." The sergeant nodded glumly. " 'Tis truly desperate. Without reinforcements from the Ninth, our men will be overwhelmed."

"That cursed Ninth! May the gods take the soul of their commander and scatter it to the winds! May it never find another warrior to reside in!"

The easy comradeship of the past few moments vanished. The two rode silently for a while, each wrapped in their own thoughts. Alena glanced up as the timber walls of the camp came into view. " 'Twill be good to get home," she muttered absently, still thinking of the perfidious Ninth. "I rode out early this morn, and would break my fast before riding with Megarric."

Praxas nodded, then looked at her in surprise when she pulled her startled mount to a sudden halt in the middle of the cobbled road.

Alena stared up at the towering walls of the Roman camp, set high on its hill. Her thoughts raced. When had this place, which had once been her prison, become "home"? When had she ceased to see the walls as barriers between Romans and Lopocares and started to take comfort in the security they represented for her, and for her people? Even with the pain of the past few months, when her lord had treated her so coldly, she'd never felt rejected here nor wished to run away. The men had taken her to their hearts, and somehow, sometime, she'd taken them to hers. In her mind, they were no longer conquerors, but simply men. She knew half the soldiers by name and understood that each had his own wants and needs, weaknesses and strengths.

As she stared up at the high ramparts, Alena felt the uncharacteristic confusion that had plagued her these past months dissolve. She straightened in her saddle. She would be damned to eternal darkness if she'd moon about any longer like some whey-faced, timid maiden. Her mind churned furiously, and a bold idea took possession of her.

"Why do you dawdle here, Praxas? Come, I have much to do this day." She gave her pony a hard kick and rode off, leaving the bewildered sergeant and his men to scramble after her.

Alena flew into the headquarters building and called imperiously for her husband's chief scribe. When the man came running, he found her sitting behind the captain's broad desk, brows drawn together in fierce concentration.

"Come in, come in, man! I would have you write a message for me. I wish to send it with all speed to my lady mother, Queen Cartimandua. Here, sit you down and take my words."

Never doubting for one moment that the scribe would take his orders from her, Alena spoke fast and furiously. The man begged her to slow down several times, but still wax chips flew in all directions as he scratched frantically on a coated wood tablet with a sharp stylus. When Alena finished, he read the message back to her and corrected it where she desired.

"I want this in my mother's hands before the moon wanes, do you understand? Send your swiftest messengers, with several changes of horse."

When the man nodded, she strode out of the headquarters and crossed the *via principalis* to her quarters. For the first time in weeks, she smiled, a wide, natural, happy smile. By the gods, it felt good to be doing something again, instead of moping about like some helpless ninny.

"Ethelyn! Bring your cloak. I go to ride with Megarric, and would that you accompany me."

The maid came running at her shout, her red hair flying behind her. "Me?" she squeaked. "Lady, you know I cannot ride."

"Aye, I know."

Ethelyn blinked at her dry tone.

"I've ordered my chariot. We'll take it to the valley where the old herb woman dwells and see what she has to settle that rambunctious babe. Sergeant Praxas escorts us. I believe he would speak with you. Mayhap on the way back you and he can take a different path and a slower pace."

Ethelyn's face glowed a shade brighter than her hair as she grabbed her cloak and followed her mistress outside.

Alena reveled in the wind and the crisp, clean air as she guided her vehicle along the dirt road leading north. Megarric rode cheerfully ahead of her on the narrow road, Praxas beside him. The half-dozen troopers comprising her escort followed behind. They made good time to the old crone's hut, and the women spent a contented hour wandering around her herb garden. This early in the spring, when traces of frost still dusted the earth each morning, only a few hardy shoots straggled upward to bask in the afternoon sun. But the stooped, ancient woman had a plentiful supply of dried herbs and gave Alena instructions for a soothing root tea to settle Ethelyn's stomach. While the women talked the business of life in the small, dark hut, Megarric and the soldiers sampled home-brewed ale and tossed javelins idly in the small clearing behind the hut. Alena was just tasting the ale herself when hoarse shouts and Megarric's high-pitched screams shattered the afternoon stillness.

Alena thrust aside the thick leather that covered the door and raced outside. Bright sunlight blinded her after the darkness of the hut. Her eyes watered as she strained to peer through the brilliant light toward the unmistakable sound of battle. Whirling, she ran toward the sound.

Before she'd taken more than a few paces her vision cleared. Fear, harsh and metallic, closed her throat. A dozen or more naked warriors surrounded the small band of Romans. The soldiers were backed into a tight circle, with Megarric in the center, fighting ferociously. But they were no match for the overwhelming numbers attacking them. Even as Alena raced forward, she saw two soldiers go down with spears through their throats. Halfway across the yard, she heard a quick movement behind her. She whirled, saw the flash of an iron sword descending, and then knew no more.

* * *

She woke to darkness all around her. And pain. Blinding, white-hot shafts of pain slashed across her head with every jarring step her horse took. The agony in her head warred with a burning ache in her shoulders. Her head dangled downward, and her wrists were bound by a rope that was stretched taut under her horse's belly and lashed to her ankles. The ungiving wood of her saddle slammed into her middle with every step her horse took. She felt nausea welling up and swallowed frantically behind the thick rag stuffed into her mouth. Did she vomit now, slung upside down across the back of a horse like this, she would choke on the contents of her own stomach. Her horse stumbled slightly, its hooves ringing on stone, and pain lanced through her in slicing, searing waves. Alena moaned.

Dimly she heard another horse draw up alongside hers. A hand thrust into her hair and pulled her head up painfully, bending back her neck until Alena was sure it would break. Involuntary tears slid out beneath her lids.

"The whore is awake."

A harsh voice rang in her ears. Her horse stopped abruptly. She felt a sawing on the rope binding her wrists, and then rough hands wrapped themselves around her waist and hauled her backward off the horse. She tumbled to the ground and screamed silently into her gag as her bruised body hit the hard earth. She lay panting, fighting waves of dizziness.

"Bring the child and the other woman."

Alena tried desperately to open her eyes. One lid was crusted shut with what she suspected was dried blood from the pounding wound on her temple. Finally she worked it open, and her vision cleared enough to fix on the body behind the voice. He stood over her, one foot planted firmly on either side of her crumpled form. She frowned, straining with every ounce of her being to bring the hazy figure into focus. Gradually the blackness drifted away and she made out the details of her captor. He was tall and naked and covered with thick blue paint. She had never seen him before, but from his markings she knew he was of the Selgovae tribe.

"Mama! Mama!"

Alena jerked her head at the sound of Megarric's frightened cries and choked against her gag as pain slashed through her head once more. She breathed deeply through her nose, opened her eyes and turned her head again, slowly. Her son was only a few feet away. When he saw her open her eyes, Megarric struggled to break loose from the man who held him. Ethelyn lay sobbing on the ground behind him, a thick rope around her neck tethering her to a naked warrior.

"Sit up, woman."

Alena brought her gaze back to the man straddling her. His lips twisted in a grim smile, and he reached down to grab a thick skein of her hair. Alena swallowed another silent scream when he pulled her up. With a rough jerk, he yanked the gag out of her mouth.

She tried desperately to swallow. Her dry throat closed against the attempts and blocked her breath. She almost sobbed in relief when the man above her grunted in disgust, then bent and held a skin to her lips. Viciously he tilted it and filled her mouth with sour, brackish water until she gasped and choked and turned her head away.

"Listen to me, woman. We take you and your whelp north, to King Beorht. We'll ride without stopping this night, until we're outside your borders. I want no whining or woman's cries from you, or I will not hesitate to knock you senseless again."

"Wait." The cry rasped painfully in her sore throat. Alena swallowed convulsively, and tried again. "Wait. Listen to me. Take me, if Beorht so commands, but send my son and the maid back. They cannot make such a ride."

When the warrior whirled angrily and hauled her to her feet, Alena called on every ounce of iron strength she possessed to hold herself rigid.

"Listen, you Roman whore, you'll give no orders, nor open your mouth unless I bid you do so. The puling Lopocare men may bow and scrape to one who spreads her legs for their conquerors, but I would as soon slit your throat as not. Do you think to survive this journey, keep your mouth shut."

Alena gritted her teeth as the man dragged her to her horse. She gave shaky thanks to the gods when he ordered her brusquely to mount, then lashed her ankles with a taut rope under her horse's belly. At least she would not be thrown across the saddle once again. Even with her hands bound behind her and rope biting into her ankles, riding upright would help her clear her head of its dizzying pain.

True to his word, the bandit leader drove them hard and fast, avoiding all villages and farmsteads. Instead, he kept them to the forests and deserted hillsides for hour after grueling hour. Time passed in a haze of pain and gut-wrenching fear for Alena. She turned constantly to check on Megarric, who rode white-faced and silent between two warriors. Ethelyn was mounted behind another rider, her wrists bound around his waist. A rag muffled her dry sobs, but tears drew tracks down her dirtied face.

Alena was given no chance to speak to either her son or her maid during the whole nightmarish journey. When they stopped to water the horses late the second night, Alena tried to slip next to Megarric. The leader of the band backhanded her viciously and knocked her into the stream. Thereafter, icy wetness added to her other aches and grinding pains.

Finally, when she'd lost all track of time and distance, they stopped on the crest of a hill. In a deep valley below lay a sprawling encampment. Hide tents were spread haphazardly across a long vale, and thousands of men huddled around cook fires in the early-morning cold. The band's leader studied the distant campfires for long moments, as if waiting for some sign. Eventually he grunted and kicked his horse onward. The weary band followed him down the hill, past picketed guards and into the maze of tents and milling horses.

Chapter Twenty-Two

Her captor sliced through the rope binding Alena's ankles, and she slid from her horse to crumple to the ground. She sat on the cold, muddy earth for long moments, too weary and numbed to do more than watch as Megarric was lifted down. The boy's lips trembled, but he met his mother's steady look and bit back his tears.

"So, Alena, we meet again."

With great effort, Alena lifted her head. Early-dawn light filtered through thin clouds and outlined the towering figure standing before her. But even if she could not see his features, she knew his voice well.

"Beorht."

The giant stood silent for long moments, staring down at her crumpled form. Alena felt a surge of disgust at her own weakness and pulled her knees under her. Awkwardly she pushed herself upright with her bound hands. The man before her made no move to help. When she finally stood on shaky legs, she still had to look up into the morning sun to see his face. He did not speak, and her pride would not allow her to. She raised her chin and waited.

Beorht reached out and took her bound arm in a cruel grip. "Come. I have much to say to you."

Alena dug in her heels. "Nay, I will not leave my son."

He turned on her, blue eyes blazing and long, flame-colored hair flying in the morning sun. One corner of his flowing mustache lifted in a snarl. "You will never set eyes on him again, nor any other living person, do you dare defy me."

Her chin went up another notch. She had laughed and ridden with and bested this man at bow and javelin too many times in their childhood for her to cower before him now.

"Your cub will not be harmed," Beorht finally ground out, then yanked her after him again. She nearly tripped over her own feet when he pushed her into a round leather tent. In the dim interior Alena made out the figure of a naked woman cowering on thin, rancid furs.

"Get out."

The woman jumped at Beorht's curt command. She clutched a mangy fur to her breast and scrambled past them on all fours. Beorht aimed a kick at her bony flanks, which sent her flying out of the tent face forward. He turned back to Alena and whipped out a long, vicious dagger.

Alena met his eyes steadily. After a long moment, he grinned and sawed through the ropes binding her wrists. When she raised trembling hands to rub her bruised skin, Beorht kicked a wooden stool across the small tent and sat, watching her closely. Even sitting, he topped her by a head, Alena noted. Like all his tribe, he wore no clothes, not even a loincloth. In battle he would catch his man-parts in a leather pouch and tie the sack to his waist, but now only smeared blue streaks covered his massive form. He scratched absently at his belly and surveyed her with cold blue eyes.

"I did not think to find you holding your head so high after whoring for the Roman captain these months."

Alena flushed. "He is my lord. I honor my vows to him...as I did to Dugald."

It was Beorht's turn to flush as remembered anger and frustration stained his cheeks. Only he and Alena knew how many times he had pressed the budding child bride to lay with him. Once he'd even tried force. But Alena had been as fierce then as she was now.

"Well, I will rid you of this unwanted husband soon. Half his army lies rotting in the sun even now, on the plain to the west. The rest will soon fall to my sword."

Alena felt the blood drain from her face. "When did you battle? We had no word."

"Three days ago. My forces swept over them like the tides on the marshes," he bragged.

"It must have been a very low tide," Alena said scornfully, "if you must fight them again. You had thrice their number, and more."

She wished desperately she'd kept her words to herself when Beorht rose, arm raised. She flung up her hands to block the blow, but even so the force of it knocked her to the dirt floor. She landed on her elbow, and the pain shot up her arm in fresh, hot waves. Beorht knelt on one knee beside her and tugged cruelly at her hair until her face was only inches from him.

"We are not children any longer, Alena. No more will you taunt me or flay me with your sharp tongue. No more will I hold back my strength or my manhood. You are but a woman, one I have long wanted. Although now I'm not sure I wish to take the leavings of Rome."

His lips pulled back in a vicious snarl. "Why did you not come when I sent for you last summer? Why did you let your bitch of a mother settle you on the Roman?"

Alena resisted the pain of his hard, cruel hand twisting in her hair. She kept her eyes steady, and her voice dripped scorn.

"Mayhap I sensed that you would use me—and the Lopocares—as you do now, with a heavy fist. I did not let you force me as a child, when you blustered and tried your muscles on me, nor will I now."

Beorht's sapphire eyes shone with a cruel light behind thick, surprisingly dark lashes. Alena forced herself not to swallow in fear at the thin sneer twisting his lips.

"Do not presume upon the restraint I used with you when we were children. I was a fool not to take what you flaunted then. If I can bring myself to spill my seed in one who has wallowed with Roman pigs, I may keep you for myself. If not, my men will use you as the whore you are. 'Twill make my victory over the Romans even sweeter when they see what happens to women who sport with them."

"Is that why you brought me here? To make an example of me?"

He freed her hair and flung her to the dirt floor again. "Aye. Your marriage is a desecration. You betrayed yourself and your people. And now you will live to regret it, most bitterly. I'll send your whelp to you so that you may make your farewells. He goes north within the hour as hostage to your behavior."

Alena waited until the tent flap closed behind him before she wrapped her arms around her middle and allowed the tremors of fear and pain she'd held at bay to wrack her body. For all Beorht's pretended disgust, she knew he would lie with her. And she knew the experience would not be pleasant. He was so much like her first husband that her stomach clenched with sick dread. Loud and blustering and quick to take his grunting pleasures, with no thought for the blood and aches left behind. Knowing what was to come was made even worse by the knowledge that the act of coupling didn't have to be so hurtful. That it could be filled with passion and laughter and breathless, blinding pleasure. Marcus had taught her that.

Alena bit her lip to hold back the terror threatening to swamp her when she thought of her husband. She didn't even know whether he lived or not. Beorht spoke of a battle, a near-victory. Surely he would have bragged about it if he'd taken the Roman leader. Surely Marcus could not be dead. She laid her head on her drawn-up knees and took deep, gulping breaths.

By the time Megarric ran into the tent, sobbing for her, she'd calmed herself enough to take him in her arms and stroke his curly head with hands that trembled only slightly. Ethelyn stumbled in behind him and threw herself at her mistress.

"Hush, hush. Come, you two, do not weep so on me. I only just dried out from my dumping in the stream."

Her light words worked with Megarric, who gave a watery chuckle and hiccuped, but Ethelyn continued to sob hysterically. Finally, knowing they didn't have much time, Alena took her arms and shook her.

The maid gulped in heaving, painful breaths. "Oh, Lady, they killed Praxas. I saw him fall, saw them plunge a sword into his stomach and twist it. His blood spewed forth, and...and..."

Alena closed her eyes. Her mind struggled to find the proper words to speed the sergeant's soul out of the darkness and into a warrior worthy of his courage, but no words would come. Promising to give sacrifices for his soul later, she shook the still-sobbing maid again.

"Listen to me! We have not much time. If you would live to birth your babe and avenge his father, you must be strong."

She turned to the wide-eyed, trembling Megarric. "You are to be taken north, as a hostage. Remember you are a king and a most valuable prize. They'll not harm you, only hold you. I will see that Ethelyn goes with you."

She caught her son's small body tight against her chest, her mind churning desperately. "She will stay with you, as your nurse, but you must protect her, my son. Tell them she must sleep in your quarters, that she . . . she was sent to you at birth as a special gift from the gods. She is your nurse, who must see to your needs. The two of you can aid each other until I come. And I *will* come! Do you understand, Megarric? Do you?"

The boy looked at her with wide, frightened eyes, but nodded. Alena pulled him against her breast again and held him there, rocking and crooning old songs, until they came for him.

Marcus stretched out full-length on the narrow stone ledge. He ignored the blade-sharp pieces of shale slicing into his legs and pricking his stomach as he wriggled forward a few more inches to peer over the edge to the scene below. His dark eyes narrowed as he tried to see through the swirls of early-morning fog. Finally satisfied with what his eyes beheld, he signaled to the guide with him and began to edge his way backward with agonizing care. The last thing he wanted to do was dislodge any of the loose stones and send them tumbling down the sheer cliff, alerting the sentries he knew had to be posted nearby.

An hour later, Marcus and the exhausted guide rode into the Roman encampment. In contrast to the scene he'd just surveyed, no cook fires blazed to ward off the chill of the early dawn. Nor did any tents dot the horizon. His army sat huddled in small groups on the hard ground, wrapped in their wool cloaks, chewing stoically on dry rations of smoked meat and hard flat bread washed down with water. The usual noise and bustle of a large army just rising to meet the dawn was missing. No bugles sounded to call the men to their meal, no centurions' harsh voices were raised to give orders or conduct the head count. Even the horses' hooves were muffled with cloth to keep their iron shoes from ringing on the hard stone. Marcus grunted with fierce satisfaction as he rode through the silent rows of huddled men. The only advantage they had now over the horde of barbarians was surprise, and his troops knew it.

"Send runners to gather the cohort commanders." He flung the order to his aide as he dismounted. "And find the senior tribune. I would speak with him immediately."

He paced restlessly while he waited for Lineas, turning his embryonic plan over and over in his mind. When the younger man came hurrying up, Marcus could barely contain his impatience.

"We have the bastard, Lineas! He's trapped himself, like a fox run to ground. I need to work the details of our battle plan with you before the officers assemble."

Marcus grabbed a scroll from the dispatch box his chief scribe carried and spread it on the ground. With a rough piece of charcoal, he made a hurried sketch.

"He's encamped here, in this deep valley two leagues to the north. Sheer mountains rise on one side. The other side has steep, wooded hills. Between the two is a long, rolling plain ending in a lake to the east. The only way out is to the west."

"Why in the world would he put himself in such a position?" Lineas frowned. "This man is no fool. He must know how vulnerable he is there. Think you it is a trap?"

"It could be, but all my instincts tell me no. His camp is strewn across the uneven ground in a haphazard way, and they've thrown up no defenses. I believe he thinks himself secure and withdraws at his own leisurely pace to choose another site for our next meeting. He knows I will come after him, but also knows we suffered great losses and need reinforcements desperately. He can have no idea we are so close."

"Nay, he cannot. I can scarce believe it myself." Lineas shook his head and hunched his shoulders tiredly. "We've shared many desperate times, Marcus, but even I would not have believed you could regroup so quickly after such a bloody battle, with so many losses."

Marcus felt his stomach clench in a surge of anger and utter, implacable determination. For as long as he lived, he would remember the nightmare battle his men had fought. In his mind's eye he could see again wave after wave of blue warriors rushing toward them in wild, undisciplined charges; his ears still rang with the echoes of hoarse shouts and screams of pain, and the incredible din of iron swords battering shields and bones.

His foot soldiers had held, protected by their armor and their interlocking barrier of shields. The ranks of archers behind them had loosed deadly fire on the onrushing enemy. But still they would have been overwhelmed by sheer numbers, had his cavalry not broken through one flank in a mad, desperate charge. Nearly half his mounted forces had been lost before the enemy line finally began to waver, to crash back into itself in the confusion and din. Marcus had led the final charge himself, slashing and stabbing with fierce, deadly satisfaction.

By the time the native forces had withdrawn, the earth was ankle-deep with blood and gore and his men were exhausted. They'd pushed through walls of dead and near-dead, screaming men to pursue the enemy. Marcus had halted the pursuit within minutes. He'd known the natives were not defeated. They had withdrawn to regroup, and would attack again, on another day, in another place. His troops could not pursue and force battle against such a superior force.

When the scouts had brought word two days later that Beorht's army had halted their withdrawal and made temporary camp, he'd pushed his men almost beyond endurance to reach within striking distance. He was determined that on this occasion the time and place of battle would be of his choosing.

He'd moved them forward with as much stealth as a great army could exercise. They marched at night, buried themselves under brush and in ravines during the day. Every sound was muffled, every order whispered, every eye strained in the darkness to follow the man in front and not trip over his heels. And it appeared this desperate march had worked. The enemy sprawled in a disorderly camp, unaware of the Roman forces just a few miles from them.

"There's a narrow path along the cliff face, the one I used this morning. It's wide enough for one man, walking carefully."

Marcus made himself speak slowly, with great precision. He would have only one chance to detail his plan to the officers circled around him, and then they would disperse. If they did not understand, or if any one of them acted precipitately, the whole scheme would fall apart. He turned to his chief engineer.

"Dismantle the light catapults and pick your sharpest gunners."

" 'Tis time."

"Aye," Marcus replied. He sat unmoving for long moments, watching the sun slip slowly behind the wall of the cliff opposite. "Give the signal."

Lineas waved to a tense, waiting band of archers. Within seconds, a flaming arrow sped into the sky. It trailed a plume of gray smoke from the burning, pitch-soaked rags wrapped around its shaft.

Marcus strained to see the distant cliffs. He had moved his forces up as close as he could without alerting the enemy pickets. Foot soldiers were massed in the woods that lined the narrow entrance to the far valley, and the remnants of the cavalry had moved to positions on the far flank, halfway up the steep hills. Now all depended on whether his men had been able to move the clumsy catapults into position on the sheer cliff opposite them.

Suddenly, bright, glowing spheres arced out from the gray cliff walls. They sailed through the deepening blue sky and broke into showers of burning, flaming pitch. Tongues of flame fell to the ground. In the distance, Marcus could hear the first screams of terrified horses and a growing swell of hoarse shouts. Another wave of flaming balls catapulted through the sky. The shouts grew louder, and the sound of pounding hooves rolled toward the waiting troops.

From his position on the hill, Marcus watched the first wave of horsemen come thundering down the valley. He waited. And waited. The men around him shifted nervously, yet still he waited. Slowly he lifted his hand. When the horsemen were halfway past, he dropped his arm. A wall of arrows flew out of the trees and tumbled the front forces to the ground. Those few who escaped the deadly rain rode only a few yards farther, then crashed into brush-covered ditches lined with sharpened stakes. Men and horses screamed as onrushing troops rode into the bodies of their own fallen comrades. Within minutes, a writhing, living, screaming barrier had formed across the neck of the valley. And still the arrows flew.

Marcus led the attack. From the hillsides, his cavalry crashed down on the milling, thrashing warriors. His men fell on the helpless enemy, who could neither go forward, because of the wall of their own fallen, nor back, because of the oncoming waves of mounted warriors.

Less than an hour later, exultant Roman officers crowded around their commander in a small clearing on the hillside.

" 'Twas a slaughter, Captain! They fell so thick and fast we almost ran out of arrows."

"Aye, and our cavalry hardly had to engage! The troopers launched javelins from a safe distance and used swords only on those few who tried to escape up the steep slopes. It's as well they retreated when they did, to give us time to rearm."

"It was like spearing fish in a marble pool, Captain."

Marcus let his officers work through their surging emotions. Their blood flowed hot and thick at the chance to avenge their near-defeat and the loss of so many comrades just a few days ago. When they finished their reports on their portion of the action, Marcus took charge.

"Aye, we have them now. They cannot retreat with the lake at their backs, nor come forward with us blocking the mouth of the valley. We'll give them the rest of this night to let their situation sink in. Tomorrow, we either take their surrender or pick them off man by man until not one of the bastards lives. Tell your men to stay alert this night. I don't think they will try to break out in the darkness, with their own downed warriors blocking them, but be prepared."

Marcus didn't sleep during the long night that followed. He made a circuit of his troops, checking their placement with his officers and speaking hearty words of encouragement to the men. When the first streaks of dawn lightened the sky above, he conducted a solemn ceremony, dedicating this day to Mars. He shared another cold, dry meal with his officers and went over their strategy should the enemy not immediately surrender.

A runner tumbled into the small clearing where the officers gathered and saluted his captain. The man was panting in his eagerness.

"Intelligence sends word back that a lone rider comes forth from the Selgovae camp. They think it is Beorht himself."

Chapter Twenty-Three

"By Jupiter, we've got the bastard. He comes to surrender!" Lineas leapt up, a feral grin on his face.

"Mayhap."

The exultant officers turned at their commander's quiet, speculative tone.

"What else could it be?" Lineas demanded. "The man must know he's trapped."

"It could be a challenge to single combat. By the gods, I would welcome that!" Marcus felt a leap of flame in his belly at the thought.

Lineas stared at his friend, all his previous excitement gone as worry washed across his face.

"Marcus, you cannot. You know the emperor forbade the practice years ago. Rome cannot afford to lose her best commanders, or a great battle, based on single, hand-to-hand combat."

"Aye, I know." Marcus would say no more. Lineas made as if to protest further, but the captain turned away. He called for one of the local guides and swung smoothly into his saddle.

"If it's a trick and I don't return, you have command, Lineas. You know the battle plan. Bring honor to the Seventh."

Marcus rode through the slowly brightening day toward the lone figure who sat, still and arrogant, astride his horse at the entrance to the valley. Gory remnants of the previous evening still littered the narrow vale. Crows and carrion picked at the dead men and horses scattered in grotesque display under the gathering daylight. Moans drifted across the morning air from wounded not yet retrieved. Marcus knew well that the stench would grow unbearable and that the moans would intensify with each passing hour. Closing his mind to the carnage around him, he drew up before the waiting warrior.

"So, Roman, we meet again." The nervous guide interpreted in a low voice.

"So, Beorht of the Selgovae, we meet again."

The red-haired giant was much as Marcus remembered from their brief combat many months ago, during the abortive attempt to steal Alena. He sat his horse easily, his huge, muscled thighs relaxed against the pony's sides. A leather strap around his forehead served to keep his flowing hair from his eyes in combat, but otherwise he wore no coverings. Under its smeared coating of blue paint, his skin gleamed like burnished bronze in the dawn light.

The warrior took his own assessment of the soldier, and finally broke the deadlocked silence between them. "I had planned this meeting between us differently."

"Aye, I can well imagine. From the leisurely way you withdrew and left yourself open to attack, you thought yourself safe. You have learned the hard way not to underestimate Rome's endurance and perseverance."

Beorht straightened in his saddle, shedding some of his lazy nonchalance.

"I will admit you surprised me. But mayhap you underestimate me, as well, Roman."

"Mayhap, although I think not." Marcus leaned forward in his saddle. "You are completely surrounded. I have only to signal, and my men will rain down fire on your camp again from the cliffs. If you try to run from the flames, you will die by arrow or sword."

"Toss your fireballs, Roman. Fill the skies with arrows. I will not surrender, nor will my men."

"Then you will die."

"If the gods will it. But you should know, your whore dies with me."

All pretense of composure gone, Beorht leaned forward, as well. His eyes narrowed and filled with hate. With an abrupt gesture, he tossed a small, glittering object toward the soldier.

Marcus reached out and caught the object in midair. He stared for a long moment at the gold ring, with its glowing bloodred stone. He didn't need to read the inscription carved around the bevel. He'd watched the goldsmith inscribe it himself. His fingers closed around the thick gold, and he raised cold, deadly eyes to the man opposite him.

"What are your terms?"

"I leave within the hour, with all my men and chattel. You and your army remain here for the rest of this day. I will send the woman back when we are clear."

"Know you, if my wife does not come to me alive and whole, I will track you night and day and peel every inch of skin from your body?"

"Do not threaten me, Roman. I honor my oaths. Although in truth you are welcome to the bitch. I thought to amuse myself with her, but find I have no taste for spoiled meat. She has lost her flavor, being so well used by rutting Roman pigs."

With every fiber of his being, Marcus wanted to slash the mocking grin off the face before him. His hand clenched and moved toward his sword, but the knowledge that Alena's life hung in the balance stayed it. He knew a tortured moment of doubt about how she might have come to this man's camp. He pushed back the dark, insidious thought that she might have flown to her old lover and now found herself used by this ruthless savage to save his own hide. Marcus knew, from the cold, evil look in the blue eyes opposite him, that did he not accede to Beorht's terms, Alena would die a slow and painful death in front of his entire legion.

"You have one hour. After that, I attack with my forces." He wheeled his mount and kicked it into a gallop.

Marcus sat rigid astride his restive horse for the next, endless hour. With his officers behind him, he watched the native army ride out of the valley, retrieve their dead and depart. Beorht's men filed past in a long, drawn-out, vulnerable column. Every now and then a derisive taunt rang out as the soldiers called down from their stand on the high hillsides to heckle the departing natives. The Selgovae knights would answer with shouted threats and promises of retribution, but for the most part a heavy, tense stillness hung over the valley.

Marcus strained for some glimpse of a tawny mane amid the milling throng that straggled past below him. He saw several women in torn, dirty robes mounted behind warriors. And one

whose flowing, tangled hair could well have been his wife's, but
he was too distant to be sure. Long after the last wagons disappeared from view, he sat rigid and unmoving, his eyes trained
on the trampled, muddied route leading out of the valley. Lineas kept his men away, knowing well the prefect would not
welcome either their violent curses that the Lady Alena had
been taken by these savages or their unspoken fears that she
would not return.

The sun crept up the morning sky. For the first time in days,
the officers gave the men leave to light fires and cook a hot
meal. With an impatient hand, Marcus waved away his orderly, who tried to bring him food. A light breeze whispered
through the bare branches of the scruffy trees and the sound of
an army laying aside its arms and settling in drifted up all
around him. None of the sounds registered. He didn't hear
anything but the pounding of his own heart and the silent oath
he kept repeating to himself, over and over. Did she not return, the man Beorht would find no sanctuary anywhere on
earth or in the realm of the shades.

Long after the sun had passed its zenith, a lone rider appeared on the far horizon. She slumped low in the saddle, on a
horse that limped along with a slow, uneven gait. Marcus was
beside her within minutes. He reached out to lift her to his
saddle and almost dropped her when she gave a harsh, ragged
moan at the touch of his hands.

When Marcus laid her on his woolen cloak in the shade of a
scrubby, stunted oak tree, Lineas sucked in his breath. "Sweet
mother of the gods!"

"Get the surgeon. And water."

Marcus brushed Alena's filthy, matted hair back from her
bruised face. His stomach clenched as his fingers encountered
crusted blood. The surgeon, a senior sergeant who had worked
his way up from the veterinary corps, brushed him aside and
knelt beside the prone woman.

"Close your eyes, Lady. This will hurt, and may cause you
to lose your senses."

"I never faint." The words drifted out, hazy and indistinct.

Alena opened her eyes to blue skies above her and a ring of
red cloaks surrounding her. For a moment, blue and red blurred

together, and she closed her eyes against a flash of pain. When she tried again, the blue stayed still but the circle of red was gone, replaced by a lone, silent figure in a mud-streaked bronze breastplate.

"So, Lady Wife, you rejoin the living."

Marcus leaned over her and slipped a callused hand behind her neck. He lifted her head to trickle clear, cool water down her parched throat. It was the first she'd had in more than twenty-four hours. She gulped greedily, painfully.

"Aye, husband," she croaked. "I tried hell, and misliked it greatly." She struggled to push herself up.

"Nay, Alena, stay still yet." Marcus held her on the grass with a firm hand on her shoulder.

"I must get up. Marcus, we must go after him. He has Megarric." Her voice was cracked, and the words were nearly unintelligible, even to her own ears. She wet her swollen lips and tried again. "Beorht holds Megarric hostage. We must go after him."

Alena felt panic rise in her when her husband sat back on his heels and stared at her with a cold, flat look. Did she not make herself understood? The only thing that had sustained her through Beorht's rage last night, when he had used her bound and helpless body to relieve his frustration at being caught in the Roman trap, was the thought that Marcus was near. That he would rescue her son. She pushed his hand away and struggled up.

"Marcus, hear me. The man is obsessed by you and all things Roman. I thought he would go mad last night when you turned his earlier victory to ashes by trapping him here. Do we not go after Megarric now, before Beorht reaches his stronghold, we will never get him out alive."

Marcus looked down at his wife for long, still moments.

"You won him back his army. Do you now send me forward to a trap, to win him victory?"

His words failed to penetrate her frantic mind at first. When they did, Alena felt the blood congeal in her body. Cold, numbing ice crept through her veins. She stared at him in stunned disbelief.

"Think you I would betray you to this man? That I would lie about my son's life?" The words came out in a slow, agonized whisper, from the depths of her soul.

Marcus rubbed a weary hand across his eyes. In despair, Alena saw the years sitting heavy on her husband's rugged face. Fine lines wrinkled the corners of his eyes, and exhaustion etched itself in the taut skin of his cheekbones. He let out a long sigh and looked away.

"I don't know what to believe. My head tells me this would be a good chance for you to rid yourself of your burdensome Roman lord. My heart tells me you would not betray me, or my men, so."

He turned back at her strangled sob. A tired grin edged his mouth. "Poison me, maybe, but not betray me."

Alena felt hot, scalding tears well up in her eyes. "Oh, Marcus, I swear I did not mean to hurt you that solstice night. I wanted to beg your forgiveness many times, but my pride would not let me. Please, please, do not hold my foolishness against me now. You must believe me. You must save Megarric."

Dry, wrenching sobs wracked her body. Tears she'd refused to shed through the terror and pain of the past days now flowed unchecked down her cheeks. Alena bowed her head, covered her face with her hands, and gave herself up to the waves of fear and hurt that washed over her.

When her husband reached out and pulled her to him, she crumpled against his chest.

"Come, Alena, cease your tears. You'll make your injuries worse."

Alena felt the soft stroke of his hand in her tangled hair before his whispered words penetrated. Desperately she struggled to swallow her wrenching sobs. Her hands trembled so much that she could barely grasp his arms.

"Please, Lord. Save my son."

Marcus looked down at her with bleak eyes. "I will try, Lady Wife. I know not yet how it will be done, but I will try."

Marcus kept his forces bivouacked in place that night. He knew instinctively that Beorht would not stop until he gained the fastness of his keep. Having once been battled to a standstill on open ground, the wily chieftain would retreat to his hilltop fortress and launch assaults on the invading forces at his own pace. In the flickering light of the oil lamps set on folding stools around his small tent, Marcus went over the maps detailing Beorht's keep with his senior officers. In frowning concentration they studied the high, jutting promontory, protected on either side by deep, rushing rivers. The only entrance—and exit—was from the north, up a long, sloping grade that offered little protection to any enemy foolish enough to attempt to rush it. Marcus listened carefully to a report from the tribune in charge of his specially trained teams, and nodded. His plan was risky, but could work. The question that burned in the prefect's mind as he listened to his officers' quiet conversation was whether even to try. If he launched an assault, Beorht would kill the child before the keep was overrun. If he withdrew, his heart told him the child would not long survive in any case.

Dismissing his officers, he turned on his leather stool to survey the woman sleeping on a cot at the rear of the tent. The surgeon had drugged her heavily, yet even now she resisted the pull of the sleeping herbs. Long after her wracking sobs had stopped, tears continued to stream unchecked down her filthy, swollen cheeks. Marcus stared at her in the dim light, trying to remember if he had ever seen her cry before. Images of Alena flashed through his mind—laughing, defiant, icily proud, panting with rage, moaning in passion. But even when he'd pulled her dislocated shoulder into place and she had gnawed her lip against the pain until she blacked out, never once had she cried. Only her fear for her son would bring such desperate, wrenching tears.

Marcus let himself out of the small tent and stood still in the darkness. Lineas detached himself from a small group around the campfire and joined him.

"How is she?"

"Still sleeping."

"We will avenge this, Marcus. We'll avenge the death of Praxas, as well."

Marcus said nothing. Lineas had been beside him when Alena told her halting, stark tale of kidnapping and slaughter. By then her words had been slurred and indistinct from the drug, but even without many details both men could guess with unerring accuracy the horror and indignities the women had suffered. A burning rage coiled deep in the prefect's gut, made worse by his shame at having let Alena see his doubts about her. He'd known in his heart that she would not betray him. For the thousandth time since he'd held his sobbing, pain-wracked wife in his arms this afternoon, he cursed himself for his stupidity in adding to her hurt.

"I'm taking a small squad out this night, Lineas—the special forces trained to scale the cliffs. You will break camp an hour before dawn and bring the legion. Stick to the battle plan we've detailed. If I'm successful and find the boy, I'll meet you in the fields to the south of Eilon Hill."

The tribune nodded. "I won't try to talk you out of this, Marcus. I've expected something like it ever since we learned the boy was taken. 'Tis almost certain suicide, you know."

"I know. I also know that I have to try." Marcus shrugged and placed a companionable arm across his friend's shoulders.

"Send Alena home tomorrow in one of the wagons, with a heavy escort. Tell her I will bring her son, and this Beorht's head."

Lineas bitterly regretted agreeing to stand in as the captain's deputy the next morning. When he told Alena that Marcus was gone and she was to leave within the hour for the rear, her fiery temper ignited. Lineas almost called the surgeon in to drug the blasted female once more.

"If you think you're sending me home in a damn baggage cart, like some worn-out camp follower, you may think again," Alena shouted when he tried to calm her.

"Listen to me, woman, Marcus will have my head do I not send you back to safety. I don't have time to argue with you about it. We move out within the hour, and I have to get you on the road."

"I will not go back! My son and... and my lord are forward. I go with you."

Lineas pushed a hand through his matted hair in exasperation. "You cannot go with us. We're already undermanned, and I can't spare additional forces to guard you should we meet the enemy."

Alena whirled and stalked up to him. Even under her patch-work of bruises, she looked so fierce that Lineas had to force himself not to step back when she thrust her face up close to his.

"If you cannot spare forces to protect me, you cannot spare them to escort me back, either. And I don't need any protection. Give me a spear and a bow and I will take care of myself."

"For the love of—! Do not make me add to your injuries, woman. If I have to knock you unconscious and tie you in that damned wagon, you're going."

Alena's narrowed, glittering eyes took in the flustered man before her. She bit back the furious arguments she wanted to scream at him. These Romans were so infernally pigheaded! She took a deep breath, softened her voice and tried a different tack.

"Please, Lineas. You must listen to me. I have nothing to go back to. If Megarric and Marcus do not survive this siege, my life is over anyway. My mother will only marry me off to some puling lord and take the Lopocare lands unto herself. I will not allow myself to be used like that again. I would rather die fighting for the two I love."

Lineas stared at her, an arrested expression in his blue eyes. "I did not think I would ever hear you admit you love a Roman."

"Well, I do, damn you! Though why I should love someone who treats me so coldly for months because of a little . . . mis-understanding, and goes off without even giving me the courtesy of a farewell to an almost certain death, I don't know."

Alena glared up at the grinning tribune.

"*Pax*, woman. Don't take out your rage at Marcus on me. You can ring your long list of grievances over his head when next you see him."

The tribune stumbled back when an ecstatic Alena threw herself against him and wrapped her arms around his neck. "Oh, Lineas, thank you. You will take me forward with the army!"

He unwrapped her arms. "Nay, I cannot. I promised Marcus. You must go back, Alena."

By the time her small escort topped the hill she had come down only a few days before, Alena had run out of curses. She pulled her horse to a halt and turned to look down, across the steep valley. In the distance, a long red column wound its way north through shrubby trees. Alena closed her eyes and offered a silent prayer to whichever gods would listen.

"Come, Lady, we must travel far before dark."

She turned back to study the short, stocky centurion who commanded her escort. He was young for such a rank, having just recently been elected to officership by the men. He watched her with a mixture of admiration and nervousness. Alena sighed, knowing well that this earnest young man would follow the tribune's orders to the letter.

She kicked her horse into a trot, then had to swallow a grimace when forgotten aches rose to taunt her. Sitting a horse may yet be painful, she thought, but at least she was not being sent home in any damned baggage wagon!

Chapter Twenty-Four

Marcus stifled an oath as his right hand slipped off a ragged rock. He could feel his fingernails tearing as they scratched against the sheer face of the rock for a hold. He hung by one straining, aching hand until the other finally found purchase, body hugging the cliff wall, face pressed against cold stone, heart pounding so hard he was sure the sentry above him must hear it.

After a long, heart-stopping moment, he gritted his teeth and pulled himself up by his fingertips once more. Muscles aching, he let go of his precarious hold and reached above him for another. Inch by painful inch, he struggled up the sheer face of the cliff. Just above, he could hear the faint, rasping breath of his lead sapper, whose agile fingers and toes found impossible holds in the sheer rock. Marcus twisted his head slowly, cautiously, to peer down into the inky blackness, but he couldn't see his other three men. They'd all stripped themselves of their white tunics and loincloths and darkened their skin with thick black mud. Even the rope wrapped around the lead's waist had been blackened with thick, oozing mud to dull it.

Marcus clenched his teeth as a sharp, jutting rock cut into his belly. The disguise certainly helped conceal them from any guards above, but didn't protect their skin—or their body parts—from the ravages of the rock. He rubbed his face against his straining arm to wipe the sweat from his eyes and reached for the next hold.

The moon slid out from behind dark, drifting clouds, and Marcus plastered himself once more against the cliff wall. He hung there, halfway up, with a hundred feet of sheer drop below him and towering cliff walls still above him. Faint sounds floated out across the dark, still air above his head. He heard a distant *clip-clop* of horses' hooves striking against stone streets, a muffled laugh, dogs barking. Perspiration rolled down into his eyes, and he wiped his face against his arm once more, smearing mud and sweat indiscriminately. He breathed a relieved sigh when the moon disappeared behind the clouds again, and began to climb once more.

After what seemed like hours, a strong arm reached down to pull him, panting and aching in every inch of his body, onto a small ledge a few meters below the clifftop. He scrambled to the back of the shelf while other dim shapes were hauled up beside him. Within minutes, the small ledge was crowded with sweaty, gasping men.

"We wait here until the last hours before dawn," Marcus whispered. "The house where our guides believe the young king is kept is deep within the center of the town. If we should be separated for any reason, or an alarm sounds before we reach the boy, do not head back here. As long as one of us remains free, the rest of us must not betray this escape route."

The men nodded in the darkness. They had reviewed the plan many times in the past hours. Each man knew that none would return if the boy did not. Briefly Marcus surveyed each soldier. They were good men. The best. He'd handpicked them himself from the many who'd volunteered for this mission.

The small band had ridden at a breakneck pace ahead of the main body of troops and then crept through the brush past enemy pickets to make their way undetected to Beorht's very walls. The last portion of their way was easier, since few patrols guarded the ground below these sheer cliffs. All afternoon, six of them had lain buried beneath brush and dead leaves at the edge of the river that rushed on the west side of the promontory, waiting for darkness. They'd seen a few peasants fishing the rocky banks of the river, and one mounted patrol, but otherwise little activity. Most of the traffic passed far to the north, up the sloping hill that led to the fort's only entrance.

When darkness fell, they had swum the rushing river. Marcus gained a whole new set of aches and bruises from being slammed against the boulders and rocks by the fierce current. He could still hear the sickening thud and muffled moan of one of his men, who'd lost his footing and hit headfirst against a huge boulder. The body had floated away from them in the rushing current before any of them could grasp it. He thanked Mars they had all stripped, knowing the body would not be readily identified as Roman.

Five of them had made it. Enough to accomplish the task, if it could be done at all, Marcus thought with a grim determination.

"All right," he whispered, rising. "Remember, use your knives and garrotes to good effect. They are to make no noise as they go down."

With great caution, a hefty soldier leaned against the cliff face and bent one knee slightly. Marcus stepped onto the knee, then lifted himself to the man's shoulders. Reaching as far above him as he could for a crack to slide his fingers into, he pulled himself up once more.

When his raw fingers felt the top edge, he gave a silent prayer of thanks. Slowly, inch by painful inch, he drew himself up until he could peer over the edge. Deep, unbroken darkness surrounded him. With his last reserves of strength, he bunched the muscles in his arms and pushed his body over the edge. Within minutes he'd tied a thin rope to a bent, twisted tree near the rim and snaked it down to his waiting men.

Crouching, silent as shades from Hades, the five men picked their way across the rocky ground toward the round huts sitting at the outskirts of the Selgovae city. Marcus thanked the gods there were no dogs snuffling in the dirt outside the closest hut as he lifted the leather covering its entrance mere inches and slipped inside.

A short time later, the soldiers came out of the hut to merge with the darkness once more. They wore the rough, woolen garb of peasants and had wiped only enough of the mud off their faces and arms to make their disguise believable. Walking upright for the first time in nearly twelve hours, they headed for a cluster of high-roofed, wooden buildings in the small town's center.

The gods were with them, Marcus thought as they neared the town center. They were stopped only once, by a drunken warrior who stumbled outside to relieve himself against a stone wall. The man turned bleary eyes on the five dark shapes com-

ing down the street. Before his slurred, stumbling voice even
finished a sentence, Marcus stepped forward, wrapped an iron
arm around his neck and slit his throat. One of the soldiers
pulled the man behind the hut and covered him quickly with
loose sticks. With any luck, they'd be gone before the body was
discovered in the morning light.

Marcus motioned the others to a halt in the shadows of a hut
and stared at two large buildings at either end of a moonlit
square. The hall to the north was built of tall timbers set in a
base of piled stone. Even in these hours before dawn, sounds
drifted out through its leather-covered door. Low voices, rumbling snores, once even the sharp cry of a woman, quickly silenced. If the guides were to be believed, this was Beorht's main
hall, where he and those of his warriors who had not their own
huts slept. The other building was a storehouse, with high,
timbered walls and a thick door designed to protect the chieftain's treasures—and hold his prisoners. For a short, sick moment, Marcus wondered if the guides were wrong. Mayhap a
child as young as Megarric would be kept elsewhere. With the
warriors themselves, or in the women's quarters. He guessed
there were nigh on a hundred huts on this rocky bluff. He hesitated, watching the two buildings with worried eyes.

As he and his men crouched in the darkness, a figure tumbled through the leather door of the main hall. It hit the ground
with a hoarse cry. The entrance covering lifted once more, and
a tall, naked warrior stood outlined by the dim light from the
interior of the house. Dropping the leather, he strolled out into
the street and stopped beside the huddled figure. Another low,
ragged cry filled the night as the warrior slammed a vicious kick
into its side.

"Get up."

The sobbing figure tried to comply, lifting herself on all
fours. She didn't move fast enough. The brawny man reached
down and pulled her up by her hair. The woman whimpered in
pain and fear.

"Be quiet, you stupid slut. You'll waken the whole camp
with your whining."

"Please," a soft, broken voice cried. "Please, let me go
now."

Marcus stiffened in the darkness. Although the voice was low and trembled with sobs, it rasped across his mind with blinding familiarity. He palmed his dagger, readying for a swift throw, when the warrior backhanded Ethelyn with a force that whipped her head to one side. For a moment, Marcus feared her neck was broken. His arm stilled in mid arc.

"Aye, go, you worthless lump of scrawny flesh. I've gotten more pleasure from sheep than from your dry, scraping hole."

The warrior scratched his belly and watched the woman creep away from him. He gave a deep grunt, then turned to go back inside the main house.

Marcus waited until the woman was almost past before he stepped out of the darkness, wrapped a hard hand over her mouth and hauled her back into the silent band of men.

She moaned into his palm and tried to shake her head loose. In her panic and fear, she didn't hear his whispered words. Marcus pressed his hand harder against her mouth to still her whimpers, clamping her nostrils shut until her feeble struggles ceased and she hung limp in his arms. He propped her upright against the wall of the hut with his own body.

"Please," she moaned a few minutes later. "No more."

"Ethelyn! Be still."

Fearfully the woman opened her eyes. In the dim light, Marcus could see them widen in fear, then fill with disbelief.

"Aye, 'tis me. I've come for you and Megarric."

Great, gulping sobs wracked the thin body beneath him, and Marcus cursed under his breath as he wrapped his palm over her mouth once more.

"Cease that wailing," he ordered in a fierce whisper. "We have not much time. I don't want to waste it while you water the damned rocks."

"Is it really you?" Ethelyn gulped, trying to swallow her sobs.

"Yes. Yes!"

"How came you here? The gates are barred shut each night and patrolled each day."

"How do you know this?"

"The hard way," she whispered bitterly. "They kept me chained the first few days, but 'twas too inconvenient for the men who wanted to take their pleasure. Now I am free to sleep

in the streets—after they're through with me. I tried the gates
the first night. They are secure. None can escape this pile of
rock.''

"We will," Marcus swore fiercely. "Come, tell me where the
boy is. Is he also left to roam unconfined?"

"Nay, he is in the warehouse yonder. I've only been allowed
to see him once. There are small rooms inside the house, each
locked. Megarric is in one."

"Who has the key?"

"The inside guard. At least he did the one time I was allowed within."

"How did you get in?"

The maid lowered her head and looked away. For a moment
Marcus thought she would not answer.

"The guard has strange tastes. He promised me a visit did I
not cry or scream while he took his pleasures."

Marcus held her against him in the darkness. The rage he'd
banked inside his belly unleashed its red-hot coils once again.
He had much to settle with this Beorht. He forced himself to
stillness, willed the anger back deep within. Too much was at
stake now to risk foolhardy, hot-blooded action.

Putting Ethelyn aside, he turned to study the storehouse once
more. Its door was wreathed in deep shadows, but even in the
darkness Marcus could make out the dim figure of a guard
posted at the main entrance. So there was one within and one
without. He turned back to the little maid.

"You must help us in this, woman. Can you go across the
square and distract the guard at the door? Just long enough for
me to slip up behind him?"

Ethelyn swallowed and nodded her dirty, matted head. "Aye,
'twill be easy. The pig would wallow in the street with me, or
any passing wench."

"Give us five minutes to slip around through the streets to the
rear of the house."

The maid nodded, then pressed herself back against the wall
as the five shadows melted away. Her legs trembled so badly
she almost stumbled as she made her way across the dirt square
a few minutes later. The guard straightened from his lazy slouch
against the wall and watched her approach. He squinted his
eyes to pick out her features in the dark.

"Well, what is this? Did you like your last visit so well you come to perform for me again?"

Ethelyn swallowed her frightened sobs as the man rubbed a rough hand across her tender breast. "Please, I've come to see how my lord does."

"In the middle of the night?" The guard hauled her against him. "Do not try to tell me you— Mmmph!"

Ethelyn jumped back to avoid the arc of blood that shot from his severed jugular. Marcus pulled her and the slumped body around the corner of the building.

"Are you all right?"

"Aye," she whispered, wide-eyed.

"Now you must get the inner guard to open the door and let you in. Can you do it?"

She nodded, barely able to breathe. She glanced down at the body rolled up against the wall and began to hope for the first time since her nightmare had begun.

"Good girl. I'll be right behind you. Just get him to open the door and let you inside."

Ethelyn felt a ripple of fear trip down her spine, but ignored it as she rapped tentatively on the wooden door. After an interminable, heart-stopping period, it opened a crack.

"What do you want, wench?"

"I want to see my little lord."

"At this time of night? Are you touched? Go away!"

The door started to close in her face.

"Wait!" she cried, frantic. "The...the other guard bade me to come at night, late, so that he could ease himself. He promised to let me in if I pleasured him."

The door opened wider. "That rutting pig. He'll get us both skewered. If Lord Beorht knew he left his post to lie with a slave girl in the street, he'd not see the next sun. Where is the stupid bastard?"

The man craned his neck to peer into the darkness. Marcus flattened himself against the side of the house, cursing silently. With every ounce of his being, Marcus willed the man to step out, to come around the corner searching for his partner. Or at least stick his damned head out far enough to present a target. This man, however, had more care for his duty.

He stared at the maid with narrowed eyes, well protected by the thick door.

"Where is he?"

"He—he said he had to... to relieve himself."

The guard gave a small, disgusted grunt. With a quick motion, he grabbed Ethelyn's arm and pulled her inside, dropping the thick bar in place before she could protest. He tossed his long pike aside and began to unbuckle his belt. Ethelyn stared, mesmerized at the bone knife and heavy sword attached to the wide leather belt. They fell to the floor with a clatter that resounded obscenely in the dim, stone-lined room.

Ethelyn shot a frantic look at the barred door, then whipped her eyes back to the man reaching casually under his woolen robe to loosen his loincloth. Both of them turned at a sharp rap on the wooden door. A thin, sneering smile spread across the guard's face.

"Finally, the fool is back from emptying his bowels. Well, he's already had his turn. On your back, woman."

Ethelyn bit her lip until she tasted blood. Slowly she lowered herself to the dirt floor. Another loud pounding sounded on the door, distracting the man straddling her. Did she not do something, quickly, the men outside would give themselves away. She closed her eyes while the guard pulled her legs apart and thrust into her dry channel. She waited while he arched, breath rasping far back in his throat, heaving and grinding her hips into the hard dirt. When he groaned and threw his head back, her outflung fingers closed around the bone handle of his dagger.

Swallowing convulsively, she rammed the knife into the man's side. He grunted in surprised pain and stiffened. Wild, disbelieving eyes stared down at her while one of his hands moved to his side.

Desperately, Ethelyn pushed at his heavy torso. She heaved with all her might, and the man groaned and tumbled off her. Scrambling backward on the dirt floor, she lurched away from his rolling, moaning form. She pushed herself up on shaky legs and started for the door.

"You bitch!"

Ethelyn ignored the agonized groan behind her. Just as her hands closed over the heavy wooden bar, a shaft of white-hot pain lanced into her back. She sagged against the door, holding on to the bar to keep from crumpling to the ground. The wood vibrated against her ear. A pounding sounded once again, mingling with the pain roaring in her ears to form a black, swirling crescendo. With her last conscious thought, she knew she had to lift the bar. She pushed up against one end of it, and felt the searing pain in her back spread to her chest. The bar clattered to the floor, and Ethelyn crumpled on top of it.

Marcus heard the bar fall and pushed with desperate strength against the weight holding the door back. The wooden panel moved, and he slipped inside the narrow opening. His men followed silently. One of them moved over to the groaning guard, still rolling on the floor in a pool of bright red blood. A quick slash brought his moans to a gurgling halt.

Marcus knelt beside the still maid, slipping an arm under her to lift her to his chest. A bone knife handle protruded obscenely from between her shoulder blades. Grimly he tugged the knife free, then lowered her back to the dirt.

"She's dead," he said curtly. "Search the guard's body for the keys, then check the rooms."

They found the boy in a small, airless room, huddled in a ball on the dirt floor. When Marcus reached down and shook the child, he woke and scrambled backward in a frightened manner that clutched at the soldier's heart.

"Nay, lad, don't fear. We've come for you."

"Marcus?"

The boy launched himself into the captain's arms with a dry, wracking sob.

By the time Marcus led his small party back through the dark streets to the far edge of the keep, he guessed dawn was not far off. When he saw the dim outline of the cliff edge ahead, relief eased the knotted muscles across his shoulder blades.

One of his men slithered over the edge, then tossed up the rope they'd left on the shelf.

Kneeling, Marcus tied the rope around the boy's waist. He double-checked the knots, then took the small shoulders in a firm grasp.

"You go to your mother now, Megarric. Trust these men. They will protect you with their lives."

"Do you not come?" Fear edged the boy's voice, though he tried to swallow it down.

"Nay, child. I have unfinished business here. Tell your mother... Tell her..."

"What, Lord?" the child whispered.

"Nothing. I'll tell her myself, when next I see her. Hold on to the rope. I'll lower you over the edge."

He checked the knots yet again, then gripped the boy's shoulder fiercely before lowering him to the waiting soldier. Swiveling on his haunches, he gave the men their last instructions. He waited, still and silent in the dark, while they inched their way back down the sheer cliff face. Eyes straining, he watched their shadows until they blended into the stone. Only when the last faint echo of their descent had died away did he rise.

For a long moment he held his face to the sky, drinking in the first feathery streaks of dawn silhouetting the mountains far to the east. The realization that this would likely be his last dawn did not disturb him. He'd been a soldier, facing death, for far too long to worry about his own inevitable demise. As he headed back toward the center of Eilon Hill, his thoughts were not of the coming battle, but of Alena.

Chapter Twenty-Five

Alena slid off her weary mount and stretched her aching muscles. Her escort dismounted, as well, and she heard their muffled moans and curses as they worked out the stiffness of a full day in the saddle. With a tired sigh, she settled down on the thick grass beside the path to share a meal of dried beef and brackish water.

She had just lifted a waterskin to her lips when the young centurion beside her stiffened.

"What is it?"

"Quiet, Lady."

The man laid himself out flat on the grass and put his ear to the ground. After a moment, he jumped up.

"Quickly—into the woods!"

By this time, Alena and the others could hear a distant rumbling, as well. They scrambled up and pulled their weary mounts into the thick brush alongside the wide path. Alena knew well this was the only route north, that the rumbling could be trade wagons or cattle or any number of peaceful travelers, but she was no more anxious than her escort to take any chances. A trooper brushed their tracks from the roadside with a leafy branch, then scrambled into the undergrowth.

They waited, hands over their mount's noses and breath suspended. The rumbling grew louder, and the ground beneath them began to vibrate. Long, breathless moments later, the first chariots rolled into view. Straining to see through the thick branches, Alena caught a flash of bright red and yellow. With a glad cry, she started forward.

The nervous centurion caught her arm and jerked her back.

"You fool!" she cried, whirling on him. "Those are my mother's colors!"

She yanked her arm free and pushed her way out of the bush, almost sobbing with relief when she saw the huge mass of mounted warriors. She estimated more than two hundred men, some in the distinctive blue and green of the Lopocare clan, most in her mother's red and gold.

It took nearly half an hour to restart the long column of chariots and horsemen. First, Alena had to brief the leader of the band, a grizzled old warrior she remembered well from her wedding. Lord Carric wanted every detail on the situation to the north as she knew it. The young centurion added his bit, with Alena translating when he stumbled over the native words. Then she had to convince the stubborn officer to let her go back with the warriors. He insisted that his orders were to take her south with all speed.

"Look you, Centurion, these troops are from my mother. I sent a message to her a week and more ago asking for men. Your captain needs them desperately, but they will not fight under a Roman officer. I must lead them, or they will not go."

She ignored the bland look on the old warrior's face. So she stretched the truth somewhat. So the men were sent with her mother's orders to do the Lady Alena's bidding, not necessarily to follow her into combat. The centurion need not know that.

The young officer vacillated, and was lost. Before he could stop her, Alena jumped up into the light chariot offered for her use, took up the reins of the two horses from the driver and drove off with a wild, exultant yell.

The Romans scrambled to their mounts as the lead chariots raced northward, the others following in a roar of galloping horses and rumbling wheels.

Alena wrapped the reins around her wrists and braced herself against the jolting, rocking movement of the wicker vehicle as it flew over the dirt road. Her aches and bruises forgotten, she prayed with every ounce of her being that they would be in time.

They rode all that night, stopping only to rest and water the horses. The miles vanished under the pounding hooves of the mountain horses. Thankfully, the gods sent a full moon scudding out from behind dark clouds to illuminate the narrow road. Their light wicker chariots traveled much faster than the heavy wooden ones brought to Britannia by the Romans.

The road bypassed the valley where Beorht had been trapped, but even from a distance of some miles the night air was heavy with the sickening miasma of rotting carcasses. Alena tried to blank her mind to all that had happened in that valley of death, and kept her face and her thoughts pointed north. Megarric and Marcus filled her mind, along with the numbing fear that she might never see either of them again.

They picked up the trail of the Roman column just as the first traces of dawn were beginning to streak the night sky. They swept on, through a high pass, then down into a broad, spreading valley. Finally they topped a high rise and pulled up. Below them stretched a deep, impenetrable forest. In the far distance, almost at the limit of their vision, the forest gave way to a high, barren plain. Crowning the plain was a sheer granite cliff, rising high into the still-dim sky. Straining, Alena could barely make out the twin rivers that bracketed the rocky promontory. Even as they watched, the rising sun edged over the horizon and turned the rivers to ribbons of liquid gold. Alena lifted her eyes from the molten streams to scan the stark, forbidding cliff. She could see a dark smudge atop the headland that she knew was Eilon Hill, Beorht's hilltop fortress.

"How far?" she asked Lord Carric, drawn up beside her.

"Several hours yet, Lady. The trail through the forest is rutted and barely passable. We'll have to move carefully and spare the horses, or they'll have no strength left for battle when we get there."

Alena bit her lip and nodded reluctantly, although every instinct screamed at her to push on, taking both men and horses to their limits. Her fear, never far from the surface of her consciousness, rose up once more. What if they were too late? Great Mother Epona, she would not be. She could not be. Her son and her husband were there, on that high, barren plain, and she would be there when they met their fate. Grimly she wrapped the reins around her aching wrists and started forward once more.

* * *

Marcus made his way back through streets just beginning to stir with the dawn. A few slaves dragged themselves through the gathering light, wooden buckets in hand, heading toward the well by the north gate. As unobtrusively as possible, Marcus fell in behind two still-sleepy, slow-moving men. Their tattered clothing matched his stolen garb, but they also wore thick iron collars that scarred and abraded their flesh. Hunching his shoulders, Marcus pulled up his rags to cover his bare throat.

His mind raced with various plans for gaining access to Beorht's main hall as he slouched along behind the two slaves. Given that he had only a razor-edged dagger with him, he decided the simplest and boldest approach was the only feasible one. He would just walk into the hall and seek out his prey, hoping to reach him before he was challenged.

As he stepped into the central square and headed for the main hall, however, the gods smiled on him. He didn't have to run down his prey, for Beorht came to him. There was no mistaking the warrior's massive form or his distinctive coloring. The red-haired giant stepped out from behind the leather door covering and into the square just as Marcus reached it. Not quite believing his luck, the soldier stood quietly in the shadow of a hut. Eyes narrowed, he watched Beorht relieve himself, then stretch and flex his muscles. The first morning rays glinted off the reddish fur covering the man's body, still streaked with the remnants of his battle paint. He carried his scabbard, with its great iron sword, loosely in one hand. Naked except for a wide gold armlet and a collar of what looked like bronze, he was a magnificent animal. A worthy opponent, Marcus thought as he shed his rags. Clad only in a thin loincloth, dagger in hand, he stepped out into the dirt square.

"Beorht!"

Marcus watched the big man turn and squint into the morning shadows. A few more warriors came out of the hall and paused beside their motionless chief.

Marcus walked out farther, to the center of the open area.

"Here, bastard!"

The big man stared at him. Disbelief was etched on his face, followed by consternation as his eyes narrowed and swept the square. Marcus knew he was searching for Roman troops, believing his keep had been overrun in the night. Beorht muttered something to the warriors beside him, and they stiffened. One reached for his sword, giving a hoarse shout to alert the other warriors.

Marcus let his smile widen, making no attempt to hide his mocking scorn as the warriors crouched and scanned the huts.

"Nay, there are no others. Only me."

Slowly, as if still not quite believing the evidence of his eyes, Beorht moved forward. When fewer than fifty yards separated them, he stopped and rocked back on his heels.

"It appears that I've underestimated you once more, Roman."

"Aye. But take heart, 'tis the last time you will do so."

The warrior frowned, eyeing the dagger in Marcus' hand. Despite the hate roiling in his gut, Marcus had to admire the man's courage. He faced an armed enemy—a lightly armed enemy, to be sure—naked and unafraid.

"Do you come to barter your life for the boy's?"

"Nay. You no longer have the boy to barter with. He's gone."

Beorht stiffened and gave the warehouse a quick glance, as if seeking confirmation with his own eyes. When he brought his gaze back, a grim smile lifted one corner of his long, flowing mustache.

"So, 'tis for me you've come."

"Aye." Marcus felt a savage satisfaction deep in his soul, knowing the moment had come. "I challenge you, Beorht of the Selgovae. To single combat. Here. Now."

A bright gleam leapt into the warrior's blue eyes. "You would decide the fate of our people with a sword and dagger?"

"Nay." Marcus shook his head and spoke carefully. He wanted to be sure the slowly gathering crowd understood as much as the giant facing him. "This is between you and me. I seek vengeance for what you did to my wife and son-by-marriage. The fate of your clan lies separate from our battle. My army marches here even now, under command of my lieutenant. He will lead them against your warriors, according to the battle plan we long ago devised."

The red-haired giant gave a bellow of laughter. His eyes lit up with the joyous love of battle Marcus had come to associate with these wild northern people.

"By the great god Camulus, I take your challenge! You are a foe worthy of the chieftain of the Selgovae. I will be proud to wear your head on my belt when I lead my warriors against this puny army of yours."

He turned to face his own people. "This Roman challenges me to combat. We fight here, to the death. Know you, whoever survives will lead his forces in great battle this morning. I swear this by Camulus, whose spirit flows in the rivers that guard our fort and give the Selgovae strength."

Marcus kept his face impassive while the chieftain's strong voice rolled out, exhorting his men, exciting their blood lust. He doubted the warriors would honor their chief's promise that, should he be the victor in their personal battle, he would be allowed to leave Eilon Hill to lead his own forces in the greater combat to follow. His heart and his mind told him he would meet his fate on this high, rocky promontory. Refusing to allow any thought beyond this moment to defuse his concentration, he focused on the man before him.

Beorht beckoned to a robust, well-muscled knight whose upper torso was covered with intricate tattos. "Give the Roman your sword and shield, then send word to the outlying camps to gather our forces on the high plain. Should I not survive, you will lead our men. Whatever happens here, the Selgovae will sweep down from the hills and destroy the dark desecrators of our land once and for all."

Beorht slipped his sword from its leather scabbard, accepted a shield from one of the other knights and turned back to Marcus with a wide, feral grin on his face. "Now, Roman, prepare to meet your gods."

Marcus thrust his dagger into the ground before him and slid the offered sword out of its embossed bronze scabbard. Keeping a wary eye on the warrior before him, he sliced it back and forth through the air a few times to assess its weight and balance. It was longer than a Roman sword, and heavier, made of iron and decorated with swirling Celtic designs along the shaft and wooden handle. He knew the barbarians used their swords to cut and slash, and mentally adjusted his own technique to the weapon he held. Hefting the rectangular wooden shield, with its central iron boss, he found it smaller and lighter than the oval shields of the legionnaires. It would serve not so much to protect the body as to deflect enemy strokes.

He barely had time to slip his left arm through the leather straps and grab the shield's handhold before Beorht gave a wild shout and banged his sword against the iron boss of his own shield with a crash that shattered the morning air. The giant leapt forward, his red hair flowing and a joyous, ear-splitting shriek on his lips.

Marcus raised his shield to ward off the murderous blow from Beorht's iron sword. Fire raced up his arm as he danced back and lifted the wooden guard once more against the arcing, slashing blade. The air around him filled with shouts. From the corner of his eye he could see the warriors and townspeople crowding into the square to form a rough circle around them. He backed farther away from the attacking warrior, taking his measure even as he took the force of his awesome strokes on a now-numb arm.

Dust swirled around them as their feet slid sideways in the dirt to find purchase. Once more Marcus raised his shield to ward off a murderous blow.

"Is this how Romans fight? Backward, with shields instead of swords?" His face now almost as red as his hair, Beorht taunted the soldier.

Marcus smiled grimly to himself. He knew his best weapon was the Celt's own reckless courage. These barbarians were brave, loved the fight itself, and would join in any fray, laughing and shouting their way to bloody victory or equally bloody death. But Marcus would pit Roman discipline against Celtic recklessness. He would keep this battle to his own plan and pace.

With another thunderous roar, Beorht charged forward once more. He swung his sword in a vicious arc above his head and brought it down with all the power of his massive frame.

Marcus darted to one side, hearing a deadly hiss as the sword slashed the air beside his ear. While the big man was still carried forward by the momentum of his blow, the Roman thrust.

Beorht twisted away just in time. The sword sliced into his side, but glanced off his ribs instead of penetrating to the hilt.

Bright red blood spilled down his body. Oblivious to his agony, he roared and charged again.

Marcus parried the blow, but the force of it knocked the wooden shield against his head. Blinding pain rocked him for a moment, and blood gushed down his face. Raising one sweaty arm, he wiped it from his eyes as best he could.

Surging heat shot through Marcus' veins as he parried each slashing blow and thrust forward whenever an opening presented itself. Sweat poured down his body. He licked his lips, tasting the sharp, metallic tang of blood. His ears rang with the crash of iron on iron and the din from the crowd around them. Mouth open, panting for breath, he balanced on the balls of his feet.

He knew he couldn't match this giant in strength, or in endurance. He had to make his move. When Beorht swung wildly once more, Marcus launched himself forward. Ducking under the warrior's guard, he thrust. Savage, exultant joy filled him when the shaft buried itself in Beorht's stomach.

The man toppled to his knees in the dust. Marcus wrenched the sword free and lifted it once more. Alena's bruised face flashed in his mind. He swung with all his might, and Beorht's head rolled into the dirt.

Alena breathed a heartfelt prayer of thanks when thick, dark forest finally gave way to the sparse brush and scrub that marked the edge of the plain below Eilon Hill. She pulled up her chariot and passed the reins to her driver. Now that they were close, he would maneuver the chariot. She would need both hands for her spear and sword.

Her forces fanned out beside her. Their eyes strained against the sun, sweeping the high, barren plain. Alena felt her heart stop when she saw movement in the far distance. Narrowing her eyes, she picked out a thin line of red. And it was moving forward. A glad cry escaped her lips, only to be cut off when the old warrior beside leaned forward and pointed urgently.

"Look, Lady, up and to the right."

Alena swept her gaze along the right flank of the thin crimson line and caught the glint of sunlight on burnished bronze on the hills surrounding the plain. A faint, raucous din floated across the thin air as a wave of chariots swept over the hill and down toward the plain, heading for the Roman line. Even from this distance, the watchers could see the wild, uncontrolled charge as Selgovae and Caledonian charioteers rampaged up and down in front of the enemy line. Alena knew the boldest knights would be standing on the chariot's yokes, holding the horses' manes with one hand and leaning forward to give their spears added distance when they thrust them at the enemy. Although she couldn't see the exchange of missiles, she could hear the faint sound of shouting and feel the low, rolling thunder of the charging chariots. Her heart in her throat, she watched the red line to see if it held against the first assault.

"There, mistress—" Lord Carric pointed "—there, to the left. The Romans are spread so thin at that point that the Selgovae will break through and turn to attack their flanks. That is where we should head."

Alena nodded, eyeing the distant line. She knew the time was at hand. Obeying an instinct older than time, she searched for an omen, a sign to speed them on their way, to hearten the warriors before battle.

"Get down," she told her driver. "Go back into the brush behind us and raise some birds."

The young man nodded. Jumping lightly to the ground, he raced back the few yards to the scrub. Alena pulled her chariot forward a few paces and turned to face the milling warriors crowded behind her.

"Battle is at hand, warriors of Brigantium, of Lopocare," she shouted. "The Selgovae attack with Caledonian support. These tribes have raided our lands and killed our people for many centuries, before the Romans ever came to our shores. Do we not stop them now, they will sweep over the Roman line and down upon our people, with fire and sword and death.

"Remember that, lest you think we fight here only to aid the Romans. We fight for our own, and because we are the bravest, the fiercest, the most skilled tribes of this land. The gods will give us a sign, to show us a way in this battle."

She nodded to the driver, who plunged into the brush, whooping and beating it with the flat of his sword. A flock of wood pigeons, startled from their nests, rose with a rush of wings beating in the thin air and flew north. Alena grinned in triumph.

"We go north! To battle!"

A great roar rose from the milling throng. Alena's driver ran back to take the reins and lead the charge across the plain. Alena gripped the wicker side with one tight hand and held her javelin raised above her head with the other. As the vehicle flew across the uneven ground, she gave one last, silent prayer of thanks to Epona for sending the birds north. She'd had other interpretations ready in case they went east or west, toward either flank, but she would have been hard put to come up with a coherent explanation if the damned pigeons had flown south. Excitement shot through her as they pounded forward, and she let out a wild, high battle cry. Her men picked it up, surrounding her with the sound of thundering hooves and fierce, exultant shouting. Following her orders, the driver turned the horses and headed the chariot to the left, where even now the Selgovae horsemen charged the Roman flank.

Chapter Twenty-Six

Marcus raised a leaden arm and wiped the blood from his face. Through bleary eyes, he surveyed the battle line stretched out before him. From long experience, one part of his mind catalogued the disposition of his forces, while another part marveled that he still lived at all to do so.

Hoarse battle cries rose above the crash of swords beating against shields and the deadly whir of javelins slicing through the air. Marcus ran an assessing glance over the wave of naked, fair-skinned warriors charging forward in their light chariots. For as long as he lived—which might not be long, he acknowledged ruefully, given the overwhelming masses facing him—he would see these people through different eyes. Cruel, mindless in their lust for battle, yet possessed of their own indelible brand of honor. These Celtic warriors were no longer savages in his mind. They lived and died by a code of arms as strong as any that drove the Roman legions.

Even with their fallen chief's body lying in the dirt, they had honored his vow. When Marcus had turned slowly to face the tattooed warrior Beorht had identified as his second-in-command, the man had stood silent and immobile in the square. Expecting death from vengeful Selgovae lords, Marcus had been at first confused, then incredulous, when he realized the warriors would not attack.

The hair on the back of his neck prickling, every nerve end screaming, the Roman had turned slowly on the balls of his feet to survey the crowd. An eerie silence had filled the square, broken only when the massed spectators shuffled apart to allow a warrior leading a horse to come forward. Still without uttering a word, the new chief had watched impassively as man and horse halted in front of Marcus.

The ride out of Eilon Hill was the longest Marcus had ever made. He kept the horse to a walk as he headed down the wide dirt street toward the gates. Blood had streamed from his brow, blurring his vision of the wide, wooden gates looming a hundred yards ahead, then fifty yards, then twenty. The silence had roared in his ears, and at each slow step of the mountain pony he'd expected to feel an arrow in his back.

But he hadn't. He'd ridden out of the camp, through slowly gathering masses of enemy troops, down the sloping road that wound toward the plain below. Only when his pony's feet left the road and he turned its head toward the south had he actually believed that he would be allowed to live, that this wasn't some cruel game. He'd kicked the pony into a gallop and headed toward the Roman columns just appearing out of the forests edging the far side of the plain.

Now he faced that same enemy once more. He straightened in his saddle and forced the exhaustion from his body. Battle was joined, and his long years of command exerted themselves. He signaled for a courier to come forward and began barking out crisp orders to relay to the cavalry battalion commander for the reinforcement of his weakening flank.

Marcus looked up in startled surprise when a scout came galloping up to report a large force charging across the expanse of plain behind them. He turned, tearing his eyes from the waves of enemy chariots rampaging up and down his line. Far behind him he could see the clouds of dust raised by the fast-moving forces.

Lineas came panting up. "By the gods, Marcus, how did the bastards get behind us? Our line holds. I swear we had pickets out right to the edges of the mountains. Unless they can pick up their chariots and fly, they could not have gotten behind us!"

The commander sat as still as stone for long moments. If he pulled his cavalry from the right flank to meet this new threat, they were doomed. Even now, the horsemen countered a fierce thrust by the savages and were fully engaged. His only reserve, the Tungarian Cohort, was already headed to the right to aid in the counterattack.

While his mind raced, his eye picked up a flash of bright colors amid the swirling dust. Red, and a touch of gold or yellow.

"Great Jupiter, those are Cartimandua's colors, Lineas!"

For a brief, mindless instant, dread coursed through him. Did the Brigantes take this opportunity to join the Selgovae and crush the Romans completely? Had Cartimandua betrayed her treaties with Rome? Was Alena part of this? But even as the thoughts formed, his heart rejected them.

"They're turning, Marcus! They head for the left flank! By the gods, they are with us!" Lineas shouted exultantly. A ragged cheer went up from the band of officers surrounding them.

"Aye, they're with us. All right, men, we must use this unexpected aid. Give the signal to move forward. And may the gods be with you."

The trumpeters sounded forward, their clarion calls ringing out sure and clear above the din of battle. Slowly the line of Romans began to advance. With grim satisfaction, Marcus saw the Selgovae warriors jump down from their chariots and begin to fight on foot. The Roman foot soldier had all the advantages over the native warriors. Their sturdy armor, larger shields and short stabbing swords were designed for close-in hand-to-hand combat. At close quarters, the long, slashing swords and lightweight shields carried by the Celts were next to useless. Marcus drew his own sword, leaned forward over his horse and charged.

By dusk, the plain was awash in blood and littered with fallen men and horses. The Roman charge had broken through the Selgovae cavalry at the center, while the Brigante horsemen had crushed their flank. The enemy faltered, stumbled over themselves in the confusion, and fell back to the hills surrounding the broad plain. They rallied briefly, but the Roman infantry and dismounted cavalry ringed the hills and vales and drove forward, forcing the enemy back upon himself. Late in the afternoon, the remaining Selgovae tried to break to the north, to head for the safety of the keep. Brigante horsemen circled behind their lines and blocked the retreat. Bloody skirmishes broke out, with every man engaged in slogging, murderous hand-to-hand combat. The battle ended when darkness fell and the troops could no longer see to pursue the fleeing remnants of the beaten force.

Marcus signaled the trumpeters to call a withdrawal. His men drew back to regroup on the broad plain. The mighty support apparatus of the Roman army ground into action, with defensive lines thrown up, tents staked out, hospital areas established and quartermasters issuing weapons and food.

The men stopped their activity to stand and stare as the troop of Brigante warriors rode slowly out of the swirling evening mists and headed toward the Roman camp. Illuminated by the flickering cook fires, they looked tall and fierce in their flowing red-and-gold plaid robes. At their head was a band of men in blue and green, an honor guard for a single wicker chariot. As the warriors rode by, a Roman centurion straightened slowly and lifted his arm in a time-honored clenched-fist salute of victory. Slowly, like a rippling wave, the camp came to its feet as soldier after soldier raised his arm in respect. A low, ragged cheer broke out, swelling to a great roar.

Alena tried to wave to the troops as she rode by. Her arm ached so that even raising it slightly took all her strength. She smiled, pulling stiff lips back against ingrained dirt and sweat, but her heart pounded with anxiety. As they neared the center of the camp, her eyes searched the small group of officers gathered there. Her breath caught on a choking sob of fear. She couldn't make out any features in the darkness, only filthy, once-white tunics now stained with blood and dirt, and dull armor glinted in the firelight.

She pulled the chariot to a stop and stepped down, heart pounding so loud it beat a steady drumming roar in her eyes. A tall figure detached itself from the group of men in front of her and strode forward. At first she didn't recognize him. His body was covered with blood and gore, and his face and arms were streaked with mud. But she recognized the small figure beside him. Her heart leapt into her throat and hot, scalding tears of joy flooded her eyes at the sight of her son.

She ran forward and fell to her knees beside Megarric, taking his small, welcoming body into aching arms. The child sobbed into her neck as she knelt on the ground, rocking back and forth, arms wrapped tightly around him. The warmth of life flowed back into her with each of his gasping sobs and

choked cries. The tight knot of fear she'd carried in her breast
for so long loosened.

It didn't dissolve completely, however, until strong hands
reached down to raise her from her knees. Her tear-drenched
eyes lifted. Gradually her vision focused on the dark figure before her. Under his covering of dried blood and streaked mud,
Marcus loomed like an apparition from the deepest chambers
of the underworld. She closed her eyes against a new wash of
tears and gave fervent thanks to the gods for his deliverance.
When she opened them, he stood still and silent before her, his
hands encircling Megarric to hold her in a grip of iron.

In the flickering firelight, she could not read the expression
in his dark eyes. Painfully she wondered why he did not sweep
her into his arms, or even speak. She swallowed and forced her
raw, hoarse throat to form the words that seared her heart.

"Thank you, Lord Husband. For giving me back my son."

"Alena, by all that is sacred, you—"

"Alena! By Jupiter, 'tis you!"

The tribune's shout interrupted her husband's low voice. She
turned as far as Marcus's hard hold would allow to greet Lineas as he rushed up to them.

"You witch! I knew I should have chained you to that
damned supply wagon. Was that you leading the Brigante
warriors? How came they here?"

His impetuous arrival released the other officers from their
paralysis. Within seconds she was surrounded by a begrimed,
stinking cluster of men who peppered her with questions. She
twisted in Marcus's hands, but he allowed her to work only one
arm free. Her other remained encircled by his hard, unyielding hand.

Even when she nodded to Lord Carric, beckoning him forward to accept the thanks of the Roman officers, Marcus held
her. The prefect bowed to the grizzled knight, thanked him with
heartfelt sincerity, and still he held her.

Not until Lineas lifted Megarric from her arms did Marcus
loosen his grip. And then it was only to shift it to her wrist.

"Come."

Alena blinked in surprised confusion as he pulled her out of
the circle of firelight and headed for a leather tent. Her first
instinct was to resist, to yank her wrist free. After all she'd been

through these last days, she deserved better, she thought. Before she yielded to the impulse to dig in her heels, another thought seeped into her tired, confused mind. She felt her lips curve up in a slow, feline smile and a tingle of anticipation dance down her spine. Instead of resisting, she forced her weary legs to lengthen their stride, matching his. Suddenly she was as eager for the privacy of their tent as was he. After the horrors of a day filled with gruesome death and dying, she hungered for an affirmation of life.

She stumbled into the tent before him, moving hesitantly in the close darkness to stand beside the cot.

"Wait here."

His voice sounded low and strained. He lifted the tent flap to duck outside, only to return moments later with a lit brass lantern. Huge, dancing shadows darkened the tent walls while he adjusted the tin reflector plate behind the lantern so that its light was thrown directly at her. Alena put up a hand to shield her eyes from the sudden glare, grimacing inwardly at the thought of the unsightly picture she must present. Well, she couldn't look any worse than her lord, what little she could see of him as he stood, tall and still, behind the lantern.

After a moment, her eyes adjusted to the light and she lowered her hand to her side. The tingle of anticipation returned, intensifying with every second he stood watching her. Eager to take the next step, Alena smiled.

"Have you no words of greeting for me, Roman?" She waited, excitement now heating her veins, for his response. Her smile widened to one of pure female invitation.

Finally he moved around the small drum table, which held the lantern, and stepped across the small space.

"I doubt you will consider the words I have for you a greeting."

Alena's smiled slipped at his dry tone. She tipped her head to peer up at him, but with the lantern now behind him, his eyes were shadowed. He closed the distance between them.

"You don't sound very grateful for the assistance of the Brigante," she told him, with just the slightest hint of acerbity. This game was beginning to pall.

"I'm most grateful to *them*. I'm trying my damnedest not to give in to the urge to beat *you* senseless, however."

Alena's jaw dropped. "What!"

"My orders were for you to be sent to safety. Lineas assured me you were en route back to Corstopitum."

"Well, of all the—! Who do you think brought those warriors to your aid? Who led them night and day, to save your—your blasted hide!"

"You did not need to lead them, woman. Lord Carric could have done so, or my own centurion who was with you."

Alena stuttered in rising indignation, unable to find the words to vent her riotous emotions. She stared up at the dark face looming so close above hers, wanting to beat at it as much as she wanted to smother it in hot, hungry kisses. By the gods, she'd never felt such overwhelming, conflicting sensations in her life. Before she could form a coherent thought in the torrent of emotions, Marcus took her arms once more and jerked her up against his chest.

"Don't you understand, you stubborn, pigheaded female? My heart stopped when I saw you drive into the camp, spattered with the blood of your foes."

Alena blinked at the force of his angry words. He shook her, hard.

"That could have been your blood. Two thousand javelins flew this day, mayhap ten thousand arrows, as well. Any one of them could have killed you."

Her head snapped back on her shoulders as he shook her once more and proceeded to tell her in graphic detail the extent of her idiocy. With every word, his voice rose until his shouts bounced off the leather walls. Alena thought she'd never heard such wonderful sounds in her life. When he stopped for breath, she held hers, as well, then let it out in a soft sigh.

"Would it have mattered so much to you had I taken an arrow this day?" she whispered.

Blank astonishment wiped all other emotion from his face. Alena bit her lip when he stared down at her, openmouthed, for long, endless moments.

"Would it have mattered?" she asked again.

"Are you daft, woman?" he shouted. "Think you I would have climbed that damned cliff to send you back your son if it didn't matter? Think you I severed that bastard's head from his shoulders because it didn't matter, because *you* didn't matter?''

"Well, how would I know?" she asked, her low voice contrasting with his heated one. "You accused me of betraying you to Beorht, then left me without another word, to be sent home under guard. What was I to think?"

Marcus stared down at her, an arrested expression in his eyes. "Why did you bring reinforcements if you thought I believed you a traitor?"

While she searched for words, enlightenment dawned. "'Twas to save Megarric, was it not?" he asked her softly.

"Nay!"

"I understand, Alena. You would move heaven and earth to save the boy."

"You don't understand at all, you blind idiot." She bit back her exasperation and tried again. "I knew Beorht would never release Megarric alive. His twisted hatred ran too deep. In truth, I—I believed I would never see him again. I wasn't sure I would arrive in time to see you, either."

"Yet you came."

"Aye. I came. I had to come, to bring you what aid I could."

Marcus took a deep, shuddering breath. Alena felt its force under her palms, still splayed against his chest.

"Alena, I ask your forgiveness for doubting you. I've wanted to scourge myself for ever suggesting you might have gone to Beorht willingly. I knew as soon as the words were out you could not have done so. Forgive me, Lady Wife."

"'Tis not forgiveness I would grant you, Roman," she told him, her voice low and sure. She barely heard her own whispered words over the pounding of her heart.

"Give me what you will, then."

A slow smile curved her lips at his humble words. Somehow she doubted this domineering male would remain meek and penitent for long. Nor did she wish him so. With unshaking certainty, she knew she wanted him proud, and strong, and radiating the quiet command she'd come to treasure.

Sliding her hands up his matted chest, she locked them behind the thick column of his neck.

"I would give you this."

Standing on tiptoe, she reached up to press her lips to his. Slow, sweet fire ignited in her blood at his familiar taste.

Later, much later, Alena twisted on the narrow cot, trying to ease her body from under his weight. She grinned in the darkness at the sucking sound their sweat-dampened flesh made. This had to be the most passionate—and aromatic—coupling she'd ever experienced. With all her soul, she longed for just an hour in the baths at Corstopitum.

"Where do you go?" Marcus rolled over sleepily and pulled her back against him.

"One of us must get water to bathe. We cannot sleep like this. The mud and…and other will harden. Come dawn, they'll find us locked together and suffocated in a cocoon of clay."

Laughter rumbled in his chest. "Just think what legends we would become."

"Well, I've no notion to become legend just yet." Alena slapped at the hands holding the naked flesh of her hips. "Let me go, Marcus."

"No, not yet. Wait here. I have something for you."

Lifting himself over her prone body, he rolled with fluid grace off the cot. Alena ran appreciative eyes down his long, lean flanks and muscled buttocks as he walked across the tent to rummage in his gear. She watched with even more approbation when he turned and came back to her. Exhausted, sated, emotionally drained beyond belief, she still felt a stirring at the sight of his maleness.

"Here. This is yours."

Marcus knelt beside the cot and took her hand in his. Firm, steady hands pushed a heavy ring onto her trembling finger. Wordlessly Alena stared at the wide golden band with its dark red stone. His hand folded hers, cocooning it in hard, warm strength, pressing the ring between their flesh.

"*Anima mea,*" Marcus whispered. "My soul."

Epilogue

Alena shifted uncomfortably from one foot to the other as she stood in the courtyard of the king's palace. She placed a protective hand under her swollen belly and lifted it gently, trying to ease the ache in her back. Great Mother Epona, this child bade fair to be bigger even than its sire—with yet a full cycle of the moon to go before its birth. She placed a hand at the small of her back and arched against the weight.

Megarric stood beside her, his golden curls ruffling in the fall breeze. Together they awaited the arrival of her mother, Queen Cartimandua. The advance guard had already arrived and dismounted. They now stood beside their horses, wrapped in their distinctive red-and-gold cloaks, waiting as she did.

The clatter of iron-shod hooves striking loose shale warned Alena of her mother's approach. She straightened and rearranged the loose drape of her blue-and-green plaid to cover her bulging front. Responding to the pressure of her hand, Megarric went down on one knee when the richly caparisoned chariot entered the courtyard. Alena knew better than to attempt a curtsy in her condition.

Sunlight glinted on the bronze metal decorating the sides of her mother's chariot and on the intricate enamel of the horses' snaffle rings. The equipage blazed with magnificent color. But it was the driver who drew Alena's gaze. Her eyes widened at the sight of the huge, heavily muscled young man in helmet and shield enameled in the queen's red and gold. He was without question the most handsome man she'd ever seen.

When he jumped down and turned to offer the queen his hand, his short tunic revealed thick, gold-furred legs roped with muscle. Alena gulped. Happy in her marriage and as pregnant as a sow about to birth a litter, she still felt an involuntary ripple of healthy feminine awareness at the man's sheer animal magnificence.

Tearing her eyes from the driver, she bowed awkwardly to the queen. A quiet pride filled her when Megarric rose and went forward.

"Welcome, Lady Queen," he said with a grave dignity.

Cartimandua stood back to survey the child before her. "Strong and sturdy and probably as stubborn as his headstrong mother," she observed to Alena. "A worthy grandson. One who will hold these lands well when he grows into his crown a bit more."

She laid an affectionate hand on the boy's shoulder and turned to her daughter.

"You'd best go inside and sit down. You look about to drop your babe even here."

Alena laughed, caressing her belly. "Aye, 'twould be more comfortable to talk with my feet up. We've an hour yet before the lords assemble for the ceremony. Come inside and refresh yourself. Lady Nelwyn has set out wines and cheeses."

She waited quietly while Cartimandua acquainted herself with Nelwyn. Strange, she thought, I have two mothers, and the one who birthed me is less known than the one who raised me. She studied the queen, as if seeking to understand how the blood bond between them could mean so little.

Cartimandua looked every inch the ruler this day, her daughter thought. She'd piled her thick hair up in a knot and captured it with a heavy golden diadem. The filtered sunlight of the great room hid the gray in her hair, picking up only rich, tawny highlights. A wide gold torque wrapped around the loose flesh of her neck, hiding much of its excess. Her crimson robe fell to the floor in heavy folds and was caught at the waist by a wide embroidered girdle. When she moved, light sparkled from the enameled hand mirror hanging from a gold chain around her waist. With her red-and-gold patterned cloak thrown over one shoulder, she presented a picture of glowing color and vibrant womanhood. Alena felt cool and pale—and distinctly bulky—in her presence.

Cartimandua nibbled at the fruit and cheese spread out for her pleasure and listened with every evidence of interest to Megarric's childish patter. She gave Nelwyn news of the last lingering remnants of Druid society and shook her head gravely over the demise of the once-powerful class.

" 'Tis gone for all time, I fear."

"Aye," Nelwyn replied slowly. "So will our songs and histories and traditions also go. Without the priests to teach them to our young, our ways as we know them will vanish."

"Mayhap. I do not wish to offend you, Lady Nelwyn, but having spent some twenty years in uneasy coexistence with these Romans, I believe we can survive. Not without change, but without turmoil. We are our own worst enemy, with our constant intertribal warfare and bloody feuds."

Alena and Nelwyn shared a quick look. They'd had word of the latest violent dispute between Cartimandua and her consort. Reportedly he had demanded a greater share of tribute for his own clan's coffers. When Cartimandua disagreed, Venutius had attacked a caravan of goods, then retreated with his stolen treasure to the fastness of his hill fort at Stanwick. Alena knew her mother would not tolerate his actions without retribution. The prospect of another bloody war hung over the Brigantes. Alena worried about the impact to her own people, and to Marcus, who would likely be sent to quell the disaffected Venutius.

Before she could ask Cartimandua for the latest news, however, servants came for Megarric. He must change and don the trappings of his kingship for the ceremony in which he would pledge his oath of allegiance to Cartimandua. Nelwyn rose gracefully when the child left and bade her own quiet farewell. Alena knew she wanted to give mother and daughter time alone to talk of the future.

Cartimandua herself broached the topic when the room was cleared. "There are troubled times ahead, daughter. Your father incites the nobles against me once more. The fool stirs up greed and their long-simmering resentment at being ruled by a woman. As if anyone else could have held these war-mad tribes together all these years!" Indignation and scorn laced Cartimandua's voice. "Narrow-minded ass that he is, Venutius will unleash their war lust, then not be able to control it."

Alena looked at her mother with troubled eyes. "We had word you petitioned the governor for troops to support a drive against my father. Mayhap Marcus himself will lead the Roman force."

"I'm sorry he's not here," Cartimandua said, stretching her long legs in front of her and relaxing in the high-backed carved wooden chair. "I wanted to speak with him about this matter. When does he return from Londinium?"

"We expect him within the week. He's been gone nigh one full moon now."

Cartimandua frowned. "I dare not linger here beyond a few days, with Venutius stirring the lords to such passions." After a few moments, she shrugged. "Well, I've brought that fool to heel before, I'll do so again. At least now I don't have to worry about those savages from the north sweeping down to harass us while I set our own house in order. Marcus Valerius is due much honor for subduing the Selgovae and ensuring peace."

"Nay, Lady Mother, honor is not due to just my lord. You, also, share in that." Alena leaned forward and spoke with sincere emotion. "I would kneel to you if I could, Lady Queen. I cannot begin to convey my thanks for sending forces when we needed them so desperately."

Cartimandua smiled into her daughter's shining green eyes. "I accept your thanks—as I did the rich tribute the governor and your lord sent. Do not think me too noble, Alena. I do whatever must be done to preserve Brigantium."

"Aye, I understand," Alena said slowly. In the face of her mother's frankness, she tried to articulate her own doubts. "I thought what I did was for my people, as well. But my heart knows it was as much for the man, himself."

"I am not overly familiar with the emotion, daughter, but 'twould appear you're afflicted with what the bards call love."

Her mother's dry tones brought a tinge of red to Alena's cheeks, but she lifted her head proudly and met her gaze with a direct, glowing one of her own. "Aye, Lady Mother. I would give my life for him," she said simply.

Cartimandua felt envy twist her heart. In her lifetime she'd known lust many times, and pleasure, and companionship. But never with the same man. And never had she experienced the passion she saw reflected in her daughter's eyes. She sighed and dropped her gaze to the chased gold goblet in her hand.

"Would that I had such a love."

"Would that you did," Alena concurred softly.

Cartimandua paused, then lifted her face. It held an uncharacteristic uncertainty. "Mayhap I do. Did you notice my driver?"

Alena laughed, a rueful twinkle in her eye. "How could I help but notice him? The man fills even my matronly head with awe."

Cartimandua smiled. "He pleasures me, daughter, in a way that no man has done in many years."

A familiar earthy gleam lightened the shadows in her mother's eyes. Alena remembered that lascivious look well. She'd last seen it fastened on Marcus. Her smile slipped somewhat, but her mother didn't appear to notice.

"He was your father's armor-bearer, until I corrupted him. Now *I* carry *his* spear—as often as these old bones will allow!"

Alena sputtered with mirth while hearty chuckles shook Cartimandua's frame. When the laughter subsided, however, the shadows were back in her eyes. "'Tis the real reason your father rebels, I fear. His pride is sorely dented this time. He has no consort with me, but objects when I take my pleasure elsewhere. As if he does not!" The queen snorted in disgust, then rose and helped her daughter to her feet.

"I had no time for you as a child, Alena, nor for your siblings. If it's not too late, I'll give you some motherly advice now. Your lord is a man among men. If the gods are kind, you will share his bed long after your son has grown to manhood and assumed his kingship. Do not let your duty to Megarric and these people come between you and such a man."

Alena frowned, trying to grasp her mother's meaning. How could one who had spent her entire life building a kingdom speak of subordinating duty to desire?

She pushed her mother's strange words to the back of her mind in the days that followed. The ceremony of suzerainty went well, filled with color and pageantry. Lineas Flavius, representing the Romans, hosted the queen—and her ever-present driver—at a banquet that began in midafternoon and flowed over into the next day. More than one Roman and Celt sported a throbbing head at the games that followed.

By the time the festivities ended, Alena's back, feet and head ached constantly. She watched her mother's escort leave with a thankful prayer, then jumped when the babe kicked against her taut stomach wall. Nelwyn saw her grimace and sent her back to the camp with stern orders to rest. Only too willing to comply, Alena sank deep into the fur covers and vowed to sleep for as many hours as the rambunctious babe would allow.

Marcus found her asleep in their bed when he returned late that night. Moving quietly in the darkened room, he slipped out of his travel-stained clothes and toyed briefly with the idea of a visit to the baths before joining Alena. The sight of her tawny hair spread in wild disarray across the bed, and her mounded stomach, convinced him the bath could wait. The feel of his wife could not.

Shedding his loincloth, he eased himself into the bed beside her. She stirred restlessly and shifted against him, trying to find a comfortable position. Marcus slipped his arm under her head and pulled her gently onto his shoulder. With an unconscious sigh, she turned to nuzzle her face into his neck. Her soft breath feathered his skin.

The room lay in total darkness when Alena started, awakened from her sleep by a hard kick.

"Ahhhh!"

"What? What is it?" Marcus shook the dregs of sleep from his head, holding her fast with one hand while his other scrabbled for his sword.

"'Tis your child, wanting to play." She took a deep breath, then turned her face up to his. "When did you get home?"

"Are you sure that's all it is? Do I need to send for Nelwyn?" Marcus loosened his hold to stare down at her in the darkness.

"Nay, I'm fine, truly. When did you arrive?"

"A few hours ago. You were sleeping so soundly I had not the heart to disturb you."

"Well, 'tis not often that I can sleep lately, so I thank you for not waking me." Alena laughed, struggling to sit up. "But now that we're all three wide awake, light the lamp and tell me what happened in Londinium."

When soft, flickering light filled the wide chamber, Marcus settled himself back in bed and Alena back in the cradle of his arm.

"Nero sent many prizes. I brought back silver medals for the commanders of foot, armbands for the cavalry leaders, and a silver spear for the young centurion who came back with you and helped lead the Brigante charge. Lineas Flavius earned two gold oak-leaf crowns, and a promotion. He's to take command of the Sixth Victrix Legion in Hispania. Also, the centurion who led the first unit over the walls when we breached the fortress at Eilon Hill was awarded a *corona muralis*."

Alena caught her breath. She knew the prized gold crown, in the shape of miniature castle walls, only went to heroes in major sieges. Nero must be grateful indeed if he had awarded one for the fall of Eilon Hill. Her heart clenched in dread at what was to come.

"And you?" she whispered. "Did the emperor recognize your leadership in this campaign?"

"Aye," Marcus replied slowly. "I was given the broad stripe of a senator's toga and designated *quaestor*, with lands in Italy and a villa in Rome."

"Oh, Marcus. How proud you must be."

By now, Alena knew how rarely men of common birth were appointed to the Roman senate. She turned her head on her husband's broad shoulder to look up into his shadowed face. He would make an excellent senator. Strong and brave and incorruptible. Just what Rome—and Nero—needed in these times of rebellion in the provinces. A flash of panic at the thought of leaving her son and this land to travel to a distant, unfamiliar Rome welled up. Firmly she stifled the fear. Her mother's advice of only a few days ago echoed in her mind.

"When do we leave?" she asked quietly.

Marcus shifted to stare down at her, his thick lashes shielding his eyes and his thoughts. Alena waited, heart beating painfully.

"We do not leave," he finally answered, reaching up to cup her chin.

Alena felt pain clutch at her heart. Her breath caught in her throat as she struggled with the knowledge that he did not plan to take her. A barbarian wife would be a hindrance to an aspiring senator, she realized in despair.

"When do you leave?" she amended, her heart breaking into tiny fragments.

His black brows drew together slowly, as if not understanding her repeated question. "I said, we do not go. I refused the honors."

Alena stared up at him, stunned. "You refused? A senator's stripe?"

"Aye, Alena. Think you I would take you from this land you love, from your son? I told the envoys I would retire when this command is done and buy lands here."

Alena struggled against the joy flaring in her breast. "Oh, no, Marcus! You should not have done so! You earned the honor. You would be the kind of leader Rome needs now."

"I want it not." He lifted her face until she could see clearly into his eyes. The deep, possessive love in them made her heart thump painfully.

"I've spent nigh on thirty years in service to Rome. My loyalty is unquestioned, and as deep as my soul. But I can serve the emperor and you, my wife, better here than in Rome. Together, we will manage your reckless sire and headstrong mother. Together, we will ensure our people prosper. This is where we will raise our children, where we will build our future."

His hand left her chin and slipped down, over her swollen breasts, to stroke the mound of her stomach with a light, caressing touch.

Alena felt tears welling up in her eyes, blurring the dark face so close to her own. She doubted this quiet man would ever say flowery words of love. He knew them not. But she fingered the heavy ring on her finger and knew that he had just given her a gift more precious than gold. He had given her the future.

"Aye, my love. We will build our life here, together."

* * * * *

CALEDONIAN CONFEDERACY

Eilon Hill
Beorht's Capital

SELGOVAE

Corstopitum
Alena's home/ Capital of
the Lopocare Clan

BRIGANTES

Isurium
Queen Cartimandua's
Capital City

Londinium
Roman Capital of
Britannia

**Territories of the Celtic Tribes
in Britannia, A.D. 67**

Author's Note

Five years ago, my husband and I took three weeks off from our respective military careers and explored northern England and Scotland. One cold, misty morning we stopped at the Roman fort at Chesters. I can still remember the eerie shivers I felt when we climbed atop Hadrian's Wall and walked for miles along the broad strip where once Roman chariots raced from milepost to milepost. That's when I first had the urge to write the story of these proud soldiers, stationed so far from their own lands, surrounded by hostile Celtic tribes.

Years later I came across the fascinating history of Queen Cartimandua. The woman's Machiavellian brilliance in managing her vast tribe, and her lusty love of life, caught my interest. I dug deeper, and was hooked! Cartimandua ruled her rambunctious clans and a rebellious husband for almost three decades after the Roman invasion of Britain in A.D. 43. She lost her throne a year after the fictional story of Alena and Marcus takes place, when she formally divorced her husband to marry her young armor-bearer. Her enraged consort once again led a force against her, this time successfully. He was finally subdued by the Romans in A.D. 71. at the Battle of Stanwick. Although the Brigantes lost much of their previous independence with Venutius's downfall, the Roman commander in the north governed the province for many years with skill and diplomacy.

While Cartimandua's daughter, Alena, and her Roman husband lived only in my imagination, it might interest you to know that a love such as theirs may well have existed. Archaeologists recently uncovered a rich find at the ancient Roman fort at Vindolanda, near where this book is set. In addition to a wealth of wax quartermaster's tablets and letters to and from Roman soldiers, explorers also discovered a woman's tomb. Within the tomb they found a gold ring, set with a glowing carnelian stone and carved with the words *Anima Mea*.